D0179443

LISA JACKSON

MEMORIES

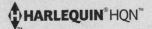

ISBN-13: 978-0-373-77876-8

MEMORIES

Copyright © 2014 by Harlequin Books S.A.

The publisher acknowledges the copyright holder of the individual works as follows:

A HUSBAND TO REMEMBER
Copyright © 1993 by Susan Crose

NEW YEAR'S DADDY
Copyright © 1995 by Susan Crose

Recycling programs for this product may not exist in your area.

HARLEQUIN®

Printed in U.S.A.

www.Harlequin.com

CONTENTS

A HUSBAND TO REMEMBER

den
The
the
hea

str
too

PROLOGUE

Steam rose from the jungle floor. The earth smelled damp though the tropical sun beat mercilessly through a canopy of thick leaves. Her lungs burned, her calf muscles ached, and she swallowed back the fear that drove her higher and higher through the hills of the island. Over her own labored breathing, she heard the surf pounding the shore far below the cliffs, but still she ran, ears straining for sounds of the man in pursuit.

Help me, God, please. Her legs were scratched from the vines and brambles and her sandaled feet tripped over exposed roots and rocks. She scrambled up the overgrown trail, hoping that at the ridge, high above the sea, there would be a place to hide, a fork in the path that would at least give her a way to escape.

"*Pare!*" a deep voice commanded. "Stop!"

of the old mission, its cross long disappeared, the walls beginning to crumble. Though deserted for years, the mission held her only hope. There was still a chance that someone was there, a tourist or local who could help her.

She started up the final hill. Biting her lip against the urge to cry out, she ran along the trail that rimmed the cliffs. Pebbles fell, dislodged by her feet to mingle with the angry white foam that swirled far below, pounding the rocky shore.

Just a few more yards.

Unless no one is there.

Unless the man chasing her already had someone there.

Behind her the man was scrambling up the trail, closing the distance. *Hurry! Hurry! Hurry!*

Tears stung her eyes, but still she ran, hearing his loud breathing, hoping that he didn't have a gun.

"Stop!" he yelled again. So close. So damned close.

A huge hand touched her shoulder and her footing gave way. Her ankle twisted and she cried out. Falling, she tried to clutch the tufts of dried grass and sharp rocks, but her fingers found only air. Her body pitched over the edge of the cliff.

CHAPTER ONE

VOICES, DISTANT AND jumbled, echoing from somewhere in the darkness, somewhere just out of reach, beckoned to her.

"You wake up now," a woman said in thickly accented English. "*Dios,* it's time for you to stop this sleeping. *Señora,* can you hear me?"

She tried to respond but couldn't, though the voice had become familiar and kind, one of the voices that ebbed and flowed on the tide of her consciousness. She'd heard many voices often in the darkness and knew that they were friendly. They were voices she could count on, voices that would help—unlike the voices in her dreams, the voices that caused her to scream in silent horror as she replayed the chase through the jungle over and over.

If only she could open her eyes.

"*Señora*—can you hear me? *¿Señora?*" The nurse was trying to talk to her again. "Your husband…he is here. Waiting for you to wake up."

Husband. But I don't have a husband…

She swallowed. Lord, was that sand in her throat? And the taste in her mouth—horrid and bitter. Metallic. Her stomach burned and her eyelids peeled back for an instant. Light streamed through the swollen slits, causing an explosion of pain in her brain. In an instant, she saw a huge woman leaning over her—a woman in white, with large breasts, worried expression, dark skin and black hair pulled into a tight bun covered with a stiff white nurse's cap.

Intelligent brown eyes stared into hers, and the nurse began speaking in rapid-fire Spanish that she couldn't begin to understand. Where was she? A hospital, she guessed, but where?

She couldn't focus, couldn't read the name on the pin clipped to the nurse's huge bosom. "The doctor, he is on his way, and your husband, we have told him you are waking up."

I'm not married, she tried to say, but the words wouldn't form, and another wave of blackness engulfed her.

"Oh, no…she is sinking again…" More Spanish as the nurse barked orders.

The darkness was peaceful and calm and cool.

"We are losing her again!" the big nurse's voice called from the darkness. "*¡Señora! ¡Señora!* You wake up. You just wake up again!" She felt strong fingers around her wrist, moving quickly, trying to edge her back to consciousness, but the sinking had begun and she floated steadily downward to the black void, grateful for the relief it brought.

"Nikki!" A man's voice called to her, but it was too late.

Nikki?

"Your wife, she will wake up soon," the nurse said.

I'm no one's wife. I'm… Panic seized her as she searched for a name, a memory, anything she could recall. But there was nothing.

"Nikki, please. Wake up." The husband again. *Husband?* Her eyes fluttered for a second and she focused on a hard face, a very male face. Severe, bladed features, thick brows and stormy blue eyes pierced through the fog in her mind. His lips were thin and sensual, his nose a little crooked, and she was certain that she'd never seen him before in her life.

"Nikki, come on. Wake up…"

But the darkness washed over her again, pulling her into its safe, silent vortex, to a place where she didn't have to wonder about her past and she didn't have to think why this man, this stranger, was claiming to be her husband.

The fragrance of carnations and roses drifted through the ever-present odor of antiseptic, and she heard music, a soft Spanish ballad interrupted by occasional bouts of static as the melody drifted through her sleep, dragging her awake. She tried to stretch, but her muscles rebelled and she felt as if she'd been lying in one spot forever. She ached all over and her head… Lord, her head… pounded shaven, shirt wrinkled and rolled at the sleeves, jean-clad legs stretched in front of him, he was tall and swarthy, his features set and grim, his lips clamped shut in a harsh, thin line. His gaze was trained past her to the hallway door, and the sound of the music accompanied muted voices and the rattle of a cart being pushed through the corridor.

A tingle of foreboding touched all her nerve endings when she looked at him. There had to be a reason he was here—but what? And who was he? Mean-looking, with a square jaw that meant business and shoulders wide enough to hide the back of the chair, he appeared not to have slept for the past week. Aside from his rumpled clothes, his black hair was mussed and hung past his collar, and there was an air about him that seemed almost dangerous.

As if he suddenly sensed that she was staring at him, his gaze swung quickly back to the bed, and eyes as blue as the Caribbean focused on her with such unerring intensity that a shiver of dread chased up her spine. *Don't be silly,* she told herself. *He's obviously a friend.*

licked her lips and tried to sit up, but pain exploded in her head.

"Hey, wait a minute." He was on his feet in an instant, big, callused palms pressing gently on her shoulders as he held her down. "Take it slow, Nikki. You'll get your chance to talk, believe me."

He knew her, but she was certain she'd never seen him before in her life.... No, there had been an instant of wakefulness when these same cold blue eyes had searched hers. She willed herself to remember, but the pain in her head caused her to wince and she felt like she might throw up. There was something she should know about him. Something important.

He offered her a sip of water from a glass on the table, bending a straw so that she could drink. The water was warm and tasted slightly metallic, and after a few swallows she shook her head and he set the glass back on the tray.

"Who...who are you?" she asked, her voice rough and squeaky, like a neglected instrument that needed tuning.

For just a second she thought his eyes slitted suspiciously. "You don't know?"

"No... I..." Panic gripped her as she searched her memory, or what had been her memory. Nothing surfaced. *Nothing*. Not just about this man or this hospital or herself. "I...I don't remember...." But how could that be? She tried to concen to say something, but stopped himself short, and the sharp glance he shot her way said, without words, that he didn't believe her.

"Who *are* you?" she demanded. She knew instinctively that she shouldn't show any kind of weakness to this man.

"You're serious about this amnesia?" he scoffed in a whisper.

"I don't—"

Suddenly he leaned over the bed, took her face between his hands and pressed his lips upon hers with the intimacy of a kiss that bespoke of a thousand kisses before. His lips molded against hers with a warm possession, and her heart, already beating in fear, began a wild tempo that pulsed through her veins. He groaned softly into her mouth and whispered, "I've missed you, Nikki. Oh, God, I was scared." His lips claimed hers again with a depth of passion that caused her to tremble and melt inside before she could collect her senses.

Stop this madness. Stop it now!

Even though his mouth and hands were persuasive, she couldn't respond, because deep in her heart she knew the kiss wasn't right—the passion and caring of this man were all wrong. There wasn't any logic involved in her thinking, just a gut feeling that the man wasn't being honest with her. She tried to struggle, but the tube in her arm restrained her and his mouth way. "She's awake," he said, shrugging with the innocent guile of a child caught stealing a cookie from the jar. All trace of the coldness she'd sensed in him had been quickly hidden.

"*Dios.* We thank the Virgin." The nurse, a big, buxom woman with copper-colored skin and eyes as black as obsidian, moved to Nikki's bedside. Smothering a smile over the tender scene she just witnessed, she shooed the man back away from the bed where he suddenly hung like a lovesick puppy.

Nikki tried to explain. "I don't know what's going on, but—"

"Shh, *señora.* Please." With trained fingers, Nurse Consuela Vásquez, according to the name tag pinned to her ample bosom, took Nikki's pulse, blood pressure and temperature. Nikki tried to protest, to ask questions, but she was told by the big woman to wait. "First we see how you are doing. Then you tell us everything. Okay?"

Impatiently Nikki waited, wanting to wiggle from beneath the stranger's stare, for his eyes, as she was examined, never left her. Finally, when Nurse Vásquez had checked the IV bag and scratched Nikki's vital information on her chart, she offered Nikki a sincere and relieved smile. "Well, Señora Makinzee, you wake up. *¿Qué tal se siente hoy?"*

Nikki's brows drew together and she shook her head. "I...I don't understand. I don't speak Spanish."

"She wants to know how you feel," the man interjected.

"Like I've been run over by an eighteen-wheeler."

"¿Cómo?"

The corners of the stranger's mouth curved upward

just a little as he explained to the nurse, and Consuela Vásquez chuckled.

"*Sí.* You are lucky to be alive. Your husband…he save your life."

Nikki's gaze moved to the man leaning over the bed. He wasn't smiling any longer and his gaze had suddenly become unreadable. Like a chameleon, always changing. "He did?" she whispered, her heart hammering and sweat collecting along her spine. She wanted to confide in the nurse, to explain about the frightening blackness that seemed to be in the spot that should have held her memory, but hesitated, wondering if it would be wise to admit as much while this man—this man who had kissed her so passionately while she was lying helplessly in the bed—was standing nearby. "My husband? But I'm not married."

The nurse's smile collapsed. "He is your husband, *señora.*"

Nikki shook her head, but a jagged streak of pain ripped through her brain and she was forced to draw in a sharp breath. "I'm not married," she said again, her gaze locking with that of the stranger, the man claiming to have married her. Was it her imagination or did the skin around the corners of his mouth tighten a little?

"But, Señor Makinzee—"

"McKenzie. Trent McKenzie." His eyes didn't warm as he said, "You remember, we were married just before we came to Salvaje for our honeymoon."

Dear God, was he telling the truth? Why would he lie? But certainly she would remember her own wedding.

"My name is—" She squinted against the blinding

pain, trying to see through the door that was locked in her mind.

"Nikki Carrothers," Trent supplied.

That sounded right. It fit, like a favorite pair of old slippers.

"Nikki Carrothers McKenzie."

The slippers were suddenly too tight. "I don't think so," she said uncertainly. Could she possibly have been married to this man? Eyeing him, she mentally removed several days' growth of beard, the tired lines of strain around his eyes, the unkempt hair. He could be considered handsome, she supposed. He was just shy of six feet with a thick chest that tapered to slim hips and muscles that were visible whenever he moved. *Lean and mean.* For there wasn't a trace of kindness in his eyes and she knew that undying love wasn't one of the reasons he'd had for staying at her bedside.

"No memory?" the nurse asked.

Try, Nikki, try. She squeezed her eyes shut for a second, willing her memories—her *life*—to come back to her. "None. I...I...I just can't," she reluctantly admitted, her head throbbing.

Consuela's worried expression deepened. "Dr. Padilla will be in soon. He will talk to you." She turned questioning eyes to Trent and then, after promising a sponge bath and breakfast and a pill for pain, she hurried out the door with a rustle of her crisp uniform. Trent followed the nurse into the corridor, and though Nikki strained to listen, she heard only snatches of their conversation which was spoken in whispered Spanish. What was she doing here in this foreign country—in a hospital, for God's sake—with no memory?

Her heart thudded and she tried to raise her arms.
Her left was strapped to the bed, the IV taped to her
wrist. Her right was free, but ached when she tried to
move it. In fact, now that the pain in her head had eased
to a dull throb, she realized that she hurt all over. Her
legs and torso—everywhere—felt bruised and battered.

Your husband. He save your life.

Her throat tightened. What was she doing with Trent
McKenzie?

She glanced around the room, to the thick stucco
walls and single window. Fading sunlight was streaming through the fronds of a palm tree that moved in the
wind just outside the glass, causing shadows to play on
the wall at the foot of her bed. The window was partially opened and the scent of the sea wafted through
the room, mingling with the fragrance of the roses, two
dozen red buds interspersed with white carnations in a
vase on the metal stand near the table.

The card had been opened. Pinned to a huge white
bow, it read: "All my love, Trent." These flowers were
from that hard-edged man who claimed he was married to her? Nikki tried to imagine Trent McKenzie,
in a florist's shop, browsing over vases of cut lilies,
bachelor's buttons and orchids. She couldn't. The man
who'd camped out in her hospital room was tough and
suspicious and had a cruel streak in his eyes. No way
would he have sent flowers. And no way would she
have married him.

But why would he lie?

If only she could remember. Her head began to throb
again.

Somewhere down the hallway a patient moaned and
a woman was softly weeping. Bells clanged and foot-

steps hurried through the hushed corridors. Several people passed by the doorway, all with black hair and dark skin, natives of this island off the coast of Venezuela. When Trent had mentioned Salvaje to her, Nikki had flashed upon a mental picture of the tropical island. The picture had been from a brochure that touted Salvaje as a garden paradise, a quaint tropical island. There had been pictures, small captioned photographs of white, sandy beaches, lush, dense foliage, happy natives and breathtakingly beautiful jagged cliffs that seemed to rise from the sea. Nikki's pulse skyrocketed as she remembered a final photo in the brochure, a picture of an abandoned mission, built hundreds of years ago at the highest point of the island. The mission with the crumbling bell tower and weathered statue of the Madonna. The mission in her nightmare.

She convulsed, her heart hammering. What was she doing here on Salvaje, and why did this man, the only other American she'd seen, claim to be her husband? If only she could remember! She slammed her eyes shut, fighting against the bleak emptiness in her brain, and heard the steady click of boot heels against the tile.

He was back. Her body tensed in fear, but she forced her eyes open and told herself that he'd inadvertently given her a glimpse of her memory when he had mentioned Salvaje, the Wild Island, and if she could, she should try to get him to give her more information, hoping that any little piece might trigger other recollections.

He strode to her bed, towering over her with his cynical demeanor and lying eyes. Nikki, tied to the rails, forced to lie under a thin sheet and blanket, felt incredibly vulnerable, and she knew instinctively that she hadn't felt this way before the fall. "Dr. Padillo has been called," Trent said with a little less rancor. "He'll be here within the hour. Then maybe we can get you out of here."

"Where will we go?"

"Back to the hotel and pack our bags. Then we'll grab the first flight to Seattle as soon as you're well enough to travel."

Seattle. Home was the Pacific Northwest. She almost believed him. "We have a house there?" she asked, and she noticed the hardening of his jaw, the slight hesitation in his gaze.

"I have a house. You have an apartment, but we planned that you'd move your things over to my place once we returned."

"We...we got married in Seattle?"

His gaze, blue and hard, searched hers, as if he suspected that she was somehow trying to trip him up.

"By a justice of the peace. A quick ceremony before we came here for our honeymoon."

No big wedding? An elopement? What about her family—her parents? Surely they were still alive. Her stomach knotted as she tried to concentrate on Seattle—the city on Puget Sound. In her mind's eye she saw gray water, white ferries and sea gulls wheeling in a cloud-filled sky. Memories? Or a postcard she'd received from some acquaintance?

Trent rubbed his shoulder muscles, as if he ached from his vigil. She watched the movement of his hands along his neck and wondered if those very hands—tanned and callused—had touched her in intimate places. Had they scaled her ribs, slid possessively along her thigh, cupped her nape and drawn her to him in a passion as hot as a volcano? And had she, in return, touched him, kissed him, made love to him? Had she fingered the thick black strands of his hair where it brushed his nape? Had she boldly slid her hand beneath the waistband of his worn jeans? She bit her lip in frustration. True, Trent was sexy and male and dangerous, and yet…if she'd made love to him, if her naked body had twined with his, wouldn't she remember?

He turned to face her, catching her staring at his back, and for a second his hard shell faded and a spark of regret flashed in his eyes. Nikki's lungs tightened and she could barely breathe, for beneath the regret, she also saw the hint of physical desire. He glanced quickly away, as if the emotions registering in his eyes betrayed him.

"Who are you, really?" she asked.

His jaw slid to the side. "You honestly don't remember me?"

"Why would I lie?"

"Why would I?"

She lifted the fingers of her left hand just a little, wiggling her ringless fingers.

His lips thinned. "Hospital rules. Your jewelry, including your wedding ring, is in the safe."

"No tan line."

"No time for a tan. We just got here when you fell."

"I fell?"

"On the cliffs by the old mission. You're lucky to be alive, Nikki. I thought…you could have been killed."

Fear took a stranglehold of her throat. "I don't remember," she lied, not wanting to hear any confirmation that her nightmare had been real, that the terror-riddled dream that had chased her in her sleep wasn't a figment of her overactive imagination.

The back of her throat tasted acrid. "Were you chasing me up on the ridge?" she asked, her voice little more than a whisper.

He hesitated, but only for a heartbeat. "You were alone, Nikki," he said, and she knew he was lying through his beautiful white teeth. "There was no one else."

"Where were you?"

"Waiting. At the mission. I saw you fall." His face went chalk-white, as if he relived a horrid memory. "I think it would be best...for you...to go home. You'd feel safer and forget the accident."

Accident? The breath of fear blew through her insides, and she wished she could run again, that her body would support her and she could get away...to...where?

"I don't think I'd feel safer—"

"But you would be. With me."

"I don't even know you," she said, stark terror beginning to seize her throat.

Sighing, he shoved a hand through his unruly mane. "Maybe we shouldn't talk about this. The doctor doesn't want you getting upset."

Her patience snapped and she threw caution to the wind. "I can't remember anything! I don't remember my life, my job, my parents, my family, and I certainly don't remember you! I'm already way past upset!"

His mouth twisted heartlessly as his cruel mask slipped easily back into place. "I think we'd better wait for Padillo. See what he has to say."

There was an edge to his voice that caused sweat to gather at her nape. She couldn't remember the men she'd dated, but she would swear on her very life that none of those men would look like a rough-and-tumble backwoodsman with hawk-sharp eyes, angular features and scuffed boots. She noticed the beat-up leather jacket tossed carelessly over the back of his chair and the worn heels of his boots. He moved restlessly as if he were a man used to looking over his shoulder. Her throat went dry with fear. He was a con man? Someone sent to kidnap her? Or was he really her husband?

Her mind raced with a thousand reasons why she might be kidnapped, but she didn't think she was rich or famous or the daughter of some tycoon. She didn't feel like a political radical or a criminal or anything.... But for some reason this man wanted her, or the people in the hospital, to think that they were married.

She couldn't remember much, but she was convinced this impostor was *not* her husband.

But who would believe her on this island? Certainly not Nurse Vásquez, who obviously thought that Trent was besotted with her. But maybe the doctor. If she could talk to Dr. Padillo alone, perhaps she could convince him that something was very wrong.

Trent peered out the window, as if he were searching for someone in the parking lot below.

"I think if I really was married to you, I'd know it," she said.

"You'll remember," he predicted, though no warmth came over his face. He rested his hips on the sill, his gaze shifting from her to the crucifix mounted on the wall, the only decoration in the otherwise stark room. "As soon as I get you out of here."

"But you can't," she said, desperation creeping into

her soul. Alone with this man—with no recollections of the past?

He smiled with cold patience. "I'm your husband, Nikki, and now that you're awake, I'm going to ask the doctor to release you as soon as you're well enough to go home."

CHAPTER TWO

"So SHE WAKES up!" the doctor said, poking his head into Nikki's hospital room. Short and round, with a wide smile, dark eyes and a horseshoe of gray hair, he strode into the room with the air of a man in charge. "*Buenos días,* you are the sleeping beauty, *sí?*"

Nikki felt anything but beautiful. Her entire body ached and she knew her face was scratched and bruised. "*Buenos días,*" she murmured, glad to finally see someone who might be able to help her.

The doctor picked up her chart from its cradle at the foot of the bed and scanned the page. His lab coat, a size too small, strained around his belly, and when he looked up and grinned a glimmer of gold surrounded a few of his teeth. Small, wire-rimmed glasses were perched on his flat nose. "I'm Dr. Padillo," he said as he dropped the chart and moved in close with his penlight, carefully peeling back Nikki's eyelid and shining the tiny beam in her eye. "*¿Qué tal se siente hoy?*"

"Pardon?"

"She doesn't speak Spanish." Trent's voice caused her to stiffen slightly.

With the small beam blinding her, Nikki couldn't see Trent, but she sensed that he hadn't moved from his post near the window. He'd spent hours sitting on the ledge or restlessly pacing near the foot of the bed.

"Dr. Padillo asked how you were feeling today." As the penlight snapped off she caught a glimpse of him, leaning against the sill, one hip thrown out at a sexy angle.

"The truth?" Nikki asked, blinking.

"Nothing but," Trent said.

"Like I was ground up into hamburger."

Padillo's eyebrows shot up and he removed his glasses. *"¿Cómo?"*

Trent said something in quick Spanish and the doctor smiled as he polished the lenses of his wire-rims with the corner of his lab coat. He slid his spectacles back onto the bridge of his nose. "So you have not lost your sense of humor, eh?"

"Just my memory."

"Is this right?" he asked Trent and Nikki was more than a little rankled. It wasn't Trent's memory that was missing, it was hers, and she resented the two men discussing her.

"Yes, it's right," she said a little angrily.

Scowling, Padillo checked her other eye, clicked off his light and glanced at Trent, who had shoved himself upright and was standing in her line of vision. His features were stern and the air of impatience about him hadn't disappeared. Dr. Padillo rubbed his chin. "You are a very lucky woman, Señora McKenzie. We were all worried about you. Especially your husband."

"Worried sick," Trent added, and Nikki thought she heard a trace of mockery in his voice. His cool gaze flicked to her before returning to the doctor.

Shifting on the bed, she grimaced against a sudden pain in her leg. "I feel like I broke every bone in my body."

Padillo smiled a bit, not certain that she was joking. "The bones—they are fine. And except for your—" he glanced at Trent *"—tobillo."*

"Your ankle. It's sprained but not broken," Trent told her, though she would rather have heard the news from the doctor himself. The thought of Trent and Padillo discussing her injuries or anything else about her made her stomach begin to knot in dread.

"Sí. The ankle, it is swollen, but lucky not to be broken."

She supposed she should believe him, but lying in the hospital bed, her body aching, Trent acting as her husband or jailer, she felt anything but lucky.

"Your muscles are sore and you have the cuts and scrapes—contusions. Lacerations. You will be—" he hesitated.

"Black and blue?" Trent supplied.

Doctor Padillo grinned. *"Sí.* Bruised. But you will live, I think." His dark eyes twinkled as he touched her lightly on the arms and neck, lifting her hospital gown to expose more of her skin as he eyed the abrasions she could feel on her abdomen and back. "This must be kept clean and covered with antibiotic cream so that she heals and does not get the infection," he told Trent. To underscore his meaning, he pointed at a scrape that ran beneath her right arm and the side of her ribs, and the air touched the side of her breast.

A tide of embarrassment washed up her face and neck, which was ridiculous if Trent really was her husband. Surely he'd seen her dressed in much less than the hospital gown. Her breasts weren't something new to him. Yet she was grateful when the thin cotton dropped over her side and afforded her a little bit of modesty.

The headache that had been with her most of the time she was awake started thundering again and hurt all over. Her entire right side was sore and she was conscious of the throbbing in her ankle. Padillo listened to her heartbeat through a stethoscope and asked her to show him that she could make a fist and sit up. She did as she was bid, then hazarded a glance in Trent's direction, hoping that he had the decency to stare out the window, but his eyes were trained on her as if he had every right to watch as the doctor examined her.

"Ooh!" she cried when Padillo touched her right foot. The doctor frowned slightly. *"Tiene dolor aquí."*

"What?"

"He says you have a pain there—in your foot."

"Mucho pain," she said, gritting her teeth.

"Sí." Padillo placed the sheet and woven blanket over her body again. "It will be…tender for a few days, but should be able to carry your weight by the end of the week." Stuffing his hands in the pockets of his coat, he added, "We were wondering if you were ever going to wake up."

"How long was I—?"

"You were in a coma for six days," Trent said, and from the looks of his jaw he hadn't shaved the entire time she'd been under. She supposed that it was testament to his undying love that he'd spent the better part of a week keeping his vigil, and yet there was something about him that seemed almost predatory.

Again she looked at his harsh features, trying to find some hint in her memory of the rugged planes of his face. Surely if she'd married him, loved him, slept in the same bed with him, she would recall something about him. She bit down on her lip as he returned her stare, his eyes an opaque blue that gave no hint of his emotions. Desperation put a stranglehold on her heart.

"The nurse will give you medication for the pain," Dr. Padillo said, making notes on her chart before resting his hip on her bed. "Tell me about the—*Dios,*" he muttered, snapping his fingers.

"Amnesia," Trent supplied.

"*Sí.* Have you any memory?"

Nikki glanced from the doctor to Trent and back again. She needed time alone with the doctor and yet Trent wasn't about to leave. "Can we speak privately?" she asked, and Padillo's brows drew together.

"We are alone…." He glanced up at Trent, his furrowed expression showing concern.

"Please."

"But your husband—"

"*Please,* Doctor. It's important!" She wrapped her fingers into the starched fabric of his white jacket.

"It's probably a good idea," Trent said with a nonchalant shrug. As if he had nothing to hide. "She's a little confused right now. Maybe you can straighten things out for her and help her remember."

I'm not confused about you, she thought, but bit hard on her tongue, because the truth was, she didn't know a thing about herself.

Trent let his fingers slide along the bottom rail of the hospital bed. "I'll be in the hall if you need me." As he left the room, his boot heels ringing softly, he closed the door behind him, and Nikki let out a long sigh.

"That man is *not* my husband," she asserted as firmly as she could.

"He's not?" The doctor's eyebrows raised skeptically, and he eyed Nikki as if she'd truly lost her mind.

"I—I'm sure of it."

"Your memory. It has come back?"

"No, but…" Oh, this was hopeless! She clenched a fist in frustration, and pain shot up her arm. "I would remember him. I know it!" Unbidden, hot, wet tears touched the back of her eyelids, but she refused to cry.

Dr. Padillo patted her shoulder. "These things, they take time."

"But I would remember the man I married."

"As you remember the rest of your family?"

She didn't answer. The haze that was her past refused to crystallize and she was left with dark shadows and vague feelings, nothing solid.

"Your home? A pet? Your job? You remember any of these things?"

She closed her eyes and fought the tears building behind her swollen lids. She remembered so little and yet she felt like she was trapped, like an insect caught in the sticky web of a spider, vulnerable and weak. She stared at the IV tube draining into her arm, the iron sides of the bed, the gauze on her arm and the tiny room—her prison until she could walk again.

If only she could remember! Why was Trent posted like a wary guard in her room day and night? Surely he trusted the hospital staff to take care of her. Or was his concern of a different nature? Was he afraid she might escape?

She closed her eyes as the questions pounded at her brain. Why the devil was she on this little island off the coast of Venezuela? And why in God's name wouldn't this doctor believe her? There had to be a way to convince him!

"I've never set eyes on Trent McKenzie until I woke up a little while ago."

"See! That is wrong. He is the one who brought you to the hospital." Padillo smiled reassuringly. "Give it some time, Señora McKenzie. You Americans. Always so in a hurry."

"Please, call me Nikki."

"Nikki, then. Do not rush this," Doctor Padillo said gently. "You have been…lucky. The accident could have been much worse."

The tone of his voice caught her attention, and for the first time she wondered how she'd become so battered. "What happened to me?" she asked, looking up at him and trying to ignore the horrible feeling that the man to whom this doctor was going to release her was inherently dangerous.

"I've talked to your husband as well as the *policía*. They concur. You and Señor McKenzie were walking along the hills by the mission. These hills, they can be very…*escarpado*…uh, sharp…no—"

"Steep," she supplied, her nightmare becoming vivid again. The jagged cliffs. The roaring sea. The dizzying heights and the mission with its crumbling bell tower.

"*Sí*. Steep. The path you were on was narrow, near the cliffs, and you stumbled, lost your footing and fell over the edge. Fortunately, you landed on a…*saliente*—*Dios*…you call it a…"

"A ledge," Trent supplied as he opened the door and heard the tail end of the discussion. His gaze was pinned to Nikki's and his mouth was a thin grim line. "You slid over the side and landed on a ledge that jutted beneath the edge of the cliff. If you'd rolled another two feet, you would have fallen over a hundred feet into the sea."

Her body jarred as she remembered pitching in the air. *So the nightmare was real. Oh, God, help me!* Her throat closed in fear, but she managed to whisper hoarsely, "And you saved me?"

His lips tightened a little. "I couldn't save you from falling over the edge—I was already at the mission. But I heard you scream." His jaw clenched. "I followed the sound and ran back to the spot where you'd fallen. Fortunately I could climb down and carry you back."

Was he lying? "How did you get down to me?"

"It was tricky," he admitted as he rolled up the sleeve of a cotton work shirt. "But I've climbed mountains."

"So you didn't see me fall?"

His eyes locked with hers, and he hesitated for a fraction of an instant. "I'm sorry. I shouldn't have gone on ahead."

Nikki wasn't convinced he was telling the truth, but the pain in her body was intense and she knew arguing with these two men was useless. Could Trent possibly be her savior as he claimed, or had he been the man chasing her, the man who pushed her over the edge? But if so, why would he have brought her back for medical care? Oh, Lord, her brain hurt.

Shuddering, she thought about her nightmare, her feet losing their purchase on the rocky trail, her body pitching toward the rocky shore hundreds of feet below the ridge. Deep in her heart she'd expected that the horrid dream was real, but she shivered with a fear as cold as the bottom of the sea. She hadn't fallen over the edge, she'd been pushed, chased by someone…someone darkly evil. Her gaze moved to Trent's face, so severe and determined. It was hard to imagine that he had saved her from death…. She almost cried out, but forced the tremors in her body to subside. She couldn't show any sign of weakness to this stranger who claimed to be her husband, and she had to come up with a plan, a way to escape the hospital and find out who she was. Oh, God, if her head didn't ache so badly, if she could bear weight on her ankle, she'd find a way to uncover the truth.

A shadow crossed her face as Trent bent over the bed. "I'll be back in a minute," he promised, his breath fanning her face. He kissed her lightly on the lips and there was a warmth in the feel of his mouth against hers that caused her heart to trip. Was it possible that she'd fallen in love with this brash, uncompromising man? Nikki couldn't remember anything about her past, but she didn't believe for a second that she would marry a man so damned intimidating, a man who just by his mere presence seemed destined to dominate everyone he met. Certainly she would have chosen a kinder, wiser individual—a thinking man.

His lips moved against hers, and it was all Nikki could do to lay stiffly and unresponsively on the bed. Trent lifted his head and, straightening, smoothed the wrinkles from his shirt as he winked at her. The smile curving his lips was positively wicked—as if he and she shared some dark, indecent secret. He patted the edge of the bed, then walked with the doctor out of the room.

Silently fuming, Nikki thought of a million ways to strangle him. His little show for the doctor was just an act. Or was it? There was no passion in this kiss, not like the one before, and yet she'd felt a spark of emotion, a tenderness she couldn't equate with Trent McKenzie or whoever the hell he was. She ground her teeth in frustration and willed her memory to surface, but only vague images drifted into her mind. She remembered a grassy field and riding a horse—no, a pony, a spotted pony. She'd been bareback. A dog had trailed after the chubby little horse, nearly hidden in the tall grass. There had been apple trees—an old orchard, perhaps—in the corner of the field and a copse of oak and fir trees on the other side of the fence line.

Had the pony been hers? She imagined cattle grazing on the stubble in the next field, but the image turned cloudy and she was left with an emptiness that she couldn't fill. "Damn it all," she muttered as she tried and failed to summon any other thoughts about her past.

What about Trent? Your husband? Any memory of him at all eluded her completely.

She shifted on the wrinkled sheets and sucked in her breath at the sharp pain at her ankle. From the hallway, she heard Trent and Dr. Padillo, talking softly in the flowing cadences of Spanish. Of course they were discussing her, but she couldn't hear or understand them. Frustrated, she tried to sit up, but fell back against the pillows. If only she could climb out of this bed, march down to the police station, or the airport, or the American embassy, if there was one on this godforsaken island, and demand to know who she was and how she got here.

Tears threatened, and she stared at the crucifix on the wall. "Give me strength," she whispered as Nurse Vásquez returned with her medication. She thought of refusing the drugs, knowing she needed a clear mind, but the pain was too great and she was thankful for the tide of sleep the tiny pills would bring her. She swallowed the sedative eagerly, waiting for the pain to slowly erode and drowsiness to overcome her. Closing her eyes, an old commercial message wafted through her brain. *Calgon, take me away...*

When she woke up...then she'd try to remember.

"I want her released as soon as possible." Trent eyed the little man who was the most highly recommended doctor on the island. However, there couldn't have been more than three physicians on Salvaje, so Trent wasn't going to linger here, hoping this man knew what he was doing. Too much was at stake.

"But you have time...you are on your honeymoon." With a knowing grin, Padillo patted Trent's arm. "Be patient."

"We have to get back to the States."

"Why must you leave so soon?"

"We'd only planned to stay a week," Trent explained, trying to keep his temper in check. He was used to doing things his own way. Having Nikki in the local hospital was inconvenient. Damned inconvenient. Probably even dangerous. *Don't get paranoid,* he told himself, but he hadn't slept much in five nights and he was strung tighter than a bowstring. Right now, he wanted to shake some sense into the little doctor, to convince Padillo to release Nikki at that very moment, but he couldn't tip his hand. Not yet.

"Salvaje is a beautiful place. You should stay here. Enjoy the climate," Doctor Padillo was saying as a nurse at the lobby waved at him in an attempt to get his attention. "Your wife...she has not seen much of the island."

"We can come back."

"You Americans," the doctor said, clucking his tongue. "Always in a rush."

If you only knew.

"I can release her within three days," Padillo said, though by the gathering of lines between his flat black brows it was obvious to Trent that the doctor wasn't happy about his decision. "But there are only a few flights to America."

"We'll find one."

"Doctor—" the nurse called, and Padillo waved her away, as if she were a bothersome insect.

"Then I'll have the necessary papers ready to sign."

"Good. Oh, and while you're at it, I'll need my wife's purse and personal belongings."

"Today?"

"*Sí.* I think she'd like to look through it before she goes home."

"If it is lost, the hospital cannot be responsible—"

"Don't worry," Trent said, thinking of the pretty woman with the battered face as she lay in a hospital bed a few doors down the dark corridor. "Just give me her belongings. I'll sign a release for everything."

Nikki wasn't sure of the time. She'd slept so much, she couldn't keep track, but it seemed as if two or three days had passed, with Trent forever in the room with her, the doctors and nurses flitting in and out, feeding her, forcing fluids down her, fiddling with the IV, concerned that she eliminate, and assuring her she would be fine.

They seemed worried about infection, anxious about her temperature and her blood pressure, but no one showed the least bit of uneasiness about the fact that her memory had all but disappeared.

When Nikki had asked Padillo about her amnesia, he assured her that her memory would return and she would remember everything about her past, most likely in bits and pieces at first, but then, slowly, all the years of her life would blend together and she would know who she was, her family, what she did for a living. She'd even remember becoming Trent McKenzie's bride.

She wasn't so sure.

When she questioned him, Trent was reticent to talk to her about her amnesia. "Don't worry," he'd told her. "It'll come. Take it easy." She wondered if he'd been coached by the hospital staff or if there was a reason he didn't want her to remember her past.

He never gave up his vigil. Sitting with her day and night, refusing the next bed, looking the worse for wear each time she awoke, he was in the room with her. He didn't bother to shave, but did manage to change into a clean shirt one day. Was he devoted? She didn't buy it for a minute, yet she was certain that there was something tying them together, something worth much more to him than a wedding ring.

Had he kidnapped her and brought her to this tiny island off the coast of South America?

No—for he wouldn't have alerted the police to her accident, and Padillo himself had talked to the authorities. Unless the *Policía de Salvaje* were not sophisticated enough to know about crimes committed in the States. Why would they doubt him? He made all the outward signs of caring for her. She, on the other hand, couldn't remember where she'd lived all her life. Of course they would believe him.

Her head began to throb, and Trent, sensing she was awake, shifted from his spot near the window to take a chair at the foot of the bed. He propped the worn heels of his boots against the mattress and folded his arms over his chest.

"Good morning," he drawled with a sexy smile.

She glanced at the windows. "It's afternoon." Her dry mouth tasted horrible.

"Well, at least you can still tell time."

"Very funny," she said, wishing her tongue didn't feel so thick. She moved her arm and was surprised that there wasn't much pain. Either she was healing, or the medication hadn't worn off.

"Feeling better?"

"I feel like hell."

He chuckled. "Glad to see you haven't lost your sunny personality."

"Never." Forcing her gaze to his, she said, "Who are you? And don't—" she lifted her sore right arm, holding out her palm so that he wouldn't immediately start giving her pat, hospital-approved answers "—don't give me any bull about being my husband."

His lips twitched and showed a hint of white teeth against his dark jaw, but he didn't argue with her.

"What do you do for a living?"

"I work for an insurance company."

"Oh, come on," she said, rolling her eyes to the ceiling. "You—a suit? No way." She would have bought a lumberjack, or a cowboy, or a race-car driver, but an insurance agent?

"Why not?"

"Give me some credit, will you? I may not be able to remember much, but I'm not a total moron."

"Believe what you want." His grin was smug and mocking and she would have given anything to be able to wipe it off his face.

"Oh, now I get it," she said, unable to stop baiting him. "You've spent the better part of the last week camped out here on the off chance I'd wake up and buy term life insurance or accident insurance—"

"I'm an investigator."

"That's more like it."

"For an insurance company. Fraudulent claims. Arson, suicide, that sort of thing." Cocking his head to one side, he said, "But the company would probably appreciate it if I could sell you some term—"

"Enough already. I believe you." She tried to sit up, couldn't and motioned toward the crank at the end of the bed. "Would you—"

Trent, dropping his feet, reached over. Within a minute she was nearly sitting upright. "Better?"

She rubbed the back of her hand where the needle marks from her recent IV were turning black and blue—to match the rest of her body. "Yes. Thanks."

He seemed less hostile today, and the restlessness which usually accompanied him had nearly disappeared. As he propped his boots on the mattress again, settling low on his back, he actually seemed harmless, just a concerned husband waiting for his bride to recover. She decided to take advantage of his good mood because she couldn't believe it would last very long.

"How did we meet?"

"I was working for the insurance company on a claim from someone who worked with you. Connie Benson."

"Connie?" she repeated, shaking her head when no memory surfaced. But the name seemed right. "Connie Benson?"

"You were both reporters at the *Observer*."

"I don't—"

"The *Seattle Observer*. You told me you've worked there for about six years."

A sharp pain touched her brain. The *Observer*. She'd heard of it. Now she remembered. Yes, yes! She'd read that particular Seattle daily newspaper all her life.... She remembered sitting at a table...sun streaming through the bay windows of the nook...with...oh, God, with whom? Her head snapped up.

"You remember."

"Just reading the paper. With someone."

He held up his hands. "Not me, I'm afraid."

She felt a niggle of disappointment. For some reason she'd hoped that his story could be proved or disproved by this one little facet of information.

"We met just about five weeks ago."

"Five weeks?" she repeated, astounded.

"Kind of a whirlwind thing."

"More like a hurricane. Five weeks? Thirty-five days and we got married?"

"That's about right."

"Oh, no." She shook her head, and his eyes grew dark. "I don't think I'd—"

"You did, damn it, Nikki! We hung out together as much as possible, decided to get married, found a local justice of the peace, tied the knot and came down here for our honeymoon."

She was still shaking her head. "No, I'm sure—"

His feet clattered to the floor and suddenly he was looming over her, his hands flat on the sheets on either side of her head, his face pressed close to hers. "Look, lady, I'm sorry if I destroyed all your romantic fantasies. But the truth of the matter is that we didn't have a long engagement or a big, fancy wedding."

"Why not?"

His sensual grin was positively wicked, and she wondered how she could have felt so comfortable with him only a few minutes before. With one finger, he traced the circle of bones at her throat in a slow sexy motion that caused her blood to flow wildly through her veins. "Because we couldn't wait, darlin'," he drawled. "We were just too damned hot."

"Liar." She shoved his hand away, but her pulse was jumping crazily, betraying her.

"That's the way it was. You can try to romanticize it if you want to, put me up on some white charger, give me a suit of shining armor, but it really doesn't wash, Nikki. I'm no hero."

Her heart was hammering, her breathing coming in short, quick gulps of air. *Oh, dear God!* Had she really married this…this sexy, arrogant bastard?

His glance slid insolently down her body. "I could lie to you. Hey, what the hell, you don't remember anyway, do you? So, if you want to believe it was all hearts and flowers, moonlight and champagne, holding hands as we walked along a beach, well, go right ahead."

"Why are you doing this?" she said through clenched teeth.

"I just don't want you to have any illusions about me. That's all."

"What about the roses?"

"The what?"

She moved her hand, motioning toward the stand near the bed. In the process, her fingertips scraped against his shirt, grazing the muscles hidden behind the soft blue denim. He sucked in a swift breath, his gaze locking with hers for a heartbeat. Her throat turned to sand and she imagined him on another bed, positioned above her, his body straining and sweating. Slamming her eyes closed, she blocked out the erotic image. He couldn't be telling the truth! He couldn't!

"Oh, the flowers. Nice touch, don't you think?" he said without masking any sarcasm.

"What do you mean? Are you saying they're just some kind of joke?"

"I thought you'd like them. That's all."

Her heart sank as he settled back in his chair again. Recrossing his ankles on the end of the bed, he asked, "Anything else you want to know?"

"Just one thing," she said, bracing herself. "Why did you marry me if you hate me so much?"

His lips flattened. "I don't hate you, Nikki."

"You've made a point to ridicule me."

"Because you can't or won't remember me."

Her heart ached, and she forced the words over her tongue. "Do you love me?"

He hesitated, his eyes shadowing for just a second, his emotions unreadable. Plowing a hand through his hair, he grimaced. "I guess you could call it that."

"Would you—would you call it love?"

Ignoring her question and the pain that had to be obvious in her gaze, he stood and stretched lazily, his muscles lengthening, his body seeming more starkly male and dangerous than ever.

"Do you love me?" she said again, more forcefully this time.

A sad smile touched his face. "As much as I can, Nik. You can't remember this, but I may as well lay it out to you. I never much believed in love."

"Then why did you marry me?"

His jaw tightened and he hesitated for a heartbeat. "It seemed like the thing to do."

"Why?"

He shoved his hands into the back pockets of his jeans and walked to the door. Pausing, he sent her a look that cut right to her soul. "I married you 'cause you wanted it so damned much."

"Noble of you."

"You really don't remember me, do you? 'Cause if you did, you'd know I was anything but noble." He sauntered away, leaving her feeling raw and wounded as his footsteps faded down the hallway.

She let out a long, heartrending sigh. Everything was such a jumble. Nothing made any sense. *Think, Nikki, think! Trent McKenzie is not your husband. He can't be. Then who the hell is he and what does he want?* Squeezing her eyes shut, she forced her mind to roll backward. He'd told her she lived in Seattle, and that felt right. He'd mentioned she'd worked for a newspaper—the *Seattle Observer*—and that, too, seemed to fit. But nothing else—not the whirlwind romance, not the quick civil ceremony for a wedding, not the hostile man himself—seemed like it would be a part of her life.

So who was he and why was he insisting that they were married? She tried to force her memory, her fists curling in frustration, her mind as blank and stark as the sheets that covered her.

In frustration, she gave up and stared out the window to the blue sky and leaves that moved in the breeze. Maybe she was trying too hard. Maybe she should take the doctor's advice and let her memory return slowly, bit by bit.

And what about Trent?

Oh, Lord!

"Señorita Carrothers!"

The woman's voice startled her. She turned her head toward the doorway and found a pretty girl with round cheeks and short black hair. Her smile faded slightly as she noticed the wounds on Nikki's face.

"*¡Dios!* Are you all right? We, at the hotel, were so worried—"

"Do I know you?"

"*Sí,* when you register—"

"Wait a minute." Nikki held up a hand but was restrained by her IV. She tried to think, to remember. "You're saying I registered as Carrothers. *Señorita* Carrothers?" Nikki asked, her heartbeat quickening. This was the first proof that Trent had lied.

"*Sí.*"

"Was I alone or was my husband with me?"

"Your husband?" A perplexed look crossed the girl's face.

From somewhere down the hallway, rapid-fire Spanish was directed at the girl in the doorway, and Nurse Vásquez, her guardian feathers obviously ruffled, appeared. Nikki couldn't understand the conversation but could tell that the nurse was dressing the girl down.

"Wait," Nikki said when she realized that Vásquez was sending away her one link to the past. "What's your name? Where do you work?" But already the girl was out of sight, her footsteps echoing down the hallway. "Please, call her back!" she begged, desperate for more information about herself.

"I'm sorry, Señora McKenzie. Strict orders from the doctor. You are to see no one but family members."

Nikki started to climb out of the bed. "But—"

"Oh, *señora,* please. You must rest…. Do not move."

"Don't let her leave!" Nikki ordered, but it was too late. The girl was gone and Nikki was left with a more defined mistrust of the man posing as her husband. As the nurse took her blood pressure, Nikki said, "Can't you at least give me her name?"

"I do not know it."

"Why was she here?"

"A visitor to Señorita Martínez, I believe."

"Please, ask Señorita her name and where she works." The nurse seemed about to decline, but Nikki grabbed her sleeve, her fingers desperate. "Please, Nurse Vásquez. It's important."

"Dios," Nurse Vásquez muttered under her breath. "I will see what I can do."

"Gracias," Nikki said, crossing her fingers that Trent wouldn't get wind of her request. For the moment, she would keep her conversation with the woman to herself.

Within the hour, she heard his footsteps and braced herself for another confrontation. He appeared in the doorway with two cups of coffee. "Peace offering," he said, setting a cup on the stand near the bed. Then he resumed his position near the window. "I didn't mean to upset you."

"I'd like to lie and tell you I'm fine, but I'm not."

He lifted a shoulder and took a long swallow. "I know. I wish I could change that."

"You don't have to spend day and night here."

"Sure I do."

"I'll be all right—"

"Wouldn't want my bride to get lonely." He offered

her a sly grin, then sipped from his paper cup, letting the steam warm his face.

"I wouldn't be."

"I was hoping that being around me would jog your memory."

Slowly, she shook her head. "Don't be offended, but...I don't see how I would ever have wanted to marry you. True, I can't remember, but you don't really seem my type."

"I wasn't." He curled one knee up on the ledge and stared through the glass. "You were used to dating button-down types."

"So why would I take up with you?" she asked.

"The challenge," he said, his eyes twinkling seductively.

"I don't think so."

"That's where you're wrong." His lips turned down at the corners. "You've always been a risk-taker, Nikki. A woman who wasn't afraid to do whatever it was she felt she had to. Your job at the *Observer* is a case in point."

"My job?" she asked.

"Mmm. You're a reporter, and a damned good one."

For some strange reason, she glowed under his compliment, but she told herself to be wary. Instinctively she knew McKenzie wasn't the kind of man who praised someone without an ulterior motive. Her shoulder muscles bunched.

"You've been bucking for more difficult assignments since you signed on at the paper."

"And was I given them?"

"Hell, no. A few people at the *Observer,* those in positions of power, like to keep things status quo. You know, women doing the entertainment news, helpful household hints, local information about schools and mayoral candidates and whose kid won the last spelling bee. That kind of thing."

"That's what I wrote?" she asked, her brows drawing together. It sounded right, but she wasn't sure.

"Most of the time, but you were more interested in politics, the problems of gangs in the inner city, corruption in the police department, political stuff." He watched her carefully as he sipped the thick coffee.

"Who was my boss at the paper?"

"A woman named Peggy Henderson...no—Hendricks, I think her name was."

"You don't know?" she asked, incredulous.

He lifted a muscular shoulder. "Never met her." When she gazed at him skeptically, he snorted. "As I said, you and I, we haven't known each other all that long." Again, that soul-searing look.

"What about my family?" she asked, her fingers twisting in the sheets. He was giving her more information than she could handle.

"Your father's based in Seattle, owns his own import/export business. But he's out of town a lot. In the Orient. You have a sister back east and one in Montana somewhere, I think, and your mother lives in L.A."

"My folks are divorced?" Lord, why wasn't any of this registering? she wondered. Why couldn't she conjure up her mother's smile, her father's face, the color of her sisters' hair?

"Dr. Padillo didn't want you to rush things," Trent said evenly. "He thinks it's best if your memory returns on your own."

"And you disagree?"

"I don't know what to think, but I'm sure the best

thing for you would be to get you home, back to the States, where an American doctor, maybe even a psychiatrist or neurosurgeon, could look at you."

Her throat closed. "Could my amnesia be permanent?" she asked, her heart nearly stopping. The thought of living the rest of her life with no recollection of her childhood, the homes she'd grown up in, the family she'd loved, was devastating. A black tide of desperation threatened to draw her into its inky depths.

A shadow crossed his eyes. "I don't know. But the sooner we get home, the better." This side of Trent was new, as if he were suddenly concerned for her emotional well-being. "Tomorrow Padillo's springing you. I'll pick up everything at the hotel, meet you here, and we'll take the first flight back to Seattle."

"I'd like to call someone."

He froze. "Who?"

"My editor, for starters. Then my mother, I guess." Was it her imagination or did his spine stiffen slightly?

"If the doctor agrees."

"Why wouldn't he?"

"As I said, I'm no medicine man. But I'll see if I can get a portable phone down here. If not, you can use the pay booth at the end of the hall."

"Now?"

"I don't think that would be a good idea."

"Well, I do." She forced herself upright, ignored the dull ache in her hip and leg, and slid over the edge of the bed. As she set weight on her right ankle, she winced, but the pain wasn't as intense as she'd expected. She didn't know the layout of the hospital, but she hoped to find Mrs. Martínez's room. If she couldn't get the information about the girl from the hotel from Nurse

Vásquez, she'd check with Mrs. Martínez. There were more ways than one to skin a cat.

"Get back in the bed," Trent ordered.

"Not yet."

"Nikki, please—"

"Help me to the bathroom," she said, tossing her hair off her face and grabbing the light cotton robe that was thrown across the foot of the bed. It was hospital issue and not the least bit flattering, but at least it covered the gaps left by the hospital gown. Balancing most of her weight on her left foot, she shoved her hands down the sleeves and tied a knot in the loose belt. "Come on, *husband*."

For a second he seemed about to refuse. "This is crazy."

"The nurse told me that whenever I felt like getting out of bed, I should. And I feel like it now."

Grumbling about hardheaded women without a lick of sense, Trent bent a little so that she could place her arm around his neck. He wrapped a strong arm around her waist and nearly supported all her weight himself. "Okay, let's go."

She was a little unsteady at first, but managed the few steps out of the room to the bathroom down the hall. She tried to ignore the warm impressions of Trent's fingers at her waist and concentrated on taking each tenuous step. The walking got easier and she became more confident.

If only she could ignore the smell of him, male and musk and leather as they paused at the bathroom door.

"*¡Señora McKenzie!*" A petite nurse hurried down the hallway. Concern creased her forehead and caused her steps to hurry along the smooth tile floor. "*¡Es-*

pere!" As she approached, she slid a furious glance at Trent. *"¿Qué es esto?"* Her black eyes snapped fire and her thin lips drew tight like a purse string.

"She wants to know what's going on here," Trent explained. There was an exchange of angry Spanish, and finally Nurse Lidia Sánchez shoved open the restroom door with her hip and helped Nikki inside. "I guess she didn't like my bedside manner," Trent offered as the door swung shut.

Nurse Sánchez was still muttering furiously in Spanish, but Nikki didn't even try to understand her. Instead she stared at her reflection in the mirror mounted over the sink. Her heart dropped and all the tears she'd fought valiantly swam to the surface of her eyes. The swelling had gone down, but bruises and scrapes surrounded her eye sockets. Thick scabs covered the abrasions on her cheeks and chin. Her hair was dirty and limp and she barely recognized herself. She hadn't expected to be beautiful, but she hadn't thought it would be this bad. Beneath the bruises she could see traces of a woman who would be considered pretty and vivacious, with green eyes, an easy smile and high cheekbones. Her chin-length hair, a light brown streaked with strands of honey-blond, held the promise of thick waves, but today the dirty strands hung limp and lusterless.

Trent certainly wasn't posing as her husband because he was taken with her beauty. She winced as she touched the corner of her eye where the scab had curdled.

"Pase," Nurse Sánchez insisted as she held open the door to the lavatory. *"Ahora."*

Nikki followed her orders, but on her way out paused at the mirror again and caught Nurse Sánchez in the mirror's reflection as she attempted to wash her hands. "Do you know which room Mrs. Martínez is in?"

"*Sí*, room seven. You know her?" she asked skeptically.

"Just *of* her," Nikki said, wiping her hands and following the nurse back to her empty room. Trent wasn't anywhere to be seen, and she felt a mixture of emotions ranging from disappointment to relief. She had started to trust him, but the girl from the hotel had caused all her doubts to creep back into her mind. Somehow she had to find a way to talk to Mrs. Martínez in room seven.

Her bed had been changed, and she lay on the crisp sheets and closed her eyes. Her surface wounds were healing. Even her ankle was much better, but her memory was still a cloudy fog, ever-changing like the tide, allowing short little glimpses into the past life, but never completely rolling away.

She was certain she remembered a golden retriever named Shorty, and that she'd never gotten along with her sisters, who were several years older, but she couldn't recall their names or their faces.

Instinctively she knew that she'd always been ambitious and that she'd never spent much time lying around idle— already the hospital walls were beginning to cave in on her—yet she couldn't recall the simple fact that she was married to a man as unforgettable as Trent McKenzie.

She was in limbo. No past. No future. A person who didn't really exist.

At the sound of the scrape of his boot, she opened her eyes and found Trent at the foot of her bed. His expression was as grim as she'd ever seen. "There's good news and bad news," he said, his fingers gripping the metal rail of the bed until his knuckles showed white. "The good news is that you get to leave this place. Padillo says that you can leave tomorrow."

"And the bad news?"

"The airline we're booked on, one of the few carriers that flies to this island, declared Chapter Eleven yesterday."

"I don't understand."

His eyebrows pulled together, forming a solid black line. "They're in bankruptcy reorganization. Everyone who bought a seat on the plane is scrambling to get passage on the other carriers. The airport's a madhouse, and my guess is that we won't get out of here for at least two days."

"Two days?" she repeated.

"Maybe longer." His jaw was tight with frustration. "I booked us another room, and I was lucky to get one. I paid for a week. Just in case." He kicked at an imaginary stone on the floor. "Looks like we're stuck here for a while, Mrs. McKenzie. Just you and me."

CHAPTER THREE

"HERE IT IS—HOME, sweet home." Trent swung open the door of their hotel room and Nikki felt the cold hand of dread clamp over her heart. So she was here. Alone with her husband.

Swallowing hard, and still holding on to Trent's arm for balance, Nikki carefully stepped over the threshold of the second-story room. It was furnished with a single queen-size bed, a small round table with two chairs situated near the terrace and a single bureau. Matching night tables in an indiscriminate Mediterranean design were placed on either side of the bed.

"Come on. You'd better rest."

"I've done nothing but rest for the past week," she objected, though leaving the hospital, the bumpy cab ride and walking through the large hotel had been more difficult than she'd anticipated. Doctor Padillo had assured her that she would feel stronger with each passing day, and she certainly hoped so.

Trent hadn't lied about the problems getting off the island. Never easy, now leaving Salvaje was nearly impossible with the major carrier to the island in a state of flux. "You haven't found us another flight yet?" she asked, though she guessed from his silence in the cab that his attempts to fly home must have failed.

"I'll work on it."

A firm hand on her elbow, he guided her to one side of the bed, pulled down the covers and let her slide onto the clean sheets. She felt awkward and silly. If he were her husband, this was no big deal. If he weren't…she couldn't even imagine where being cooped up alone with him might lead.

"There's a phone here. Good luck getting an overseas line. Everyone who's stranded here is trying to call out."

"Great," she muttered, though she hadn't expected better. He'd tried to help her make a call to her mother from the pay phone at the hospital. She propped the second pillow behind her head while she scanned the room. It was airy and clean, with a paddle fan mounted from the ceiling and bright floral bedspreads that matched the curtains. The closet door was half-open, and she spied her clothes—at least, she assumed they were hers—hanging neatly. A yellow sundress, khaki-colored jacket and white skirt were visible. She'd hoped seeing some of her things would jog her memory, but she was disappointed again. It seemed as if she'd never put together the simple pieces of her life.

As if reading her thoughts, Trent opened a bureau drawer and withdrew a cowhide purse.

In a flash, she remembered the leather bag. "I bought this in New Mexico," she said as he handed her the handbag and she rubbed the smooth, tooled leather. "From Native Americans. I was on a trip…with…" As quickly as the door to her memory opened, it closed again and she was left with an empty feeling of incredible loss. "Oh, God, I can't remember."

"A man or a woman?" he asked, his voice suddenly sharp.

"I don't know." She turned her face up to his, hoping he could fill in the holes, but he lifted a shoulder.

"I wasn't there. Before my time." He walked to the door, shut it and snapped on a switch that started the paddle fan over the bed moving in slow, lazy circles.

Nikki wasn't going to be thwarted. The keys to her life were in her hands and she was determined to find out everything she could about her past. Leaning back against the headboard, she tossed back the purse's flap and dumped the contents on her lap. Brush. Comb. Wallet. Tissues. Sunglasses. A paperback edition of a Spanish-English dictionary. A pair of silver earrings. Several pens. Address book. Passport. Small camera.

"All the clues to who I am," she said sarcastically.

"Not quite. I think I've got a few more." Reaching into the pocket of his jeans he withdrew a sealed plastic bag. Inside were a pair of gold hoop earrings, a matching bracelet and a slim gold band.

Her throat seemed to close upon itself, and she had to hold back a strangled cry at the sight of her wedding ring. Proof of her marriage. With trembling fingers she withdrew the tiny circle of metal and slipped it over her finger. "You bought me this?" she asked, her eyes seeking his.

"At a jewelry shop near Pioneer Square."

She licked her lips and stared at her hands. The ring was obviously a size too large.

"You wanted to keep it for the honeymoon, and we planned to have it sized back in the States."

"Is that right?" she said under her breath. Why couldn't she remember standing before a justice of the peace, her heart beating crazily, her smile wide and happy as the love of her life slipped this smooth ring over her finger. *Because it didn't happen!*

"I don't remem—"

"You will," he told her, his gaze steady as he stared down at her.

She shook her head, mesmerized as she scrutinized the ring. Her head began to throb again. "I should remember this, Trent," she said, her frustration mounting. "A wedding. No matter how simple. It's not something anyone forgets."

"Give it time."

Give it time. Don't rush things. It will all come back to you. But when? She felt as if she were going crazy and her patience snapped. "I'm sick of giving it time! Damn it, Trent, I want to remember. And not bits and pieces. I want the rest of my life back, and I want it back now!"

"I'd give it to you if I could." Plowing his hands through his hair in frustration, he spied her wallet. "Here." He tossed it into her hands. "Maybe this will help."

"Maybe," she said, though she didn't believe it for a minute. Sending up a silent prayer, she opened the fat leather case and sifted through her credit cards and pieces of ID. Nothing seemed to pierce through the armor of her past, and she was about to give up in futility when she saw the first picture.

"Dad," she whispered, her heart turning over as she recognized a photograph of a distinguished-looking man with a steel-gray mustache and jowly chin. For a second she remembered him in a velvet red suit and long white beard, tiny glasses perched on the end of his nose, as he dressed up as Santa Claus each year for his company party…. The memory faded and she tried vainly to call it up again.

"Hey…take it easy." Suddenly Trent sat on the edge of the bed, his warm hand on her forehead. "It'll come."

If only she could believe it. "So everyone says. Everyone who can remember who they are."

"It's been less than a week since you woke from the coma."

His harsh features seemed incredibly kind, and she felt hot tears fill her throat. She fought the urge to break down and cry because she couldn't trust him—even his kindness might be an act. There were other pictures in her wallet, some old and faded, none that she recognized, until she saw the family portrait, taken years ago, before her parents had split up. Her father still had black hair back then; her mother, a thin woman with a thrusting jaw, was a blonde. Her older sisters—why couldn't she remember their names?—looked about fourteen and twelve, and Nikki was no more than eight, her teeth much too large for her mouth.

"Janet," Trent said, pointing to the oldest girl with the dark hair. "Carole." The middle sister with braces. "Your mom's name is Eloise. She and your dad—"

"Were divorced. I know," she said, saddened that she couldn't recall her mother's voice or smile, couldn't even remember a fight with her sisters. Had they shared a room? Had they ever been close? Why, even staring at pictures of her family, did she feel so incredibly alone? If only she could sew together the patchwork of her life, bring back those odd-shaped pieces of her memory.

"Look, why don't you try calling your dad?" Trent suggested, though his eyes still held a wary spark. "He's still in Seattle and you always have been pretty close to him. Maybe hearing his voice will help." He snapped up the address book, opened it to the *C*'s and scanned the page. "It's still early in Seattle, so you might catch him at home."

He picked up the receiver and started dialing before she could protest.

"Have you talked with him?" she asked.

"No."

"You didn't call and tell him about the accident?"

"I figured he'd take the news better from you. I've never met him. As far as I know, he doesn't even know we're married, and since your life wasn't in danger, I didn't see a reason to worry him."

"And my mother—"

He held up a hand. *"¿La telefonista? Quiero llamar Seattle en los Estados Unidos. Comuníqueme, por favor, con el número de Ted Carrothers..."* He rattled off her father's number in Spanish, answered a few more questions, then, frowning slightly, handed her the receiver.

Nikki's heart was thudding, her fingers sweaty around the phone. "Come on, Dad," she whispered as the phone began to ring on the continent far away. She was about to give up when a groggy male voice answered.

"Carrothers here."

"Dad?" Nikki said, her voice husky. Tears pressed hot behind her eyelids, and relief flooded through her. She felt like she might break down and sob.

"Hey, Nik, I wondered if I'd hear from you."

"Oh, Dad." She couldn't keep her voice from cracking.

"Is something wrong, honey?"

"No, no, I'm fine," she assured him, shooting Trent a grateful glance. "But I did have an accident...." She told him everything she could remember or had been told of her trip, leaving out her amnesia so that her father wouldn't worry. As she talked, bringing up the fact that Trent McKenzie had been the man who had rescued her, she let her gaze follow Trent, who, whether to give her some privacy or to get some air, left her and walked onto the veranda. The wind had kicked up, lifting his dark hair from his face and billowing his jacket away from his lean body.

"Nikki! You could have been killed!" her father exclaimed, all sounds of sleep gone from his voice.

"But I wasn't."

"Thank God. I knew going to Salvaje was a bad idea. I tried to warn you not to go."

"You did?"

"Don't you remember? I thought that was why you hadn't called, because you were still angry with me for trying to talk you out of the trip."

Now wasn't the time to mention her loss of memory. "Well, things worked out. And I got married to Trent."

"You *what?*" He swore under his breath. "But I've never heard you mention him. Nikki, is this some kind of joke? You could give me a heart attack—"

"It's no joke, Dad. I'm really married." *At least, that's what everyone tells me.* She heard his swift intake of breath. "It...it was a quick decision," she said, giving him the same spotty information she'd gleaned from Trent.

"To a guy named Trent McKenzie. A man I've never even heard of?" *Here it comes—the lecture,* she thought. "Holy Mary! I can't believe it. What about Dave?"

"Dave?" A lock clicked open her mind.

"Dave Neumann. You know, the man you've been dating for about three years. I know you two had a spat and that you said it was over, but hell, Nikki, that was barely six months ago. Now you've gone and eloped with this...this stranger?" Anger, disapproval and astonishment radiated over the phone. "I know you've always been impulsive, but I gotta tell you, this takes the cake!"

"You'll meet him as soon as we get home," Nikki assured her father, though her stomach was tying itself into painful little knots.

"I'd damned well better. You know, Nikki, for the first eighteen years of your life I got you out of scrape after scrape—either with the law or school or your friends or whatever—but ever since you turned into an adult, you've been on this independence kick and nothing I tell you seems to sink in. I warned you not to go to Salvaje, didn't I? I knew that it would be trouble. Maybe if you'd told me you were going on your honeymoon, or at the very least confided that you'd found a man you were going to marry, things would have turned out differently and you wouldn't have ended up in some run-down, two-bit hospital!"

She felt her back stiffen involuntarily. "How would your knowing change anything?"

"Hell, I don't know. But you've gotten so damned bullheaded and secretive! Lord, why would you try to hide the fact that you were getting married, unless you were ashamed of the guy?"

"It...it just seemed more romantic," she said, trying to come up with a plausible excuse.

"Romantic, my eye. Since when have you, the investigative reporter, the champion of the underdog, the girl who fought every damned liberal crusade, been romantic? Don't tell me he's one of those long-haired left-wing idiots who chains himself to nuclear reactors or sets spikes in old-growth timber to keep loggers from cutting the stuff."

"I don't think so, Dad," Nikki said, smiling to herself as she watched Trent lean against the railing, his broad shoulders straining the seams of his jacket. She couldn't imagine him in a protest march.

"Good." He sounded a little less wounded, as if the news had finally sunk in. "I just don't understand why you didn't bring up his name or have the guts to introduce me to him."

"It's...it's complicated. I'll explain everything when I get back."

There was a slight hesitation on the other end of the line, then a quiet swearword muttered under her father's breath. "There isn't something more I should know, is there?"

She felt sweat collect between her shoulder blades.

"I mean, if there was a...problem...you'd come to me, wouldn't you?"

She bit down on her lip. What was he saying?

"If you're in any kind of trouble..."

Oh, Dad, if you only knew.

"These days you don't *have* to get married. There are all sorts of options...." His voice trailed off, and she realized what he was implying.

"I'm not pregnant, Dad."

A sigh of relief escaped him. "Well, I guess we can thank God for small favors."

"I'll call when I get home."

"You'd better. Now, wait a minute. Let me get my

calendar. Where is the damned thing?" he asked himself, his voice suddenly muffled. "Okay, here we go. So when will you be back home? I'm supposed to take off for Tokyo next week."

"We'll be back as soon as we can catch a flight. There's a problem with the airline we flew on."

"I read about it. But there are other flights. Try and make it home before I leave."

"I will," she promised. They talked a few minutes more and she finally hung up feeling more desperate than ever. She had wanted to confide in her father, tell him that she wasn't sure of her past, couldn't remember the man who'd become her self-appointed guardian—her *husband* for God's sake—and yet she'd held her tongue. She was an adult now and responsible for herself, and she realized that the animosity she'd felt over the phone only scratched the surface of the rifts in her family.

Slowly, she pushed herself up from the bed and made her way to the veranda. The breeze, warm and smelling of the sea, lifted her hair and brushed against her bruised face. Thick vines crawled up the whitewashed walls of the hotel and fragrant blossoms moved with the wind. Poised on a hillside, the hotel offered a commanding view of the island. From the veranda, Nikki looked over red roofs and lush foliage toward the bay. Fishing vessels and pleasure craft dotted the horizon, and as she cast a glance northward, she saw the sharp cliffs rising from the ocean, the rugged terrain that wound upward to the highest point on Salvaje and the crumbling white walls of the mission tower.

Her heart seemed to stop for a minute and her teeth dug into her lower lip. Fear, like a black, faceless monster, curled her soul in its clawlike grasp, and suddenly she could barely breathe. She held on to the rail in a death grip and her knees threatened to buckle.

Trent had slid a pair of aviator glasses over his eyes and his expression was guarded. "Memory flash?" he asked, his jaw tense.

She shook her head. "Not really."

"Your father shake you up?"

She snorted and blinked against a sudden wash of tears. "A little. He's not too keen on the fact that he didn't meet you."

"He'll get over it."

"I wonder," she said. Leaning forward on her elbows, she ignored the cliffs and forced her gaze to the sea, where sunlight glittered against the smooth waves.

"Look. I know you don't remember me or trust me. That's all right. I can be incredibly patient when I have to be." That much she believed. Like a tiger stalking prey, Trent McKenzie knew when to wait and when to strike. That particular thought wasn't the least bit comforting. His lips grew into a deep line. "But I want you to know that I'll keep you safe."

She wanted to believe him. Oh, God, if only she could trust him, but she remembered the girl in the hospital, Mrs. Martínez's friend, and once again she doubted him. Her gaze flew to his and she trembled slightly. "I think I was the kind of person who took care of herself."

A cynical smile slashed his jaw. "Then I'll help."

Her heart cracked a little, and she noticed the handsome lines of his face disguised by the scruffy beard and dark glasses. It would be too easy to fall for him, to trust him because she didn't have much of a choice.

But she was still her own woman, and though she'd grown to depend on him, she had to trust her own instincts, make up her own mind. "My father mentioned that I was going to Salvaje. I'd told him. But I hadn't mentioned you."

"Your choice."

"Why wouldn't I tell him?"

"Because you were afraid he might try and talk you out of it," Trent said simply, turning his face to the horizon again. "You and your dad don't always get along, Nikki, and he didn't like you taking off to some small island so far from what he considers civilization."

"So I snuck behind his back?" she asked, disbelieving.

"You just didn't mention me."

"Why not?"

He snorted and his eyes turned frigid as he assessed her. "Because you were afraid he wouldn't approve of me." He leaned an insolent hip against the rail and crossed his arms over his chest. "From what little I know of your old man, you were probably right. Ted Carrothers would probably hate me on sight."

"Why is that?"

"Because he had someone else picked out for you."

"Dave," she said, without thinking.

"That's right." The corners of his mouth pinched in irritation and he shoved his sleeves over his elbows. "Remember him?" She shook her head, and he grinned that wicked smile. "Well, he was a real Joe College type. Big, blond, shoes always polished. Went to Washington State on a football scholarship and graduated at the top of his class. Ended up going to law school and joined a firm that specializes in corporate taxes. Drives a BMW and works out at the most prestigious athletic club in the city."

"This was a guy I dated?"

"The guy you planned to marry," he corrected.

"You know him?"

"I know *of* him."

Was it her imagination or did he flinch a little?

"How?"

"I checked him out," he said with more than a trace of irritation.

"When?"

"Before we left Seattle."

She wanted to argue with him, but there was something in his cocksure manner that convinced her he had his facts straight, that she had, indeed, been the fiancée of the man he described. "I assume you know why we broke up?"

He lifted a shoulder. "He was too conventional for you. Your dad loved him. Even your mother thought he was a great catch, but he wanted you to give up your career and concentrate on his. You weren't ready for that."

"Thank God," she whispered, then, realizing how that sounded, quickly shut her mouth. But it was too late. Trent's eyes gleamed devilishly, and Nikki was left with the distinct impression that he'd been conning her.

She plucked a purple bloom from the bougainvillea and twirled the blossom in her fingers. Could she trust Trent? Probably not. Was he lying to her? No doubt. But what choice did she have?

He slapped the peeling wrought iron as if he'd finally made an important decision. "I've got to go out for a while. Check things at the airport. You want to come?"

She shook her head. "I'd like to clean up, I think."

"Just keep the door locked behind me."

"Afraid I might run off?" she asked, unable to hide the sarcasm in her words.

He glanced at her still-swollen ankle. "Run off? No. But hobble off—well, maybe. Though even at that I don't think you'd get far. Besides, there's really nowhere to run on this island."

Her temperature dropped several degrees at the realization that she was trapped. Her mouth suddenly turned to dust.

Trent cocked his head toward the French doors. "Come on, I'll help you into the bathroom."

"I can manage," she said stiffly, and to prove her point, she stepped unevenly off the veranda, walked into the bathroom and locked the door firmly behind her. Wasting no time, she turned on the taps of the tub and began stripping. As steam began to rise from the warm water, she glanced in the mirror, scowled at her reflection and noticed the greenish tinge to the bruises on her rump and back. The scabs were working themselves off, but beneath her skin, blood had pooled at the bottom of her foot and ankle. "Miss America you're not, Carrothers," she told herself, then stopped when she realized her name was now McKenzie.

"Nikki McKenzie. Nicole McKenzie. Nicole Louise Carrothers McKenzie." The name just didn't roll easily off her tongue. She settled into the tub and let the warm water soothe her aching muscles. As best she could, she washed her hair and body, then let the water turn tepid before she climbed out of the tub and rubbed a towel carefully over her skin and hair.

Wrapping the thick terry cloth around her torso, she walked into the bedroom, but stopped short when she found Trent lying on his side of the bed, boots kicked off, ankles crossed, eyes trained on the door.

His eyelids were at half-mast and his gaze was more than interested as it climbed from her feet, past her knees, up her front and finally rested on her face.

"I—I thought you'd left," she sputtered, clasping the towel as tightly as if she were a virgin with a stranger.

"I decided to wait."

"Why?"

"It didn't make sense to leave you alone in the bathroom where you could slip and hit your head, or worse."

"I'm not an invalid!"

"I didn't say you were."

"And I don't need a keeper."

He let that one slide. "I just wanted to be handy in case you got into any trouble."

"The only trouble I've gotten into is you," she said, willing her feet to propel her toward the bureau where she snatched clean panties, bra, shorts and T-shirt from one of the drawers. It crossed her mind that he'd unpacked her clothes, touched her most intimate pieces of apparel, but she ignored the stain of embarrassment that crawled steadily up her neck. After all, if she could believe him, they'd been intimate—made love eagerly. So who cared about the damned underwear?

She started for the bathroom. "Don't leave on my account," he remarked, and when she turned to face him, her wet hair whipping across her face, she saw a glimmer of amusement in his cobalt eyes, as if he enjoyed her discomfiture.

"You mean I should just let the towel fall and dress at my leisure?"

"Great idea." He stacked his hands behind his head

and watched her. Waiting. Like a lion waits patiently for the gazelle to ignore the warning in the air and begin grazing peacefully again.

Just to wipe the smirk off his face she wanted to let go of the damned towel, stand in front of him stark naked and call his bluff. Would he continue to tease her, playing word games, or would he avert his eyes, or, worse yet, would he, as he'd implied earlier, be unable to control himself and sweep her into his arms and carry her to the bed? How would she respond? With heart-melting passion? Oh, for crying out loud!

She turned on her heel and with as much pride as her injuries would allow, marched rigidly into the bathroom.

"Don't forget the antiseptic cream," he ordered as she slammed the door shut. Wrinkling her nose, she mimicked him in the mirror, trying to look beyond her skinned face and scabs. Some of the smaller scrapes were beginning to heal and her eye wasn't as discolored as it had been. "And stay inside," he ordered from the other side of the door. "The doctor warned you about getting too much sun."

"Yes, master," she muttered under her breath. Her teeth ground together as she thought of him barking orders at her. It seemed as if all her life someone was continually ordering her around. Her parents, her older sisters, her teachers, her editor at the paper, and now Trent.... She froze, her heart hammering wildly. She remembered! Nothing solid, but teasing bits of memory that were jagged and rough had pierced the clouds in her mind. Little pieces of her personality seemed to be shaping. Suddenly she was certain that she'd always been stubborn, resented being the smallest sister, the youngest woman on the staff of the *Observer!*

She'd also resented the fact that her work had been looked upon with a wary eye, just because she was young and sometimes because she was a woman. She'd had pride in her work, a great passion for journalism and an incredible frustration at not being taken seriously.

She wanted to share the news with Trent, to tell him that it was truly happening, her memory was coming back, but she held her tongue. She still didn't remember anything about him, about her trip to Salvaje, about the reasons she married him.

And what if she suddenly remembered that it had been he who had been chasing her, he who had pushed her over the cliff? She couldn't really believe that he'd want to hurt her, as he'd had plenty of opportunity to do so since the accident, but there was something deep in her unconscious mind, something dark and demonlike and frightening, that warned her to tread softly with this man. If he were dangerous and her memory was the key to uncovering his deception, he might turn violent.

A shudder of fear ripped through her. *Take it slow, Nikki,* she told herself. You can't trust him. Not yet. Until she had something more concrete, she'd keep her small discovery—that her memory was beginning to surface—to herself.

By the time she'd dressed, dried her hair and applied some salve to her face, he was gone, and she was grateful to be alone.

With the aid of her dictionary, she dialed room service and managed to order a pitcher of iced tea. She found some bills in her wallet and gave the waiter a healthy tip before locking the door behind him.

On the terrace, she poured herself some tea and looked through the pictures in her wallet again. There was one she'd missed earlier—a snapshot taken in the wilderness. A rushing river and steep mountains were the backdrop and two people were embracing before the camera. She recognized the woman as herself, but the man—blond and strapping with even features—wasn't Trent. *Dave,* she mouthed, though she felt no trace of emotion as she touched his photograph with the tip of her finger. No love. No hate. No anger. As if he'd been erased from her mind and heart forever.

"What a mess," she said, but decided not to dwell on her misfortune. She'd been feeling sorry for herself for nearly a week, but it was time to take charge of her life. She wasn't laid up any longer. She could walk, though admittedly she wouldn't win any races just yet, but she didn't have to depend upon Trent or a bevy of doctors to take care of her. She was a grown woman, and, if everyone were to be believed, a strong-willed and independent person who could handle her own life. An investigative journalist, for crying out loud.

She should be able to figure out if Trent was who he claimed to be. She watched the lemon dance between the ice cubes in her glass and decided that it was time to find out if Trent was her husband or an impostor.

Before it was too late. Before she made a horrible, irrevocable mistake.

Before she slept with him.

CHAPTER FOUR

THE MAN WAS known as *el Perro,* the Dog, and Trent thought the name fit. Small and wiry, with long black hair tied in a stringy ponytail, *el Perro* slouched behind the wheel of the beat-up old Pontiac, squinting moodily through the smoke curling from the cigarette dangling at the corner of his mouth. His beady black eyes were ever vigilant as he surveyed the empty, dusty road. Harsh sunlight baked the hood of the car, filtering through the grime on the windshield and causing the temperature in the Pontiac to rise to over a hundred degrees, despite the fact that the windows were down.

The car was parked on a desolate patch of ground. Dry weeds grew heavy between the two dusty tracks on the hillside. Far in the distance, the sea was visible. Below, the town of Santa María stretched along the beach, whitewashed buildings almost blinding as they reflected the sun, and high above on the hill, the ruins of the mission were visible through the trees.

El Perro drew on his filterless cigarette, pulling smoke deep into his lungs. "You want me to watch this one." He jabbed a grubby fingernail at the photo of Nikki with her sisters, a copy Trent had made.

"Yes."

"Qué bonita."

Trent couldn't argue. Nikki Carrothers was one of

the most beautiful women he'd ever met. Her smile was nearly infectious, her green eyes intelligent and warm, her hair thick and lustrous. But it wasn't her beauty that intrigued him. No. His fascination for her went much deeper. Too deep. He felt as if he were drowning. Nikki messed with his mind. She had from the first time he set eyes on her. He slid his gaze away from the photograph and gritted his teeth.

"She is in danger, eh?"

"She's in danger and she's dangerous. Both."

El Perro chuckled. "A *tigre, ¿sí?* Wild like the island."

"She's my wife," Trent said with a meaning that bridged the language and social barrier between the two men. Silently he cursed the fact that he had to deal with this lowlife. But *el Perro* came highly recommended. The best on Salvaje.

"You need another man to watch your wife?" With a disgusted snort, the sullen man said, "I trust no one but myself with my woman. No other man—"

Trent grabbed the front of *el Perro*'s shirt, the sweaty cotton wadding between his fingers. He shoved his face so close to the native's that he could see the pores in the smaller man's skin and acrid smoke from the Dog's cigarette burned Trent's eyes. "Get this straight, *amigo,* you're not to lay a hand on her, you're not to speak to her and you're not to be seen by her. You got that?" He gave the shirt a jerk.

El Perro's eyes slitted and he drew hard on his cigarette. Smoke drifted in angry waves from his nostrils. "You do not frighten me," he snarled, though his eyes grew black as the depths of hell. "For your money, I will watch your woman. She will never know that I am near."

"Good."

Releasing the other man's clothing, Trent settled back against the broken springs of the car, reached into his jacket pocket and withdrew a small envelope. He tossed the payment onto the stained seat and climbed out of the Pontiac, leaving the door ajar. "The rest when the job is done."

"How will I know when it is finished?"

"I'll find you," Trent vowed, surprised at the force of his emotions.

El Perro grinned lazily, showing off a slight gap between stained front teeth. "It is not always easy to find the tracks of the Dog, eh?" He tossed the butt of his cigarette out the open window.

"I'll find you," Trent promised, his lips drawing into a cruel smile. "You can bet on it."

No suits!

Not even a sports jacket. Nikki rifled through the clothes in the closet, searching for a clue to Trent's identity. She'd worked quickly, her fingers dipping into each of his pockets, rummaging through a denim jacket, two pairs of jeans, a pair of shorts and several shirts. For all her efforts, she discovered an opened pack of gum, loose change in American money, and a pair of nail clippers.

"Okay, Nancy Drew, what next?" she asked herself as she hobbled into the bathroom. His shaving kit was there and it held nothing more than shaving cream, a razor which obviously didn't get much use, a bar of soap, toothpaste and a brush. "Great. Just great," she muttered under her breath and wondered when he'd return. How much time did she have? If he were to be believed, the airport was overflowing with concerned tourists trying to make connections back home, and he would be standing in line for hours.

Feeling like a traitor, she picked up the telephone and with the aid of the operator, managed to get through to the hospital, though Nurse Sánchez was not on duty. Nor could Mrs. Martínez come to the phone. In heavily accented English, the hospital operator assured Nikki that Nurse Sánchez would call her when her schedule permitted.

"Great," Nikki mumbled in frustration as she eased back on the bed. There had to be a way to check him out. Another way. She picked up her address book and flipped through the pages, stopping at the section marked *M,* but nowhere in the pages had she scribbled Trent's name, address or telephone number.

Though the little book was half-full of entries, there wasn't even a notation for the man she'd married.

Names that were vaguely familiar caused little sparks to flare in her memory, though the faces that swam in her mind were blurred and fleeting.

In the section for people whose surnames started with *J,* she found Janet Jones, then saw that the address had been crossed out with a note to look under *C,* where her sister Janet had landed after resuming use of her maiden name.

Her sister's face came to mind, and she remembered a teary confrontation where Janet had confided that her husband, the love of her life, had left her for another woman, a younger woman with no children and a lot of money. Janet had been nearly suicidal and she'd sworn off men for the rest of her life. It had been rain-ing heavily outside, the water sheeting the windows of her apartment....

Nikki sucked in her breath. Suddenly she remembered where she lived—a small walk-up in the Queen Anne section of Seattle. The rambling old house had originally been built in the 1920s, and later divided into four apartments. Her studio was located on the uppermost floor in quarters originally designed for servants. The ceilings were sloped, the windows paned dormers, but there was a brick fireplace, tons of closet space under the eaves of the old manor, and a gleaming hardwood floor. Long and narrow, the roomy apartment was filled with plants and antiques.

Heart racing, Nikki remembered the braided rug she'd picked up at a garage sale, an antique sewing machine she used as an end table and a rolltop desk positioned near the windows. Her computer table was in the corner near a built-in bookcase and her lumpy couch, a hand-me-down from…from…oh, Lord, who gave her the camel-backed couch? Her great-aunt Ora!

Warm tears gathered in her eyes at the thought of her relatives, now with faces and names. She thought about her home, a place she remembered. Her sister Carole had been at the teary meeting as well, telling Janet to divorce the bum and get on with her life. As Carole rationalized, Janet could "take Tim to the cleaners."

Had there been happy moments with her sisters? Nikki concentrated, but no other memory of either woman drifted through the foggy corridors of her past.

Sniffing, Nikki tried to think of Trent, of the times he'd been there. Had he helped her cook in the tiny kitchen alcove? Had he been around to patch the leak in the roof near one of the windows? Had he swept her into his arms and made love to her there on the rug before the fire or on the daybed tucked under the eaves?

Her throat filled, but she remembered nothing but the incessant pounding of the rain when her sister had poured out her heart, alternately crying and swearing about Timothy Jones, DDS and SOB.

Heartened by the breakthrough, Nikki became impatient, trying to force more memories. She sifted through the address book again, stopping at the section marked *N*. Sure enough, David Neumann's name, address and phone number were neatly recorded. Yet she hadn't even scribbled Trent's number in the book. Strange.

She tossed the little address book aside and looked through her wallet, stopping again at the family portrait. Had Janet remarried since her divorce from Tim? And Carole? Did she have a husband?

Do you? a voice in her head demanded. She glanced at her wedding ring, shining and mocking, a symbol of possession that felt awkward around her finger. Why couldn't she remember Trent slipping the little band of gold on her hand? Had there been music at the ceremony? Probably not. A bridal bouquet? A wedding dress of any kind?

"Stop it!" she growled at herself. All she was doing was creating a headache of mammoth proportions, and she didn't want to have to take any more medications for pain. Right now, while she had time alone, she needed a clear head.

In frustration, she walked back to the closet and pawed through her own clothes, half expecting to find a cream-colored linen suit suitable for a wedding, or a plethora of negligees, or...what? Discovering nothing, she turned back to the bed and her heart nearly stopped beating. The camera! Biting her lip, she picked up the 35 mm and checked the back. Nine pictures had already been taken. Her throat went dry. Surely, if she'd been on her honeymoon, some of the snapshots would be of Trent. Her fingers were sweaty as she clicked open the back of the camera, removed the film cartridge and slipped the undeveloped film into her purse. What would she do if Trent wasn't in the pictures? And, oh, Lord, what would she do if he was?

The shadows in the room were getting darker as the sun dipped behind the ridge of mountains to the west. It was still daylight, four in the afternoon by her watch. Trent would be back soon and she hadn't accomplished much. Her stomach growled, reminding her that she hadn't eaten since breakfast at the hospital, but she didn't have time for food. Not yet.

Propped on the bed, with her Spanish-English dictionary lying facedown on the night table, she gathered her strength and tried to dial her mother in Los Angeles, but was told by the operator that all outside lines to the United States were busy.

Wonderful, she thought sarcastically and made a mental note of the people she needed to call. Her family, of course, and her editor at the *Observer,* Peggy Hendricks. Also, she'd call Connie Benson, a co-worker and close friend. If Nikki really had been seeing Trent in the few weeks before she'd flown to Salvaje, certainly someone she'd known had met him—a friend or a co-worker, if not the members of her family.

She had to work fast. Searching the room for an extra room key, she found nothing. Well, that wasn't going to stop her. She slung the strap of her handbag over her shoulder, locked the door behind her and made her way through the hall to the elevator.

With a groan of ancient gears, the lift arrived and she climbed in with an elderly couple and a teenage girl draped in a beach towel. With a deep tan and perpetually bored expression, the girl glanced at Nikki, flinched, then slid her eyes away. Blushing, Nikki noticed that the little old lady with apricot-tinted hair was staring at her face.

"My goodness, what happened to you?" she said, her eyes concerned behind owl-like glasses.

"I... It was an accident. I, um, fell off my bike," Nikki replied, hating to lie, but not wanting to tell her life story to the anxious woman.

The woman clucked her tongue. "Well it looks like it's healing. In a few days, you'll look much better. But you've got to keep the scabs soft. With vitamin E—"

"Phyllis, please." The gentleman shook his head. "I'm sorry, Miss. My wife used to be a nurse and she can't ever give up her profession."

"It's fine," Nikki assured them both, glad to hear good old American English.

"Don't you go out in the sun too much," Phyllis advised as the elevator shuddered to a stop. "Wear a hat. The sun's no good for you, anyway. Causes wrinkles. Just look at me."

"Come on, Phyllis."

The teenager slid out of the car as soon as the door opened, and the gentleman shepherded his wife toward the front doors. Nikki started toward the registration desk on the far side of the lobby.

The hotel was old, with thick plaster walls, paddle fans and rich-hued carpets spread over cool tile floors.

In the center of the lobby, a screened aviary lent guests a view of brilliantly colored birds and lush tropical plants that flourished around a central pond and small waterfall. Goldfish and koi swam beneath the lily pads while a toucan screeched from an upper limb of a small palm.

If she were feeling better, if she believed that the man who claimed to be her husband was whom he said he was, if she could remember more of her past, Nikki knew she would enjoy this beautiful old hotel with its dark furniture, whitewashed walls, slow-moving fans and graceful ironwork.

She made her way to the desk and tried to speak with the thin man at the register, but her halting Spanish wasn't any better than his attempts at English. Trying to avoid staring at the scabs on her face, he forced a smile and located an older man with thick silver hair, glasses and a ruddy complexion.

"How can I help you, *señora?*"

Hiding her nerves, she told the man that her husband had mistakenly taken the room key and she'd locked herself out of her room. The lies came easier as she went on, and with very little explanation, she was given her own key. She asked to see their registration form, and the man, though his white eyebrows lifted slightly, showed her the receipt Trent had signed. An imprint of an American Express card identified him as Trent McKenzie. Skimming the rest of the information, she noted that he lived in Seattle, though the address meant nothing to her. She forced her tired mind to memorize the street and telephone number, then asked the man behind the desk about a camera shop or a place she could develop pictures.

"For the film?" he said, his lower lip protruding

thoughtfully. "On the waterfront. José's. He can get you pictures in two, maybe three days."

Three days! "Doesn't anyone here do it in an hour?"

The ruddy man laughed. "Santa María is not New York," he said. "Talk to José. Maybe he can...rush the job for you."

She turned away and nearly tripped on a boy of about five who was staring at her. His eyes were round and he pointed at her face before running to catch up with his mother, a tall, graceful woman in a voile dress. The woman glanced at Nikki, offered a smile filled with pity and promptly scolded her son for staring.

Nikki cringed inside. She wouldn't be able to get out without drawing attention to herself. Though her scabs were healing and her black eye had nearly disappeared, she would still attract attention wherever she went.

She needed a disguise. Something simple. Dark glasses and a hat with a scarf attached that she could wrap over her face. With the traveler's checks still tucked in her wallet, she could buy something inexpensive. All she needed was a shop, and certainly a hotel this large catering mainly to tourists, would have a little store.

Thanking the clerk, she walked as quickly as she could down a corridor leading to an exit when she felt someone watching her. Her heart slammed against her ribs as she saw him, lounging lazily in a chair near the terrace doors, his eyes trained on her, one boot propped on a table. Slowly, Trent pushed himself upright. His face was impassive, devoid of emotion, as he approached his "wife."

"Been busy, haven't you?"

Oh, God, did he hear her ask about developing the

film? Her throat was as dry as cotton. "I couldn't stand being in the room a second longer."

"So you decided to check up on me."

She wanted to deny it, but wasn't going to lie. Well, not much, especially when she'd been caught red-handed. She inched her chin up a notch. "Look, Trent, I can't recall diddly-squat about my past, I don't remember you, or why—or even *if*—we were married. You haven't acted much like a bridegroom on his honeymoon, and I feel like you're hiding things from me, so why wouldn't I come down here and try to put a few of the pieces of my life together?"

"You *want* me to act like a bridegroom?" he asked, taking a step closer. "Is that what you want? To barricade ourselves into the bedroom for three or four days?"

"No, I—"

"It can be arranged, you know. Just say the word and I'll carry you upstairs and we'll get down to it."

"*You* don't understand—"

"You don't understand, damn it! I've tried hard not to rush you, Nikki. I figured that it would be better to wait until you wanted me as much as I want you." His lips flattened over his teeth and he grabbed the crook of her arm roughly. "You want to go upstairs? Now? Just you and me?"

"No!" her voice was strangled, and she felt fear mixed with awe at the pure animal lust in his eyes.

"I didn't think so." In disgust he dropped her arm and shoved his hair from his eyes. "This is driving me crazy!"

"You? At least you have a past."

"You will, too," he said, his voice harsh.

"Easy for you to say."

"Why can't you trust me?" he asked, his eyes an arresting shade of blue. For a second she saw a flicker of despair in his gaze, but it was quickly hidden.

"I don't know you."

He looked as if she'd slapped him. "Oh, hell, I'm not arguing about this again! Come on." He grabbed hold of her wrist and started for the elevator.

"No!" She refused to budge and nearly stumbled as he tugged on her arm. Several old men who had been smoking near a window cranked their heads in Nikki's direction.

"Let's go," he ordered through clenched teeth.

"I already told you I don't want to go back to the room."

His jaw worked and a vein throbbed at his temple. "Either you go willingly into the elevator or I bodily carry you up there."

"You can't—"

He leaned closer, so that his lips were nearly brushing her ear. "I've got news for you, baby. I can do anything I damned well please. You're my wife, I'm your husband and, if you haven't noticed, this ain't the good old U.S. of A."

"That doesn't mean—"

"This society isn't quite as sophisticated as ours. Women's rights haven't been an issue down here. In fact, I think it's legal for a man to do just about anything he wants to the woman he marries."

She could barely breathe. "That's archaic!"

"Welcome to Salvaje."

"Great place for a honeymoon," she muttered. "Who planned this vacation? The Marquis de Sade?"

"You."

She went cold inside. Who was this man, this monster, whom she'd married? He tried to propel her toward the elevator, but short of being dragged, she wouldn't move. Inching her chin up mutinously, she decided to call his bluff. "If you're going to carry me, then get on with it. If not, then let me go!"

Grinding his teeth, he dropped her arm again. "What is it you want from me?"

"Answers. Straight answers."

"I've given you answers."

"Not enough."

He closed his eyes for a second and pinched the bridge of his nose between his thumb and finger. "Okay," he said slowly, as if forcing himself to be calm, "why don't we go to dinner and you can ask me anything your little heart desires?"

He was mocking her, but she didn't argue. All she wanted was the truth. Again he took hold of her elbow, but this time his grip was less punishing, and he guided her through double glass doors to a restaurant with a garden. She insisted they sit outside, and Trent, though he looked angry enough to spit nails, didn't object.

The maître d' led them through the potted plants to a private table positioned near the rock railing. Beyond the short wall was a view of the ocean, darkening with the coming night. The scents of jasmine and lemon wafted on the sea breeze and soft Spanish music floated on the air from speakers hidden in the lush vines and flowers surrounding the tables.

"It really is beautiful here," she said, nervously. She wondered how she would feel if she'd never fallen over the cliff, never lost her memory, and was deeply in love with this mysterious stranger who insisted they were wed.

"If you say so."

A waiter in red shirt and black slacks appeared, and Trent ordered wine for her and a beer for himself. The waiter glanced at Nikki, his soulful eyes lingering on her face a fraction longer than necessary before he disappeared.

"You sure you want to be here?"

"Of course I do."

"People stare."

"Let them. I'm not contagious," she said, and Trent settled back in his chair. Though he outwardly appeared relaxed, Nikki knew better. There was a restless tension lying just under the surface of his calm demeanor. Hands tented under his chin, he stared at her accusingly. "You should have waited until I got back before you came out of the room."

"I told you, the four walls and I had run out of conversation."

"I was only concerned that you might fall on that ankle."

"The ankle's a lot better."

He didn't respond, but glanced casually around the garden, as if he were an interested tourist, but Nikki couldn't fight the impression that he was looking for something or someone lurking in the shadows.

The drinks arrived, and after quickly scanning the menus, Trent ordered for both of them. He exchanged words and a chuckle with the waiter and slid a sexy glance in her direction. Nikki refused to be intimidated, though her stomach was churning nervously. She thought of the camera in her purse and bit her lip. She couldn't very well develop the film with Trent around, and yet she saw no way of getting away from him today.

Placing her napkin over her skirt, she heard snatches of conversation from tables tucked between the pots overflowing with flowers. Quiet conversation and the clink of glasses were punctuated with soft bursts of laughter. People enjoying themselves, relaxed and happy, on a tropical island for a vacation.

"So you think you're ready to take on the town," he said, eyeing her.

"The whole island, if I have to."

He took a swallow from his beer, then picked at the label of his long-necked bottle. He scanned the garden slowly, as if gathering his thoughts, but his gaze was wary, his lips a little too tight over his teeth.

"How'd things go at the airport?"

"Not great. We got reservations out of here, but not for a few days."

Her heart sank a little. It was crazy, of course, and she wanted to return to her home and her life, but she felt cheated, as if she'd come to this Caribbean island with a purpose not yet served. Even if her plan had simply been to sightsee, she'd been robbed. And if this trip were truly her honeymoon, then it had become a disaster, because she and the man seated across from her were at odds, more enemies than lovers.

The waiter returned with steaming bowls of a thick fish chowder, which burned all the way down Nikki's throat. Her conversation with Trent lagged and she sipped her wine throughout the meal of swordfish, a spicy rice dish and sautéed vegetables.

She was nearly finished with her second glass of wine when the waiter returned with a dessert cart.

She shook her head. "I can't," she insisted, and Trent grinned widely.

"I was beginning to think you were a bottomless pit."

"After watery gelatin, gooey oatmeal and wilted, tasteless vegetables at that hospital for the past week, everything looks good."

"Except dessert."

She grinned and finished her wine. "Maybe later."

"In bed?" he asked, his gaze locking with hers. She couldn't move for a second and unconsciously she licked a final drop of wine from her lips. She thought of the film hidden in a pocket of her purse. Would it develop into snapshots of Trent, smiling and carefree on his honeymoon? Bare-chested and incredibly sexy, with the wind in his hair and desire burning bright in his eyes? Suddenly the ring around her finger seemed heavy and tight.

Trent paid the bill, then helped her from her chair.

"I—I don't want to go upstairs yet," she admitted.

"You're not tired?"

"It's barely eight," she pointed out. "Besides, it seems like I've been in bed forever."

"Not with me," he said, and her pulse leapt wildly. He took her arm, and she wondered if he was being helpful, or making sure that she wouldn't bolt, that he wouldn't lose her.

Through the opening in the rail, they walked along a sandy path that wound through the grounds of the hotel. They crossed a wide flagstone patio and passed clusters of umbrella tables. Hurricane lanterns were lit, their flames warm and steady with the coming dusk.

"I tried to call my mother and my sisters today," Nikki admitted as they strolled past the pool. Children were still splashing in the water, but the sunbathers had left for the day, the chaise lounges empty.

"And?"

"No luck. The phone lines were jammed."

He nodded. "My guess is telephone service here isn't all that great to begin with, and now, with the airline fiasco, it's nearly impossible to call out. We were lucky to get through to your dad."

The night closed in around them. Insects droned and flitted around the lanterns and a million stars glimmered in the purple sky. Stuffing her hands in the pockets of her skirt, she said, "Tell me exactly how we met."

He slid her a glance. "It's not all that exciting."

"I don't care."

"I was working on a claim for Connie Benson. Her car had been stolen and I had some questions for her. You were with her when I showed up and we were introduced. Later in the week we ran into each other at a restaurant on the waterfront. We started talking and didn't stop until the place closed down. From that point on, we saw a lot of each other." He slid her a sly glance. "You practically moved into my place that first week."

"No!" She blushed as they walked, the heat climbing up her neck to redden her cheeks. "I couldn't be that impulsive."

"For God's sake, Nikki, why would I make this up?"

"I...I don't know," she admitted, wishing the holes in her memory would heal. "I realize I'm stubborn. 'Strong-willed,' I think my mother used to say, but I'm also somewhat methodical and careful, and I wouldn't marry someone I didn't know well."

"It felt right, Nikki, so don't beat it to death."

"Okay," she agreed, as they followed stone steps covered with sand. "Then what about you? You don't exactly seem like the marrying type."

"I'm not." He lifted a shoulder. "But with you—" Hesitating, he stopped near a crooked palm tree and his hands slid up her bare arms "—I lost my head." He said it with a sound of disgust. "Believe me, I tried to fight you, but—" his rough hands surrounded her arms and he pulled her against him "—I lost." His lips clamped over hers and his arms slid around her. Warning bells went off in her head, but she ignored them and felt the barriers she'd so carefully erected against him begin to erode. His lips were magical and demanding, warm with the promise of passions yet untouched. She trembled slightly, and his arms tightened around her, dragging her close. "You're a mystery to me, Nikki. I've never felt this way before. You make me do things that seem entirely irrational, and yet I do them willingly, *eagerly,* for you." His face was a mask of perplexity, as if he couldn't understand his own motives. "I thought when I met you that I would get you out of my system. We'd have a hot affair and that would be the end of it."

"Is that your usual relationship with a woman? A 'hot affair.'"

One side of his mouth lifted. "I don't have 'usual' relationships. In fact, I don't have any relationships at all."

"Am I supposed to be flattered?" she asked, not trusting him for a minute. She tried to step backward, to put some space between his body and hers, but the arms around her tightened like iron bands, holding her close, refusing to let her go.

"I'm just answering the questions."

"So you're into one-night stands?" she asked, her voice breathless, her gaze searching his face.

"I'm not 'into' anything."

"They're not safe, you know. Not in today's day and age."

"Don't lecture me, Nikki, 'cause it doesn't matter. Until I met you, when I saw a woman I was attracted to, I ran like hell. The last thing I wanted in my life was any emotional entanglements."

That much she accepted. But her heart was thundering and she couldn't ignore the feel of his body pressed anxiously against hers. Through the soft barrier of their clothing, her flesh was warmed by his. "But you want me to believe we're married."

"We are."

"I don't believe—"

"Believe," he commanded before kissing her again, his tongue rimming her lips, prying her mouth open so that he could taste all of her. Deep in a dark corner of her mind, she knew she should stop him, but she couldn't, not when her skin was on fire, her blood flowing wantonly.

He crushed her to him and her breasts began to ache. His hands moved slowly and sensually up and down her spine, touching the sensitive area at the small of her back.

"This…this can't happen."

"It is happening."

"No, please—"

"Listen, damn it!" he said, jerking his head back long enough to stare deep into her eyes. "I can't tell you anything else. I can't explain *how* it happened. It just did. It's not as if this was planned, you know. I took one look at you and told myself to make tracks and quick, but for some reason, and I can't explain why, I ran to you instead of away from you. Maybe it was because you weren't interested at first."

"I thought you said I was…how did you so romantically put it? *So damned hot,* wasn't that it?"

"That was later." He grinned, running a hand down her back.

"But not much later."

"I kept pursuing you. You gave me the cold shoulder at first because of Neumann. You were still licking your wounds over him."

Dave. Her throat caught. She'd thought she loved him, planned to marry him, but he'd never intended to walk down the aisle with her. She couldn't remember their breakup, but suddenly felt the emotional abandonment, the pain and humiliation. Her memory teased her, rose to the surface of her consciousness only to submerge and leave her feeling raw and bereft.

"Are you saying I married you on the rebound?" she asked, her emotions electric and jumbled.

"I'm saying you didn't want to get seriously involved, but I wouldn't give up, and when things started getting hot and heavy, you insisted on marriage."

Would she have jumped so suddenly? Her father had said there had been six months since she and Dave had broken up. Would she have been so paranoid, so downright archaic to demand that this man marry her and prove that his intentions were honorable? "And you just happily went along with my idea," she scoffed, knowing instinctively that Trent McKenzie wasn't a man to be manipulated.

"I wanted you. Period." His voice was husky and raw, ringing with a conviction that tore at her soul. "I would have done anything to have you. Anything."

"Even marry me."

"Even that."

Her breath got lost in her lungs, and when his eyes touched hers, they burned with an inner fire that caused the denials to melt on her tongue. There was no doubt of his sexuality or the passion that simmered in his blood.

He lowered his lips to hers and kissed her softly at first, but with more hunger as each heartbeat passed. As her arms wrapped around his waist, she told herself to remember that this was the man who could not profess to love her, who often seemed cold and distant. So why now would he open his heart to her?

His lips moved over hers and his tongue rimmed her mouth, touching, enticing, prodding her lips apart to slip into the dark, wet recess. She closed her eyes and moaned as the tip of his tongue flicked against the roof of her mouth, dancing and parrying, teasing her own reluctant tongue to life.

Nikki's knees buckled, and his arms surrounded her, holding her close, pressing her against him, forcing her breasts against his chest. He prodded her legs apart with a knee that deftly cleaved her skirt and shoved her against the palm tree. Her blood was on fire, her breaths short and rapid, and the denials singing through her brain earlier all but silenced.

She knew that becoming intimate with him was taboo, that danger lurked in his dusky kisses, and yet she couldn't stop herself. Her body screamed for him, her breasts ached for his touch, and deep inside she felt a molten fire, like the boiling lava of a volcano about to erupt.

When he lifted his head, she sagged against him.

"This is how it's always been with us," he said, his

breathing ragged, his gaze tortured. He smoothed a stray strand of hair from her face. "And that, lady, is why I married you."

CHAPTER FIVE

NOW WHAT? COME ON, Nikki. You're a smart woman. Or at least you were once upon a time. So now what're you going to do?

Trust him. For God's sake, Nikki, follow your heart and trust him!

She stood on the veranda, her fingers curled around the iron rail, the breeze teasing her hair and brushing softly against her cheeks. From the open door of the hotel room, she heard water running, the sound of Trent in the shower. Trying to come up with a plan, she stared at the winking lights of Santa María. Strung jewel-like along the inlet, the city lights reflected on the water and kept the dark night at bay.

She didn't have much time. Soon she'd have to sleep with a man who, by casting her a single glance, could set her blood on fire. A mystery man who claimed to be her husband. A man she instinctively felt was dangerous. If only she could trust him. But trust, she knew from some vague experience in her past, was earned, not given casually. She rubbed her arms as if suddenly chilled and thought about the night ahead, sleeping in the same bed with him, feeling him close. Her stomach tightened and she knew she couldn't make love to him. Husband or no, she didn't trust him. She decided the best way to avoid making love to him was feigning sleep. Surely he'd understand that, after days of lying in the hospital, the move was hard on her and she was worn-out.

Truth to tell, she knew she'd barely sleep a wink with his body only inches from hers. What a mess, she thought, blowing her bangs from her eyes and glancing down at the garden patio where several people were still gathered, laughing and talking and sipping from island drinks. Older couples laughed over glasses of wine, and a couple in their mid-twenties held hands as they walked by the pool. Lovers, she thought, with just a twinge of envy.

Shaking off her worrisome thoughts, she hurried inside, and as she listened to the water still running in the bathroom, she quickly shed her skirt and blouse and yanked on a pair of satin pajamas. The fabric molded to her breasts and hips, and the deep *V* of the neckline offered a view of more of her skin than she would have preferred, but the pink pajamas were the most sedate bedroom apparel she'd brought to the island. It made sense, she supposed. A flannel nightgown and robe that would keep her warm through the wet and cold Seattle winters would have no business on a tropical island. *Especially on your honeymoon.*

The shower spray stopped, and her heart began an erratic tattoo. *Oh God,* she thought, her throat so tight she could barely swallow.

Quietly, she slipped between the covers, rolled on her side and offered her back to the other side of the bed. Squeezing her eyes shut, she heard him running the water again, probably at the sink, taking his damned sweet time, while she prayed for sleep. She realized she was acting like a child, a neurotic virgin, but as she was still laid-up and vulnerable, she felt the best course of action was deception. Just until she had her full faculties back. Once her memory returned, she would be able to deal with him more openly.

However, the pretense bothered her more than she expected, and she realized that Nikki Carrothers, in her other lifetime, had never sunk low enough to deal in lies. *These are extenuating circumstances,* she told herself as she plumped her pillow and tried to relax.

The water at the sink stopped suddenly. Nikki tensed. Through her slitted eyelids she noticed the lightening of the bedroom as he opened the door. *Act groggy,* she told herself, though she felt a fool.

He didn't say a word. She heard his keys jangle on the nightstand near his side of the bed, felt the movement of the blankets as he threw back the covers, smelled the scents of soap and shaving cream and musk as he slid between the sheets and the mattress creaked. Her heart was thundering as he turned out the light on his night table and scooted closer.

She stiffened as his arms surrounded her waist with easy familiarity. He pressed his body against hers intimately, his breath warm against her neck, the stiff hairs of his chest brushing against the slick satin covering her back. "You're not fooling anyone," he said, his hand splayed possessively across her abdomen. "I know you're awake."

She didn't reply. *Fake it, fake it, fake it! Just breathe in and out as naturally as if you don't feel his warm body cuddling yours!*

"But don't worry. I won't force you."

Her muscles relaxed a little, and he took advantage of the moment, drawing her closer still. His legs, bare from what she could feel through her pajamas, tucked against hers and he seemed to fit perfectly, his knees and hips bending at the same angles as hers. She tried to remember this feeling of closeness and intimacy, of sharing a bed with him, but no pleasant, warm memory surfaced. He kissed the back of her neck, and her pulse jumped crazily. "There's no need to rush, darlin'," he said in a sexy drawl that caused her stomach to turn over in anticipation. "We've got the rest of our lives."

Oh, God, why couldn't she remember?

Trent knew he should keep his hands off her. Touching her like this was dangerous, and yet he couldn't resist. He hadn't lied when he'd told her that she was the most fascinating woman he'd ever met. From the moment he'd first seen her in Seattle, he'd wanted to make love to her.

And yet he had to hold back. She was still in pain, still confused, still distrustful. There was so much he wanted to tell her and so much he still couldn't divulge. But as soon as they were back in the United States and he was assured of her safety, things would be better. He smelled the lilac scent of her shampoo on the hairs that spilled across her pillow and the desire already flowing through his blood created an ache in his loins. It would be so easy to start kissing her, to brush his fingers across her breasts, to rub up against her and nudge her legs apart....

"Hell," he ground out, forcing himself to roll over and cling to the side of the bed. He'd never been a hero, and there had been a time in his life when he hadn't really cared what a woman thought of him before or after he'd taken her to bed. But now, with Nikki, things were different. Complicated. Dangerous.

He grimaced and stared at the ceiling, knowing she wasn't sleeping. Any way he thought about it, the night was going to last forever!

Nikki climbed out of bed as soon as the morning sunlight streamed through the window. Hazarding a glimpse of Trent, she felt her throat catch as she saw his face, cleanly shaven, in complete repose. His jaw was strong and square. Dark lashes brushed his cheek and his mouth was without its usual cynical twist. His black hair fell over his forehead and his bare shoulders, even relaxed, were sculpted with sinewy muscles. Bristly hair swirled over his chest and disappeared beneath the sheet. A handsome man, she thought, but who the devil was he? Husband? Lover? Enemy?

"Are you gonna stand there all day and drool over me, or are you gonna come back to bed and do something about it?" He patted the spot where she'd been lying without cracking open an eye.

"You—"

With a slow, deliberately sensual smile, he levered up on one elbow and the sheet fell away, revealing a washboard of lean abdominal muscles. "I what?"

"You were awake," she said, deciding it wouldn't be wise to insult him just yet.

"Mmm." He stretched his arms far over his head and settled back against the pillows. Yawning, his slumberous eyes dark with an unnamed passion, he said, "You're lucky I didn't try to take advantage of you."

She couldn't help rising to the bait. "Maybe you're the lucky one," she teased, hurrying into the bathroom and locking the door firmly behind her before she decided she was being childish. He was her husband—right? He could see her naked. Or could he? Taking in a deep breath she unlocked the door. He could make the next move if he wanted to.

Telling herself that things were as normal as they could be given the circumstances, she carefully applied a little makeup and was grateful that her face was beginning to heal. A few of the scabs had become loose and some had actually peeled away to reveal pink skin that contrasted vividly with her tan. All in all her body was healing, she decided as she applied antibiotic cream and vitamin E skin oil to her abrasions. If only her mind would mend as well.

After brushing her hair and changing into shorts and a T-shirt, she returned to the bedroom where Trent, dressed only in faded Levi's, was pouring coffee into two cups. "Cream, no sugar, right?" he asked.

"Yes." For years she'd tried to wean herself off cream, she remembered, but hadn't been able to drink coffee black. Somehow Trent had been around her long enough to know her habits. It was frustrating, this being in the dark.

Handing her a cup, he huddled over a newspaper at the table and she tentatively took a seat across from him. She tried not to stare at the sharp angles of his face as she blew across her coffee, but she watched him, hoping that a glance, a gesture, a word would trigger memories of their whirlwind courtship and marriage.

"Tell me about your family," she suggested as he scanned the front page.

"Not much to tell."

"Your parents?"

"Still married and living in Toledo. Dad's retired from working in the steel mills. Mom's a nurse. She'll retire in a couple of years."

"Brothers?"

"Just one snip of a sister. Kate. Stubborn, single and a pain in the backside." He glanced up and smiled. "Anything else?"

"How did you end up in Seattle?"

Frowning, he folded his paper neatly on the table. "What is this—twenty questions?"

"Yes. Or thirty. Or fifty. Or a hundred. Whatever it takes."

"I didn't want to end up like my old man, with a bad back and a bum hip, so I managed to get a scholarship. That, along with working nights, put me through school. I graduated in law enforcement, decided I couldn't stand working for a boss and gravitated toward being a private detective. I moved around a lot. Things were slow and I heard about a job with the insurance company where I could make my own hours, and so I took it. I was living in Denver at the time and ready to move on."

"And that's it?"

"My life history."

She sipped from her cup and burned her tongue as she considered his story—encapsulated as it was. He didn't say anything she could dispute, but it seemed so cold and sterile—no hint of warmth when he talked about his folks, no smile when he mentioned his home town, no mention of a family pet, or a friend, or anything that might show a hint of his emotions. As if his past has been manufactured and printed off a computer screen.

You're letting your imagination get the better of you, she told herself. *Why would he lie?*

He snapped his paper open again and scowled at the articles written in Spanish. "Makes you wish for a copy of the *Observer,* doesn't it?"

Crash!

Glass shattered on the veranda.

Nikki jumped, sloshing hot coffee onto her hands and the table.

Trent kicked back his chair. "Stay back," he ordered, his expression grim. On the balls of his feet, his muscles tense, his jaw tight, he said, "Stay back!" He threw open the French doors. A stiff morning breeze skated into the room, billowing the drapes and rustling the newspaper.

Despite his warning, Nikki inched forward and saw thousands of glass shards, the remains of a hurricane lantern, scattered over the decking.

Trent, seemingly oblivious to the glass and his bare feet, had run to the edge of the veranda, where he stood, surveying the grounds and nearby breadfruit trees, as if he expected a prowler to leap out at him.

He started to move, and she yelled, "Watch out or you'll cut yourself."

"I thought I told you to stay inside!"

"I don't like being ordered around."

"It's for your own good."

"I can take care of myself."

"Can you?" With a sharp glance over his shoulder, he raked his gaze up her body to land on the scrapes on her face.

Squaring her shoulders, she lifted her chin. "I may not know a lot about my past, but I'm sure that I was more than self-sufficient!"

The look he shot her spoke volumes.

"I don't know why you're so rattled, anyway," she said, motioning toward the sparkling shards of glass. "It was just the wind."

"Maybe." Apparently satisfied that no one was lurking nearby, he bent over and began picking up the larger pieces of broken glass.

"You were expecting someone?" Nikki, too, gathered the chunks of sharp glass and dropped the jagged pieces into a trash can.

"No." He shook his head, as if convincing himself.

"Then what is it you're afraid of?" she asked.

"Afraid of?"

"You act like you expect someone to jump out at us."

The lines around his mouth tightened a little. "I was startled, that's all." Angrily, he threw the last of the broken lantern into the metal trash can, and it clattered loud enough to wake the dead.

"You don't strike me as someone who would startle easily. Come on, Trent, something's going on. You want to get me off the island as soon as you can. You practically have me locked away in this hotel room. Every time I'm out alone, you act as if something awful is going to happen."

He followed her into the hotel room and leaned a shoulder against the carved wood door frame. Crossing his arms over his chest, he stared at her, his lips compressed, his eyes narrowed slightly, as if he were weighing a heavy decision. "You've already been hurt once and spent too much time in the hospital. I just don't want to take any chances."

"On another accident occurring?"

His lips thinned, and instinctively she backed up,

steadying herself on the edge of the bureau. He still scared her a little, and yet she decided it was time for a showdown. She'd been walking a high wire with him, afraid that any misstep would send her plummeting into a black oblivion that she couldn't escape. She couldn't stand it a minute longer. "I get the feeling that you're hiding something from me."

"I'm not."

"Liar."

He advanced on her, his bare toes touching hers as they peeked from her sandals. For a second he didn't say a word, just studied the contours of her face, and her breath got lost somewhere between her lungs and throat. She stared into eyes a deep, mysterious blue, eyes that seemed to see into the most secret parts of her. Her palms began to sweat a little, and for a breathless instant she wondered if he was going to kiss her. *Get a grip, Nikki!*

"I just want to get you out of here before you really get hurt."

"So you're superstitious."

"I don't follow."

"Because the *accident* happened here, you want to leave. That doesn't make a whole lot of sense. Unless you think I'm only accident-prone when I'm on Salvaje. Or unless you know something more than you're telling me."

"Like what?" Frowning, he locked the door firmly behind him.

"I have nightmares, Trent, and I relive falling over the cliff, only I don't just take a misstep and pitch toward the ocean on my own," she said, catching his full attention. His head snapped up and the muscles in the back of his neck grew strident. "I know someone was chasing me and that same person gave me a shove over the edge." The room was suddenly so close, she had trouble getting enough air into her lungs. His gaze narrowed on her, and he didn't move.

"Who?"

"I...I don't know. I don't remember. But it's so real, it's got to be true."

"You think I pushed you," he said, his voice flat, his nostrils flaring slightly.

Her pulse throbbed in her brain. "I don't know what to think. But I know that you haven't been completely honest with me."

"Oh, Lord," he said on a heavy sigh. Rubbing a hand around the back of his neck, he shook his head. When he looked at her again, his gaze had sharpened. "Part of your dream is real, part illusion. It's true I didn't see you fall over the edge. I was already at the mission, waiting for you. But no one was following us."

"You're certain?"

He didn't answer. "Why would anyone push you, Nikki?"

"I don't know." She shook her head, trying to remember.

"Oh, Nikki." Muttering a curse under his breath, he placed his hands on either side of her body, trapping her against the bureau. He leaned forward, his nose nearly touching hers. "I know you don't like the idea, but you're going to have to trust me. I'll get you home. I'll make sure you're safe."

"You'll be honest with me?"

He hesitated, but only briefly, then one side of his mouth lifted into a sardonic smile. "Of course I will,

darlin',", he drawled, and she knew in an instant that this
man was an inveterate liar, a man who would say or do
anything in order to accomplish his goals.

Despite all that, regardless of her gut feeling not to
trust him, a part of her wanted to lean on him, rely on
him, trust him with her life. If only she could let herself
feel safe with him. He smelled clean and male and...
She bit her lip as he tilted her chin with one finger and
whispered, "Just trust me, Nikki. We'll be home soon
and you can see your own doctor. You'll get your memory back. Things will be better."

Trust me. Her heart twisted. She wanted to trust him.
More than anything in her life, she wanted to believe
that he was telling her the truth, that they were married, that there wasn't anyone on Salvaje or anywhere
else who would want to hurt her.

He kissed her then. Slowly and deliberately, his
hands placed on either side of her head, his body pressed
close to hers. His lips were warm and persuasive, his
tongue a gentle prod against her teeth. She knew she
should stop him, that kissing him was courting disaster, yet she closed her eyes and parted her lips willingly, and his hands moved slowly down her face to
her shoulders and lower still to her buttocks. His bare
chest rubbed against her T-shirt, and she was lost in the
smell and feel of him.

With a groan, he drew her closer, pulling her hips
against his so that she could feel the hardness of his
desire against her abdomen. Her blood was pounding
through her veins as his kiss deepened.

As suddenly as he'd grabbed her, he let go, swearing
and planting his hands on his jean-clad hips. He closed
his eyes and his jaw became hard as granite. "Son of

a bitch. Son of a goddamned bitch!" Raking his hands through his hair, he growled, "I've got to get out of here.... *We've* got to get out of here."

She couldn't agree with him more. Being cooped up in the small room, with only each other, was playing with fire.

"Come on," he said, stuffing his arms through the sleeves of a bleached denim shirt. "Let's have some breakfast and then we'll check out Santa María. Do some sightseeing. Something. Wait a minute." He closed the gap between them once more, and with his shirt still open, he surveyed her wounds. His thumb brushed across the scab still clinging to her cheek. "But we can't be out long. The doctor doesn't want too much sun on—"

"I know. I'll wear a hat," she said, angry with him or herself, she didn't know which.

"I just wouldn't want that beautiful face to scar."

"I'll be careful." She felt a sudden elation at the prospect of escaping the prison walls of the hotel room and realized this would be her chance, if she ever was alone, to have the film she'd found in her camera developed.

A sharp needle of guilt stabbed at her, but she quickly shoved it aside. She had the right to learn everything there was to know about her "husband," even if she had to sneak behind his back to uncover the truth.

He changed into walking shorts and a T-shirt, slipped a pair of aviator glasses over the bridge of his nose and headed outside. The sunbaked driveway to the front of the hotel was filled with idling cabs and cars. Trent took her hand and led her past the taxi stand to a shaded bench where the driver of a horse-drawn carriage was dozing.

At the sound of approaching footsteps, the horse—a big bay gelding—snorted, and the driver's black eyes opened. "Ah, *señor,*" he said, tipping a wide-brimmed hat. "A ride for the lady?"

"Sí." Trent fished in his wallet for a bill and asked to be taken downtown.

"To see the beautiful *Santa María*—just like the name of Columbus, his boat, no?"

"Right," Nikki said, grinning. It felt good to be out in the sunshine, to see the shadows of swaying palm fronds play across the ground, to talk to someone other than Trent, to feel young and carefree despite the worrisome fact that she remembered so little of her past.

Trent helped her into the leather seats, and the driver climbed onto his perch and flicked his whip over the gelding's ears. The carriage began to creak as it rolled forward, bouncing a little on the uneven street of time-worn cobblestones.

With a hat to shade her face and huge sunglasses to cover her eyes, Nikki nearly felt normal. Sitting next to Trent, feeling the length of his leg rest against hers, smelling the soap and leather scent of him, she could almost imagine herself a bride on her honeymoon. Almost.

Trent threw one arm behind her shoulders, though he didn't draw her close, and his fingers tapped restlessly on the tucked upholstery supporting her head. His eyes, hidden by his aviator glasses, were restless, always on the move. His jaw was stern, his lips compressed, and never once did he seem to relax.

It was as if he was looking for something. Or someone. Expecting danger. Lines of strain carved his skin at the corners of his mouth and his fingers kept up their nervous beat. Like a restless, wary animal, he watched and listened.

Nikki refused to let his anxiety infect her. It had been ages since she'd been out among people, and she hadn't realized what a social creature she was. Delighted, she watched street vendors try to hawk their wares from umbrella-covered pushcarts parked on the street corners. Bicyclists and motorbikers vied for room with a few cars and ancient pickups that clogged the streets. Yet the old horse plodded on, undisturbed by the noise and motion of this lazy city.

Overhead, suspended from lampposts, baskets of flowers blazed in a profusion of color. Deep purple blooms and bright pink buds trailed from long vines and fluttered in the breeze, perfuming the air already filled with the scents of saltwater, fish and seaweed.

It was a glorious day. The sun was blazing with tropical heat, but the breadfruit trees and palms offered some shade. As the carriage moved slowly downhill, Nikki stared past the driver and haunches of the draft horse to catch glimpses of the ocean, azure and sparkling with sunlight. Schooners and fishing rigs skimmed the bay, and to the north, jagged rocks, small islands unto themselves, rose like the spiny backs of ancient sea monsters hidden deep in the water.

Involuntarily Nikki shuddered, and her good mood dissipated on the wind. She looked upward to the cliffs above the city to see the crumbling bell tower of the old mission, barely visible through the dense foliage of the hills. Why had she been running up the steep path and who had pushed her? For, despite Trent's claims otherwise, someone had deliberately shoved her over the embankment, hoping that she would plunge to her death on the rocky shoals.

The driver pulled the horse to a stop, and as Trent tipped the driver, Nikki hopped to the ground, careful to land on her uninjured foot. For a second she felt as if someone was watching her, and she turned quickly, looking at the throng of tourists crowding the street, half expecting to meet a stranger's malevolent gaze, but none of the tourists or locals wandering through a central square of shops and cafés near the park were paying her the least bit of attention. Most were walking slowly, a few had found a seat in the ornate wrought-iron benches to eat, read or smoke, still others threw scraps of food to the flock of birds that had gathered in the shade of several grapefruit trees.

She told herself that she was being silly—that some of Trent's tension had infected her, but she couldn't re-capture her lighthearted spirit of only moments before.

The sound of music from a steel-drum band floated on the breeze as Trent led the way along the sandy boardwalk that rimmed the water. People strolled along the docks, stopping to barter at outdoor booths and carts, chattering in a variety of languages.

At a small café, Trent ordered breakfast of fresh fruit, fried bread and scallops. They sipped fresh orange juice and thick black coffee and watched the ocean, which glittered in the sunlight.

"You didn't tell me about any of the women in your life," she said as she finished her coffee.

"You didn't ask."

Leaning both elbows on the table and balancing her chin in her hands, she said, "I'm asking now."

He grinned. That slow, sexy smile that caused a nest

of butterflies to erupt in her stomach. "All the gory details?"

"Every one," she replied, though a pang of jealousy surprised her. The thought of Trent with another woman was unsettling.

He took a long swallow from his cup, then frowned into the dregs. "There isn't really much to tell. I had a high school sweetheart in Toledo, but she ended up marrying another guy—someone more stable, which translates into dollars. The kid's dad owned one of the biggest steel mills in the Midwest. I moved from one college to another, didn't put down any roots or leave many broken hearts."

"You haven't been married before."

He shook his head.

"Never came close?"

"Not as close as you," he said, tilting his head to one side and surveying her. "You still don't remember Dave?"

She thought back, trying to conjure up some memory, some link to a man she'd nearly married. He was handsome and athletic—she'd seen that much in the snapshot she'd found in her wallet—but there was something else about him, a personality trait, that seemed to surface in her mind. "Not really, but I have this feeling he was very dominating."

Trent lifted a shoulder, but Nikki was on a roll. "That's right. Not overtly demanding, but always subtly suggesting that I should dress a little differently, act more sophisticated, get a job more suitable for a woman…." She felt an old emotion break through the void in her mind. "He…he took me somewhere once, to the symphony, or the opera, or something, and he bought me a dress because he didn't like the clothes I'd been wearing." She remembered opening the box, excited until she'd seen the black sheath with the gauze sleeves and skirt so short she wouldn't be able to sit comfortably.

"It'll look great on you," Dave had insisted, and to keep him happy, she'd worn the dress, even letting him tell her to pin her hair up in a French braid. All evening she'd felt uncomfortable. He'd introduced her to friends, showing her off as if she were another acquisition, just as he'd proudly displayed his new top-of-the-line sports car and his gold watch. Though he'd cared about her, Nikki had always gotten the feeling that his love hadn't gone past the surface, that if she'd been born ugly or scarred, he wouldn't have cast her a second glance. Lips curling wryly, she wondered what he'd think of her now with her battered face.

"I do remember Dave," she said. "In some ways he was like you."

Trent snorted, but his gaze never left her face.

"You know—demanding, arrogant, pushy," she teased, unable to resist baiting him.

He reached over and clasped his fingers over her wrist. "Watch it, lady," he warned, "or you'll find out just how pushy I can be." She might have been frightened, but the fingers around her wrist were warm, the curve of his lips seductive.

They wandered through the small town, and Nikki never stopped looking for a camera shop. As they window-shopped, pausing to finger trinkets of silver and gold, agate and shell, she never forgot the roll of film hidden deep in her pocket.

They passed carts laden with flowers, fresh fruit,

handcrafted jewelry, sweaters and kites. On the docks, fishermen sat and smoked while repairing their nets or selling their catches. Past the boardwalk, the white sand stretched in a lazy crescent surrounding the bay. Sunbathers lay on towels, soaking up rays, drinking from tall glasses. Children waded near the shore and snorkelers waded deeper into the glimmering surf.

An island paradise, Nikki thought. *A perfect spot for a honeymoon.* She almost believed it was true. However, one glance at Trent and her romantic fantasy crumbled. She remembered nothing of him. While staring at his rugged, handsome features, no image of being with him surfaced in her mind. Slowly she was glimpsing small, murky fragments of her memory, but never had Trent appeared in any of the tiny vignettes of her past. Why not?

Because he's a complete stranger, that's why!

That thought hit her like a blow, and she realized that she'd let herself get caught up in this ridiculous fantasy, that she was beginning to believe, if only a little, that he was her husband.

Even the undeveloped pictures might not prove that he wasn't her husband.

In the early afternoon, Nikki began to tire. They stopped to rest at an outdoor café situated on the north end of the boardwalk. Trent ordered drinks when Nikki spied the sign, a painted board attached to a short stucco building that housed José's camera shop, which was located less than a block from the café.

She hesitated, but told herself there was no time like the present. The waiter deposited a frosty beer on the table in front of Trent and an iced lemonade for Nikki. They didn't talk much, just sipped their drinks slowly, watching as the tourists, young and old, moved along the street. The canister of film felt hot against her thigh, and she watched the minutes roll by, hoping for some excuse to leave him.

A loud woman in a straw hat, chasing a slim youth, caught her attention before blending into the crowd that drifted slowly along the street. The seconds ticked by. Trent was nearly finished with his beer.

Nikki was taking her time, slowly drinking her lemonade, hoping for a reason to leave the table. She watched a black man without any teeth, who was playing a guitar in a doorway on the other side of the street. A thin old dog was lying at his feet, sunning himself and moving only to lift his head and sniff the air before letting out a low growl and lying back down again.

She felt Trent's eyes on her and took another swallow. But her throat was nearly clogged and she had trouble drinking. At a nearby table, a single man was nursing a beer, and though his back was turned, Nikki felt as if she'd seen him before…in the hotel lobby or… As if he knew she'd spied him, he paid for his drink and left, never once glancing over his shoulder.

You're imagining things, she told herself, turning back to the guitar player who was playing the soft calypso strains of an unfamiliar song. Nikki watched the crowd and noticed a tall, thin native dressed in white. A red sash was his belt and a green parrot was perched on his shoulder.

The dog lifted his head, sniffed, and spying the bird, jumped to his feet, barking loudly. The parrot flapped its great wings and squawked, trying to escape.

Nikki flinched, knocking over her glass and Trent's beer. Liquid and ice cubes sloshed across the table, beer foaming into lemonade as it drizzled over the edge, spilling onto her lap.

"What the devil?" Trent demanded, looking from the dog, now being dragged into the building by the toothless man, and the parrot, unable to fly away because of its leash, to Nikki.

"Oh, God, I'm sorry," she apologized, grabbing at her glass as it rolled toward the edge. "What a mess!"

Trent hardly blinked, just shouted to a passing waiter as Nikki dabbed at the table with a napkin. Her shorts were soaked, her blouse sprinkled with the beer and lemonade that still oozed through the cracks in the table and dripped to the brick patio.

"Señora, por favor..." A waiter with cloth in hand came to the rescue, and in the confusion, Nikki touched Trent's sleeve. "I'd better try to rinse this in the women's room," she said, motioning toward her clothes. "So that they won't stain."

"Let's just go back to the hotel."

"No!" Her fingers tightened over his arm. "We've had such a good time, let's not spoil it. Order another couple of drinks and I'll try not to be so much of a klutz." Without waiting for any further protests, she dashed into the building, ostensibly in search of a restroom.

She took the time to look back through the window and spied Trent talking with the waiter. Good. As quickly as possible, without causing a scene, she ducked through a side door and dashed along the shady side of the street to José's. Her ankle began to throb, but she kept running. A tiny bell tinkled as she entered the shop. A young, dark-skinned girl was at the register, helping another customer, a man with silver hair and a cane.

Nikki waited impatiently, wishing she could push the older man aside. As he paid for his purchase, he turned, and his gaze collided with Nikki's. For a second, Nikki felt as if she should know the man, as if she'd stepped into the bottom of a dank well. A seeping coldness crept along her skin as she stared into eyes devoid of emotion. Her heart nearly stopped. The old man forced a smile that was well-practiced but friendly. The wintry feeling she'd experienced dissipated. "Pardon me, miss," he said in perfect English. With a tip of his straw fedora, he walked slowly out the door.

She gazed after him, but she didn't have time to wonder who he was—probably just some old guy who was surprised by her bruised face. She yanked her roll of film from her pocket and set it near the register. With the aid of her dictionary, and in halting Spanish, she asked the girl to process the film *pronto*. Nervous as a cat, she kept checking her watch while the pretty salesgirl took her sweet time about filling out the paperwork. Sweat began to collect on Nikki's palms, but eventually the salesgirl told her the film would be ready in two days. Nikki said a quick thanks and hurried out of the shop.

Breathless, she slipped back through the side door of the café and into the restroom, where, still dressed, she splashed her blouse and shorts with water before attempting to wring out all the liquid from the clumps of material she could squeeze in her fingers. She looked a mess, but couldn't worry about the half-baked job. Forcing her breathing to slow, she returned to the table where Trent, cradling his new bottle of beer on his stomach, was waiting.

He cast a glance at her wet clothes. "Okay?"

"Mmm." A fresh glass of lemonade was waiting on the clean table. She took a long swallow and hoped that she appeared calm, that she didn't show any sign of pain from her ankle or look as if she'd been running.

"Took long enough."

"It was a busy place." Smiling sweetly, she picked up a peanut from the dish on the table and popped it into her mouth. "I guess a lot of women had spilled on themselves."

He lifted a brow over the rim of his sunglasses but didn't comment. She wanted to squirm under the intensity of his gaze, but managed a smile as she lifted her glass to her lips. Feeling a tiny drop of sweat slide down her temple, she silently prayed he didn't notice that she was nervous as a mouse trapped in a rattler's cage.

"Cheers," she said, touching the rim of her glass to the top of his dark bottle. "To the honeymoon."

The muscles in his face flinched a little. "Cheers," he muttered, but his eyes didn't meet hers. Instead, he scanned the sea of people strolling past the umbrella tables situated in the courtyard.

Inwardly, Nikki breathed a sigh of relief. The lemonade was tart and cool, and now that she'd accomplished her mission, she could relax. They finished their drinks, and though Nikki protested, Trent insisted they return to the hotel.

She wanted to argue with him, but he was insistent and guided her back to the carriage stop. She decided it was better not to do battle just then. Besides, the sun was blistering, heat waving up from the cobblestone streets. Only the breeze off the ocean offered any relief. Nikki's face began to hurt again and her ankle throbbed.

Trent helped her into the carriage.

Two days, she thought, as the horse trudged slowly up the hill. Only two days. Then she would pick up the pictures. Finally she might have an answer or two about Trent McKenzie, the heretofore mystery man.

So what would she do if she discovered no sign of her "husband" in the shots? Worse yet, what would she do if he *was* in the photographs, holding her hand, kissing her, flashing his sexy smile toward the camera?

Her stomach did a nosedive. What if she found out that she really was married to this stranger?

CHAPTER SIX

"I WANT TO go back to the mission," Nikki said calmly as she shuffled the cards she'd been playing with for nearly an hour. Slowly but surely she was going out of her mind, cooped up with this man she wanted to trust, but couldn't let herself. She'd spent most of the time since they'd gotten back from the carriage ride pretending to play solitaire, surreptitiously studying him from beneath lowered lashes, willing herself to remember, knowing in her heart that a man like Trent McKenzie was unforgettable.

"You're not serious." He was stretched out on the bed, half listening to some Spanish program on the television while flipping through the pages of a sports magazine devoted solely, it seemed, to soccer. He'd been restless, as restless as she, since returning from the carriage ride. Like the clouds gathering in the tropical sky, the tension between them had grown heavy and oppressive.

"I'm dead serious, Trent. I think I should go back to the mission."

"Are you out of your mind?" He tossed his magazine aside.

"What mind?" she quipped, though the joke fell flat and he raked his fingers through his hair in the frustration that consumed them both.

She knew the mission was a dangerous topic, but going back up that trail was something she'd decided she had to do. Before they left the island. While she still had the chance.

Sitting at the table near the French doors, she looked back to his long body lying so insolently over the mussed bed covers and tried not to notice the dark hair on his legs or the open V of his shirt and the chest hairs springing from darkly tanned skin. She even tried to dismiss the concern and worry darkening his gaze.

She continued shuffling cards, listening to them ruffle rather than think about how that atmosphere in the room had become sultry. She'd caught him looking at her, staring at her with eyes that seemed to burn straight to her soul. She flipped a card faceup. The jack of diamonds. "I think if I went back up there, to the 'scene of the crime,' so to speak, I might remember something. Something important."

"There's no road that goes all the way to the mission. You'd have to walk, and that ankle of yours—"

"We could ride." She flipped another card. Queen of hearts.

"Ride? Ride *what?*"

"Motorbikes."

"Too bumpy."

She slapped down several more cards. "Horses, then. There's got to be some way up there."

"I don't think you're ready to go horseback riding."

"It doesn't matter what you think."

"Like hell!" He leaped from the bed and strode across the room. In one swift motion, he shoved her cards out of the way and placed his palms flat on the table so that his head was level with hers. "You're my wife, damn it. My responsibility. I'm not going to have you hurt yourself again and—"

"I'm a person!" she shot back, glaring at him, nose to nose. The air seemed to crackle between them, and she could see the streaks of gray in his blue eyes. "Whether you're my husband or not, I'm an adult. Able to make my own decisions." Oh, Lord, she'd had this conversation before. A long time ago. With…with someone else…. Her father! They'd been arguing—about trust and responsibility—and her father's face had been flushed, his lips tight with anger at his wayward daughter.

"You can't decide anything until you're well!"

His words snapped her back to the present, and all the old anger mingled with her new fury. "And who decides that?" she demanded, thrusting her chin out mutinously. "You or God?"

His eyes sparked. "You are the most aggravating female I've ever met!"

"Great reason to get married, isn't it?"

Like a panther springing, he grabbed her. He dragged her into his arms, clamped his lips over hers and kissed her with a hot desire so wild she couldn't break free. Her blood was already pounding through her veins, and now his rough kiss caused her heart to thud and her mind to spin.

She yanked her head away from him. "Let go of me," she ground out.

"Not until you start making sense!"

He kissed her again. Harder this time. She tried to fight him, for she knew that kissing him, relying on him, giving herself up to him, was an irretrievable mistake. But his tongue was playing magic upon her lips, prying them open, pressing inward, and he'd all but climbed over the table to force his body close to hers.

Heat swirled inside her. Liquid and white-hot, desire coiled in wanton knots that slowly unwound and slid through her bloodstream.

"God, you make me crazy," he said when he finally lifted his head and stared into her eyes. His chest was rising and falling, his breathing torn from his lungs.

"You *are* crazy."

"Only with you, darlin'." He dropped his hands and gritted his teeth, desire still flaming in his hot blue eyes. By sheer force of will, he walked away from her. "Only with you."

Nikki rubbed her swollen lips and bit back another sharp retort. This was no time for her temper to take command of her tongue. If he chose to be autocratic, so be it. She'd wait him out. It shouldn't be all that hard. There was no way he'd spend an entire day tomorrow cooped up in the hotel, and when he left, she'd do exactly what she damned well pleased.

Flopping back on the bed, he picked up the phone and ordered room service for dinner. With one hand over the receiver, he asked, "What do you want?"

"Anything you order for me, O lord and master."

"Knock it off."

"I have no right to make decisions," she said sweetly, though her eyes were shooting daggers. "Remember?"

Jaw tightening, he ordered for her in Spanish, hung up and said, "Hope you like liver and chickpeas in a hot pepper sauce."

"My favorite," she replied with a smile.

Growling about unappreciative women, he strode to the veranda, slammed the door behind him and stared at the dusky sky.

Liver and chick-peas! Still fuming, Nikki went into the bathroom, locked the door and soaked in a tub of warm water. She didn't know if she could stand another moment of being alone with Trent.

Forty-five minutes later, refreshed and ready to do battle, she returned to the room and found him seated at the table, waiting. The dishes from room service had arrived and were still covered. A glass of white wine shimmered, waiting, next to her plate while a long-necked bottle of beer was sweating on the table in front of his chair. There were smaller dishes of bread, butter and dessert as well.

"Didn't want to start without you," he said, kicking out her chair as she rounded the table wearing a bathrobe over her pajamas.

"Noble of you."

He snorted as she took a seat opposite him. She felt his eyes linger on her a little too long before he slid his gaze away. "May as well eat. Wouldn't want that hot pepper sauce to cool down." With a flourish he lifted the lid from his dish and steam rose from the platter of whitefish, sautéed vegetables and pasta covered with a cream-and-garlic sauce. "Specialty of the house."

Nikki braced herself and uncovered her meal to discover that Trent had ordered the same for her.

"All out of the other stuff," he explained as he twisted off the cap of his beer.

"Sure."

"Maybe tomorrow." He was teasing her, and his eyes glinted seductively.

"After the ride to the mission."

"Don't start with me," he warned, his lips pulling into a harsh frown.

"Okay, okay!" She lifted her palms outward. "Truce."

"Is that possible?"

"God only knows," she said with a smile before lifting the glass of wine to her lips.

She tried her best not to antagonize him during the rest of the meal. They ate in companionable silence, and the food was delicious. Tender and flaky, the fish was the best she'd eaten in a long, long while.

She tried not to stare at him, attempted to make small talk, but there was only so much that could be said about the hotel, the weather and the town of Santa María.

She was nearly stuffed when he lifted the lids on two small dishes. "Oh, I couldn't," she said, shaking her head at the small custard cup filled with a crème pudding, covered by brandied bananas and drizzled in sauce.

"Come on. It's an island specialty." He poured them each a cup of coffee and added a slim stream of cream into her cup. She watched the lazy white clouds roll to the dark surface and wondered how many times in the past Trent had poured her a cup of coffee. How many times had they eaten, just the two of them at a table like this? How many times had they fallen into bed and made love until dawn?

Her throat felt suddenly dry, and she took a long drink from the coffee. She had to quit thinking about him like that—to stop her mind from running away with these fantasies. She glanced at him over the rim of her cup and her stomach turned over. He stared at her with such intensity, such hot-blooded desire, that she forced her gaze away.

Nerves tight, she tackled the dessert, eating most of the sweet concoction, until, belly stretched, she shoved the cup aside. "That's it. No more."

"You sure? There's more coffee—"

"No way. Go ahead." Yawning, she stretched in her chair and noticed that his eyes slid to the V of her neckline.

"Nah. I, uh, think I'll go clean up."

He shoved himself away from the table and walked straight to the bathroom. He locked the door behind himself and wondered how in the hell he'd get through the next few days. Didn't she know what she was doing to him? Didn't she care? Or had she changed so much since the accident? He didn't want to force himself upon her, not until she was ready, but damn, being this close to her, sleeping with her, for God's sake, and trying to keep his hands off her was driving him up the wall.

You're losing it, man.

Muttering under his breath, he turned on the shower spray. He kicked off his boots, yanked off his clothes and stepped under the ice-cold spray. Closing his eyes, he hoped the frigid water would temper his blood and take care of the erection that seemed to sprout every time he was alone with her.

The water stung. Sharp, cold needles against his skin. He leaned against the tiles and waited, forcing all thoughts of Nikki from his mind. He had other things to worry about. Tomorrow, first thing, he'd have to check with *el Perro,* just to make sure she wasn't up to any funny stuff. At the thought of the disgusting little man,

Trent scowled, wishing he never had to deal with the likes of the Dog.

Unfortunately it was all part of the game.

Nikki took advantage of her time alone in the room. She was still angry that he thought he could tell her what she could and couldn't do. Well, he had another think coming. Trent wasn't going to get the best of her. She might not remember her past, but she wasn't some mindless wimp who didn't know what was best for her! With one ear tuned to the running water, she dug through his jacket and pants pockets and came up with his wallet.

"Bingo," she whispered, opening the leather with shaking fingers and a cat-who-ate-the-prized-canary smile. What would she do if she discovered he wasn't Trent McKenzie, that he had several aliases, that he'd lied to her? Her heart was pounding so loudly she was certain he could hear it through the closed door and above the shower's spray. With clammy fingers, she opened the wallet and held her breath.

The Washington state driver's license confirmed that his name was, indeed, Trent McKenzie, and that his address was the same as he'd listed on the hotel registration. His picture stared up at her, his harsh glare challenging her, and she felt like a thief. For a second she thought about returning the wallet, but she knew she might not get a second chance to discover more about him.

She told herself that going through his things was all part of investigative journalism, her job. Besides, if he truly was her husband, then he shouldn't mind. Quickly, she flipped through the cards stuffed neatly in special slots: social security, American Express, MasterCard, Visa, Puget Sound Insurance and an oil company card issued to Trent McKenzie. There were no pictures in his wallet, no clues to the inner man, but he was carrying a few hundred dollars in cash and traveler's checks worth nearly two thousand. She was about to flip the wallet closed when she checked one final recess. Her heart stopped beating as she read the permit to carry a concealed weapon.

Because he was a private investigator. She supposed she should feel comforted, but a knot of worry tightened in her guts and she bit her lip against the fear that shot like ice-cold bullets through her bloodstream.

The shower stopped and, with clumsy fingers, she hastily returned the wallet to his pocket. She slid between the covers, snapped off the light, settled her head on the pillow and again feigned sleep. The ruse of dozing wouldn't work indefinitely, she knew, but until she was ready to suffer the consequences of making love to her "husband," she was more than willing to sink to deception.

He left her alone the next morning. Exhausted, she'd fallen asleep sometime after midnight, despite his strong arm thrown around her waist and his warm, steady breath against her nape. Once in the middle of the night, she'd awakened and noticed that his hand had cupped her breast, as if he had every right to touch her anywhere he pleased.

She had shifted and the hand fell away, but it left her feeling empty and frustrated and wishing—oh, God, *wishing*—that she knew who she was.

He'd left a note on the nightstand, telling her that he'd be back before eleven and that she should order room service again.

"Not on your life," she said, flinging off the covers. She had to work fast. After dressing and combing her hair in record time, she dialed the overseas operator and was able to connect with the United States and the offices of the *Seattle Observer*. With any luck, Connie would be working the early shift. Nikki crossed her fingers. Within minutes, a pert female voice, thousands of miles away, answered on the fifth ring. "Connie Benson."

"Holding down the fort?" Nikki asked, her voice lowered though Trent wasn't due back for a few hours.

"Who is this?"

"Nikki. Nikki Carrothers."

"Are you kidding?" Connie said, her voice suddenly friendly. "I thought you were somewhere in the South Pacific."

"The Caribbean," Nikki corrected, trying to keep her voice steady. She took a deep breath. "On my honeymoon."

"On your *what?*" Connie screeched. "Hey, who is this? Is this some kind of joke or what?"

"It's no joke," Nikki said, explaining the circumstances as best she could, though she didn't admit to her amnesia. For now, she decided, the fewer people who knew about her loss of memory, the better.

"I don't believe it! You. Married." Connie chuckled, and Nikki saw the image of a red-blond, big-boned woman with freckles and laughing gold eyes. "Well, you know what they say—never say never."

"What's that supposed to mean?"

"You know, after that Dave fiasco, you swore off men for good. So who's the lucky guy and why didn't I meet him?"

"You know him," Nikki said, crossing her fingers. This was her first chance to catch Trent in a lie. "His name is Trent McKenzie and he works for—"

"The insurance company? Puget Sound Insurance?" Connie said on a long breath. "God, he's gorgeous!"

"Then you remember him?"

"How could you forget a man like that?" she said. "And you *married* him?"

I wish I knew.

"Let me tell you, if I ever snag a man like that I'll hire one of those sky pilots to write it in the sky over downtown Seattle and I'll have the biggest wedding this town has ever seen just to show him off! Come on, Nikki, why didn't you tell me?"

Nikki was ready for that one. "We wanted to surprise everyone."

"Oh, God, how romantic!" Again a long, envious sigh. "Wait until I tell Peggy. She's gonna flip. She'll think you'll want to give up your job, stay home and raise about fifty kids."

"I don't think so," Nikki said, but grinned. It felt good to speak to someone she knew she could trust. "So you remember introducing him to me?"

"Of course I do. It was that claim I had a few months ago. He was checking it out. Came into the office to talk to me, and you were there."

So far, so good. Trent's story was holding up, but there was still something wrong, something out of sync. "How's the job going?"

"Same old grind," Connie said. "It looks like there's been some scam down at the docks. One of the union bosses has been skimming off of the dues and there's a drug ring working out of Tacoma, but, of course, John and Max were given those assignments. I got to cover the arrival of Jana, that big-time fashion model from Europe, but other than that it's the same old, same old. You know, school district stuff, city council news, nothing earth-shattering. As for your friend Crowley, he's still up to his old tricks, but no one seems to be able to prove a thing. If you ask me, Max has dropped the ball on that one."

A little spark of memory flared. "Crowley?" she said nonchalantly, though her heart was thundering. There was something about that name, something important.

"Yeah. You know, Peggy went to bat for you to cover the story, but it was the higher-ups. Frank Pianzani, he's grooming Max for his job, so he put the thumbs-down on a woman covering the senator. Sometimes I think the women's movement never made it through the doors of the *Observer*. Sure, we can talk it up all we want, and report it—God knows we'll get all the information into the paper—but practice it? That'll never happen. Not as long as Pianzani and some of his pals are in charge."

Nervously, Nikki twisted the phone cord. "So tell me about Crowley."

"The good senator has been keeping his nose clean and his face out of the paper for the past couple of weeks," Connie said. "I've been too busy to pay much attention to him. Gotta get all the hot news on the school lunch menu, you know. Someone's got to report if they're serving hot dogs or jo-jos." She laughed and Nikki smiled. "You know, my most interesting story since you've been gone is whether there's too much fat in the food that the schools are serving."

"It's a dirty job, but someone's got to do it."

Connie laughed.

"I think I'll come back home and dig into the Crowley story again," she said, hoping Connie would fill her in on the details.

"I'd expect it."

"Just where did everything end?" Nikki persisted, her hands twining in the telephone cord. "What with getting married and all, I barely had time to think about it."

"Like I said, he's keeping a low profile. If he's into anything shady, he's hiding it well. Anyway, it'll wait until you get back. Besides, you know we agreed we shouldn't talk about it on the work lines."

"Oh." So this was big enough that they didn't trust other people at the paper overhearing their conversations? What could it be? Try as she might, she couldn't remember.

"You know, all this talk about the senator started about the time you met Trent."

"I...I...know," Nikki said, though she felt as if she'd been hit by a sledgehammer. Was there a connection between Trent and Senator Crowley and if so, what? *What was going on?*

"Look, I'll talk to you when you get home. And if you want, I'll nose around."

"That would be great."

"Consider it done!"

Nikki was more mystified than ever. Who the devil was Senator Crowley?

They talked for a couple of minutes longer, and Nikki explained that she'd be home in a few days. She didn't have a lot of time before Trent showed up again, but she was still reticent to sever the connection to her friend and her past.

She hung up and sighed. *So Trent hadn't lied.* She didn't know whether to laugh or cry. One thing was for certain, she couldn't give up trying to remember everything she could about her life before the accident, and the two items at the top of her list were Trent McKenzie and Senator Crowley.

Glancing at her watch, she decided she had time enough to talk to her mother. If she could get through. Her luck held and in a few minutes, her mother's high-pitched voice echoed in her ear. Eloise seemed genuinely glad to hear from her. Though the background noise was loud, and more than once her mother had to cover the mouthpiece to shout at one of her teenaged sons, she seemed relieved to hear from her youngest daughter.

"Thank God you finally called," she reprimanded gently. "Your father phoned. Told me about your accident, but didn't know where you were staying. Then dropped the bomb that you'd gotten married to some stranger. Nikki, I just never thought you would do anything so rash. Now, Janet, that's a different story. When she married Tim, I knew it was a mistake. I wouldn't be surprised if she called me up from Reno or some other place like that and told me she'd gotten married again. But you…well, you were always the sensible one. You know I was awfully fond of Dave…."

"I know, Mom," Nikki said, hating the deception. "But it didn't work out."

"And this Trevor, he's—"

"Trent, Mom. Trent McKenzie."

"I could've sworn your father told me his name was Trevor. That man, I tell you…" she grumbled, then let the rest of her thought die. "Look, just come down to L.A. as soon as you can. I'd love to meet him and so would Fred. He thinks of you girls as his own, you know."

Fred's affections, Nikki remembered, were anything but directed at his stepdaughters. And her mother knew it. Why she continually tried to deceive them all was beyond Nikki. Fred Sampas had never given any of Eloise's daughters a second glance. "Extra baggage," he'd once complained to a friend, and Carole, Nikki's middle sister, had overheard the comment. "Tell Fred I said hello," she said, hiding the sarcasm in her voice.

"I will, honey, but first you tell me all about your accident. Your father was sketchy but he said you're all right. He wasn't lying, was he? He wasn't just trying to spare my feelings."

"No, Mom, I'm okay. I've still got a few scrapes and a couple of bruises, but I'll be fine in a day or two." She filled in most of the details of her fall and recovery, and her mother, over the crackly long-distance wire, seemed satisfied.

"Thank the Lord you weren't hurt any worse! You know, Nikki, I don't know why you can't slow down a little. Now that you're married, you should take things easier, quit trying to prove yourself to that darned paper."

"Is that what I do?"

"Well, you want them to treat you like a man, and you're not one. I guess you know that now."

"I just want to be treated equally."

"There is no equal. Not in this world. Just like there's nothing fair. You know that as well as I do." Nikki didn't bother arguing, but she realized that she wasn't close to her mother and probably never had been. They talked for a few more minutes before Nikki's half brothers commanded her mother's attention and they had to disconnect.

Nikki fell back on the bed and tears burned at the corners of her eyes. Her mother and father had never been happy together, that much she knew, and the divorce had been, for them, a relief, but there had always been a bit of pain, and a little prick of guilt that Nikki had never dislodged. She was old enough to know that she hadn't caused the deep, angry rift between her mother and father, and yet she'd felt real jealousy that Eloise seemed so content with Fred and her new sons. She let out a slow, shuddering breath. "Quit feeling sorry for yourself," she chided.

This wasn't the time to dwell on the sorrows of her past, so she pushed her painful memories—tiny as they were—of her mother aside and concentrated instead on the call with Connie. Their conversation had served to whet her appetite to know more, find out everything she could, and the most certain way of throwing off the dark shadows of her nightmare was to face her past and the accident. The first step was the mission.

"Let's go!" Nikki, skirt bunched around her thighs, nudged her heels into the mare's dappled flanks. The little gray darted forward, galloping up the rocky path leading to the mission. Short, dark legs lengthened stride and the mare's ears flattened against her head. In the blur that was her vision, Nikki saw tall grass and wildflowers bend as the breeze over the ocean blew inland, carrying ominous clouds and oppressive heat. They rimmed the dark forest where, in her nightmares, she'd been chased in a life-and-death race for...what?

Nikki glanced at the gray sky nervously. Dressed in a skirt and a T-shirt, she wasn't ready for a tropical storm. Besides, she had to work fast. Before Trent caught up with her.

Renting the horse hadn't been easy. A driver of one of the horse-drawn carriages had told her of a man who had horses that could be leased for the day, but Nikki's halting Spanish, her half-healed face and the desperation in her tone had made the owner cautious. Only after paying him extra did she wind up with the spunky little mare.

"Don't worry about it," she told herself. But she felt anxious, partly because of the storm brewing, partly because she was deceiving Trent again and partly because, ever since leaving the hotel, she'd had the uncanny feeling that she was being followed. "Oh, stop being a ninny!" It was just the smell of the storm and the fact that her nerves were strung tight as piano wire. Nothing else.

Ignoring the pain that was beginning to throb in her ankle, she ducked her head closer to the horse's neck, smelling the scent of animal sweat and hearing the gray's breathing as she struggled uphill.

"We're almost there," Nikki said, hoping to encourage the horse. The wind in her hair and the pounding of hoofs against the gravel-strewn path reminded her of another time, another ride deep in the closed recesses of her mind. She was sure she had ridden often; the leather reins felt right in her hands. Instinctively she moved with the mare, anticipating subtle changes in the horse's gait, but she couldn't remember a single instance when she'd ridden.

It'll come, she told herself, frustrated that she couldn't control the timing of her memories. As they rounded a curve, the mission came into view, the once-white walls crumbling and gray in ruin.

The path veered closer to the edge of the cliff.

Nikki's heart nearly stopped and she drew back on the reins, yanking hard, causing the horse to shake her head and slide. "Whoa, girl, it's all right," Nikki said, as much to convince herself as the game little mare. Prancing and sidestepping, the gray snorted as she dismounted. Nikki could barely breathe, and the sound of the surf, pounding against rocks and sand hundreds of feet below, seemed to echo through her brain.

Fear, winter-cold and numbing, clutched her heart, but she made her way closer to the edge. Her throat felt dry and raw, her fingers twined in the leather straps of the reins as she inched toward the precipice and looked beyond the earth. Oh, Lord! Her heart plummeted as if to the angry depths below. Jagged black rocks pierced the swirling aquamarine water. Foam and spray swirled around the shore.

The nightmare seemed to close in around her. She felt herself falling over the side, and the edge of her vision seemed to grow dark. The hairs on the back of her neck lifted and she glanced swiftly over her shoulder, certain that she would see someone hidden in the shadows of the forest's growth, eyes hot as he spied upon her. Goose bumps stood on her flesh. For most of the day she'd felt she'd been followed but had never seen anyone tracing her tracks. Now, standing alone on the very ridge from which she'd been pushed, she felt alone and filled with a dread she couldn't name.

She turned back to the ocean. A flock of birds gathered in rookeries on the uppermost points of the rocks suddenly rose in a startled, frantic cloud toward the ominous sky. Rubbing her arms, Nikki tried to remember the birds. In all of her nightmares, the noisy flock hadn't existed. "Come on, Nikki, think!" she muttered under her breath in utter frustration. Why couldn't she call up anything, any damned thing? She kicked a stone in frustration and watched the pebble tumble over the cliff.

The image in her mind switched suddenly. With blood-chilling certainty, she remembered the feel of a harsh hand upon her shoulder, the reeling blow that had pitched her forward, over the edge—

"Nikki!"

She shrieked, nearly jumping out of her skin. The horse snorted, starting to rear, but Nikki held on to the reins and whirled around to find Trent, astride a sorrel gelding, emerging from the thick copse of trees. So he'd been following her! No wonder she'd been on edge. Steeling herself for another one of his lectures on going out alone, she watched as the sorrel raced up the hillside.

Trent moved with the horse, as if he'd ridden for years. His black hair was wild in the wind, his face tanned and harsh, his shirttails flapping. His eyes were covered with aviator glasses but his expression was severe. It didn't take a genius to realize that he wasn't pleased.

He leaped off as the gelding slid to a stop, and Nikki's already thudding heart accelerated.

"What the hell do you think you're doing?" he demanded, advancing on her.

"What the hell are *you* doing here? You nearly killed me, sneaking up on me like that and shouting my name!"

"I thought you might jump."

"Are you crazy?" she demanded, her fury seeping a little as she saw, behind his colored glasses, the fear in his gaze. She inched back from the edge and breathed in a deep, calming breath. Tossing her hair from her eyes, she reminded him, "I told you I wanted to come back here."

"And I said—"

"I know what you commanded," she said, poking an angry finger at his chest. Her horse, pulled by the bridle, followed her. "But I don't take orders from you or anyone else."

"You tried to sneak off behind my back!" He glowered down at her but she refused to be intimidated.

"That's right! Because you wouldn't bring me up here yourself." All her anger reignited in a blast of fury. "I'm tired of you telling me what to do for my own good. And I'm sick to death of lying around trying to piece together my life. If we're married, and I'm not saying I believe that we are, then you'd better get one thing straight, McKenzie, I'm not the kind of woman who wants to be coddled, or treated like a fragile doll, or commanded around like a slave!"

He stared at her, the wind moving his hair, his eyes hidden by the shaded lenses of his glasses, his mouth set in a thin, unbending line. In faded jeans, a white shirt with the sleeves rolled up and the tails flapping freely, he looked sexy and unpredictable and mysterious. Tanned and proud, he glared down at her, and Nikki didn't know what to expect.

"What if you would have hurt yourself?"

"I didn't. No thanks to you."

"No one knew where you were."

"You found me," she sassed back.

"I got lucky."

"Then there's nothing to fight about!"

"Like hell. If you haven't noticed, lady, there's a storm rolling in off the ocean."

"I've been through storms before."

"This isn't Seattle."

"*That* much, I remember." Angrily she wound the reins in her hands, the leather cutting into her palms. "You can come with me or you can go back to the hotel. I really don't care," she said as she placed her left foot in the stirrup and mounted. "I'm going up to the mission. I missed it last time around. Don't want to make the same mistake twice. Hiya!" She kicked her mare and the horse sprang into a gallop, leaving Trent to eat her dust.

"Serves him right," she told the gray. "I've never seen such an overprotective, arrogant, self-important macho jerk! I *can't* believe I married him!"

But he wasn't a man to be put off by a few strong words, or so it seemed as she heard the sound of approaching hoofbeats. Hazarding a quick glance over her shoulder, she saw Trent, riding hell-bent for leather, the gelding's longer strides easily closing the distance between the two horses. "How about that," she muttered, nudging her mount faster. She felt a perverse satisfaction that he'd been compelled to follow her. For some reason he'd taken on the responsibility of her protector, or at least that was what he had hoped she would think.

The mare was breathing hard by the time Nikki drew in on the reins near the mission. Dropping to the ground, she surveyed the ruins. The walls of the centuries-old church were still standing, though cracked and beginning to collapse from years of fighting a grueling and losing battle with the weather. The roof had succumbed long ago. Pieces of red tile were still visible, but there was a gaping hole exposing cross beams and rotting rafters.

The bell tower was beginning to crumble, the stone fence surrounding the mission in ruin and the place was deserted, as if only ghosts resided therein. Nikki felt a chill of apprehension as she tied the mare to a low-hanging branch of a breadfruit tree and walked through a sagging arch to an area where tangled weeds were all that remained of once-tended gardens.

"The monks who lived here left nearly a century ago," Trent said, tethering his horse before he followed her through the ruins. She slid through the opening left by a door no longer in existence and ventured into the church vestibule. The stone floor was cracked and weeds grew between the worn-flat stones leading to the raised platform which had once supported an altar. Vines grew on the inside of the walls, testament to the uselessness of the remaining roof.

"Why'd they leave?"

He lifted a broad shoulder. "Lack of interest, I suppose. The mission was already beginning to need a lot of repairs, and the population of monks had dwindled. Salvaje wasn't as populated as some of the other islands. Off the trade routes, it also didn't develop as quickly."

"I'd think monks would like that kind of solitude."

"A few stayed, but eventually died. The last, Brother Francis, lived here until 1930, I think, but he was murdered in his sleep by a woman who swore he was the father of her child. Rumor has it that he still walks the ruins at night."

The ghost's footsteps seemed to crawl along her flesh. "You're kidding," she said. "Tell me you're kidding."

"I've never seen him myself, but a lot of the natives are superstitious and they believe that his soul is still earthbound."

"That's kind of creepy." Nikki ran her fingers along one rough wall, and encountered the web of a large black spider. She quickly stuffed her hand into the pocket of her skirt. "Why were we coming to visit this place the other day?"

"Sightseeing."

Her brow puckered, and she remembered the dream, running through the steamy jungle, her feet stumbling as she broke from the dense foliage to the grassy headland rising over the sea. She'd heard a voice—a harsh male voice issuing orders to her in Spanish.

¡Dama! ¡Por favor! ¡Pare! She'd only run faster, the voice of her assailant spurring her upward toward the mission though her lungs had burned like fire with each breath.

"Oh, Lord," she whispered, leaning suddenly against the wall. Yes, she'd seen the path, taken it a few short steps, and then a heavy hand had pushed her over the edge and she was falling, falling...

"Nikki." She jumped at the sound of Trent's voice and the feel of his hand on her arm. "Are you all right?"

The vision faded and she was staring up at him, shivering though the temperature was sweltering, the humidity high enough to draw beads of sweat on her forehead. "I keep thinking about the dream."

"It's over," he said.

"I don't think so." She rubbed her arms and walked to a window which no longer held glass but offered a view of the changing horizon. Schooners, their masts devoid of sails, were harbored near the town, and the beach was nearly empty. Overhead, the bellies of heavy clouds had turned a deep purple hue and caused the ocean to swirl in dark, angry waves.

"We'll be home soon."

"And that will make everything right?"

"I hope so."

He was placating her, she could feel it, and she was torn between trusting him with her very life and running from him because he was dangerous—if not physically, at least emotionally. He kept her off balance; one minute she found him incredibly attractive on a purely sensual level, the next she feared he was part of some murky master scheme to do her harm. But why? Who was behind the plan? Why would anyone want to hurt her? Why did she feel like a pawn in some game of political intrigue?

The thought struck her like a lightning bolt. *Political intrigue. Politics!* She felt as if she'd inadvertently tripped over a major clue to her being on the island. But what? Her head was beginning to pound all over again. What was it Connie had said, that the women reporters at the *Seattle Observer* weren't allowed on the big, newsworthy stories? That they were kept away from political scandal and corruption and anything that could potentially be award-winning material? The thought was there, just under the surface of her consciousness, niggling at her, something that would give her a clue to her past as well as her present. She concentrated, but try as she could, the thought slipped away, into the black oblivion that was her past. Damn! Damn! Damn! Why couldn't she remember something this important?

"I think we should get back." Trent tugged lightly on her arm, but she yanked her hand back. She stared at the empty, ruined church and shook her head.

"Why did I pick Salvaje as a place for the honeymoon?" she demanded as suddenly as the question popped into her mind.

"I don't know. It appealed to you, I guess."

"But why not Jamaica or Bermuda or Hawaii? Why an isolated island like this?" She walked through the crumbling archway and viewed this island from the highest point. Little more than the top of a great, submerged mountain, Salvaje was as wild as its name. To the east lay the sea, a deep angry blue that looked as threatening as the darkening sky. To the west, the jungle, hot and sweltering and untamed. Far below, the city of Santa María, a small speck of civilization. She walked to the far side of the ruins, where the horses were tethered. Trent's arms surrounded her and he laced his fingers over her abdomen.

"Salvaje appealed to you."

"Didn't you think it was odd?" she asked, turning in his arms, wishing she could yank off his aviator glasses and stare into his eyes—search for the truth.

"We wanted to be alone." A stiff breeze ruffled his hair and he adjusted his sleeves, already pushed over his forearms.

Her stomach did a strange little flip. "But there are tourists, other people…." He stared at her lips and she had to fight the urge to rim them nervously with her tongue. She saw him swallow and wondered what it would be like to touch his broad chest, to trace the small scar at his hairline, to feel his lips warm and wet against hers.

As if reading her thoughts, he lifted one side of his mouth in a crooked smile that caused her pulse to leap. "We'd better get going. There's one helluva storm brewing and we don't want to be caught out here."

"Don't we?" she said, thrusting out her chin as the wind billowed her skirt. "I thought you said we couldn't keep our hands off each other, that we were so hot we had to get married, that we came here because it was so damned isolated. So why is it now, when we are alone, not a soul in sight, you want to run back to the hotel?"

His back teeth ground together. "I'm only thinking of you."

"Are you?"

"Your injuries—"

"I don't believe you, Trent. This whole thing doesn't wash. I think I came here because…because of some story I was working on at the paper, or because I was running away from something or because I had to get away, but I don't believe that I came here to be alone with you— Oh!"

His mouth claimed hers. As the wind began to howl and the little mare whinnied and reared, Trent pulled her still closer and his lips molded firmly over hers. Gasping, she tried to struggle free, but he wouldn't let go.

His tongue gently prodded her lips apart to slip into the moist secrets beyond her teeth. Nikki knew she should stop him, that she was playing with fire by goading him, but she couldn't help it, and as his tongue flicked against the roof of her mouth, her knees threatened to buckle. The palms that pushed hard against his shoulders moved as her fingers curled to grab his shirt and feel the warm flesh beneath the cotton fabric.

Stop him, Nikki! Stop this madness! her mind screamed, but her reeling senses, already spinning out of control, demanded more. She couldn't get enough of the male smell of him, the feel of his hands splaying against her back, the taste of his mouth on hers.

Her heart was thundering wildly as, with his weight, he pulled them both to the ground. When he lifted his head from hers, he ripped off his sunglasses and searched the contours of her face. "You make me do things I shouldn't."

"Like…like this?" she asked, her voice catching as his blue, blue eyes gazed into hers.

"Like everything I've done since the first time I saw you."

Clouds moved through the sky as he traced the line of her jaw with one long, callused finger. "I told myself to stay away from you, that you were more trouble than I needed, to run like hell until I forgot your name."

"But you didn't," she prodded.

"Couldn't."

But still he didn't love her. She swallowed hard as he

wrapped his fingers in her hair and settled his mouth on hers again. She returned the passion of his kiss. Their tongues met and danced, stroking and mating, thrusting and parrying.

Nikki's blood ran hot. Her body began to ache with a willful need that tugged at her heart and burned deep within her. He kissed her eyes, her cheeks, her neck. She was breathing so raggedly her breasts rose and fell, aching to be touched. She barely felt the first drops of rain.

Trent's lips moved easily down the column of her throat and his hands found the hem of her T-shirt, moving upward to scale her ribs, her skin feeling branded where he touched.

Don't do this, Nikki! Don't! one part of her mind screamed, while the other cast caution to the wind. So far she hadn't caught him in a lie. He was, after all, her husband, and even if he wasn't, he was the most damnably sexy man she'd ever met.

His tongue traced the circle of bones at her throat, and a liquid heat started to build deep within her. She moaned softly and he responded, slowly lifting her T-shirt over her head. As the cool air touched her bare skin, she felt her nipples stiffen, and the delicious warmth swirling within her, stretching and reaching outward from the deepest, most feminine part of her, caused all rational thought to cease.

He kissed the tops of her breasts, brushing his lips across the filmy lace of her bra. Had he kissed her this way before? She couldn't remember, but didn't stop his hands from lowering one strap to unleash her breast, its proud, dark nipple puckering in the wind.

"God, you're gorgeous," he whispered, his hot breath fanning the wet tracks of his kisses on her skin. "So damned gorgeous." She stared up at him. The darkening sky was a backdrop for his strong, chiseled features, a slightly crooked nose and a jaw that meant business. She reached upward, dragging his head downward so that his lips encircled her breast.

Like an electric current, a shock ripped through her. His teeth and lips tugged and played, his tongue tickled and teased, and she arched upward, thrusting her hips closer to his. "God, Nikki, we're playing with fire," he admitted as he stripped away her bra and kneaded the soft flesh of her breasts, pressing them together and burying his face in the deep cleft between.

"It's all right. We're married," she said, her equilibrium long gone, desire overtaking common sense.

Growling, he kissed her again, and one of his hands delved beneath the waistband of her skirt, sliding along her spine, touching deeper and deeper until she was writhing beneath him.

"Nikki—" he whispered roughly, as he withdrew his hand.

"Please." She bucked upward and he groaned, his eyes glazing.

"I don't think this is a good idea."

"You started it."

"We'll both regret it."

"Why?" she asked, sensing that he was trying to tell her something, to break the wall of passion that surrounded her mind.

"The doctor said—"

"He's not here."

"We're getting wet."

"Not the first time. We're from Seattle, remember?"

She smiled up at him, teasing him, baiting him as rain began to pepper the ground.

His gaze moved from her just-kissed lips to her breasts, and his eyes turned smoky with passion again. "God help us," he said before his lips claimed hers again. Her fingers found the buttons of his shirt and ripped them free, so that she could touch the swirling black hair covering his chest, feel the muscles flex as her fingers grazed his nipples, watch his abdomen curve inward to allow her fingers access to the buttons of his fly.

"You make me crazy," he said.

"The feeling's mutual, I think."

With little effort, he stripped her of her skirt and kicked off his jeans. She saw him for the first time, naked and lean, strident muscles tense as he prodded her legs apart. "You're sure of this?" he asked.

"Trent, please."

Closing his eyes and muttering something under his breath, he thrust into her. Nikki gasped as she enveloped him, felt him start his magical rhythm. She moved her hips to his, and her fingers dug deep into the muscles of his shoulders as the tide of sweet pleasure washed over her in hot, anxious waves. He moved faster, and she kept up with his pace, her breathing wild, her heartbeat pounding in her ears, rain sliding down his smooth, sleek muscles.

"Nikki!" he screamed, throwing back his head. "Nikki, Nikki, Nikki!"

As if the universe exploded, she convulsed, her thoughts swirling, her mind soaring. She quivered in aftershocks and sighed in a voice she didn't recognize as hers as he fell against her, murmuring her name, his body glazed with a salty sheen of sweat.

"Oh, Nikki," he whispered hoarsely, his hands gently brushing the wet strands of her hair from her face. Rain slid down his neck. His face was tortured and pained as he kissed her lips. "What have I done?"

CHAPTER SEVEN

"…AND STAY IN the room until I get back," Trent ordered through the open door of the cab. Rain ran down his neck and under his collar as Nikki sat in the backseat of a battered old Chevy that smelled of must, sweat and stale cigarette smoke. They'd returned the horses and now Trent was sending her back to the hotel. Alone.

"Where will you be?"

"Back at the airport, trying to find out how bad this storm is supposed to be and if our flight will take off tomorrow."

"I could come with you—"

His lips thinned in silent reproach. "Go back to the hotel and dry off before you catch pneumonia."

"I'm not going to—"

"I'll be there as soon as I can." He slammed the door closed and the cabbie stepped on the gas, leaving Trent standing in a puddle of rainwater and a cloud of blue exhaust.

"Serves him right," she muttered, still steaming. After they'd made love, he'd become as sullen and brooding as before, insisting they return the horses and she go back to the hotel.

Wind whistled through the palms and banana trees that lined the street which was all but deserted as pedestrians waited for the storm to pass.

At the hotel, Nikki paid the cabdriver and dashed through the rain to the hotel lobby. Her skirt was muddy, her hair lank and dripping as she took the elevator to the second floor and entered the room. As beautiful as Salvaje was during the mild weather, the island seemed dark and menacing in the storm.

Shivering, she stripped off her clothes and took a quick, hot shower, lathering her body and shampooing her hair with a vengeance. Her skirt was probably ruined, stained as the result of making love to Trent in the wilderness. The passion between them had been earth-shattering, and yet afterwards Trent had treated her no differently than he had before. He was still a cynical, overbearing bastard.

Dressed in a robe that covered her bra and panties, she sat before the bureau mirror and combed the tangles from her hair. The woman staring back at her looked better than she had a few days before. Most of the scabs on her face had fallen off, and though her skin was pink, with the right touch of base makeup, blush, lipstick and shadow, she would look almost the same as she had before she'd lost her memory.

The phone rang. She picked up the receiver on the third ring and, telling herself that the caller had to be Trent, said, "Hello."

"For the love of St. Peter, why are you still on that godforsaken island?"

She couldn't help but grin when she conjured up a picture of the crusty man who'd spawned her. "Probably for the same reason you're forever on a jet between Seattle, Tokyo, Seoul and Sydney. Scheduling."

He chuckled a little. "Don't patronize me, girl. I'm worried about you, and won't feel right until your feet touch down on home soil. What with the storm warnings and all, it's enough to drive me nuts. I'm lucky I got through to you."

"It's good to hear from you, Dad," she said, flopping back on the bed and staring up at the ceiling, watching the blades of the paddle fan rotate slowly.

"Then you're not still mad at me?"

"No way," she said, wishing she could remember what they'd argued about before she'd left Seattle. He'd mentioned several times that he hadn't wanted her to fly to Salvaje, but she couldn't remember why.

"Good. 'Cause you were way off base."

"Off base?" she said, prodding him. "I don't think so."

She heard him exhale an exasperated breath. "'Course you were. Jim's above reproach. Always had been."

"Jim?" she repeated. *Jim who?*

"Why you thought that you had to investigate him after all these years…I don't know what got into you."

Investigate him? She didn't want to tip her hand, but she was dying to know who.

"He and I go way back, long before he was elected, and I won't have you trying to smear his name."

Elected? A politician? Oh, Lord. Her mind spun back to her conversation with Connie at the *Observer*. "You think I'm on a campaign against Senator Crowley," she said, gambling.

"Oh, for the love of Mike, of course the senator!" he growled in exasperation. "What's gotten into you?"

"Nothing," she lied, crossing her fingers.

"Well, you must be in love, 'cause you act as if you've lost your mind."

If you only knew, Dad. She wanted to confide in

him, to tell him about her memory loss, but a feeling, a strange, uncomfortable warning buried deep in the depths of her mind, held her tongue. There was a reason, a reason she couldn't begin to fathom, that she couldn't talk things over with her father. She sensed it now—that unspoken barrier that existed between them had always been there. "So we fought about Senator Crowley," she said, trying in vain to remember.

There was a long pause on the other end of the line before her father said, "Honey, are you all right?"

"Fine. I'm fine," she lied. Why would she and her father argue about the senator? Connie had mentioned that Nikki was interested in some scam the senator might be pulling, but why would her father care? Was her father or his business involved? Did he think she was trying to smear the name of a good man, or did he think the senator was dangerous and he feared for Nikki's safety, or was there something else…something hidden much deeper in the recesses of her mind?

"When are you coming home?" Her father's voice was filled with concern.

"Tomorrow—unless the flight is canceled."

"We'll talk then."

"Dad! Wait!" Fortunately he hadn't hung up. "I…I bumped my head in the accident," she admitted, hoping the truth might elicit more information now that she so desperately needed it. "So I don't remember everything."

"You don't remember? For crying out loud, what's going on down there?"

"I've got a slight case of amnesia," she admitted, as rain sheeted against the French doors and wind began to rattle the panes. "Some things slip my mind. Like Crowley."

Her father swore long and hard under his breath. "I don't know whether to be worried out of my skull or relieved," he admitted, adding to her confusion, "but you get yourself on the first plane off that damned island and come home. I'll call Tom and—"

"Tom?"

"Tom Robertson. *Dr.* Robertson. The physician you've seen all your life. Hell, Nikki, now you've really got me worried."

"I remember *you,* Dad," she said, to alleviate his fears.

"Thank God for that!" His voice choked a little. "And when I meet that husband of yours, let me tell you, there's going to be hell to pay. I don't know what he's thinking, letting you—"

"Dad, I'll be all right," she said quickly. "Dr. Padillo thinks the amnesia is only temporary, and I'm already remembering a lot more than I did right after the fall. I'll be okay."

"Well, I don't know Dr. Whatever-the-hell-his-name-is from Adam, but I don't trust him. Could be a damned quack. You come home, Nicole. We'll take care of you."

She felt suddenly on the verge of tears. Here, at last, was her rock. "All right, Dad."

"Damned straight!"

He hung up still muttering oaths at doctors who had gotten their medical degrees by mail or worse! Nikki knew there wasn't any use in explaining that she had absolute faith in Dr. Padillo. The friendly physician seemed knowledgeable, competent and concerned, and if he'd only spoken more English, she would have been completely at ease with him. As it was, his prognosis had proved right on the money. Her wounds were healing according to his timetable and her memory was returning, in sharp little bits and pieces.

The only wild card so far was Trent. Her husband. The man who, with one cocky smile, could cause her heart to race out of control. The man to whom she'd given herself eagerly in the middle of a downpour.

Tomorrow she'd have answers. Once she went to the camera shop, she'd know if Trent had been with her before the accident. *And what if he wasn't?* a nagging part of her mind questioned. *What then? Will you be able to sleep with him? Will you confront him? What?* Without any answers to those questions, she considered her trip home to Seattle. Surely the familiar scenery would jog her memory.

But what would she do about Senator Crowley, and why did she feel that he was part of the reason she'd chosen Salvaje as a spot for her vacation…her honeymoon?

Her father's conversation echoed in her brain, names he'd spoken swimming in the murk that was her mind. Dr. Robertson. Senator Crowley. She remembered a slight man with wire-rimmed glasses, an easy, gaptoothed smile and huge nose. Because she pictured him in a white jacket, she assumed he was the doctor. As for Crowley, she had no image of the man. Senator Jim—no, James—Crowley. How had she met him? Why did she care? What was the story that she thought surrounded him? Her skin crawled as she considered the fact that somehow Trent might be involved with the man. Maybe that was why he claimed they were married. Head beginning to pound, she stared down at her wedding ring, a gold band that was too big for her finger, and the circle of gold seemed to mock her.

Yet she'd made love to him. Abandoned herself to him as if he were indeed the man she loved. She couldn't help blushing when she remembered the intensity of his lovemaking and the wanton, wild way she'd responded, with no thought of the future. She'd lived for the moment, given herself wholly to the man, and now, lying on the bed she shared with him, she closed her eyes and knew, with gut-wrenching certainty, she'd make love with him again.

It was only a matter of time.

She must've dozed. Groggy, still lying on the bed, she heard the door of the veranda rattle. She rolled over, trying to ignore the sound, but the noise was persistent. As she stretched, she climbed off the bed and noticed the darkness outside. The storm was still blowing hard and Trent had been gone for hours. A pang of worry caused her to bite her lip, but she rationalized that Trent was a man who could take care of himself, probably better than any man she'd ever met. Of course, she thought wryly, she couldn't remember most of the men she had met. Her stomach growled and she wondered if she should order room service or wait for Trent.

The rattle sounded again. Rubbing the kinks from her neck, she walked to the glass doors and reached for the knob, when her hand paused in midair. She froze. The hairs on the back of her neck raised. Her throat gave out a strangled scream as she saw him. Someone. A figure on the veranda. The light from inside the room and the pelting rain distorted her view, but she knew very clearly that a man was on her veranda, a man with dark hair and wet jeans and a slick jacket. His features were blurred. He was about Trent's height and build, but... He vaulted the rail, his jacket billowing as he threw himself against the building, probably to climb down the vines.

"Oh God, oh God, oh God," she whispered half in prayer as she backed up, fumbling for the interior door, then suddenly stopping. What was to prevent him from going into the lobby and waiting for her? She ran across the room, checked the lock on the veranda doors and quickly threw the drapes closed. She checked the hall door, found it locked as well, and with trembling fingers dialed the main desk.

"I want to report a stranger lurking outside on my veranda, a Peeping Tom or something—"

"Señora, por favor—"

"Get me someone who can speak English. Oh, God! Uh, *¿Comprende Ud.?* Do you understand? There was a man, a damned Peeping Tom or worse, on my veranda! *¿Habla Ud. inglés?* I need help!"

The lock on the hallway door rattled. Nikki dropped the phone. Heart thudding, she reached for the bedside lamp—a weak weapon, but all she had—and watched in horror as the door swung open and Trent, his hair wet and plastered to his head, the shoulders of his leather jacket soaked, entered. She nearly collapsed against the wall and her fingers let go of the base of the lamp. "Thank God," she whispered.

Trent took one look at her face and his eyes slitted in concern. "What happened?" he demanded, crossing the room. "Nikki, are you okay?"

She nodded, though she couldn't find her tongue, and when he wrapped his arms around her, she sagged against him like a silly woman who couldn't take care of herself. Relieved, she clung to him, trying not to embarrass herself by breaking into tears. He smelled of the outdoors—rainwater, leather and salt air—and though she wanted to crumple into his arms like a lovesick fool, to trust him with all of her heart, to quit torturing herself with worries about him, she stiffened her spine and gently stepped out of his embrace.

"What's wrong?"

"I saw someone on the veranda."

"Who?"

She shook her head, trying to conjure up the man's image. "I don't know. Some man. It was too dark to recognize him, but he was built like you, had on a dark jacket...bare head..." She noticed Trent's dripping hair again and his flushed face. He seemed to be breathing hard, but there was no reason for him to spy on her. No reason on earth. Not when he had a key to the room. Her sick mind was playing games with her again.

Trent threw open the drapes and French doors. Rain and wind blew into the room as he dashed outside just as someone began banging on the hotel door. *"¡Señora McKenzie!"*

In three swift strides, leveling a staying finger at Nikki, Trent was across the room. "Who is it?"

"¡Policía!"

Trent yanked open the door, and two hotel security guards, weapons drawn, burst into the room.

"It's all right," Trent assured them, and one of the men, the beefier of the two, walked to the night table, picked up the phone, muttered Spanish into the receiver and hung up.

Nikki wrapped her arms around her middle and sat

on a corner of the bed as Trent acted as interpreter. She told him of the man on the deck, and he, in Spanish, repeated it to the two guards. The questions about the man's identity and description were rapid, and Nikki had to admit that the figure she'd seen was dark and blurry through the rain-washed window.

"We have no idea who it was," Trent said as the security guards were finishing their interrogation. "At least, I don't. Nikki?"

She shook her head. Who would spy on her? "I can't imagine."

The guards talked between themselves and with Trent, even sharing a joke that Nikki couldn't begin to understand. They eventually left, apologizing to Nikki for her fright and promising to look for any suspicious characters.

"They assume it was just another burglary attempt," he said after he'd closed the door behind them. "There have been quite a few in the major hotels around here. A ring of thieves after rich tourists' money or jewelry."

"They wouldn't have found much here," she said, unconvinced. Her eyebrows drew down over her eyes. "Besides, I'm not sure that it had anything to do with a robbery."

"Why not?" He threw both dead bolts before sitting on the foot of the bed and nudging off his boots.

"Because I've had this feeling that I've been followed."

He cast an interested glance over his shoulder, but didn't say anything.

"Earlier. When I was riding the horse, I felt it, and then you showed up, so I just assumed *you* were the reason I felt as if I'd been watched. But now...I'm not so sure." She tucked her feet up close to her bottom and hugged her knees.

"So you think the man on the veranda might have been following you?"

"Yes. But I don't know why!" Sighing in frustration, she decided to gamble a little. "I think it might have something to do with Senator Crowley."

Was it her imagination or did the cords in the back of his neck tighten a little?

"Crowley? What's he got to do with anything?"

"I don't know," she admitted, "but I talked to Connie at the paper and later my dad called. They both brought up our illustrious senator. Connie seems to think I was hoping to do a story on him, uncover some sort of political dirt, I suppose, and Dad...Dad was even stranger. He acted as if he and I had fought before I left for Salvaje, and that the argument had something to do with Crowley." Stretching, she fluffed her still-damp hair with fingers that shook a little. "The thing of it is, I don't even know what the man looks like. I could barely remember his name."

"James," Trent supplied as he kicked his boots into the closet. "Diamond Jim Crowley. Attorney-at-law, private businessman and senator. A Republican who hails from Tacoma." He pulled off his jacket and hung it over the back of the vanity chair before stretching out on the bed beside her. "Connie's right. You were interested in him. You thought he might be involved in something shady."

"What's that got to do with Salvaje?"

"Nothing."

"Then why did my father and I fight about him?"

"Because your dad is a die-hard Republican who

owns his own business. You obviously don't remember, but you and your dad have always been about as far apart politically as any two people can get." He was moving closer to her, his head on the pillow next to her rump. Nikki tried to ignore the feel of his breath, warm even through her robe. She wanted to move away from him, told herself it only made sense, but there was an irresistible pull that kept her seated on the bed, her robe tucked around her legs, her breathing jumping irregularly.

"How shady?"

"Huh?"

"The senator. What was my theory?"

"I don't know. You wouldn't discuss it. Very hush-hush. I'm surprised your father and Connie knew about it."

Connie, too, had insisted that it was something they had to keep quiet. But what? Nikki racked her brain and felt Trent's wet hair rub against her thigh. Her stomach rolled over slowly as desire began to warm her blood.

"What did you find out at the airport?" she asked to keep her head clear, but his hand encircled her bare ankle. Her heart dropped into her stomach and she could barely concentrate on anything but the warm grip around her leg.

"The storm's supposed to die down and we're booked on a flight that takes off at three. Barring any more catastrophes, we'll be home by midnight tomorrow."

She should have felt overwhelming relief. Instead the nagging feeling that she was leaving something in Salvaje, something undone, kept teasing at her.

He moved his hand. His fingers gently glided up the inside of her calf. Her throat grew tight and she could barely breathe. Biting her lip, she glanced down at him, his head angled on the pillow so that his gaze met hers.

"I don't know if this is such a good idea," she said in a voice she didn't recognize as her own.

His palm brushed her knee and moved upward. "I know it isn't."

"Maybe we should stop— Oh!" Her protests were cut off when he moved suddenly, shifting on the bed so that his body was stretched over hers, his lips finding her yielding mouth just as his fingers touched her panties.

"I can't," he admitted, his lips claiming hers with the same wild passion that had touched her soul only hours before. "Don't you know that by now? When I'm with you, I just can't stop."

Trent spied *el Perro* seated at the bar. The Dog was sipping from a tall glass and trying to make time with a long-legged redhead. The Luna Plata, or Silver Moon tavern, was busy for early afternoon, the air thick with cigarette smoke and laughter, glasses clinking, ice rattling, bawdy jokes thrown about in Spanish. The barkeep, a portly man with a handlebar mustache, was busy making drinks. Waitresses in short ruffled skirts and low-cut tight bodices wiggled quickly between the booths and round tables.

Trent slid into the empty stool next to the Dog. Their eyes met in the mirror behind the bar. As Trent ordered a beer, *el Perro* whispered something into the redhead's ear, grinned at her response and patted her on her rear as she slid from her stool. Only when Trent had paid for his beer did the two men move into one of the back booths near a loud poker game that protected their conversation.

"Your woman, she is sly like the fox, eh?" *el Perro* asked, his dark eyes burning with malicious mirth in the dark tavern.

Trent's blood boiled a little, but he managed a thin smile. "She's smart enough."

"Too smart for you, eh?"

"Maybe," Trent allowed, taking a long pull from his bottle.

El Perro snorted a laugh and lit a cigarette. "She leaves you to wipe the table and does her business alone."

"What business?" Trent asked, though he suspected he already knew. "You mean the camera shop?"

The smaller man exhaled a plume of smoke and seemed mildly disappointed. *"Sí."*

"I expected that."

"Did you know she met the silver-haired one?" *el Perro* asked, sliding a glance in Trent's direction. "The man with the cane."

Trent's composure slipped. His muscles tightened and he held his bottle of beer in a death grip. "Crowley?" he whispered, his throat raw. "She met Crowley?"

"Sí." El Perro was obviously enjoying himself, but Trent wanted to rip his throat out.

"And?"

"And nothing. She did not recognize him."

That didn't solve the problem. "What about him?"

"He looked long at her, but said nothing." The Dog leaned across the table. "The silver-haired one, I do not trust him, *amigo*. His eyes, they are dead."

Amen. Trent's fists clenched. "Anything else?"

"Nothing."

Trent pulled out a thin envelope and threw it across

the table. "You were sloppy," he said. "She saw you on the veranda."

The swarthy man's brows drew together. He shifted his cigarette to one side of his mouth and counted the bills. "Sloppy. Not *el Perro*." Satisfied that the money was all there, he squinted through the trailing smoke of his cigarette. "I was never on your veranda, *amigo*."

Nikki checked her watch. Trent had been gone nearly forty-five minutes. He'd told her he was going down to the lobby to talk to the manager about tighter security, and she'd expected him by now.

The storm had blown itself out during the night, and the day was bright and clear, the afternoon sun once again streaming through the windows.

She glanced at the bed and felt her neck burn scarlet. How many times last night had they made love? Three times? Four? She couldn't remember. Not that it mattered, she supposed, but their lovemaking had been so wild…so…desperate, as if they both knew it would suddenly end. *Stupid woman with silly-girl dreams*.

Trent had promised her they could stop in the town to do some last-minute shopping before they left, and she was anxious to pick up the film. She would have to find a way to ditch him again, for only a few minutes, but that shouldn't be difficult.

She heard his key in the lock and smiled when he entered. "I thought I'd lost you," she said, but noticed the air of urgency in his step, the grim line of his mouth.

"Not so lucky," he said, but never smiled. "Are you packed?" He noticed the bags near the door and nodded. "Good. There's a chance we can catch an earlier flight, but we've got to get to the airport in twenty minutes."

Her heart dropped to the floor. "Wait a minute," she argued as he picked up her suitcase and garment bag. "I thought we were going into town—"

"No time."

"But you promised," she said, desperation gripping her heart in a stranglehold. "I told you I wanted to go shopping and—"

"Sorry."

"I'm not leaving until—"

"You're leaving and you're leaving now. With me," he said, his voice brooking no argument.

"In case you haven't heard, this isn't the Dark Ages, McKenzie! You can't just order me around like you're some lord and I'm your sorry little servant girl— Oh!"

He grabbed with hands tight as manacles circling her forearms. "It's not safe here anymore."

"What do you mean?"

"The man on the deck. I think you were right. He wasn't a burglar."

"Who was he?" she asked, trying to keep the fear from her voice.

"I don't know, but we're not sticking around to find out." He dropped her arms at a knock on the door and allowed the bellboy in to help with their bags.

Nikki was beginning to feel desperate. "It would only take a minute."

The phone rang loudly and Trent reached for the receiver. "Hello?"

The conversation was one-sided as he listened, and his eyes narrowed upon Nikki, his lips compressing.

"*Gracias,* I'll tell her," Trent said before slowly replacing the receiver.

Nikki's insides froze.

"That was Nurse Sánchez from the hospital. She says Mrs. Martínez's friend was a girl named Rosa Picano. She works at a hotel on the south end of the bay. Want to tell me about her?"

Leveling her gaze straight at him, she said, "I've wanted to tell you about her for a long time. She saw me in the hospital. She knew me. Called me Señorita Carrothers. Not Señora McKenzie."

One of Trent's eyebrows lifted. "And that surprises you?"

"Yes. Why would she call me—"

"Because there was a mix-up when we got here. At the first hotel. You signed us in while I took care of the baggage, and all of your credit cards, all of your identification, even your passport, is in your maiden name. It was easier to go by Carrothers."

"The girl didn't remember a husband."

"That's because I dealt with the manager directly because the plumbing in our first room didn't work."

She wanted to trust him, to believe in him and yet she couldn't. There were too many things left unexplained. "You're telling me the truth?"

"Yes, but I don't know what I can do to convince you," he said in irritation. "Come on. We've got a plane to catch." He propelled her to the elevator and through the lobby to the front of the hotel where a taxi was waiting in the circular drive. A copper-skinned cabbie shoved their bags into the trunk. "You can't do this," she hissed as Trent forced her into the back of the cab, climbed in beside her and ordered the driver in Spanish to get them to the airport.

"Watch me."

"I'll scream," she warned.

"Go right ahead. We're married, and as I told you before—on this island a husband's rights are rarely questioned. If I say something is good for you, whether you like it or not, that's the way it is."

"That's barbaric!"

His eyes glittered in anger. "Absolutely. That's why it works."

"But—" She wanted to argue, to scream, to pummel him with her fists as the cabdriver turned onto the concrete slab of a road that drove them straight to the airport, avoiding the city of Santa María altogether. Her spirits sank as low as they had been since she'd woken up in the hospital all those days ago. At that moment she hated Trent!

"I want a divorce," she blurted out angrily.

His answer was a slow, sexy smile. "That's not what you were begging for last night."

Without thinking, she drew her hand back and started to slap him, but he caught her wrist in mid-arc and clucked his tongue. "I wouldn't, if I were you."

"If you were me, you'd probably shoot me with that damned gun you've got a permit for!"

"Probably," he allowed, his smile returning as the palm trees gave way to the airport, which was hardly more than a few low-slung buildings and a couple of cracked runways. Nikki had no choice but to follow him into the terminal. She couldn't scream that she was being kidnapped, because he was only taking her home, and truth to tell, she did believe that there was some sort of danger on the island. Why else his case of nerves?

But there was something else here on Salvaje, something that had drawn her to this little speck in the Caribbean, some reason she had wanted to come here in the first place, and whatever that reason was, she knew in her gut that she hadn't found it.

She was still fuming as they boarded the small plane. She sat near the window, strapped her seat belt over her lap and listened to the flight attendant go over the safety procedures. She knew that Trent was watching her, but as they took off, she stared out the window, to the wild island where she'd lost her memory, the paradise she'd come to visit for her honeymoon, the place where she'd lost her heart to a man she alternately hated and loved. Oh, what a horrid mess!

The plane circled, and high above Salvaje, Nikki Carrothers McKenzie looked down to see the crumbling mission visible through the fronds of ancient palms. Her heart jerked painfully as she remembered her nightmare and the first day she'd woken up in the hospital and found herself married to a man she couldn't remember. Her throat grew tight as the island disappeared from sight.

They flew in silence until they reached Miami, where they went through customs, transferred planes and headed west. Nikki watched the movie, a romantic comedy she'd seen before, rather than have to make small talk with Trent. She dozed, ate, and after one final transfer, was on her way to Seattle.

Seattle. The largest city on Puget Sound. Sprawling around Lake Union and Lake Washington, with a series of freeways that could barely handle the traffic that had grown in recent years. She remembered the downtown area as incredibly hilly—she'd long ago given up a manual-shift car—and the waterfront as cool and windy.

She'd worked for the *Observer* for...five or six years. Leaning back against the headrest, she thought about her job and couldn't remember particular incidents, but knew that she had a deep dissatisfaction with her work and a burning need to prove that she was as good as most of the men on the staff. Slowly a memory surfaced.

"You know what they say. 'You can't fight city hall,'" Peggy had announced, slapping a file on Nikki's cluttered desk. Peggy, five foot two in three-inch heels was a petite redhead with big eyes, glasses that slid to the end of her nose and a temper that matched her coloring. "I tried, Nikki."

"I didn't get the story."

"'Racketeering,' and I'm quoting here, 'is better handled by men. They'll give the story the hard edge it needs.' End of quote." Peggy had reached in her purse, looking for a pack of cigarettes though she'd given up smoking eight months earlier. "Damn," she'd muttered under her breath. "It's enough to make me want to burn my bra all over again, and I gave that up in seventy-two."

Nikki, though furious, had managed a laugh. "We can't let them beat us."

"They think they're doing us a favor."

"Oh, so now taking the good stories is chivalrous." Nikki seethed inside. "Well, I guess we'll just have to prove them wrong."

"Nikki—" Peggy's voice held a warning note.

"I think it's Pulitzer Prize time."

"I don't like the sound of this," Peggy said, then wrinkled her nose. "Well, actually I do, but I'm supposed to go along with the decisions of the chief editor. That's my official stance."

Nikki had lifted a shoulder but knew what she had to do. The next big story that came along, wasn't going to pass her by. In fact, she'd been gathering information on a couple of stories, one of which was starting to look like it might be worthwhile—the one involving Senator James T. Crowley. "And your unofficial stance?"

Peggy pushed her glasses back to the bridge of her nose and her tiny chin was set in determination. "Go for it."

Now, circling above Seattle, Nikki's heart began to pound. So that's how she became interested in the senator, but she couldn't remember why. He was involved in something dirty, that much she'd determined, and somehow her trip to Salvaje—her *honeymoon*—was connected with the story. But how?

The plane began its approach, and Nikki glanced out the window. As they dropped through the clouds, a million lights, set in connecting grids, came into view. She tightened her seat belt. Soon she'd be home. Surely then her memory would return. She cast a glance at Trent. The mystery around him would be answered.

Her stomach twisted like a fraying rope. What if she found out they weren't married, that for whatever reason, now that she was back in Seattle, he had no further use for her? True, she believed that he cared for her, if just a little, but never once had he claimed to love her. Her heart tore a little and she told herself she was being a ninny. For the past ten days or so this man had been the very bane of her existence. So what if she melted when he kissed her, so what if she couldn't help staring at the way his hair fell over his forehead, so what if she tingled each time he took her hand in his?

Romantic fantasies! That's all. She'd been alone with him on a tropical island, sensing danger and adventure. Of course she'd become infatuated with him.

But it was over. She was home. He slid her a glance that echoed her own feelings and her heart turned to ice. Frowning slightly, Trent reached into the inner pocket of his jacket, withdrawing an envelope.

"I thought you'd want to see these," he said cryptically as he dropped the envelope into her lap. Her heart nearly stopped beating as she recognized the package containing photographs from the film she'd left at José's camera shop. "Go ahead, Nikki," he said with measured calm. "Open it."

CHAPTER EIGHT

NIKKI FELT COLD inside, as if a ghost had stepped across her soul. Only seven pictures had developed and those photographs were taken in a city near water, but a modern, busy city that she should recognize, a town that was far from the rustic Caribbean town of Santa María. She flipped through the few shots. Not one snapshot of Salvaje or Trent.

"Looks like Victoria," he said, when she just stared at the photographs and felt the hot stain of embarrassment climb up the back of her neck. "British Columbia."

She rolled her lips over her teeth. Victoria. She'd been there. Probably on her last vacation, the last time she'd used the camera.

"All that trouble for nothing," Trent remarked as she slid the snapshots into the envelope.

Clearing her throat, she slid him a suspicious glance. "Were you spying on me?"

"I was just trying to take care of you." His face was set in defiance, as if he dared her to argue with him. "But you never believe me."

"I don't know what to believe," she admitted. The plane touched down with a jolt and the chirp of tires on the runway. Nikki stuffed the pictures into her purse. Some investigative reporter she'd turned out to be. No wonder her stories had included covering the state fair, a Boy Scout jamboree and the governor's daughter's wedding. Hot stuff.

Now she was no closer to knowing if she was married to Trent than she had been before.

Once in the terminal, they picked up their bags and took a shuttle to the parking lot, where Trent's Jeep was parked. With more than its share of dents and a paint job that needed serious attention, the Jeep brought back no memories. She slid into the passenger seat that creaked beneath her weight, waited for Trent and was certain she'd never been in the Jeep before in her life.

Yet, here she was. With her "husband." Lord, when would she ever remember?

Tires humming on the pavement, the Jeep picked up speed, melding with the thick traffic that streamed northward into the heart of Seattle. A thick Washington mist drizzled from the sky and the wipers slapped rain off the windshield as Nikki peered desperately through the glass. Certainly here, in her hometown, she would remember. She waited, crossing her fingers and silently praying that with a rush of adrenaline and the familiar sights and sounds of Seattle, she would be instantly cured and her life would be complete—a past, a present and a future.

The rain-washed streets were familiar. The bustle, noise and bright lights of the city brought a familiar ache in her heart. Wispy fingers of fog rose from the asphalt. The chill wind of October blew eastward, crossing the dark waters of the Sound and rattling up the narrow, steep streets surrounding Elliott Bay.

Yes, this city was home. She'd lived here all her life and remembered driving downtown with her mother and sister, taking the monorail into the shopping district where they would wander through stores and meet their father for lunch. Those happy trips hadn't happened often and they were long ago, before the rift between Eloise and Ted Carrothers had become so deep it could never be repaired. Nikki, the youngest, had been oblivious to the undercurrents of tension between her parents in the early years, but as she grew older and approached adolescence, she'd begun to realize that her mother was deeply unhappy. Being married to a man who expected his dinner on the table at six-thirty without fail, his shirts washed, starched and ironed, and the house and children kept in spotless condition in case he brought a big client home for dinner had finally taken its toll.

The glass of wine her mother had consumed before dinner soon had stretched to two and eventually three. Sometimes Eloise had drunk an entire bottle before the meal, and as soon as the dishes had been stacked in the dishwasher, she had retired upstairs with a "headache."

Eventually she had barely been able to stay awake through the meal, and the fights that had erupted between Nikki's parents had rocked the timbers of their Cape Cod-style house in the Queen Anne district.

Nikki remembered lying on her bed, her quilt tucked over her head, trying to block out the sounds of anger that radiated throughout the old house. Even now, more than fifteen years later, the pain cut through her heart. She blinked back tears and told herself everything had turned out for the best—her mother was happy in Southern California, remarried to a real-estate man and living not far from the ocean, and her father, still single, seemed to enjoy his bachelorhood.

Trent wheeled the Jeep into the drive of an old English Tudor home that had been converted to apartments. The rig bounced over a couple of speed bumps before landing in a parking space beneath an oak tree with spreading branches and brittle, dead leaves.

Nikki stared at the building as she slammed the door of the Jeep shut. Home. Seeing the old house should bring back wave after wave of memories. Nervously, she scanned the house, trying to see past the windows which glowed brightly, though the drapes had been drawn against the night. Who were these people who lived so close to her? An old white pickup and a new Ford wagon were parked near the Jeep, but try as she might, she couldn't conjure up faces for the people who drove the vehicles and shared the same plumbing and roof with her.

Disappointed, she followed Trent as he carried her bags up the exterior stairs to the third-floor landing. Each step was covered with strips of rubber for traction and the rail was well used. Once on her small porch, Nikki fumbled with the keys and, hunching her shoulders against the steady drizzle, unlocked the door.

She dropped her suitcase and purse on the faded Oriental rug and breathed deeply of the musty, stale air. As if from habit, she kicked off her shoes and padded in stocking feet through the long, narrow attic that served as her living room and bedroom. Her hands trailed along the backs of chairs and across the dusty surface of the table, and a sense of belonging wove its way into her heart.

"It's good to be home," she admitted huskily, feeling, for the first time in two weeks, that she had some bearings. She glanced at the quilt tossed over the back of her camel-backed couch, smiled at the flowers, now dry and dropping petals, on a small table near one of the windows and noticed that her brass teapot was sitting empty on the stove.

"You remember?" Trent asked.

She shook her head and glanced back at him. Was there just a hint of relief in his gaze? "Not really. No images. Just feelings. But…I think it's coming." She crossed to a window and unlatched the panes, allowing the hint of an early autumn breeze to infiltrate the stuffy apartment as she walked to the fireplace. Cool, damp air swirled into the room and followed after her as she ran her fingers along the mantel, picking up a fine layer of dust, looking for any photographs or mementos of the man she'd married. There was nothing. Not a solitary snapshot to verify his claims.

Frowning, she eyed her desk. The calendar lay open to a date that was nearly two weeks past. Chuckling at the "Far Side" cartoon, she flipped forward two weeks. Every page was blank. Aware of Trent's gaze following her, she turned back a few pages, noted some of the appointments she'd made and kept, she supposed, but realized that there wasn't a single notation about Trent. Not even his initials. No dinner date or lunch appointment, no mention of a movie or drinks or anything. As if he'd never existed.

She glanced up at him, half expecting him to come up with some explanation, but his face was unreadable, allowing her to draw whatever conclusions she wanted. "Didn't we go out?" she asked. "You know, for dinner or something…a date?"

His mouth lifted in the corner and his eyes turned smoky blue. "We started out way beyond the dating stage."

"But there's no mention of you. Not one clue...."

Lifting a shoulder as if her concerns were unimportant, he balanced on the overstuffed arm of the couch. The muscles in the back of his neck tightened and he seemed to grapple for the right words. "It was all very spontaneous. I didn't analyze it. Neither did you."

She had no reason to believe him, no proof to substantiate what he was saying. Rubbing a kink from her neck, she sighed and glanced at the telephone recorder, its red light flashing impatiently. With a feeling of dread, she pushed the playback button and the tape rewound quickly.

The first four calls were hang-ups. Then Jan's voice, strained by older-sister concern, echoed through the room. *"Nikki? It's Jan. What the hell's going on? Mom called and said you were on some island in the Caribbean and you got married there, for God's sake. To some guy no one in the family's ever met."* Nikki's gaze collided with Trent's. *"Is this all on the up-and-up? Call me when you get back and be ready to spill everything! Geez, Nikki, what happened to you! This is just so...I don't know—impulsive, I guess. I thought you'd finally gotten over all that."* There was a weighty pause when Jan sighed. *"Look, it sounds like we're trying to shut the barn door and the horse has already escaped. I guess I should congratulate you.... Well, just call me."*

"We don't have time for this," Trent grumbled as the phone buzzed and clicked over a series of hang-ups.

"Sure we do."

The next voice on the phone was a computer message about a fabulous deal on a time-share vacation in Colorado; the next, someone taking a survey about television programming.

The final call was more urgent. *"Nikki? It's Dave."* She stiffened. Trent's lips curled into a humorless smile. *"For heaven's sake, what's going on? I called your office and talked to Connie and she let it slip that you're married to a man you barely know! Is this some kind of a joke or something? Connie said you'd hardly dated him before taking off for that island. For crying out loud, Nikki, call me and tell me it's a lie or a joke or...or* anything. *I know we had some problems, but I thought we just needed a little time and space to work them out."* There was a lengthy pause and a long sigh. *"Look, if you're really married, I hope this guy is worth it, because you deserve the best...."* Nikki closed her eyes and she remembered Dave, big and blond, neat and tidy, spit and polish. At one time, he had seemed to care for her, but the images strobe-lighting through her mind weren't filled with love or tenderness or passion. She realized that she probably had never truly loved him. He'd just seemed like the right guy at the wrong time in her life. And he'd been the one who had wanted his "space" and a little more "time," if she remembered correctly.

His voice filled the emptiness again. *"But...well, if this is all a big lie, call me. Or if the guy doesn't turn out to be Mr. Perfect, for God's sake, give me a buzz.... Believe it or not, Nikki, I miss you. I just didn't realize how much until now.... What's the saying about being a day late and a dollar short? Well, it seems to be the story of my life. I love you, Nikki. I always will."* He hung up abruptly and his words hung on the air, silent, invisible sentinels that stood as strongly as a wall of steel between Nikki and Trent.

"Eloquent," Trent muttered, his lips thinning into a hard, flat line. "Maybe you married the wrong man."

"Maybe I'm not even married."

His mouth curved sardonically and he raked fingers of frustration through his coal-black hair. "Right now I don't give a good goddamn what you believe, but we're getting out of here." He picked up the suitcase she'd dropped and slung the strap over his shoulder. The fingers of his other hand wrapped around the handle of her garment bag as he cocked his head in the general direction of the door.

Nikki refused to be intimidated. "When did we get married?" she demanded, not budging an inch.

"On the Friday we left. At noon."

Still standing at her desk, she glanced at that particular date on her calendar, but it was, aside from a reminder to pick up her dry cleaning and a note as to the time her plane was scheduled to take off for Salvaje, blank. As if Trent McKenzie, before he'd appeared at her bedside at the hospital in Santa María, hadn't existed. "I didn't write it down."

"Of course not." Dropping both pieces of luggage, he strode to the desk as if he'd walked through her home a thousand times. "We didn't know when we were getting married until that day. So we just hightailed it down to the justice of the peace and did the dirty deed." His eyes narrowed on her, as if he were challenging her to call his bluff.

"So it's on record."

"With the city of Seattle and King County," he said,

reaching around her and drawing her into the circle of his arms. Sighing, he brushed a lock of hair from her face and struggled with his temper. "Come on, Nik. Throw some things together and we'll go to my place."

"Is that what we planned?"

"I think it's best."

"We could stay here."

"Nikki." He rested his forehead on hers. Tenderness softened his features. "We're both tired. Let's not argue—just get your things together and—"

"Wait a minute." She couldn't let him sweet-talk her. As warm and inviting as his embrace was, she yanked herself free and tried to think clearly. She was running on adrenaline now and she was back in her own home. No one, especially not a man she couldn't even remember, could order her around. "This isn't Salvaje, Trent. You can't use your caveman tactics on me."

"And I thought I was being nice," he said, rolling his eyes to the sloped ceiling.

"I want answers, answers you should have given me the first day I woke up."

His jaw slid to one side. "When we get to my place."

"How about right now?" She was on a roll and she wasn't going to stop. "Why did you follow me?"

"What?"

"On the island," she said, stepping farther from him, putting much needed distance between her body and his. When he held her, she found it impossible to think and remain levelheaded. Right now, back in the United States, they had a helluva lot to straighten out. "You did follow me, didn't you?"

"I was worried about you."

"That's not an answer."

He muttered something and shoved his hands into his pockets. "I hired a man to keep his eye on you."

"You *what?*"

"A private investigator."

Her temper flamed white-hot. "You low-down, lying son of a—"

"Stop it!" he warned, his nostrils flaring slightly as his temper began to slip. "I wanted you to have a little freedom, but—"

"Not too much. You were just giving me a slightly longer leash, is that it? Why? So I could strangle myself?" She marched back to him and tipped her chin upward. Heat radiated from beneath her skin and she knew her eyes were throwing off sparks of fury. "You're keeping something from me. No, I take it back—not something, but everything. You've been pointedly vague when I asked about your family, you've sidestepped a million questions about our romance, and you act as if we're in some sort of dire jeopardy. Even now. When we're home. You told me I wasn't pushed over that ledge, and yet you're nervous as a cat, acting like someone's planning to do us—well, me, at least—in. What is it, Trent?"

"I told you I'd explain when we get home."

"We *are* home." She planted her hands on her hips and decided to force his hand. "Why don't you tell me what all this…secrecy and cloak-and-dagger stuff has to do with Senator Crowley?"

His jaw hardened a little. "So you're still onto that, are you?"

"Absolutely." She skirted him, walked to her computer and snapped the power switch. The machine hummed to life. "I figure I'll know everything I want to know and a lot of things I don't want to know about good ol' Diamond Jim when I find my notes in this thing." She tapped the top of the monitor with her fingernail. "Maybe your name will come up, too."

"We don't have time—"

"Don't we?" She whirled on him, her hair slapping her in her face. "What happened to 'all the time in the world.' Or 'the rest of our lives'? On Salvaje you wanted me to think we could take everything slow and easy, but now we're back in Seattle and it's rush, rush, rush. Are you going to enlighten me, Trent?" she asked as the monitor glowed.

Exasperated, she plopped into her desk chair, pressed a series of buttons and scanned her files. "Let's see, how about under 'Crowley' for starters?" Deftly, she typed the senator's name, but the machine beeped at her and told her no such file existed. "Okay." Her brow puckered and she tried to think. "How about 'government'?" Only a half-finished story on a mayoral candidate. "Politics" was no better. "This can't be," she said, typing quickly, one file heading after another. She reread her work-in-progress menu again. No Crowley. No Diamond Jim. No political intrigue. Something was wrong. Biting her lip, she brought up other menus, from articles she'd finished. Not a clue.

"Why are you so damned certain that you were working on this story?" Trent asked, eyeing the screen skeptically, then sauntering to the fireplace and picking up pictures of her family. He fingered a color photo of her sister, Carole.

"I wasn't assigned the story—not officially—but I have this gut feeling that..." Her voice trailed off as she noticed Trent move easily around the room, glancing through the windows, stuffing his hands in his back pockets, closing a closet door with a faulty latch, as if he knew the place inside out. As if he belonged.

Her throat went suddenly dry. Could he have erased her story on Crowley? Destroyed all records she had on the senator?

But why? Good Lord, her head was beginning to pound again. Maybe Crowley was the key to why Trent claimed to be her husband. Goose bumps raced up her arms. This whole theory gave her the creeps and it didn't make a lot of sense. She swallowed hard and kept her gaze on the screen, unable to look into Trent's eyes for fear he might read her thoughts. She didn't want to believe he would sabotage her. Why would he lie about something so easily checked? What would be the point? And if he planned to hurt her…well, he had ample opportunity in a faraway country where the United States government couldn't touch him. Her palms were slick with nervous sweat. "I think we need to talk," she said, switching off the computer and swiveling in her chair to face him. He met her eyes in the oval mirror mounted over the fireplace as the machine wound down. Nikki's throat squeezed, and his gaze, flat and unreadable, didn't falter.

"You're right. But we have to do it at my place."

"Why?"

"Because it's not safe here, Nikki."

"This is my home and—"

"For God's sake!" He whirled and stormed back to her, drawing her to her feet. "Get your things—now! We don't have a lot of time."

"You're serious about this danger thing?"

"Dead serious."

"And when we get to your place?"

"You can ask me anything you want. But move it, now, before it's too late!"

His harsh countenance convinced her. Swallowing a knot of fear in her throat, she stumbled to the closet and pulled out a couple of pairs of jeans and some sweaters which she stuffed into an empty bag. "Are you going to tell me what we're running from?" she asked, picking up her makeup case as he grabbed the suitcase she'd dropped on the floor. She struggled into her Reebok sneakers and denim jacket and glared at him. "Because I'm going to remember, damn it, and when I do, there will be hell to pay if I find out you're a fraud, Trent McKenzie!"

Trent had never been above telling a lie, not if the situation warranted stretching the truth a little, but this time he'd played out his hand and was about to ruin everything. He'd managed to get himself so emotionally tangled in his own web of deceit that he was trapped. Like a damned fly in a spider's web.

Mentally abusing himself, he took the corner a little too quickly and the old Jeep slid a bit before the tread-free tires caught hold of the slick street.

He slid a glance at her, small and huddled against the passenger door. Confused, half her memory gone, the other half distorted by people she couldn't even remember. He tightened his fingers around the steering wheel until they ached.

It wasn't supposed to happen this way. He wasn't supposed to care for her. When he'd met her he'd been attracted to her, of course—hell, what red-blooded

American male wouldn't be? She was put together well, with curves in the right places and a face that could stop traffic. Whether she knew it or not, Nikki was a knockout. Even now, with the remainder of the abrasions from the accident casting parts of her face in pink, she was drop-dead gorgeous, in a way never exploited by fashion magazines.

Her eyes were clear and could cut to a man's soul, her hair was thick and wavy and shimmered under any light and her mouth was bowed into a thoughtful little pucker that caused the crotch of his pants to seem suddenly way too tight.

Her looks had attracted him, and her personality, part pit bull, part banty rooster and another part pure sexy feline, had kept him interested. He'd been around enough good-looking women not to fall into the usual traps, but with Nicole Louise Carrothers he'd swan-dived off a tall precipice and was still falling. Straight into the depths of emotional hell. The woman had a way of getting into a man's blood and there was no getting her out.

"Damn," he swore softly. She cast him a quick glance, then stared steadily ahead, through the rain-peppered windshield to the curving streets that wound along the shore of Lake Washington.

Tugging on the steering wheel, he pulled out of traffic and into a long drive that wound through tall fir trees and dripping rhododendron bushes no longer in bloom. The drive was lit by small lights. They rounded the bend, and the house, awash in the exterior lamp-light, was visible through the trees.

"This is where you live?" she asked, her voice tinged with disbelief.

"Home sweet home."

He cut the engine in front of the garage and she stared up at the house, a long, rambling brick cottage that rose to two stories at one side.

"Somehow it doesn't fit with the Jeep."

"I just like to keep you guessing."

"That much, you do," she admitted, stepping out of his battered rig and hauling her makeup bag with her. Flipping up the hood of her jacket, she let out a low whistle.

Trent unlocked the door with a key on his ring.

Inside, the house smelled of cleaning solvent, wax and oil. As they walked along wood corridors, Trent snapped on the lights unerringly, his hands finding switches in the dark, but still Nikki felt cold as death. Though she couldn't remember her past, she was certain that she'd never set foot in this house in her life. The living room was situated near the back of the house. Furnished in high-backed chairs, ottomans and a couch in shades of cream and navy, the room offered a panoramic view of the lake, now dark and brooding, only a few lights reflecting on the inky surface.

Nikki stared out the window and wrapped her arms around herself. Brass lamps pooled soft light over mahogany tables and the smell of pipe tobacco and ash from the fireplace tinged the air in faint scents. "I've never been here before," she said flatly.

"You'll remember."

"I don't think so." A chill skittered up her spine. "I would remember this. I would remember being here with you!" She trailed a finger along the window ledge, then turned tortured eyes up to his, hoping to feel a sense of security, of belonging.

"You're just tired." His voice was rough as sandpaper. Jaw tight, he took her hand and walked along a short, carpeted hall to the bedroom, where he placed her suitcase on the foot of a massive king-size bed with square posts and a carved headboard. The carpet was thick burgundy, the quilt was patterned in tan, burgundy and deep forest green.

A fireplace filled one corner, and Trent struck a match to the bottom of his boot and lit the dry logs resting on ancient andirons.

She felt a sudden sense of trepidation as she looked around the room. Something wasn't right; she could feel it in the very marrow of her bones.

Flames began to crackle against desert-dry kindling and the moss popped as it was consumed by the hungry fire.

Trent straightened, rubbing the small of his back, then stretching. Nikki's heart turned over at the sight of a slice of his skin just above the waistband of his low-slung jeans, visible as his hands reached toward the ceiling. She noticed the smooth muscles of his back and the cleft of his spine. "It's been a long day," he said, shrugging out of his jacket and tossing it carelessly on the foot of the bed. "We should turn in."

The room felt suddenly close and she could barely breathe. She'd slept with him while they stayed in the hotel on Salvaje, but she'd salved her guilty conscience with the knowledge that she'd had no choice. She'd made love to him hungrily because she was a willing prisoner and the rest of her life had seemed so far away and remote.

But now they were back home. Or in a place he

claimed belonged to him, and the prospect of falling into bed with him was suddenly terrifying. Now the choice was hers. Or, at least, it should have been. An American woman on American soil in her own hometown. He wasn't tying her to the bed, nor did he have to drag her here. True, he'd used his considerable powers of persuasion, but she had enough of her mind left to be able to say no if she'd really wanted to.

Truth to tell, she wanted to be with him. Here. Alone. As dangerous as he sometimes seemed, she couldn't stop wanting him. Maybe he hadn't lied. Maybe his story about the two of them held some water. The hot part was right. He yanked off his shirt, and Nikki watched as the firelight played upon tight, dense muscles sprayed with coarse chest hair.

He lifted a brow in her direction. "You want to take a bath or something?"

"You said you'd give me answers."

"That I did." He walked slowly to her, took the suitcase from her hand and dropped it onto the floor. With his gaze fastened to hers, he shoved her jacket over her shoulders and it dropped in a denim pool at her feet. "I just thought we should take care of a few more important things first."

"You're stalling," she said, but her voice was breathless, and she couldn't break the magnetic pull of his gaze as he searched her face.

He kissed her, his mouth molding over hers hungrily. Nikki closed her eyes and kissed him back, feeling the rough texture of his chest hair through her blouse, her fingers digging into the sinewy muscles of his shoulders.

"Nikki, oh, Nikki," he whispered roughly. Her mind

spun backward to another time when she was kissing another man, a man whom she thought she loved. But his kisses held none of the passion of this man's, and she'd never felt the wild abandon that this man created deep in her soul. Yet they were confused in her mind, the then and now, the here and before. Trent or Dave? Her husband or fiancé? She couldn't think and she tried to regain her disappearing equilibrium. "Dave?" she whispered as his lips traveled down her neck and touched the sensitive skin below her jaw.

He froze. His hands dropped. Stumbling backward, Nikki almost fell on the bed. She was dazed, her body still anxious and wanting.

His face was a mask of fury. "What did you call me?"

"Oh, God," she said, her fingers trembling as she grabbed a clump of long hair and held it at the base of her skull. What had she been thinking? "I called you Dave," she admitted, seeing a streak of pain slash through his eyes. "I...I was confused."

He snorted and crossed his arms over the expanse of his chest. "You thought I was Neumann."

"No—not really," she said, shaking. Oh, Lord, why was she so rattled?

"But you called me—"

"I know. It's just that I remembered," she said, shaking her head as if to clear away the horrid cobwebs that kept wisping through her mind and distorting the past.

"Remembered what?"

"Kissing Dave."

"Great," he said, flinty anger sparking in his eyes. "Well, how do I compare?"

"Compare... No, I didn't mean to—"

"Just what the hell did you mean?" he demanded

through lips that barely moved. Brow furrowed, deep lines cleaving his forehead, he raked a gaze down her front.

"You could be happy for me!" she countered, her temper flaring, her chin thrusting forward rebelliously.

"Happy!"

"This is a breakthrough."

"Wonderful." He snorted in derision. "And if we make love, are you going to pretend that I'm Neumann? And am I supposed to applaud?"

"You can do whatever you damned well want!"

"But it might just happen, right? You confusing the two of us?"

"Right. It's a chance we'll both have to take," she said, her breasts rising and falling with each uneven, furious breath she drew. Where did he get off, turning this around so that she felt like some cheap tramp? "Maybe you should take me home."

"This is home."

"Prove it," she threw out, angling her head up at him, letting her hair fall down one shoulder. "Show me the marriage certificate!"

The air between them grew still. Aside from the sizzle of the fire and the soft tattoo of rain against the window, there was no noise. Nikki knew she'd thrown her trump card on the table, but he didn't flinch, didn't move one solitary damn muscle.

"I don't have it," he said, his eyes moving to her lips. She tried not to notice, shifted her gaze downward, to the wide expanse of his chest, then lowered it still farther to rest on the huge silver buckle of his belt. Her throat tightened. This wasn't working.

"Where is it?" she asked, forcing her eyes upward to meet the smoky hue of his stare again.

"At my office."

"What?"

"Downtown. We left it there on our way to the airport." He stepped a little closer to her, close enough that she fought the urge to retreat. There was nowhere to run. Her calves were already pressed against the footboard of the bed.

"I don't believe you."

"Doesn't matter." He reached for her and she swatted his hand away. "You haven't believed me from the start."

"It matters. Big-time."

"We'll pick up the damned certificate." He reached forward again, one finger hooking on the V of her blouse. This time she didn't stop him. She couldn't.

"When?" she asked, hoping she wouldn't stammer, but hardly able to focus on the conversation. The tip of his finger brushed the flesh over her sternum and caused her blood to tingle and heat.

"Tomorrow. You'll want to go into the *Observer*. We'll stop by my office then."

Dear God, if only she could think clearly, but his touch was driving her wild. Standing close enough to feel his breath against her skin, she shivered as he slowly, and oh, so deliberately began working at the buttons of her blouse, his fingers prodding each tiny button free of its bond.

With all her willpower, she grabbed his wrist. "You're changing the subject."

"There is no subject." Leaning forward he kissed the shell of her ear and she melted inside.

"You—you could be lying to me."

"I could be." He nibbled at her neck. The blouse parted and he slid his hands around her. His fingers were warm and familiar against her skin as he pulled her closer.

"I need to know that you're telling the truth," she protested, though her mind was already spinning. "Please…"

"Later."

"Trent, please—" He cut off her pleas with his lips, hot and hard and wanting as they claimed hers. He groaned into her mouth and his tongue sought entrance past the barrier of her teeth.

"Come on, Nikki," he murmured, "let yourself go."

"I can't—"

"Of course you can. You're as hot and wild as that island we just left."

She sighed, and his tongue slid quickly into the wet interior of her mouth. Her knees threatened to buckle and a growing heat spread outward from her center and through her limbs. Her arms encircled his neck and his fingers scaled her ribs to cup her breasts.

Electricity shot through her bloodstream as he slid the blouse off her shoulders and kissed the swollen mounds above the lace of her bra. "God, you're gorgeous," he whispered, his lips wet and hot against her skin.

Lolling her head back, she gave him a full view of her neck. He nibbled and licked her flesh before returning to her breasts, which were now much too tight for her bra. With little encouragement, one rosy-tipped globe spilled free of the lavender lace and he eagerly swept the nipple into his mouth.

Nikki mewed deep in her throat as he tugged and suckled, laving the anxious point until she pressed her hips easily against him. "That's it, love, let go...." His fingers caught in the silky, honey-colored strands of her hair. His body weight pushed her gently and together they tumbled onto the cool quilt. Trent's mouth found hers again, his tongue probing, his hands moving to the small of her back to knead the soft flesh.

Nikki's thoughts were tangled, her emotions tied up in distant memories that teased the surface of her mind only to disappear again. But she wanted this man. Lust streamed through her bloodstream. She lowered her head and ran her tongue across his jaw and neck. Air whistled through his teeth as he sucked in his abdomen and she moved lower, enjoying the power of her body, watching in fascination as his flat nipples tightened at her touch. She took one tiny button into her mouth and he groaned, his fingers working anxiously in her hair.

"You're dangerous," he growled.

"So are you."

He tasted salty and male as he slipped her bra off her shoulders and pressed his lips to the hollow of her collarbone. "You make me do things I should never even think about," he said, his voice rough with emotion as he kissed her again. His fingers moved to her breasts and his thumbs grazed her nipples.

Thrusting her hips to meet his, Nikki was lost, her doubts all fleeing into the dark night. Her fingers dug into the rippling muscles of his back and she closed her mind to all the doubts and fears. She wanted this man, perhaps loved him, needed him as she was certain she'd needed no other. His touch set her ablaze and the drumming passion in her bloodstream refused to be denied.

Ignoring the future as her mind blacked out her past, she lived for the moment, for the hot-ice touch of his lips that burned against her skin and surrounded her heart.

She felt her jeans slide over her hips at his insistent tugging, blinked her eyes open long enough to see him kick off his faded Levi's as well.

"Tell me you want this," he whispered hoarsely.

"I want you."

Bracing himself on one hand, he palmed her breast, making the nipple stand erect again. "Tell me again."

"I...I want to make love to you," she whispered as he lowered his head and his lips surrounded her puckering nipple. "Ohhh."

"That's right." His breath was warm and teasing against the wet little bud, stoking the hungry fire within her. Again she arched up, her naked hips touching his. He held her for a moment, one hand cupping her buttocks. "God, Nikki, I don't want to ever stop," he admitted before prodding her knees apart and settling over her.

"Never," she murmured.

As rain slid against the windowpanes and the fire popped and burned, Trent claimed her as his own. He closed his eyes as she gazed up at him, her heart thudding, the tension in her tight as a piano wire. She reached upward and touched the dark strands of his hair, while capturing the sway of his lovemaking and moving her hips in time with his.

Lying with him felt so right against the soft, down-filled comforter. With firelight playing upon his sleek muscles and throwing red-gold highlights into his dark hair, he looked tough, and strong and male. His face was strained, little beads of sweat dotting his brow as he thrust into her, again and again.

Closing her eyes, she gave herself to him, body and soul, telling herself to trust him as her thoughts spun out of control, her blood ran hot, her body gathered the momentum of a steaming freight train. She felt their worlds collide, rocking her to her very soul, catapulting her into a realm of dizzying heights she was certain no woman before had ever scaled.

She heard a voice, realized it was hers and clung to him as he fell against her, breathless and covered in a sheen of sweat.

"Nikki, sweet Nikki," he murmured, crushing her to him. As afterglow claimed her, she snuggled against Trent, secure in the knowledge that for this night, this reckless, passionate night, nothing existed but Trent and the heart-stopping fact that she loved him.

Trent held her close, but the demons in his mind would allow no sleep. He'd made mistakes in his life, too many to count. And he knew he'd made more than his share with Nikki, but he couldn't help himself.

If he had to, he'd lie, he'd steal, probably even kill for her. But he knew that no matter how many times he told her, she'd never believe him.

He pulled her closer and kissed the hollow of her shoulder. She murmured his name and sighed softly, and the sound wrenched him to his very soul because he knew that, try though he might, he was destined to lose her.

He'd gone too far, let himself get caught up in his own fantasy because he couldn't imagine ever living without her. Yes, he'd lied, and someday surely she would condemn him to the very bowels of hell, but he hadn't been able to stop himself. She was a woman the like of which he'd never met before and though he'd wanted to resist her, the task had proved too difficult.

"Oh, Nikki," he said on a sigh as he kissed her temple. "If you only knew."

CHAPTER NINE

HOT, CLOYING AIR burned in her lungs and covered her skin like a moist, invisible blanket. She kept running, vines clinging to her legs, her feet stumbling as leaves slapped her face. Sweat poured from her skin and the sound of footsteps, heavy, evil and moving with the quickness of a jungle cat, crashed after her.

Help me!

The sound of the sea drew her like a magnet, though she knew the ocean was no savior. But the malevolence breathing hot upon the back of neck propelled her unwilling legs steadily up the hill, chasing her. Fear drummed in her ears and she sent up prayer after prayer.

Please, God, help me!

"*¡Pare!*" a deep voice yelled. Oh, God, he was so close! In her peripheral vision, she saw his shadow looming big and black and moving swiftly.

She ran harder, her lungs burning, her legs straining.

"Nikki! Nikki!"

Trent's voice, somewhere in the distance.

The shadow stretched out its arm, targeting a gun toward her back. Nikki tried to scream but her voice froze in her lungs.

The gun cracked—

"Nikki! Nikki! Wake up!"

Shrieking, Nikki sat bolt upright in bed. Shaking, her

voice raw from her own screams, she collapsed against Trent and lost a battle with hot, terrified tears.

"You're all right," he whispered against her crown. She buried her face into the curve of his shoulder, her fingers digging into his flesh. "Nikki, shh. You're safe now." His arms, strong and possessive, wrapped around her, and he cradled her against his chest, slowly rocking her, kissing her crown of mussed hair, willing his strength into her trembling body.

"It was so real," she whispered, her insides quaking. Swiping back a tear with her fingertips, she felt like a fool. Her fears had crystallized in the dream, the same damned nightmare she'd had off and on for two weeks.

"You were back on the island again," he said, holding her.

She nodded against him, her cheek rubbing his solid flesh. Over the sound of her breathing she could hear the steady beat of his heart. Squeezing back more tears, she leaned against him, her arms surrounding his naked torso, her sighs ruffling the dark swirling hairs of his chest.

Trent held her until her breathing was regular, until she no longer trembled in his arms, until the guilt eating at him was too great to bear. He stared at the clock. 5:00 a.m. The fire was reduced to a few glowing coals in a bed of cool ashes, and the rain had stopped. Through the window he saw the first few lights winking from the homes of early risers who lived across the lake.

Her arms tightened around him and he gritted his teeth against the deceit that tore at him like cat's teeth. For two weeks he'd lied to her, and sooner or later he would have to own up to the truth. He'd planned to set the record straight the minute their plane had touched down at SeaTac, but he hadn't, partly from fear, partly because he was so damned selfish. For the first time in five years he longed for a cigarette and a fifth of Jim Beam and wished the ache beginning to harden between his legs would go away.

Time was running out and the lie was growing bigger.

In a matter of hours, she would be able to check the records herself.

He hated weakness and he was weak where she was concerned. Had been from the beginning. That much hadn't been part of the lies. His lust for her had been overpowering and he'd given into carnal pleasure at the expense of her trust. Hell, what a mess.

The time was right. There was no going back. Slowly he disentangled himself from her. "Maybe you should try and get a little more sleep," he suggested, then mentally kicked himself for putting off the inevitable.

Yawning, she stretched, her hands reaching upward, the bedcovers slipping down to reveal her breasts, round, dark-tipped mounds that begged for his attention. The little peaks were tight from the cold and he had no trouble imagining what they would feel like in his hands or how they would taste....

"I can't sleep," she said, smiling a little.

His insides turned to jelly. Didn't she know how damned sexy she was with her gold-brown hair falling in sensual, tangled waves to her shoulders, and her eyes, still dark and slumberous, focused on him?

The hardness in his crotch was becoming unbearable. He slid to the side of the bed, threw his legs over the edge of the mattress and struggled into his suddenly too-tight Levi's. The room smelled of charred wood, perfume and fresh air, permeated with the heady aroma of sex.

"I can't sleep, either," he admitted, conscious of her gaze on his back. If he'd only known a few weeks ago how painful this would be, the consequences of his actions, he might have done something different. Now, of course, it was too late. Much too late. "There's something I've got to tell you." He was facing the opposite direction, but he sensed her stiffen, knew that her calm had given way to wariness again.

Hell, McKenzie, how could you have been such a fool? Turning, he rested his hips and hands against the edge of the bureau. "I don't know how to tell you this," he said, measuring his words and hating the brutal effect they would have on her. "But you were right. We aren't married."

For a moment there was no sound. Nothing changed except the temperature in the room, which seemed to suddenly drop to freezing. Her big eyes stared up at him, nearly uncomprehending yet she was wounded to her soul. "I...I don't think I heard you—"

"I lied."

She sucked in her breath, as if he'd physically slapped her, then closed her eyes for a minute, gathering strength, like clouds roiling before the storm. "We're not married," she clarified, her eyelids flipping open to reveal a face ravaged by fury, a face as white as death. "And never have been."

"That's right."

"Oh, God," she wailed, her gaze turning toward the ceiling in abject misery. "Why didn't you tell me? Why?"

"I couldn't."

Blinking hard, her lips flattening, her chin jutting in anger, she whispered, "I knew it. I just knew it and I let myself be fooled by you!"

"Nikki—" He took a step toward her, but she lowered her gaze and pinned him with all her righteous fury.

"You bastard. You miserable, low-life, lying bastard. You let me believe—"

"I had no choice."

"No choice?" she hurled back at him as she scrambled off the bed. For a second she hadn't moved, had seemed caught in a freeze-frame of time, but now she was all motion, her feet landing on the floor and her hands skimming the ground for the clothes. "No choice!" She snorted out his feeble excuse.

"They were going to kill you."

"They?" she repeated, her skepticism brassy.

"The men who were chasing you."

"Oh, now the story's changed. Lord, I've pulled some dumb ones in my life—well, at least, I *think* I have—but this must take the cake!"

"Yes."

"Convenient," she said, yanking on her jeans and her blouse before pulling a sweater over her head. She didn't bother with underwear as she grabbed the handle of her suitcase and started for the door.

His fingers locked around her wrist. "Where do you think you're going?"

"Home," she said succinctly. "The one I remember."

"You can't."

"I can damn well do what I please." She sneered down at the hand manacling her wrist. "Let go of me, McKenzie. Unless you want me to call the police and have you up on charges of kidnapping me and holding me hostage, as well as assault."

"I never hurt you." She blanched and he swore under his breath. "Not physically."

"Just take your damned hands off me before I scream," she warned, her eyes narrowing in pure hatred. A piece of his soul seemed to shred, but he held firm, his face tightening into a mask of impatience.

"You could at least let me explain."

"You had your chance. Over and over again. I *begged* you to tell me the truth, *pleaded* with you to be honest, and how did you respond? With lies and promises and God only knows what else!" She was nearly shouting by this time, her breathing uneven, her anger seeming to crackle in the air.

"So now you don't have time for the truth."

"From you? Never. I wouldn't know what to believe."

"For God's sake—"

She kicked him then. With the toe of her soft Reebok. She nailed him in the shin and jerked away, but he sprang on her like a cat and snarled, "Just a minute, darlin'."

"Go to hell."

"No thanks. I've already been there," he shot back, his eyes snapping blue fury, his nostrils flared and his rugged face flushed.

"So have I." Glaring at him pointedly, she yanked herself free, ripped the ring from her finger and tossed it at him. "I think this is yours."

He snapped the ring out of the air and the muscle in his face stretched taut. "I was only protecting you. It was the only way I could admit you into the hospital without a thousand questions being asked, the only way I could stay in the room and make sure that no one got to you—"

"Oh, is that what it was?" She cocked her head toward the bed. "You know, that's the first time a man's taken it upon himself to have sex with me to 'protect' me."

His teeth ground together. "You're impossible."

"At least I don't resort to lying to score."

"That's enough!" Both his hands opened and clenched, and Nikki had the distinct impression he wanted to put them around her throat and strangle her. Well, she wanted to strangle him, too! And yet a part of her—a silly, irrational, very feminine part of her still loved him. Lord, she was a fool! *Be strong, Nikki.*

"You're right about that, McKenzie," she said as she picked up her suitcase again and slid past him. "It's way more than enough!"

"For once, just listen."

"I've listened, Trent. Over and over again. And all I keep hearing are lies. Lies, lies and more lies! Thanks, anyway, I don't need any more!"

He didn't bother to try and restrain her and she didn't know whether to be grateful or sad. A part of her still longed for him to take her into his arms, but her realistic nature kicked that silly notion right out of her head. She didn't love him. She couldn't love him. She would never love him and never had. Anything she had felt for him was a wasted, empty emotion—a fantasy that made having sex with him convenient and guilt-free.

Married to the man! Imagine! Even with the holes in her memory she should have known he wasn't her type.

She threw open the back door and walked into the gray light of dawn. Mist rose from the ground in ghostly spirals, and the lake, down a steep incline covered with fir trees still moist from the night's rain, was calm and gray. The still water seemed to stretch for miles to the opposite shore where, tucked in a dark ridge of hills, house lights were beginning to glow.

In a flash of memory, she saw herself on a sailboat, her father at the helm, her sisters, in fluorescent orange life jackets, scrambling over the deck. The mainsail had billowed, catching the wind, and the boat had dipped, skimming across a choppy surface of whitecaps.

The wind had been winter-cold and raw, but Nikki hadn't cared. Jan had complained about her hair losing its curl. Carole was sure she had frostbite, but Nikki had laughed in the wind, feeling the grip of frigid air tearing at her ponytail and stinging her cheeks.

"Let's go all the way to Alaska," she'd cried, holding on to the boom for dear life.

"Aye, aye, matey," her father had replied and she'd loved him with all her young heart.

"I'm not going to Alaska," Jan had yelled over the cry of the wind. "I've got a date."

Nikki hadn't been impressed. "Big deal."

"It is a big deal! I have to get home in time to wash and blow-dry my hair!"

"For Paul Jansen. Save me." Nikki had laughed.

"That's not a date. It's a death sentence," Carole added with a wink to her youngest sister. "But Alaska's too cold." Carole's teeth had begun to chatter loudly. Her words came out in choppy little puffs. "C-can't we g-g-go to Hawaii or L.A. or…"

At the mention of the City of Angels, Ted Carrothers's grin had turned into a gritty scowl. Their mother had already moved to Southern California and had hinted to her daughters that there was another man in her life. "Just forget it," he'd muttered to his would-be sailor daughters. Then, spying Jan, he added, "Don't worry, you'll be home in time for your date."

"Good." She'd tossed her head and sniffed at her victory.

"No way! Come on, Dad," Nikki had pleaded, her dreams crumbling. She ached for adventure and she didn't want to go back to the empty house their mother had vacated two years earlier. "Let's sail into the Sound."

Her father had scanned the flinty sky, but even before he turned his eyes back on his youngest daughter, she'd known what he would say. The mood had been destroyed. "Ah, well, we'd better be heading back. I've got a lot of paperwork to catch up on if I'm going to be ready for the meeting in Seoul next week."

Now Nikki stood staring at the calm lake greeting the dawn. Steel gray and cold. She shivered and didn't realize Trent was beside her until a twig snapped beneath his boot.

"Second thoughts?" he asked. No longer was there any anger in his voice. Only regret.

She shook her head. "But thoughts, just the same." She was surprised how quickly they came now. All at once, in a jumble, sharp, vivid memories that last week had been lost to her.

He touched her shoulder and she flinched.

"I don't have my car," she said, as if in explanation. "Since I don't know the bus schedule, and cabs don't cruise by this section of town at daybreak—"

"I'll drive you."

"No way. I'll call a cab."

"Don't be silly."

"Silly?" She laughed mirthlessly. "I've already been played for a fool. I'm not really concerned with silly."

"You know what I mean. Get in the Jeep."

He actually sounded concerned. But then, he was a consummate actor. Hadn't he convinced her that they'd been married? That they'd *loved* each other? Her heart wrenched at his story. So simple. So deceptive. Despite the fact that no one she knew had known of their romance, they'd fallen in love, hightailed it to the nearest courthouse, tied the knot and flown off to a small, out-of-the-way island in the Lesser Antilles for a romantic honeymoon and while they were there she'd fallen off a cliff and nearly killed herself. Lucky for her he was around to snatch her from the jaws of death, carry her off to his bed and lie, lie, lie to her. Her fingers tightened around the strap of her purse.

"Come on, Nikki." His voice was a caress.

"Not if your damned Jeep was the last vehicle on earth." She hitched her bag on her shoulder and started for the main road. She'd stick out her thumb if she had to, though that might be a little risky.

His fingers clamped around her arm. "Get in the Jeep."

"You can't manhandle me."

"I'm doing you a favor."

She snorted. "Your kind of favors I can do without."

He propelled her toward the door of the rig, pulled on the handle, and with a groan of metal the interior was open to her. "Get in."

"I'm not going to—"

"If I have to shove that beautiful butt of yours into the seat, I will," he warned, and she believed him. Her pride still bleeding, she climbed into the damned Jeep and gritted her teeth as he slammed the door shut. This was crazy. Pure, dumb insanity.

He slid into the driver's seat and twisted the key in the ignition. He slammed the door shut and rammed the rig into Reverse. Within seconds they were driving along the rain-washed streets, joining the first few cars and trucks heading toward the skyscrapers swarming along the shores of Elliott Bay.

Inside the Jeep the air was thick. Steam rose on the windshield and Trent flipped on the fan. Cramming her back against the passenger door, Nikki told herself she was the worst kind of fool. She crossed her arms and glared at him. "Just who the hell are you?"

"I told you."

"McKenzie's your real name?"

"You saw my ID, didn't you? When you went through my wallet." The barb stung. Oh, well, Sherlock Holmes she wasn't.

"ID can be bought."

With a sigh, he flipped down the visor, ripped the registration from its holder and shoved it under her nose. "No aliases, okay?"

The beat-up vehicle was registered to Trent McKenzie. He wheeled into the drive of her apartment building.

"Okay. So now I know your name." She shrugged as if she didn't care, but couldn't help asking, "What do you do for a living?"

"I'm a freelance investigator. Primarily I work on insurance fraud. I told you all this." He shifted down and the Jeep slowed.

"You told me a lot of things."

The rig slid to a stop, idling near the doorway of one

of the first-floor apartments. "I didn't lie about the way we met, Nikki." He cut the engine, and when she tried to open the door, he caught her arm. "Just hear me out."

"I've heard enough. Two weeks of lies is more than anyone should have to swallow, don't you think?" She managed to pull on the door handle, breaking a nail in the process. Too damned bad. "You lied to me, McKenzie, and what's worse, when I knew you weren't telling the truth, you kept piling on more and more lies." Her words raced out of her mouth. "Not only that. You took me to bed, brought me back here under false pretenses, *used* me, and only when you knew the lies would begin to fall apart, did you finally come clean. But not until we made love! Excuse me, what I meant to say is not until we had sex!" So angry she was shaking, she threw off his arm. When he tried to reach for her again, she scrambled out of the Jeep, grabbed her suitcase and ran up the wet steps. He was on her heels, chasing after her, climbing the stairs behind her.

Her dream returned, surreal but no less terrifying as he followed her. It was as if they'd played this game before. At the landing, she whirled on him. "Leave me alone, Trent," she ordered, but he was too close. He planted his hands on the door frame near her face, trapping her with his body.

"I can't, damn it. Look, Nikki, I didn't mean for it to turn out this way." His mouth curved into a self-deprecating frown. "I should have told you sooner, but I couldn't. Once you were released from the hospital, I…I wanted to stay with you. To keep you safe."

"To sleep with me."

"Yes!"

The air crackled with his admission, and Nikki's

throat was suddenly clogged. "Well, lucky you," she said angrily, but the sharp honesty in his gaze cut through the armor of her defense. "You could have stopped things," she whispered.

"I would have."

"Sure," she mocked, and she finally worked up the nerve to ask a question that had been nagging at the back of her mind. "Just who do you think you were protecting me from?"

His lips thinned a fraction. "Crowley."

She sucked in her breath. "So I was right."

"Maybe."

She had a picture of the silver-haired man with his smooth black cane. She'd met him in the camera shop! Her heart nearly stopped. Yes, there was something deadly about him, the gleam in his eye was cold as an arctic well. But she didn't believe he had the strength or stamina to run her down through a jungle. "But he wasn't chasing me."

"I don't know that anyone was."

She felt as if she'd been kicked in the stomach. "But my dream. Everything else fits. And who was the man lurking on the veranda, huh? Was that you?"

"Of course not."

"Well?"

"I thought it might have been a man I had following you."

"Oh, great! Just great! Now you're trying to tell me that one of the so-called good guys is a Peeping Tom?"

"No. *El Perro* denied it."

"His name is *el Perro?* Doesn't that mean wolf or something?"

"Dog."

"Oh, come on." She threw her hands toward the sky—in desperation or supplication, she didn't know which. "This is too damned unbelievable."

"Is it?" He shoved his face so close she could see the small lines of impatience around his mouth. "You asked what I was trying to tell you and it's simple. You're in danger. From Crowley or one of his goons. Just because we're back in Seattle doesn't mean that you're safe. I overheard you talking to Connie. I knew you were onto Diamond Jim. That's when I started doing my research on you—because there was something about you I couldn't forget. The senator's dangerous, Nikki."

She felt her throat tighten in fear, then shoved the feeling aside. No man, especially not a pathological liar, was going to tell her what to do with her life. "I don't know why I should believe you." She reached behind her, found the doorknob and pushed. It didn't budge.

"Why would I lie?"

"You asked me that before and it took me two weeks to find the answer." She dug through her purse, came up with her ring of keys and wedged the house key into its lock. With a click, the latch gave way. She shouldered open the door and stood on the opposite side of the threshold. "I'd like to say something profound here, something you could remember me by, but I can't think of a blessed thing, so I'll just say goodbye."

"I'm not leaving." To prove his point, he stuck the toe of his beat-up leather boots into the apartment.

"I'll call the police."

"Fine." He didn't budge an inch, and she felt the steam rising from the back of her neck.

"You've spent the last two weeks bullying me, Trent McKenzie, but it's over," she lied knowing that, in her heart, it would never be finished between them. But she couldn't think of *that* now. "I'll have you up on charges of harassment, fraud and kidnapping. And if those don't stick, I'll find some that do. So you'd better haul yourself out of here."

He slid into the room, rested his hips against the wall, crossed his arms over his massive chest and nodded toward the phone. "Now *I* don't believe *you.*"

She couldn't make good her threat, didn't dare call the police. Whatever story she was working on concerning Senator Crowley, it wasn't yet ready to break and she had to be careful that Diamond Jim didn't catch on to her. If she pressed charges against Trent, there was the matter of public record to consider, and there would be questions about their trip to Salvaje. Her story was half-baked and bizarre, her memory not yet a hundred percent. No, she had better keep the police out of this. For the time being. She looked up at Trent's impassive face and wished she could shake some sense into him. He had backed her into the proverbial corner and he knew it.

"Why don't you get ready for work and I'll drive you."

"You don't have to—" For the first time she realized she was missing her car. She half ran to a window, wiped the glass with her sleeve and stared down at the parking space assigned to her. Empty. Her red-and-white convertible wasn't in its usual spot. "I don't suppose you know what happened to my car?"

"My guess is it's at the airport."

"The airport!" she cried, her temper flaring again. If he'd only been honest with her earlier, she'd have her own set of wheels by now.

"But then again, maybe not. You didn't have a parking ticket on you."

"How do you know?" she demanded, but the answer was clear as the glass top of her coffee table. He'd been given her purse at the hospital when she'd been lying in that tiny room trying to piece together her memory—attempting to recall taking vows with the mysterious, bad-tempered man who had claimed to be her husband. He could have put anything in her purse or taken anything out. Hence, the wedding ring—that blasted symbol of deceit. "Oh, Lord, this is a mess," she said with a sigh as she sank onto the couch and closed her eyes. "What am I going to tell everyone? My entire family thinks I'm married. And Connie. What can I say to her?" She cast an accusing glare in his direction. "When you plot to turn someone's life upside down and inside out, you don't miss a trick, do you?"

Trying to stay calm, she rested the heel of one of her Reebok shoes on the tabletop and wondered how she was going to face the day. There would be questions about her accident, her face, her honeymoon, her husband. What would she say? What could she?

"You don't have to tell anyone what's going on."

"Oh, right! Next you'll be suggesting that I keep pretending that we're married." She lolled her head back on the couch and sighed.

She heard him skirting the coffee table as he walked to the fireplace. "What would it hurt?"

"It's a lie." She cracked open one eye.

"It doesn't have to be."

Her heart stopped for a second, before she found her voice. "Yes it does," she said, quietly. A part of her wanted to take the easy way out, keep the lie going until things settled down and to stay with this dangerous, erotic man. Then she could tell her friends and family the truth. Later she could leave him...or would she ever find the strength to let go? Slowly she shook her head and forced her gaze to meet his. "It'll only get worse."

As the words fell from her lips, she remembered her older sister, Jan, on bent knees, examining a cut on Nikki's chin as she had sat, white-faced and trembling, on the edge of the bathtub. "Geez, you look horrible," Jan had said.

"Thanks," Nikki muttered, fighting tears.

Her elbow ached and her face felt as bad as it probably looked. There was still gravel ground into the skin of her forearm and blood had dried all the way to her wrist. "So what happened?" Jan had asked, seeming uncertain as to how concerned she should be.

"I fell off my bike."

"And how." Jan reached into the medicine cabinet for a dangerous-looking brown bottle and gauze.

Tears welled in Nikki's eyes. Tasting blood in her mouth where her teeth had bitten into her lower lip, she told Jan the truth. Nikki had been riding her bike with her friend, Terry Watson, a devil-may-care girl whose sense of adventure appealed to Nikki. With her pale blond hair, round blue eyes and quick smile, Terry was popular and had a reputation for being a little bit daring. That day, while Nikki was supposed to have been studying for a history test at Terry's house, Terry had shoved her books aside and come up with an alternate plan. With only a little persuasion, Terry had convinced Nikki that they should ride their bikes down to the big Safeway store that was three miles away. The only trouble was that the store was located far beyond the boundaries their parents had agreed upon.

The girls had taken off, full of adventure, thrilled to be doing something just a little bit naughty. They had planned to be back by the time Terry's mom got off work. No one would have been the wiser.

The traffic had been wild, four lanes going fifty-five miles an hour, and the clouds that had been threatening all day suddenly let loose, pouring rain onto the streets, creating rivers flowing into the gutters and turning the day dark as night.

Headlights flashed on, tires sprayed water onto the sidewalks. Rather than ride to the crosswalk, Terry had decided to zigzag across all four lanes of traffic.

"Wait for me!" Nikki had yelled, and Terry, hearing her voice, had turned her head. A car, rounding the corner, had skidded as the driver slammed on his brakes. Horns had blared, tires had squealed. Nikki had squeezed on her brakes. The bike had shimmied in loose gravel, then slid. Nikki had fallen, scraping her knees and elbows and face, her bike flying into the traffic to be crumpled beneath the wheels of a pickup.

"Crazy kids!" The truck's driver had been livid. "I could a killed you both!" Built like a lumberjack, with a full beard and snapping blue eyes, he'd walked over to Nikki, full of wrath until he saw the scratches on her face and arms. "Hey, kid, are you all right?"

"Fine," she'd stammered, though she felt wretched. But she'd known her injuries weren't nearly as bad as the fear that settled around her heart. Her parents would kill her when they found out.

A lady dressed in a long raincoat and huge round glasses speckled with rain, had climbed out of her small compact car with its emergency lights flashing. Shoulders hunched against the downpour, she'd said, "I think we should call an ambulance."

No! "I'm okay, really." Nikki had fought to hide her pain and she reached for the handlebars of her bike just as Terry, face pale as death, had wheeled up.

"We gotta get out of here," Terry had insisted.

"Now, honey, the police—"

That did it. Nikki had hauled her bike up on its bent frame and jumped onto the seat. The rear wheel had rubbed against the fender, and she was stuck in third gear, but she hadn't thought, just ridden, like the proverbial bat out of hell, as fast as her legs could pedal, all the way home.

"And that's what happened," she had admitted to her sister as she'd tried to balance on the edge of the tub.

Jan had rolled her eyes. "Big trouble, Nik. Big, big trouble." She'd swabbed Nikki's cuts with iodine and as Nikki sucked in her breath through teeth that felt looser than they had earlier in the day, Jan predicted, "Dad's gonna kill you."

He hadn't. In fact he'd been downright kind as he'd sat on the foot of her bed, hands clasped between his knees, his suit rumpled from the drive home. "I'm just thankful you're alive," he'd said, his voice filled with reproach.

Nikki had wanted to burrow down beneath the covers of her twin bed and never come out. She'd let him down and she felt miserable. Tears had drizzled from her eyes and she'd rolled her lips inward and clamped down hard to keep from sobbing.

"I hope you've learned your lesson. I trusted you to

be where you'd told me you'd be. I thought I could believe you."

Nikki had blinked hard and swallowed that ever-growing lump in her throat. If only she could undo what had been done!

"But now...well, we'll have to start over, Nicole. Trust isn't just given out—it's earned, you know."

"I'm sorry, Dad. I'm so, so sorry."

"So am I, sweetheart, but this time sorry isn't good enough. You could've been killed. For the time being you're not to see Terry unless it's at school, and you're grounded for...well, until I can trust you again."

Her future had stretched out endlessly before her. She'd been certain she'd become an old maid before he believed her again. Oh, she'd wanted to die right then and there. *Take me, Lord, I'm ready. I can't stand the thought of being cooped up here until he trusts me again. He never will. Never, never, never!*

God, that had been a long time ago. Nikki rubbed her arms and realized that Trent was staring at her. Waiting for her to respond. "I'm not going to lie about it," she said, then realized how ridiculous her words sounded. "Well, I'm not going to lie anymore. I'll just say that it didn't work out, we rushed into things and that we're separated." Cringing inside, she heard "I told you so" being repeated to her over and over by her family and friends.

Pain darkened his gaze and he cleared his throat. "It would be best if we played along with the charade a little longer," he said, measuring the words.

"Why?"

"Until this mess with Crowley is straightened out."

A cold trickle of fear slid down her spine, but she hid

it. "Why don't you tell me all about the good senator? And since we didn't go to Salvaje together, why were you down there? I can't imagine that you spend your vacations in the tropics hoping for some woman to lose her memory so you can pounce and take advantage of her."

His eyes flashed dangerously. He rubbed his chin and swore, as if he didn't want to divulge anything to her. "It's been rumored, but hushed up for the most part, that the senator's into taking bribes. Nothing's been proven, of course, and with public officials there's always a lot of conjecture, and our boy Diamond Jim is as slippery as he is popular. Nothing can be pinned on him—he just seems to slide away from scandal."

"What's this got to do with you?"

One of his fists closed for a second and a wave of tension tightened every muscle in the back of his neck. "I know the senator. I have a bone to pick with him."

"What bone?" she asked, surprised that he was opening up.

"It's personal."

"Don't you think I'm involved, *personally?*"

"Let's just say I wouldn't cry if he went down in flames."

"So you and I went down to the island independently."

"That's right. That's why Rosa, the clerk, recognized you and didn't know me."

"And then what?" she said, watching as emotions, strong and angry, played across his face.

"We weren't on the same flight. I'd followed Crowley earlier. You showed up a couple of days later and I recognized you and I thought you might be headed for trouble. I didn't want to blow my cover, so I just kept

my eye on you. I figured, from overhearing your conversation with Connie at the *Observer* that you'd be
tracking down Diamond Jim as well."

"So...you were following me."

"And Crowley."

She clucked her tongue. "Busy boy."

"By that time I'd done my research on you, your
father, your boyfriends, your interests. Everything. I
knew all about you."

"Charming," she muttered with more than a trace
of sarcasm.

He ignored the dig. "Obviously Crowley knew you
were onto him. He must've recognized you since he's
in tight with your dad. But I don't think any feelings
he has for your old man would affect his ambitions and
you, lady, were and are a threat to him."

"How would he guess?"

"He's a powerful man with more than his share of
connections. I wouldn't be surprised if one of your co-
workers is in the senator's back pocket."

"Who?"

"That much I don't know," he admitted, scowling slightly. "So I kept dogging you and I knew you'd
planned to see the mission because I'd overheard you
talking to the concierge at the hotel, asking directions.
I made sure I got there ahead of you and then..." Guilt
shadowed his eyes and he rubbed a hand over his mouth.
"...I wasn't paying attention and suddenly I heard you
scream. I ran as fast as I could and found you on the
lower ledge. The rest you can figure out."

"What about the man who pushed me?"

Trent shook his head. "Didn't see him." When he realized she was about to protest, he held up a hand. "I'm

not saying he didn't exist, I'm just telling you I didn't see him. He could've hidden, I suppose. All I was concerned about was getting you to safety."

"And deciding to pretend to be my husband."

"As I said, originally I did it so that I could stick close to you and keep you safe. That hospital didn't have the best security in the world and I thought Crowley might send one of his goons to make sure you didn't talk. That part worked."

"But only because I didn't regain my memory. What would have happened if I'd suddenly remembered everything?"

A muscle worked in his jaw. "That was one bridge I thought I'd cross when I came to it."

"And that's why you didn't…rush things in the bedroom."

He slid his jaw to the side. "I told myself that I'd keep my hands off you. Your injuries were enough reason."

"But—"

"Oh, hell, Nikki," he exploded, "I couldn't help myself! I knew it was wrong, but I didn't exactly rape you now, did I?"

She blushed darkly. "You took advantage of me."

"So sue me! Call the damned police! Do whatever you have to, but, for God's sake, believe me! I couldn't keep away. I wanted to. Hell, I knew making love to you would be a mistake, but it was a risk I had to take."

"You didn't *have* to do anything."

He sighed loudly. "It happened, Nikki."

Her heart started to crack again, but she refused to play the part of the wounded victim. Unfortunately part of what he said made sense and the truth be told, she didn't want to leave him. Not yet. Not until she was stronger. Climbing to her feet, she said, "Okay, we'll go along with the charade, for just a few more days, until I can figure out how the hell to divorce you quietly. Then, a clean break."

"Fine." He seemed relieved. The lines of tension around his eyes became less prominent.

"But I am going to work."

He started to argue, thought better of it and nodded curtly. "I'll drive you and pick you up, then we'll go to the airport and try to locate your car."

There was no sense belaboring the point. At least the ground rules were set down, not that they might not shift at any minute. She found a set of towels in a cupboard and, after announcing she was going to take a shower, locked the bathroom door behind her and turned on the old spigots. Steam rose to the ceiling as she stripped off her clothes. So she wasn't married. Good. Soon Trent would be out of her life forever.

She pushed aside the shower curtain and stepped beneath the hot spray. As she reached for the shampoo bottle, she noticed her ringless left hand and bit down hard to keep from sobbing. What was wrong with her? He was a phony! A sham! A liar! No better than Judas Iscariot or Benedict Arnold!

So why did she still love him?

CHAPTER TEN

"CONGRATULATIONS!" CONNIE, PERCHED on the corner of Nikki's desk, dropped a white package with a big silver ribbon next to Nikki's computer monitor. Rawboned and strawberry blond, she'd grown up in West Texas and had never gotten rid of her drawl. Her long legs swung freely from beneath a short black skirt and when she smiled her eyes sparkled like liquid gold.

"What's this?" Nikki asked, but with a sinking sensation, she knew. The silver wedding bells on the wrapping paper gave the gift away.

"Open and find out."

"I can't."

"Sure you can." Connie pretended to look wounded. "Unless you want to wait until Trent's around—"

"No!" Nikki grabbed the package, read the card and pulled off the ribbon and wrapping paper. Inside was a cut-crystal vase with fluted sides. "Oh, Connie, it's beautiful," she said, feeling like a thief. "I...I don't know what to say."

Connie grinned. "You don't have to say anything. Now, check your schedule. Some of us want to throw you a belated wedding shower, probably early next month." She leaned over the desk and flipped through the blank pages of Nikki's calendar. "How about the tenth?"

"I...I don't think so," Nikki said, touched, but trying to come up with some reason to avoid the celebration. She felt like a phony and a fraud, a person who would lie to get whatever she wanted.

"It'll be fun. Jennifer knows a male stripper and—"

"Oh, Connie, really, don't," Nikki pleaded. Everything was snowballing too quickly and she felt as if her life was beginning to career off course. She touched Connie on the back of the hand and decided she had to confide in her friend. "Look, I've got to tell you something," she said, glancing over her shoulder.

Max Van Cleve was striding toward her desk. His wavy blond hair was combed perfectly, his white shirt starched.

"Later," Nikki said to Connie. "I'll tell you everything at lunch."

"What is it? Trouble?" Connie guessed from the lines of worry that seemed intent on permanently etching Nikki's brow.

"Just wait, okay?" She didn't want Max overhearing any of their conversation, and thankfully, Connie seemed to finally get the message.

"I hear congratulations are in order," Max said, showing off perfect white teeth. "How about a kiss for the blushing bride?" He was teasing, she knew. He'd been married to his wife, Dawn, for three years and the two of them still acted as if they were on their honeymoon. At that particular thought, Nikki's stomach did a little flip. Honeymoon. Salvaje. Trent.

"First of all, I don't blush, and secondly, I wouldn't want to make Dawn jealous," she quipped back. She felt like such a traitor. For years she'd prided herself on her honesty; she knew that much from the bad taste in her mouth every time she tried to lie.

"Me?" He pointed a finger at his chest. "Do anything to upset my wife? Never. Just the same, you owe me one." He rapped his knuckles on the edge of her desk and walked toward the reception area.

Nikki blew out a sigh of relief, ruffling her bangs in the process. It was good to finally be alone, though her peace lasted less then forty-five minutes, when Connie returned bearing a steaming cup of coffee and a toasted bagel.

"Fresh off the cart," she said, sliding the bagel, napkin, coffee and small container of cream onto a stack of Nikki's mail.

"You're a lifesaver." Nikki poured in the cream and sipped from the hot coffee.

"Well, I'm glad you're back. Things have been dull with a capital *D* around here since you've been gone." A set of slim gold bracelets jangled as she motioned toward Frank Pianzani's glassed-in office. "Worse than ever. Frank seems to think the only stories I can handle all have to do with triplets being born or teachers being fired. Heavy stuff." She winked lashes thick with mascara. "You'd think someone would tell that man we're closing in on the twenty-first century."

"I know just the woman to do it," Nikki said pointedly.

"Moi?" Connie pointed a red-tipped nail at her sternum and shook her head. "And chance losing my job? Uh-uh. I'll leave all that brave and noble business to someone else. I'm just a working girl."

"Sure," Nikki said as Connie strolled back to her desk.

She finished her bagel, dusted her fingers and sipped coffee while continuing to scan her notes, read her mail, skim the last few issues of the *Observer* and generally catch up with the rest of the staff. Time still seemed out of sync for her, and whether from jet lag, her amnesia or her stormy relationship with Trent, she couldn't concentrate fully on her work. Relationship. Ha! What she shared with Trent was no more than cold lies and hot sex.

That thought turned her stomach sour, and she tossed back the rest of her coffee, crumpling the cup and casting it into the wastebasket as she tore open an envelope. But work didn't come easily. She wasn't used to the noise and activity of the office. Secretaries clicked by in high heels, mail carriers pushed carts along the aisles between the cubicles housing individual desks, phones jangled, conversation wafted past soundproof barriers, and the fluorescent lights overhead hummed while offering a surreal light to the inner workings of the *Observer*.

She couldn't seem to dislodge Trent from her mind. His face swam behind her eyelids and his vague accusations against Senator Crowley kept playing back in Nikki's head like a record that was stuck. She twirled a pencil between her fingers and wondered about the connection between Crowley and Trent. Why was Trent so hell-bent to see Crowley destroyed?

Scratching the back of her head with the eraser end of the pencil, Nikki pulled up the files of stories she was working on before she left for Salvaje. Most of her work was finished and printed: old news. Only a few articles and interviews hadn't been completed, but not one of the articles had anything to do with politics or

Diamond Jim Crowley. As she read over her work, try
ing to feel some connection to this job, she experienced
an undercurrent of dissatisfaction, solidifying her earlier guess that she'd been unhappy here at the *Observer*.

Max had written an article on Senator Crowley a few
weeks back, but the piece read more like a campaign
advertisement than a piece of cutting-edge journalism.
It was little more than a reminder that James Thaddeus
Crowley was working hard in Washington, D.C., for the
people in Washington state. For jobs. For the economy.
For the environment. For everyone. Nikki's stomach
roiled. Something stunk to the very gates of heaven. She
was sure of it, and in a flash of memory she recalled
that she had planned an exposé of Crowley, there was
something…some scandal he had covered up. What was
it? She worried her lip between her teeth and tried to
concentrate, but other than her image of the cold man
with the cane in the photography shop in Salvaje, she
remembered nothing. Trent had said something about
bribery. *Think, Nikki, think!*

Nothing came. Not one measly thought.

"Terrific," she growled in disgust and let out a per-
turbed sigh. Disgusted with her lack of memory, she
rifled through the new stories she'd been given: an update on new bike paths near Lake Washington, an in-
depth article on the new director of the symphony, a
story on the import/export business in Seattle, with a
note that she could use her own father as one of her
sources as he owned one of the largest import/export
houses on the Sound.

Nothing of any substance. No investigative journalism. No dirt. Not one thing that really mattered.

No wonder she'd been after Crowley. Tapping her

pencil on her desk, she squinted at her computer monitor. But what was Trent's connection to the senator? He'd been in Salvaje, dogging Diamond Jim, just as she had. He'd been worried enough to pretend to be married to her. But worried about her safety? Or worried about what she might print about the senator? What was his ax to grind? She didn't know, she thought, leaning back in her chair and frowning at the screen, but she damned well planned to find out!

"Not really married!" Connie's jaw nearly dropped into her spinach salad. "But—you called. Said so." Her face crumpled into a mask of confusion and a wounded shadow crossed her eyes as she stared at Nikki.

"Look, I'm sorry. I didn't know myself." While picking at her crab Louie, Nikki confided in Connie, leaving out nothing save the very painful fact that she was falling in love with the very man who had started this phony charade in the first place. She even told her friend about her amnesia and the fact that she could remember little.

"You're kidding!" Connie whispered in the crowded restaurant. She glanced over her shoulder as if she expected to find, in the company of reporters, stockbrokers, secretaries and junior executives, a gun-toting mob hit man sitting in a caned-back chair, huddled over a plate of fettuccine, his gun and silencer visible when his jacket slid open as he reached for the garlic bread.

"Look, it's not that bad."

"Not that bad, are you out of your ever lovin' mind?" Connie hissed.

Nikki pronged a slice of egg with her fork.

"You fall or are shoved off a cliff, barely escape with

your life, can't remember a damned thing, and your rescuer, nearly a total stranger who just happens to be on an island few people have ever heard of, claims you're married to him. Later, after you tell your family and friends that you're married, he admits it was all a lie. And why? To keep you safe? I think I'd take my chances with a barracuda."

"But you know him," Nikki said, feeling the unlikely urge to defend Trent. Rolling an olive over a bed of lettuce, she tried to explain. "Look, I know it sounds bad—"

"Bad isn't strong enough. Fantastic is more like it. Unbelievable is damned close, or downright deceitful is even better yet. God, the nerve of the guy. And, for the record, I don't know him. Yes, I met him when I had that auto claim. Someone stole my BMW, remember? The one my folks gave me when I graduated from college." She munched on some lettuce. "Did I tell you it was stolen by a guy who was involved with a ring of car thieves? Trent, working for my insurance company, exposed the entire operation."

"So he's not all bad."

"Few people are. And he's definitely not hard on the eyes. But I don't trust a liar, Nikki, and neither should you. This guy lied to you. In a major way. If you ask me he should be strung up by his…well, his hamstrings or worse!" She tore off a piece of bread and leaned across the table. "So tell me, when you thought you were married to him—"

Here it comes! Nikki picked up her water glass and swallowed against a dry throat.

"What did you do… Well, you were supposed to be on your honeymoon. How'd you handle all that?"

Nikki nearly choked, but this time the lie—the half truth, really—rolled easily off her tongue. "I was hurt. My face, my ankle, my whole body. Trent acted as if my injuries were reason enough not to get too involved. Besides, you should have seen me. I wish I had pictures. My face was so ugly, no man would be interested."

Connie lifted a skeptical brow, but didn't argue, and Nikki felt like a heel. Why couldn't she explain everything? Because the truth of the matter was she'd fallen for the louse.

"That's why I can't accept the wedding gift," she added as she pushed her half-eaten salad aside. "It's beautiful, but I'm not married."

Connie managed a smile. "Keep it," she said. "It was worth hearing all about this."

"I can't."

"Consider it an early birthday present."

"My birthday's in May."

"A late one, then."

They argued, and finally Nikki gave in, agreeing to buy lunch in partial trade, just to keep Connie happy.

"Now, about that missing memory of yours. Maybe I can fill in a few blanks," Connie said. "You were really unhappy before you left and you were on this…vendetta, I guess you'd call it, against Senator Crowley. You wanted to do an exposé on the man, and Frank refused to let you. Even when Peggy went to bat for you, he insisted that Max or John be given the story, and we all know that Max thinks Diamond Jim can walk on water. When Peggy insisted that you be given a fair chance, Frank put his foot down. The quote went something like, 'Men just have a clearer insight into matters political.' You know, something pompous and asinine and way off base. It goes without saying that it caused your blood to boil." Connie cast Nikki a sly smile. "I think you were working on the story, anyway. You must've been if you found Crowley in Salvaje. What the devil was he doing down there?"

"I wish I knew," Nikki said as the waiter slipped their bill onto the table. She picked up the receipt, determined to find out everything she could about Senator James Crowley, as well as Trent McKenzie.

By late afternoon, the drizzle had disappeared. Sun began to dry the wet pavement, leaving puddles only in the deepest cracks and holes of the sidewalks and streets.

Nikki walked through the revolving door and took in great lungfuls of fresh air from the bay. The sky was still overcast, but a few rays of sunshine pierced through the clouds to sparkle on the concrete.

Tucking her umbrella under her arm, Nikki spied Trent, hips resting on the fender of his Jeep, arms folded over his chest. He was double-parked in an alley, but didn't seem the least concerned about a ticket. He lifted a hand when he saw her and she couldn't help the stupid little skip of her heartbeat at the sight of him. As if they truly were newlyweds. What a joke! When was this hoax going to end? Wrapping her arms close around her, as if she could guard her wayward heart, she side-stepped the deepest puddles.

He grinned at the sight of her, that sexy slash of white she found so unnerving. "Found your car."

"You did? At the airport?"

"Right where you left it."

She climbed into his rig, as if she truly belonged

there, and the scents of leather and oil seemed suddenly familiar. This was getting dangerous. Though she was always a little unsettled by him, there was something intimate and secure in being with him.

He adjusted the seat, started the engine, flipped on his blinker and merged with southbound traffic, skirting the Sound.

True to his word, he drove her directly to one of the parking lots near the airport where her little Dodge ragtop was wedged between a Toyota wagon and a Cadillac.

"How'd you find this?" she asked.

He grinned. "Professional secret."

"Give me a break." She opened the passenger door of the Jeep but before she could step out, his hand surrounded her wrist. "I'll meet you at your apartment later," he said, and she felt her pulse jump a bit.

"I don't think that would be such a good idea."

"Got to keep up appearances, don't we?"

"For whom?" A part of her was anxious to be alone with him, to continue their little lie—make that *big* lie—to be with him in the apartment, to sit in front of the fire with a glass of wine, to kiss and hold him and touch every inch of him, and yet she knew that the longer she put off the inevitable, the more time she wasted pretending they were in love, the harder their eventual breakup would be. She needed to protect her heart.

He rounded the Jeep's hood and stood next to her as she forced her key into the compact's lock.

"Don't," she warned before he laid one finger on her.

"Nikki—" He tried to touch her, but she drew away.

"I really can't go on living this lie," she said, her voice hitching a little. Oh, Lord, she wasn't going to break down now, was she? She jammed the key harder into the lock and twisted.

"You have to."

She stiffened.

"For your safety."

That was too much. Whirling to face him, she left her keys dangling from the lock. "Oh, for crying out loud! Let's not get into this again. You know where I live, where I work, all about my parents, family, even my ex-boyfriend, for God's sake. And what do I know about you? Nothing! Not one blessed thing. But I'm supposed to feel 'safe' with you. Give it up, McKenzie."

"You can't get rid of me."

"Sure I can. As of now, we're divorced."

He barked out a laugh that bordered on cruel, then grabbed her quickly and swung her against him. She gasped as his mouth descended on hers, kissing her so hard she couldn't breathe. Her knees buckled and her head was spinning. *Don't let him do this to you!* a part of her brain screamed, but another part sighed in contentment.

Propped against the still-wet side of her car, the door handle and her keys digging into her buttocks, she tried to call up every reason in the world to push him away, attempted to recover her hard-nosed stance and insist that they had to end their affair, but her heart was pumping wildly, her body ached for the touch of him, and her determination seemed to slip away, inch by inch, just as the sun slid slowly beneath the horizon.

Her senses swam, and it seemed natural to wind her arms around his neck and tilt her head eagerly to feel his mouth against hers. His tongue parted her lips and she shivered with anticipation of that glorious invasion as it touched and danced with hers.

When he lifted his head, his breath came out in a rush and she swallowed with difficulty. This felt so right and she knew it was so wrong. Loving him would only cause more heartache, more pain.

Touching his forehead to hers, he held her close. "Let's not argue about this, okay. I'll meet you at home."

"*My* home," she clarified.

"Yes, Nikki, *your* home."

He didn't move as she slipped into the driver's seat of her convertible. The upholstery molded to her contours; the seat was the right distance from the throttle for the length of her legs. Shoving the gearshift into Reverse, she backed the car out of its tight slot, slammed into Drive and, with a squeal of tires, threaded her way through the parking lot.

Trent watched her go and wondered how in the hell he was ever going to ease back into his old routine. Once this Crowley mess was settled, there would be no reason to see her, no reason to find excuses to be with her, no reason to scheme ways to get her into his bed.

Angry at himself, the world in general, and most pointedly at Diamond Jim, he kicked at the tire of his Jeep, felt a jarring pain all the way from his foot to his hip and swore under his breath. From the first time he'd seen Nikki Carrothers he'd felt his heartbeat catch, suspected that she was a woman like no other he'd ever seen. When he'd found out that she was working on a story about Crowley, he'd learned everything he could about her. The more he knew, the more fascinated he'd become until, like Crowley, she had become his obsession. One good. One evil. A balance.

But Trent hadn't expected to become more entranced with her as the days had passed. His intuition had been right, he thought grimly as he stepped into the Jeep. She was different. Stubborn, determined, relentless— not exactly female qualities that he'd hoped to find in his wife.

His hands poised in midair over the steering wheel. Wife? What was he thinking? He didn't want a wife, never had and especially would never want a bull-headed, prideful, arrogant woman like Nikki. No, he'd always gone for the softly feminine type, curvy, flirtatious, not too many brains. Those kind of relationships were easy to end.

There had been a few intelligent women in his life, women who were attractive to him on a level he didn't trust, women who had a chance of toying with his heart and his mind, and he'd avoided them like the proverbial plague. But with Nikki, things were different.

He jammed his key into the ignition, punched the throttle and roared after her. A cynical smile curved his lips. At first he'd played the role of her protector for the singular reason of keeping her safe, but as the marriage charade had worked and he'd been forced into close contact with her, he'd found his attraction to her impossible to fight. She'd been vulnerable and alone in the hospital, frightened, but as the days had passed and she'd healed, Trent had caught a glimpse of the woman within, the woman who seemed to have wrapped her long fingers around his heart and given a hard tug.

Hell, what a mess! And now, here he was, chasing her. Fitting, he thought with more than a trace of irony curving his lips. He couldn't help wondering if he'd be chasing her for the rest of his life.

* * *

Nikki felt a new power as she drove. Following a nonending stream of glowing red taillights, working her way from freeway to exit, turning on the radio to stations that were as familiar as a favorite old robe, she realized she was beginning to understand herself. Memory flashes were coming as rapidly as the street signs, milestones of her past flashing through her brain.

She remembered a little black dog named Succotash, her favorite doll, her mother lighting a cigarette and warning her never to pick up the habit herself, the fights that seemed to wave from her parents' bedroom every night when she was in junior high school, her mother's increasing fascination with wine, the splitting of her family, painful and hard. She'd felt as if the underpinnings of her entire world had been ripped away, all the security she'd known had been stripped from her. That bleak period in her life was the only time she could remember seeing her father cry. Her chin wobbled a bit before her thoughts centered on happier moments, her senior prom and the sparkly white chiffon dress she'd worn only to spill orange punch on the skirt.

Tears studded her eyes as her life began to make sense and the holes and gaps in the jigsaw puzzle of her existence became smaller. She had a life—a life she could recall.

She remembered dating Dave Neumann. Dave. He was her first truly serious relationship, the first man she'd ever considered marrying. He was handsome and witty and they'd spent hours together, planning a future that somehow hadn't quite jelled. He'd wanted a condo in the city and she'd wanted a house in the suburbs. He'd wanted to wait at least ten years for children and wasn't sure that babies and diapers and midnight feedings would ever fit into his well-ordered life. He'd planned vacations around his work schedule and insisted that he go where he could "write off" the trip for business purposes rather than choosing a spot for fun or adventure.

No wonder the relationship had died a slow and painful death.

As she wheeled her little Dodge off the freeway, she considered herself lucky. They'd broken up "temporarily" to "test their relationship" to "find out for sure that they weren't making a big mistake." It had been Dave's idea and had all sounded so rational. So clinical. So lacking passion. Well, to hell with that. If Trent had taught her anything, it was that she was a passionate person. Sexually, intellectually and morally. For that, she supposed, she should be thankful.

Trent. Oh, God, what was she going to do with him? It had been easier to deal with him when she'd believed they were married, but now, knowing that there were decisions looming ahead—hard, painful, future-determining decisions—she was frightened. After the breakup with Dave, she'd told herself that she would never, *never* get involved with a man who tried to run her life. Well, Trent certainly had bulldozed his way past any barriers she'd put up and lied, *lied* to get what he wanted.

Her teeth gritted. She was still galled at the deception.

Then there was the matter of trust. For years she'd trusted and depended upon her father, never questioning his opinions, though recently, before the trip, they had argued, and it hadn't been the first time. She remembered Ted Carrothers's anger, not a red-hot fury, but a quiet seething that she'd suddenly become a woman with a mind of her own, as if he couldn't quite accept that his baby had developed into a free-thinking, high-spirited female.

"Leave Jim alone," he'd warned her just before she'd left for Salvaje.

Now, while driving into the parking lot, Nikki shook herself out of her reverie and stood on the brakes to avoid hitting the side of the apartment house. Her throat turned to dust as she thought about the argument. They'd been seated in the shade of a striped umbrella in a restaurant on the waterfront. The scent of brine had drifted upward through the plank decking and the wind had been brisk, ruffling her father's short hair. She and Ted Carrothers had been the only souls on the deck, all the other diners having been sane enough to seat themselves on the other side of thick glass windows.

"Jim's a friend of mine," her father had said as he'd motioned the waiter for another glass of gin and tonic.

"But he's involved in a lot of shady deals, Dad," she'd replied, tilting her chin up with determination, the wind whipping a long strand of hair over her eyes.

"He's a politician. It goes with the job."

"No way. I don't believe that. Just because someone's an elected official doesn't mean that he has to turn into a crook."

"The temptations—"

"Everyone has them, Dad. You do in business. I do in my job, in my life. It takes moral fiber to walk away from them."

Her father had shaken his head, then slipped into silence while the slim waiter, clad in a green polo shirt, white jacket and black slacks, had slid another drink in front of him. Ted had taken a long swallow, compressed his lips, then stared past her to the Sound, where noisy sea gulls floated on invisible air currents high above the water and ferries churned across the dark surface, leaving thick, foamy wakes. Pleasure craft and freighters had vied for space in the choppy waters and her father had smiled sadly as he viewed a sailboat skimming along the water. He glanced down at his drink. "I felt the same way you do thirty years ago, Nicole, but as you get older, have children, face the fact that the world isn't perfect, you accept the way things are."

Nikki hadn't conceded. She'd never thought of her father as weak, not once considered the fact that he might be getting old and world-weary. "I'll never believe that all men in power are corrupt."

"Not corrupt, Nicole. Just human. Take my advice. Leave Jim alone."

Now her stomach twisted into a painful knot as she locked her car and headed up the stairs to her apartment. She felt cold to the bone, as if a northern wind had howled through her soul, and for a second she had the same unsettling feeling, the same uncanny awareness, that she was being watched. Perhaps even followed. "That's paranoia, Carrothers," she told herself, but her skin crawled and she glanced over her shoulder, hoping to hear the roar of a Jeep's engine, or catch the wash of headlights splash over the shrubbery of the parking lot. She saw no eyes hidden in the thick rhododendrons and vine maples, no evidence that anyone was watching her. Still she shivered, but Trent didn't appear like some mystical medieval knight to save her.

Lord, she'd be grateful for him now and her heart

nearly stopped beating at the thought. She stopped dead in her tracks, midway up the stairs.

She depended on him? Oh, no! Giving herself a swift mental shake she climbed the remaining stairs, unlocked the door, flipped on the lights and tossed her coat over the back of the couch. Opening the door of the refrigerator, she cringed, then yanked out a quart of milk gone sour and bread that had started to mold. So much for dinner.

She snapped on the disposal and poured globs of sour milk and slices of fuzzy white bread down the drain. Kitchen duty accomplished, she checked her messages and listened while her sister, Jan, started asking a dozen questions on the tiny tape. *"I thought you were going to call me. Come on, Nikki, I'm* dying *to know what's going on."*

Her mother, too, had called, expressing concern about Nikki's injuries and hasty marriage. *"I just hope you know what you're doing, and if your father decides to put on some kind of reception, you know that Fred and I will want to help. You're my daughter, too, you know."*

Funny how that sounded from a mother who had left three half-grown children to find herself and a new family in L.A.

The last message was from Dave. *"I don't know why I'm calling. Just a glutton for punishment, I guess. But I need to see you and know that you're happy."* Oh, sure. The truth of the matter was, Nikki suspected, that Dave was suddenly interested in her because she was no longer available. Now that someone else wanted her, he did, too. She laughed a little. She wasn't married. Her relationship with Trent was doomed, but there wasn't a snowball's chance in hell that she'd ever try to patch things up with Dave again. If Trent had taught her anything, it was about her need for independence and the sorry fact that she needed a stronger man than Dave Neumann for a lifelong partner.

She didn't want to return any of the calls, but decided there was no time like the present. Besides, she'd rather speak without being overheard by Trent.

She dialed from memory and smiled to think that something so simple was such a relief. Jan was out, her mother was worried, and she had just left a simple message on Dave's recorder when there was a quick rap on the door, a click of the lock, and Trent, balancing two sacks of groceries, appeared on the other side of the threshold.

Startled, Nikki asked, "How'd you do that?" but, with a sinking sensation, she guessed the answer before he even replied.

"I have a key."

"You *what?*"

"When we were on Salvaje. I had one made."

She opened and closed her fists in frustration. Certain there was no male more maddening on the face of the earth, she narrowed her eyes on his arrogant expression. *As if he belonged here!* "You don't live here."

He didn't bother to answer, just set the bags on the table and began placing groceries in the refrigerator and cupboards. "I figured you were out of just about everything."

"Did you hear me?"

He sent her a sizzling glance over one leather-clad shoulder. "Loud and clear, lady."

"You can't just waltz in here like you own the place, like we're *married,* for the love of Mike. No way."

"Until this all dies down."

"What? Until what dies down?" she said, closing the distance between them in long, furious strides. "Crowley."

"Right."

"What the hell have you got to do with it?"

"Crowley's dangerous. You've figured that much out, I assume." His gaze skated down the side of her face that had been so bruised and battered.

Her shoulders stiffened involuntarily.

"I know you think you've got to do some damned exposé on him, but I think you'd better leave Crowley to me."

"What will you do with him?" she asked, shoving a sack of groceries out of the way, grabbing Trent's arm and forcing him to face her. A head of lettuce rolled off the counter and onto the floor, but she didn't care, didn't give a damn about the food.

Trent's face hardened. "I'll handle him."

"Will you?" she tossed back at him. Her piece on Crowley came back to her, a series of articles about bribery and special interests. If her sources were correct, the senator not only took care of the few and the wealthy, he also accepted large gifts from corporations in the state of Washington and all along the Pacific Rim.

She was still holding on to Trent's arm. "Look, Nikki, you can believe what you want about me, I don't really care, but I don't want you getting hurt." His words were soothing, and she stepped away from him, away from the magic of his voice, the seduction in his eyes.

"Don't start this again, okay?"

"It's true, damn it!" Muttering under his breath, he dragged her into his arms and she froze. How easy it would be to let her knees and heart give way; to fall against him and rely upon him, to let him make decisions for her, to depend upon his judgment. She wanted to tell him to leave her alone, take his hands off her, take a long walk off a short pier…

But she couldn't. Bracing herself against the refrigerator door, she turned her head and her curtain of hair fell over one shoulder. He pressed his advantage, his lips brushing the back of her neck. Tingles of anticipation raced along her nerves and his arms wound around her waist, pulling her close, her buttocks wedging against the hardness forming in his jeans. She wanted to melt against him. Her bones were turning liquid as his mouth moved along the bend of her neck and his hands splayed over her abdomen, thumbs brushing the underside of her breasts.

"Don't," she whispered raggedly.

He didn't stop.

Swallowing against the urge to fall down on the floor and wrap her arms around him, she pulled his hands away. "Don't," she said more firmly, and he reluctantly stepped away.

Turning, she pressed her back against the refrigerator. "Don't use sex as a weapon."

"Is that what I was doing?"

She narrowed her eyes at him. "You know damn well what you were doing. And I can't go along with you on this Crowley thing," she said, picking up the head of lettuce and tossing it into the sink. "It's too important."

"He's just one crooked senator."

A hard smile curved her lips. "But one I can take

care of." She tossed her hair over her shoulder. "I must be doing something right, or he wouldn't have tried to do me in on Salvaje."

"He's dangerous, Nikki, and apparently desperate. You can't take any chances."

Waving away the argument she saw in his expression, she strode to her computer and snapped on the power switch. "There's got to be something," she said, drumming her fingers impatiently as the machine warmed up. "Something in here. If only I can find it."

Trent gave up arguing, and as she pulled up her chair, he propped his jean-clad hips along the side of the desk, bracing himself with his hands, crossing his ankles and watching her. She felt a rush of adrenaline as she settled her fingers over the keys and started entering commands. She'd been working on the Crowley piece for a couple of weeks behind her editor's back. Dissatisfied with the turn of her career, she'd decided to take matters into her own hands when she'd been denied, yet again, a chance to write something more interesting than a story about the winners of a local bake fair.

She intended to prove to God himself, Frank Pianzani, that she could work with the big boys. She'd been trained as an investigative journalist and never been able to prove what she could do. Well, this time, people at the *Observer* were going to sit up and take notice.

Unless she got herself killed first, she thought with a shiver.

She scanned her work files, but nothing showed up. She flipped through the disks near her desk, shoving each one into the computer and viewing the documents on each one. Still a big zero. "Where is it? Where? Where? Where?" she mumbled, biting off the urge to scream in frustration. Impatience surged through her. The story and her notes had to be here. Somewhere.

Unless everything had been conveniently erased. Trent had a key and access to her apartment when she was gone. There were times when she left him alone in this room. When she'd taken a shower, when she'd been at work… She ground her teeth together in frustration. He was a proven liar of the worst order and he would do anything to stop her, for whatever reasons, noble or otherwise.

Her fingers didn't move as her thoughts clicked steadily through her brain.

"Problems?" he asked, and when she looked up at him she expected to see mockery in his blue eyes, but he seemed genuinely concerned.

"I can't seem to locate my file."

Rubbing the stubble on his chin, he said, "Mind if I look?"

"Be my guest." Warily she rolled her chair away from the desk, stood and stretched her back as he slid in front of the machine. Fascinated, she watched as his long fingers moved quickly over the keys. He was as familiar with her machine as was she, or so it seemed.

"You must have it under some kind of code," he said, and she left him there, trusting him just a little. While he kept searching, she played the part of a domestic wife, washing the damned lettuce and using the groceries he'd picked up as the start of dinner. Her stomach rumbled in anticipation, but her mind was on the computer screen and her missing files.

She boiled linguine and cooked a shrimp, garlic and cream sauce while her thoughts swirled around Crowley. If he were behind her attack on the island, then good old Diamond Jim, her father's *friend,* had tried to kill her. So he knew she was onto him. How?

She glanced at Trent and her throat grew tight. He wouldn't! She licked the wooden spoon as she thought. What had Trent said—about a leak at the *Observer.* Connie? No! Frank? Max? "I can't remember any code," she said loud enough for Trent to hear. "It's one of the last foggy details, I guess." It was frustrating. Damned frustrating. Most of her memory had returned and yet this one important piece of information kept slipping her mind. "Come on, give it a rest. I'll feed you."

"Domestic? You?" He cracked his knuckles and stretched out, looking way too huge for her small desk chair.

"I figured I owed you, since you went to the trouble of restocking the larder." She motioned him into a chair at the small table, where she'd set out place mats and lit candles. "Don't get used to it," she teased, but her laughter died in her throat when she remembered that their relationship was only temporary. Surprisingly her heart felt a little prick of pain at that particular thought and she disguised her sudden rush of emotion by pasting a smile onto her face and setting a wooden bowl of salad next to the pasta and sauce.

It was silly really. She slid into her chair and waited as he poured them each a glass of wine. The clear chardonnay reflected the candlelight as it splashed into the bottom of her glass.

Oh, Lord, she would miss him, she realized with a

sinking feeling that swept into the farthest reaches of her heart. She'd gotten used to him, looked forward to his laughter and his lovemaking.

He touched the rim of his wineglass to hers. "To marriage," he said, and her heart felt as if it had been smashed into a thousand painful shards. He was kidding, of course.

She painted on another false smile and said, "And to divorce."

"Can't wait to get rid of me, eh?" he asked, and she thought she saw a shadow of pain cross his eyes.

"As soon as possible." Tossing back the cool wine, she imagined the small circle of gold around her ring finger, and her throat grew so thick she could barely swallow. A new, fresh pain cut through her at the thought that no matter what, soon Trent would be just another murky memory in her mind.

They finished dinner in silence, each wrapped in private thoughts. As she put the dishes in the dishwasher, he started a fire, and they finished the bottle of wine with their backs propped against the couch and the flames crackling against dried moss.

When he turned to her, it was as natural as the wind shifting over the sea. His lips settled over hers and she fought a tide of tears that stung her lashes. His arms were strong and comforting, his hands possessive.

He slipped the buttons of her blouse from their bindings and she gave herself to him, body and soul, knowing deep in her heart that she'd never love another man with the same blind passion that now ruled her spirit as well as her life.

She was his wife. If only for a few more days. If only

because of the lie that bound them together and would, as surely as the moon tugged at the currents in the sea, pull them apart.

Nikki woke up with a start. Sweat streamed down her back, and her heart was pounding a thousand beats a minute. The nightmare had stolen into her sleep, burning through her conscious and terrifying her. Even now, snuggled against Trent, one of his arms flung around her, she shivered. Would the fear never go away?

She glanced at the clock and groaned. Four-thirty. The bed, tucked in the corner under the eaves, was warm, rumpled, smelling of sex and Trent, and through the window she saw stars, clear and bright, glittering above the city.

Letting out a long breath, she cuddled against Trent, when suddenly the memory slammed into her like a freight train running out of control. She remembered what she'd done with the Crowley file. The last wisps of her fear disappeared like night melting into the dawn. She slid from the bed. Trent growled and rolled over, his breathing never disturbed. Tossing on her robe, she walked to her computer, not bothering with lights. A few glowing embers smoldered in the fireplace, casting red shadows on candles that had burned down to pools of blue wax, their flames long ago extinguished, the wine bottle left empty on the coffee table, the wrinkled afghan where they'd made love left carelessly on the floor.

Her heart caught for a second before she told herself to quit being a romantic fool. She had work to do. On the day before she'd left for Salvaje, the very day she'd argued violently with her father, she'd decided to hide her information on Crowley, just in case someone from the *Observer,* or someone in Crowley's employ, wanted to know what she was up to. She'd carefully hidden all her notes and the computer disk in a box of Christmas ornaments on the floor of one of the closets tucked under the eaves.

Quietly, she opened the closet door and yanked on the hanging chain dangling from the exposed rafters. With a bare bulb for illumination, she worked around the mousetraps and pulled out a heavy box with the stand for the tree, then dug through another crate filled with ornaments and lights.

On the very bottom, tucked in a cardboard envelope, was the disk. In a manila folder were her notes. "Son of a gun," she whispered, pleased that her memory had finally come through. Leaving the closet door open, she carried her prize to the desk and snapped on the green-shaded banker's light.

Trent snored softly and rolled over again.

Almost afraid of what she might find, she clicked on the computer, and as it hummed to life, she rifled through old newspaper articles, magazine clippings and her own notes. "Great stuff," she congratulated herself. She felt a sudden sense of pride in her job and in her life, and she wanted to share it all with Trent.

She glanced over to the bed. He'd blinked his eyes open and was watching her, his black hair mussed, his beard dark, his naked torso bronze in the reflection of the dying embers. Stretching, he glanced at the clock and groaned. "You're out of your mind, Carrothers," he said, patting the warm spot on the bed that she'd recently vacated.

"I know, but I remembered!"

"Hallelujah!" he growled sarcastically as he rubbed the sleep from his eyes. "Couldn't it wait?"

"No way." She held up the old articles and pictures. "Evidence, McKenzie. That's what this is."

He levered up on one elbow and his brows drew over his eyes. "You're sure?"

"I think so. My guess is that good ol' Diamond Jim owes favors to some of the most influential businessmen in Tokyo, Seoul and Hong Kong." She couldn't restrain a smile of pride as she flipped through the articles taken from newspapers around the world.

"You've got old news," he said. "People have been trying to tie Crowley to a bribery scandal for years. Nothing ever sticks."

"This will," she said, as she skimmed her notes. "What ties it all together is a tip I received from someone who used to work for him. He claims that the senator did all his dirty deals, taking the cash and laundering it into a Swiss bank account, through a small island in the Caribbean."

"Let me guess," Trent said, his eyes no longer slumberous, every sinewy muscle of his shoulders and chest tense. "Salvaje."

"Bingo," she whispered. "That's why I was down there." She glanced through the window to the lights of the city winking through the trees. "That's why he tried to have me killed."

"Nothing you can prove."

"Yet," she said, determined to get the fat-cat senator. She dropped the clippings onto the desk beneath the lamp, and one yellowed article slid away from the rest. Along with the report was a picture of Senator Crowley with the head of an automobile company headquartered in Japan.

She reached for the article, but her fingers stopped in midair. Another man was in the grainy photograph, a man standing just behind the shorter industrialist, a man she recognized. Her world stopped and tilted as her future and past collided. She swallowed against the bitter taste of deception as she stared down at the unmistakable, rough-hewn features of Trent McKenzie.

CHAPTER ELEVEN

NIKKI STARED AT the picture in disbelief. Anger surged through her bloodstream. He'd lied to her again! God, why had she trusted him, believed in him?

"What is it?" Trent asked, his voice rumbling and deep with recent sleep.

"I, um, found something interesting." A cold settled in the pit of her stomach. Her first impulse was to shove the damning piece of evidence under his nose, demand answers, rant and rave about truth and justice and the pain in her heart. Instead, she told herself to be calm, and with trembling fingers, she forced herself to tuck the picture deep into the notes.

"What?"

"More evidence. I have to talk to one of the aides who used to work for him. Barry Blackstone," she said, remembering a name she'd seen mentioned several times. "He quit working for Crowley a few months back and I've written a note to myself that indicates he can give me inside information."

"Blackstone?"

She stood and walked on wooden legs to the edge of the bed where she dropped onto the quilt near the lying son of a bitch…the man she loved. "What can you tell me about him?"

Trent's jaw tightened and his skin drew flat over his

features. He tried to reach for her, but she pushed his hands firmly away.

"Not now," she said, disguising the fact that her heart was breaking, that she'd never let him hold her again, that they would never again make love. Here, with the scent of sex still clinging to the sheets, she vowed never to fall into his tempting trap again. To shove temptation from her grasp, she moved to the couch and leaned against its lumpy back. A world without Trent. It seemed so bleak. Suddenly world-weary, she crossed her arms over her chest. "You've heard of him, I assume."

"I've met Blackstone," Trent said, regarding her warily, as if he sensed the silent accusations charging the air. He slid into his faded Levi's. Threadbare at the knees and butt, the pants threatened to split as he strode barefoot to the fireplace, crouched down to lay a piece of dusty oak onto the grate and blew into the coals. Sparks glowed bright, catching on the moss and dry bark. "I used to work for our friend, the senator," Trent finally admitted, stirring the warm ashes with a poker.

Nikki couldn't believe his admission. Had he read her mind—known that she'd caught him in yet another evasion? Her heart began to pound and she didn't know if she wanted to hear the rest of his story. Would it be the truth or a lie? Would he admit that he was in league with the man who had tried to have her killed? "You never said anything."

"Never seemed like the right time." Red embers pulsed against the charred pieces of firewood. "A few years back, I was one of Crowley's bodyguards for a few weeks."

Too convenient. He must suspect that you saw a photo of him or read his name in one of the articles.

Still, she played along, wondering whether if she kept giving him more rope, he would hang himself. "But you're off the payroll now?" Nikki asked. Betrayal, like a serpent, coiled around her insides and squeezed.

"Yep." He shoved another hunk of wood onto the crackling, hungry flames. "I quit four years ago."

"Why?"

He hazarded a glance over his shoulder. His mouth was drawn into a hard, cynical line. "I didn't like the working conditions."

"Meaning?" She knew she was pressing him, but she couldn't stop herself. After this one last time, she promised herself, she'd never again listen to his half truths and lies.

Standing, he dusted his hands on his rear, then slapped his palms together. "Meaning I was beginning to suspect that Jimbo wasn't on the up-and-up. A few things had happened that I didn't like. I suspected he was on the take, from international lobbyists as well as from corporations here in the States. I confronted him." A nostalgic, satisfied grin curved his lips. "He told me to take a hike."

"You were fired?"

"*Terminated* is the word he used, I think," Trent replied. "Nice, huh?"

Nikki shivered and rubbed her arms. *Don't believe him. Not a solitary word he says.*

"But it was too late, anyway. I'd already turned in my resignation." Shoving his hands into the front pockets of his jeans, he sauntered toward her, the firelight playing in red-and-gold shades upon the smooth skin and sleek muscles of his torso. She tried not to notice the webbing of black hair that swirled across his chest

and narrowed to a thin line that dipped seductively past
the straining waistband of his jeans. She avoided staring
at the sinewy ridges in his shoulder muscles or the way
his eyes, deep-set and so blue, stared at her.

Her heart did a stupid flip, but she didn't even smile.
"You lied to me." The whisper echoed to the rafters and
swirled around them like a cold whirlpool.

"We've established that already."

"No, I mean you lied to me again. You didn't want
me to know that you were connected with Crowley.
Why?" She angled her head up defiantly as he stopped
just short of her, his bare toes nearly touching hers, his
gaze delving deep into hers.

"I didn't want to talk about it."

"What about me? Didn't you think I might want to
know?" she demanded, anger burning through her blood
and controlling her tongue. The nerve of the man!

"What good would it have done?"

"This isn't about good and bad, Trent! This is about
the truth and lies, about trust. You expect me to pretend
you're my husband, let you live in my house, allow you
to have a key to my door, for crying out loud, and you
can't even show me the consideration of telling me how
you're connected with Crowley!"

"You didn't ask."

"I did," she corrected, her lips curling. "You said it
was personal."

"It was."

Throwing her hands up and grabbing the air in frustration, she shook her head. "How could I have been
such a fool—such a damned fool?"

"You're not." His fingers folded over her arm. "I

should have leveled with you, but it didn't seem important."

"Not important?" She yanked her arm away and strode to the fireplace, feeling a tide of misery swell in her heart. She loved him and he'd used her. Again. That was the sole basis of their relationship. It could never be anything more. "We're talking about my life here. Because of what I'm doing I was nearly killed, and you don't think it's important!"

A shadow crossed his eyes. "I'm trying to protect you."

"Then just stop. Okay? Get the hell out of my house and the hell out of my life! Leave me alone, Trent." *For God's sake, leave me alone to lick my wounds and start over.*

But he didn't. Cursing under his breath, he walked straight to her, and his expression was a mixture of anger, disgust and fear. "I can't, Nikki."

"Oh, spare me the protector routine. It's wearing a little thin."

"I love you."

The words echoed through her apartment and reverberated through her soul.

"I always have."

He reached for her, and she slapped him with a smack. "Don't say it, Trent. No more lies!" she cried as the red welt appeared on his cheek. Horrified that she'd struck him, she took a step backward but not before he caught her wrist and yanked her hard against him. His eyes slitted and she remembered once thinking that he was cruel.

"I've lied about a lot of things, Nikki, and I'm not proud of the fact, and I'm not going to tell you that all my reasons were noble, because they weren't. I slept with you, made love to you because I couldn't stop myself, damn it. I even rationalized that it was necessary, but I didn't count on falling in love with you." His fingers dug deep into her flesh. "If there was any way I could have prevented falling for you, you'd better believe I would have."

Her throat worked painfully. "I don't believe you," she choked out. How could she trust a man who had lied to cover lies? The words were music to her ears, but like a false melody they would fade quickly, disappear when the time was convenient, never to be recalled again.

"I love you, Nikki."

Again, those horrible, wonderful words. Her heart wanted to explode and tears filled the back of her eyes.

"I think I fell in love with you from the first time I saw you." He sighed loudly, playing out his role. "Don't get me wrong. I'm not a sentimental sap. This isn't like me, but I fell in love with you, and I swear, as long as I live, I'll never love another woman."

Oh, God! She wanted to believe him. With all of her heart, she wanted to trust and love this man, but she couldn't. As tears slid in tiny streams from her eyes, she tossed off his arm and shook her head. "And I swear to you, as long as I live, Trent McKenzie, I'll never trust you." Feeling as if she were shattering into a thousand pieces inside, she stepped away from him and brushed the tears from her eyes. "It's too late."

"Nikki—" He reached for her but she stood on wooden legs, refusing to go to him.

"Even if there was a chance for us once upon a time, it's over. Leave, Trent," she insisted, fighting the urge to run to him.

"But—"

"Just drop the key on the counter and walk out that damned door!"

He studied her long and hard, looking for cracks in her composure, then, grimacing, he turned on his heel, grabbed his jacket and walked out of her life. The door slammed with a thud, shaking the room.

Her knees started to give way. She grabbed the corner of a table and afraid she might fall into a puddle and cry for him to come back to her, she ran to the bathroom, locked the door, turned on the shower and stripped off her robe. Steam billowed, filling the room and her lungs as she stepped under the warm spray and prayed that the hot needles of water would wash away the pain in her heart. She loved Trent, was destined and doomed to love him all of her life, but she wouldn't let him know how she felt. She had already experienced too much pain at his hands—she'd never be fool enough to give him the chance to hurt her again.

She cried in the shower, quietly sobbing and letting her tears mix with the water. These, she swore, were her last tears for a man who could lie and say he loved a woman without batting an eye.

When she finally turned off the spigots and shoved the wet hair from her face, she felt stronger. She would survive. Somehow she'd live each day without him and the pain would lessen, not quickly, but she would live with it and go on with her life. She'd learned long ago, during the pain of her parents' divorce, that she was a survivor and that she could accomplish just about anything she wanted to. Right now, she wanted Trent out of her life.

Cinching the belt of her robe around her waist, she

YOUR PARTICIPATION IS REQUESTED!

Dear Reader,

Since you are a lover of our books – we would like to get to know you!

Inside you will find a short Reader's Survey. Sharing your answers with us will help our editorial staff understand who you are and what activities you enjoy.

To thank you for your participation, we would like to send you 2 books and 2 gifts – **ABSOLUTELY FREE!**

Enjoy your gifts with our appreciation,

Pam Powers

SEE INSIDE FOR READER'S SURVEY

For Your Reading Pleasure...

YOUR READER'S SURVEY
"THANK YOU" FREE GIFTS INCLUDE:
▶ 2 FREE books
▶ 2 lovely surprise gifts

PLEASE FILL IN THE CIRCLES COMPLETELY TO RESPOND

1) What type of fiction books do you enjoy reading? (Check all that apply)
- ○ Suspense/Thrillers ○ Action/Adventure   ○ Modern-day Romances
- ○ Historical Romance ○ Humour   ○ Paranormal Romance

2) What attracted you most to the last fiction book you purchased on impulse?
- ○ The Title   ○ The Cover   ○ The Author   ○ The Story

3) What is usually the greatest influencer when you <u>plan</u> to buy a book?
- ○ Advertising   ○ Referral   ○ Book Review

4) How often do you access the internet?
- ○ Daily ○ Weekly ○ Monthly ○ Rarely or never.

5) How many NEW paperback fiction novels have you purchased in the past 3 months?
- ○ 0 - 2   ○ 3 - 6   ○ 7 or more

YES! I have completed the Reader's Survey. Please send me the 2 FREE books and 2 FREE gifts (gifts are worth about $10) for which I qualify. I understand that I am under no obligation to purchase any books, as explained on the back of this card.

191/391 MDL F45L

FIRST NAME	LAST NAME

ADDRESS

APT.#	CITY

STATE/PROV.	ZIP/POSTAL CODE

clamped her teeth together and unlocked the bathroom door. She paused, took in a long, bracing breath and, in a cloud of steam, walked through the door.

Trent was gone. She knew it before she even glanced through the shadowy apartment. From the atmosphere in the room, the lack of life in the air, she knew that he'd left. And she realized that she'd been wrong. Just when she'd been foolish enough to think that she was fresh out of tears for Trent McKenzie, she found a few thousand more.

"I just don't see why I can't meet that husband of yours." Ted Carrothers touched the crook of his daughter's arm and propelled her across the street. He'd called while Nikki was at work and they'd agreed to have dinner together.

"He's busy," Nikki hedged as they threaded through the crowd of pedestrians hurrying along the sidewalks. Umbrellas, boots, newspapers and purses tucked beneath arms, raincoats billowing, everyone walked briskly, as if each person was in his own personal race with the world.

Unlike Salvaje, where the pace was slow, the weather warm and lazy, Seattle's gait was brisk, in tempo with the winds that blew chill off the Pacific. Fog was rolling through the streets and a slight drizzle threatened. Ted shoved open the door of his favorite Irish pub, and the sounds of hearty laughter, clink of glasses, and noise from a television where a boxing match was being shown, greeted Nikki. Smoke hovered over the bar and the smell of beer was heavy in the air.

"In the back. Rosie has a table for us," her father said as they moved past the long mahogany bar that had been a part of Rosie's Irish Pub since the great fire. "Here we go." Ted weaved through the tightly packed tables and, true to his word, found a booth in a corner near the back wall.

Nikki slid onto the wooden seat while Rosie, without asking, brought two frosty mugs of ale. Not believing that she could trust anyone to manage the place, Rosie worked day and night as a waitress and hostess. "Bless ya, Rose," Ted said with a wink.

"Come here often, do you?" Nikki teased, scanning her menu.

"As often as possible. And don't bother ordering. It's already done."

"Don't you think I might like a say in what I'm eating?"

His blue eyes twinkled. "Not when I'm paying the tab."

"This is the nineties, Dad."

"But I like the old ways better."

She wasn't in the mood for another fight. "Fair enough," she said, watching the small flame of a glass-encased candle flicker as they talked.

"Now, about Trent. Who the devil is he?"

Good question. "I met him through a friend." Not really a lie, just stretching the truth a bit. She took a long swallow of the dark ale. "You remember Connie Benson? I work with her, and she had her car stolen earlier in the year…" She perpetuated the lie and didn't have the heart to tell her father that her marriage was over. Or even that it had never existed. Over bowls of thick clam chowder and crusty bread, she rationalized that her love life wasn't any of her father's business and she would have to deal with Trent on her own. Rosie cleared the empty bottles and bowls and arrived with a platter of grilled salmon and planked potatoes. The conversation drifted back and forth, and each time Trent's name was mentioned, Nikki hid the quick stab of pain in her heart.

By the time she'd eaten half her salmon, Nikki thought she might burst.

"So where is Trent tonight?" her father asked as he pronged a potato and studied it. "Why couldn't he join us?"

"He's working late. Lots to catch up on."

"A private investigator…. Ah, well, I thought you'd marry someone…" He searched for the right word, and Nikki felt her temper start to simmer.

"Someone more conventional?" she asked. "Someone like Dave Neumann."

Her father lifted a big shoulder. "He's not a bad guy, but, hey, since you're married, let's leave him out of the conversation."

"Good idea." Nikki picked at the pieces of pink salmon flesh, but her appetite had disappeared. She felt like a fool and a fraud, defending a man who had not one ounce of compunction about lying to her.

Her father asked about her amnesia, tested her and, satisfied that her memory was intact, nodded to himself. "Glad you're feeling better. I was worried about you, Nicole."

"I know. But I'm okay. Really." They smiled at each other and some of the old feelings of love between them resurfaced. She remembered trusting him implicitly, never questioning his ultimate wisdom.

Finally, her father shoved his plate aside. Rosie, as if she'd been hovering nearby waiting, swooped down and swept up the dirty dishes. She asked about another round of drinks, but neither Nikki or her father was interested. When she finally left, Ted set his elbows on the table and tented his hands. "Aside from the honeymoon and the accident, how was your trip?"

"Salvaje's an interesting place. Semitropical. Warm. I'd like to go back someday."

Her father's lower lip protruded. "What about Jim Crowley?" Nikki's insides jelled and she looked up sharply, but her father just seemed to be making conversation as he swirled the remainder of his ale in his mug. "I know he was down there at the same time as you. I thought you might be dogging him."

"I was on my honeymoon, Dad," she said. "I didn't even talk to him." Nikki's tongue felt thick and twisted as she tried to evade the issue without lying to her father.

"He's…well, he's not really a friend of mine, but I know him. I've done business with his law firm for years. I deal with his son, James, Jr. Hell of an attorney. Smart as a whip."

"What you're saying, Dad, is that because Jim's son is a great attorney, I should back off on any story dealing with the senator. Especially if it shows our favorite son in a bad light?"

"Just don't hound the man, Nikki." Ted tossed back the remaining drops of his dark beer. "You people with the press, always digging, always looking for dirt."

"He's a politician, Dad."

"So he asked for it?"

"So he's got to keep his constituents' best interests at heart. He can't be playing to special interest groups and he's got to keep his nose clean. It comes with the territory."

"I think he's a good man, Nikki. I wouldn't want his reputation destroyed on some drummed-up charge. It wouldn't be fair and I wouldn't want my daughter a part of it."

"I'm a reporter, Dad." Her chin inched upward a notch in pride. "I try my level best to write the truth without being biased or opinionated. Now, that's tough given my gene pool, but the best I can promise you is that if Crowley's nose is clean, I won't harass him."

Her father sighed. "I guess that's the best I can expect."

"Damn straight."

Her father paid the bill and walked Nikki to her car. She gave him a quick peck on the cheek and wondered how they, who had been so close, had drifted so far apart politically. Age, probably. Disillusionment.

She drove to her apartment and had the uncanny feeling that she was being followed. Again. Lord, she was getting paranoid. If she didn't watch out she'd end up on some shrink's couch, paying big bucks to find out that she was insecure because her parents had split up when she was young.

And because a man deceived you into believing that you were married to him.

Oh, Lord. She tapped her fingers on the steering wheel and told herself that she should never see Trent again. Let the memories fade on their own. Let sleeping dogs lie.

As far back as she could remember, she'd never let one sleeping dog slumber in peace. Her curiosity, her sense of justice, her desire to set wrong to right, overcame her good judgment. She'd never been one to take the easy way out, or pussyfoot around an issue, and she wasn't going to start now. If she planned on being the best damned reporter that the *Seattle Observer* or, for that matter, the *New York Times* had ever seen, then she'd better quit thinking like a coward.

Sliding her jaw to the side in determination, she threw her convertible into Reverse, turned around and, tires screaming in protest, headed for Lake Washington. She was going to have it out with Trent McKenzie, right or wrong.

She drove with her foot heavy on the throttle, moving quickly in and out of traffic, suddenly anxious to see him. For weeks she'd been shackled by her injuries, by her amnesia, by Trent's lies and by the love that she'd begun to feel for him, but now she was in control, her life in her own hands again, though those very hands shook a little as she clutched the wheel.

A part of her still loved him. That stupid, female, trusting section of her brain still conjured up his face and thrilled at the memory of his touch. "Idiot," she growled, honking impatiently as a huge van pulled into the lane in front of her.

What would she say to Trent when she confronted him? She didn't know. Scowling, she caught her reflection in the rearview mirror and decided, when she caught the worry in her eyes, that she'd have to wing it. She'd done it before.

She ran a yellow light and turned off the main street. Pushing the speed limit, she drove onto the curvy road that wandered over the cliffs surrounding the lake. Steeling herself for another painful session, she wheeled her sporty car into the drive of his house.

The sun, already hidden by high clouds and clumps

of thin fog, was beginning to set and the tall fir trees surrounding the rambling old house seemed gloomy and still. She slid to a stop near the garage and bit her lip. Trent's Jeep wasn't parked where he'd left it the previous night.

"Wonderful," she muttered, then walked to the front door and rapped loudly. No answer. She pushed hard on the doorbell, hearing the chimes ring. Still no footsteps or shouts from within.

She rubbed her arms and felt an overwhelming sense of disappointment. "Stop it," she chided herself. He wasn't going to weasel out of this showdown, not after she'd worked up her courage to face him. She walked to the back of the house and found a note on the back door, which she read out loud. "'Wait for me.'"

Her throat squeezed. He'd expected her. Or someone. The hairs on the back of her neck raised as she opened the door and stepped into the kitchen. Snapping on a few lights, she felt better, but the sight of the bedroom made her stomach wrench. The huge bed was made, the fire long-dead, the curtains drawn, but in her mind's eye she saw the room as it had been. A warm fire threw red and gold shadows across the bed that was mussed and warm. Trent's body, so hard and taut, was stretched over hers, his lips grazing her breast, his eyes gazing deeply into hers.

Love or lust?

She bit her lip in confusion. What she'd felt had been love. She'd welcomed his kisses, embraced his lovemaking, given her heart to him, and she'd do it time and time over, if she ever got the chance again. Sick at the thought, she realized she'd become one of those women who are inexplicably drawn to the wrong men,

men who will only hurt and use them, men who are careless with their love, men who can never truly let a woman touch their souls.

Welcome to the real world.

The sound of a car in the drive brought her out of her reverie. Trent! Annoyed at the quick spark of anticipation in her pulse, she strode to the front door, intent on greeting him in person and giving him a healthy piece of her mind.

"Where the devil have you been?" she demanded, jerking the door open.

Standing on the front porch, his eyes a brittle blue, his expression a mirror of her own surprise, was Senator James Thaddeus Crowley.

Her insides shredded. "Oh," she whispered.

Crowley leaned heavily on his cane and his face was lined and weathered. A man stood next to him, one step back, and as Nikki's gaze moved to his face, her stomach clenched. She faced her own death. This tall man with the short-clipped black hair, feral eyes and long nose was the man who had been chasing her, the man whose swift steps had followed her through the steamy undergrowth of the jungle on Salvaje. In a blast of memory, she recognized him as the man who had placed his meaty hand on her shoulder and given her a shove. Oh, God!

"Miss Carrothers," the senator said smoothly, recovering as she began to sweat. "Well, well, what do you know? First on the island and now back here."

"What do you want?" Danger sizzled in the air around them and she looked for a chance of escape, but the two men blocked her way to her convertible and the senator's silver Mercedes was parked nearly on her car's bumper. No way out.

"I'm looking for McKenzie." Crowley's frigid eyes narrowed a fraction. "Your husband? Or is that just an ugly rumor?"

"He's not here right now," she said, trying vainly to calm the racing beat of her heart. Her fingers were slick with sweat where she still touched the edge of the door.

"No?" Crowley slid a grin of pure evil to his compatriot and said something in Spanish that caused Nikki's skin to crawl. She didn't understand the language, but the meaning was clear and deadly. She slammed the door shut, threw the deadbolt and tried to remember where all the doors in the house were. Oh, God, she couldn't. She didn't know how many entrances there were, how many ways a murderer could get into the house.

Trapped. Fear brought a metal taste to the back of her throat. Barely able to breathe, she ran to the bedroom, found the phone and dialed. "Please help me," she whispered as the dispatcher answered. "My life's in danger and—" She saw the face of Crowley's goon in the window and dropped the phone, running to the far end of the house. She heard a door creak open and her heart plummeted. She hadn't locked the kitchen door behind her.

It was only a matter of time until he tracked her down.

Fear, like ice, seemed to clog her blood and keep her feet from moving, but she forced herself to run. She found the door to the basement, left it open and quietly ran up the stairs to the second floor. On the landing she waited, her heart thudding loudly, her blood thundering in her ears. Holding her breath, waiting for her doom, she heard him. Inside. Walking like a predatory cat.

Trent, where are you?

She heard the steps creak and the door to the basement bang open farther.

She moved quickly, silently, diving into the first room she found. A bedroom with twin bunks and a window. Without thinking, she threw open the sash and stepped onto a shingled roof that was pitched gently. On her rump, she slid down the shakes, catching herself on the gutter. She had no choice but to jump. Wrapping her fingers on the sharp metal near a downspout, she lowered her body, heard the gutter groan in protest and dropped, landing in a crouch. She had no plan of escape, only hoped that she could run to a neighbor's house. But the neighbors on this stretch of the lake were few and far between, separated by dense forest or a long stretch of water.

Sprinting across the backyard, she raced into the thick shrubbery that rimmed the lake. In the distance she heard a car's engine roar to life and she thought that the senator had only been bluffing, that he was leaving. Through the leaves she saw the flash of silver. His Mercedes. Thank God. But her relief was short-lived. In the upstairs window of the house, the very window she'd opened, she spied the henchman, his face set in an ugly anger, his eyes searching the grounds.

"God help me," she whispered silently, realizing that Diamond Jim had left this cruel man to do his work. He'd make tracks, be far from the scene when her next accident occured. Heart in her throat, she concentrated. *Think, Nikki, think! Use that damned brain of yours!*

She couldn't risk running to the front of the house.

From his eagle's nest view, the would-be assassin could see her. Her only chance was the forest. Surely she could make her way through the thicket to the next house.

Running quickly, shoving aside branches and berry vines, she plowed through the undergrowth. Dry leaves and cobwebs clung to her face, vines and sticks tripped her.

She heard a shout in Spanish and her heart turned to mush. He'd seen her! *Run, Nikki, run for your life!*

A limb behind her snapped. Oh, God. He was closing the distance. Her heart was beating like machine-gun fire. *Run! Run! Run!* Her legs couldn't move fast enough.

Déjà vu! This is how she'd felt in Salvaje and in her nightmares. Running, running, being chased by the evil. Footsteps pounded behind her. Closer. Closer. "Please, God, help me!" Her lungs felt ready to explode.

A gunshot cracked and she stumbled, scraping her knees and scrambling back to her feet.

She broke through the thicket and found herself on the edge of the cliff, looking down at the lake, far, far below. "No!" she cried as the footsteps plowed closer.

In terror, she looked over her shoulder and saw her attacker, large and looming, his face, cut by twigs and thorns, twisted into a hideous snarl.

"Now you will not escape," he said, smiling and breathing hard.

Nikki stepped backward, felt her feet teeter and shifted her weight.

He lunged and she stepped to the side. "You bastard," she cried, kicking at him as she began to fall.

"Nikki!"

Another blast from a gun, the charge roaring in her

ears as her attacker fell. Screaming, she felt strong arms surround her, saving her from sliding down the cliff. Trent dragged her back to safety. "You're all right," he whispered, his gun outstretched in one hand, his other arm a steel band around her middle.

"Oh, God, Trent!" She clung to him, sobbing, holding him as a spreading stain of dark red seeped from beneath Crowley's man. He groaned in pain and writhed.

"Don't move!" Trent warned him, and Nikki, collapsing, buried her face in his shoulder. He smelled of leather and sweat and gunpowder and he was shaking as violently as she. "Hang on, Nikki, I'm here," he whispered across her crown. "And I always will be."

She couldn't let go. Trembling, she clung to him as if to life itself. Time stretched endlessly, the minutes ticking by, her heartbeat slowing, the man on the ground moaning pitifully.

She listened to Trent's uneven breathing as, in the distance, sirens screamed loudly, people shouted and eventually the police and neighbors arrived. The events played out in slow motion in Nikki's mind. She remembered Trent talking to one of the officers, taking a drag from a cigarette and pointing toward the house.

A female officer took her statement, and Nikki was surprisingly calm as she gave it, though her mind seemed disjointed and she kept watching Trent. She was aware of the helicopter and the paramedics who life-flighted the attacker away, over the serene waters of the lake, to be deposited in a nearby hospital, but the events seemed surreal and confused and she was grateful when Trent helped her into his Jeep and they drove to the police station.

Under the harsh lights, answering harsher questions,

Nikki drank several cups of bitter coffee, explaining over and over what had happened. There was talk between the officers, as if they found her story preposterous then finally believable. The man in the hospital had been willing to spill his guts, it seemed. He was going to survive, and his story corroborated Nikki's and Trent's.

According to the would-be assassin, Crowley had known that Nikki had followed him to Salvaje with the express purpose of gathering information to expose him. Crowley had ordered the "accident" to end her life even though he knew her father. Nikki was too determined, too dogged and Crowley recognized her for the enemy she was. The senator had learned of her obsession to expose him from a friend of his…good ol' Max who worked at the *Observer* and was jealous of Nikki's ambition and hard work.

Eventually, hours later, she and Trent were allowed to go home.

"You all right?" he asked as he tossed his jacket over her shoulders.

Bone weary, she offered him the shadow of a smile. "I think so."

He helped her into the passenger side of the Jeep, then slid behind the wheel, but he paused before jamming the key into the ignition. Closing his eyes for a second, he turned to her, and when his blue gaze caressed hers, he sighed. "I'm sorry," he said, touching her cheek.

"For?"

"Everything. I shouldn't have left you alone."

"You didn't have a choice. I had to go to work. I have a life. You couldn't have followed me minute by minute."

"I should have." Guilt slid stealthily over his features. "I'd hoped you'd come back, but I wasn't sure, so I left the door open and went to your apartment. When you didn't show up there, I got worried, returned home and saw Crowley hightailing it out of there. Your car was in the drive and I thought…" his jaw clenched convulsively "…I thought I might be too late. Nikki, if anything would have happened to you…" He leaned heavily back against the seat. "That bastard will pay. He's come up with an alibi, you know. Good old slippery Diamond Jim." Trent's lips curled into a line of satisfaction. "However, his alibi isn't that airtight. I know the guy who claims to be having drinks with him, and he can be persuaded to tell the truth."

"How?" Nikki asked.

"The man has a gambling problem. Connected to the wrong circles, owes a lot of money. I know, because I used to deal with him those few weeks when I worked for Crowley. Jimbo's slipping. He could've bought himself a better story, but he didn't have a lot of time. He didn't know you'd be at the house or that you'd recognize Rodriguez as the man who'd tossed you over the cliff on Salvaje.

"Besides, Jim thought you wouldn't escape this time. He wanted it to look like an accident, just like before." Turning, he gazed deep into her eyes. "We'll nail them, Nikki. Together. You've got yourself the story of a lifetime."

The story of a lifetime. Proof that she could be "one of the boys" at the *Observer.* Why did it seem so little? "And you. What did you get?"

"I've got a monkey off my back. At first when I worked for Crowley, I thought he was honest and upright and the best man to represent the people of this state. But I found out he was dirty and crooked and I've spent the last few years determined to bring him down."

"So now your life's quest is over," she said, attempting to sound lighthearted when her insides felt weighted with stones.

"Yep. Suppose so." He stepped on the throttle and twisted the ignition. The Jeep's engine caught, and within a few minutes they had merged into the slow stream of traffic heading away from the center of the city.

Through the night, Trent drove to her apartment. He parked, and without asking, helped her up the stairs and inside. "Why did you come back to see me?" he asked as she slid out of her jacket.

"I thought we needed to have it out."

"It?"

"Everything." She snapped on the lights, trying to break the intimacy, the spell of being with him. She looked into his eyes and wished that things were different between them. "You lied to me."

"And you'll never forgive me."

Her teeth sunk into her lower lip. "I don't think I can."

He looked about to say something, changed his mind and turned toward the door. "I wasn't lying when I told you I loved you, Nikki. And I've never been so damned scared in my life. When I saw you on the cliff…" He leaned back against the door and his face turned the color of chalk.

Her heart turned over. *Love him! Trust him! Forgive him! He did it for you!*

"When I figured out that you were on Salvaje digging up dirt on Crowley I thought I should try to protect you. I didn't lie when I said that I took one look at you in Seattle and lost all perspective. Seeing you on the island only reinforced my feelings. That's why I came up with the cock-and-bull story about being married. I just wanted to get you safe and hustle you off the island as quickly as I could. I thought that if we traveled together, posed as husband and wife, Crowley and his men wouldn't be so suspicious. It might have worked, too, if it hadn't been for the storm." His mouth twisted into a sad smile.

"What if I hadn't lost my memory?"

A muscle twitched in his jaw. "I don't know. I would have come up with something else."

"You took one helluva chance."

He stared at her. And the words, *I did it for you* didn't come to his lips. Instead, he read the censure in her eyes, slid one final look down her body and said, "You know how I feel and you know where I live. Oh, by the way, it's not really my house."

Another lie.

"I rent it from a friend."

Well, not so bad.

He opened the door. "Goodbye, Nikki." With a quick glance over his shoulder, he was gone, the door shut behind him, and giving into the exhaustion that overcame her, she slid to the floor, dropped her head in her hands and cried.

Nikki sipped a cup of coffee and stared at the small television on Frank Pianzani's desk. It had been nearly a week since her story broke, and in that time she'd become Frank's new star reporter. Max, having been exposed for tipping off the senator, had been fired.

Frank was pleased with himself. Thanks to Nikki, the *Observer* had scooped all the competition, and now the outcome of her incredible work was on the evening news.

Nikki stared at the screen and watched as Senator Crowley's face, showing signs of strain, appeared. His voice, however, still rang like an orator's. "I categorically deny the charges. They are absolutely false and all the constituents of the state of Washington who have voted for me over the years know that I've never accepted a bribe, nor have I accepted gifts from special interest groups."

"What about the man in the hospital? Felipe Rodriguez?"

"I don't know much about him. He's only been on my payroll a month or two. But the man is obviously suffering from delusions. His story is too bizarre to be believed. Why, just look at my record—"

"Rodriguez claims that you met on Salvaje, that you were recently there and that you paid him to kill an American citizen, Nicole Carrothers, a reporter for the *Observer*."

"As I said—delusions. His story is preposterous. Now, if you'll excuse me, I have no further comment."

Frank snapped off the set. "Looks like old Diamond Jim isn't going to seek reelection."

"Good."

"And the senate ethics committee will look into your allegations."

"More good news."

"It just keeps coming and coming," Frank said,

standing and stretching. His white shirt was wrinkled, and he snapped his suspenders happily. "You know, I don't think I ever gave you enough credit around here."

"You didn't," Nikki said.

Frank rubbed the back of his neck. "Well, I'll make it up to you."

"Too late."

"What?"

Nikki offered him her most ingratiating smile. "I quit."

Frank looked as if she'd beaned him with a bowling ball. "Quit? You can't quit!"

Reaching into her purse, she pulled out a long, white envelope. "Just watch me."

"This has something to do with that husband of yours, doesn't it? Just because things aren't working out between you two…" Realizing he'd overstepped his bounds, Frank grabbed his reading glasses off his desk and shoved them onto his nose. "Don't tell me, the *Times* offered you more money."

She grinned, but the deep-seated satisfaction she hoped to feel didn't surface. How could she explain that she'd proved her point, made her statement, and now had to move on? Her life had been turned upside down and inside out in the last week and never once had she seen Trent.

Everyone else, but not Trent. Her father, mother and sisters had rallied around her in her time of need. Calling and visiting, sick at the thought that she'd nearly lost her life. There had been many questions about her husband, and Nikki had ducked them all, saying only that the marriage wasn't yet on stable ground and after the events of the past few weeks, they'd both decided they needed some space.

Her family had thought the reaction odd, but she'd muddled through, dealing with the police, other reporters, interviews and her job. Through it all, she'd felt lonely and empty inside.

Well, today her life was going to change. One way or the other. Grabbing her coat, she took the elevator to the parking garage and climbed into her little convertible. The backseat was filled with the clutter that had been her desk: notes, pens, paper, recorder, Rolodex file, books and general paraphernalia that she'd accumulated in her years with the *Observer.*

It was time to move on. Crossing her fingers, she put her car into gear and hoped that she would be moving in the direction she hoped to.

You know where I live.

Nerves strung tight, she eased her way through traffic, flipped on the radio and hummed along to an old Bruce Springsteen hit. But her thoughts weren't on the lyrics or even the melody; her thoughts were with Trent and what she had to say to him.

She turned into the drive of the house on Lake Washington and her heart sank. His Jeep was missing and the house looked empty and cold, as if no one lived there. The police tape, denoting a crime scene, had been stripped away, but there was no sign of Trent.

She knocked loudly on the front door and waited.

Nothing. Not one sign of life. A few dry leaves rattled in the old oak trees before floating downward and being caught in a tiny gust to dance for a few seconds before landing on the ground. *Just like us,* Nikki thought, watching with sadness. She and Trent had danced for a few weeks and drifted apart.

Wrong. You pushed him away. She walked around the house and an uneasy feeling wrapped around her, a feeling that she was stepping on her own grave. Rubbing her arms, she followed the path she'd taken on the day she'd been attacked, saw the broken branches in the forest, noticed the footprints, observed the dark stain on the grass and dry leaves where the blood of her attacker had pooled.

Trent had risked his life to save her.

Shivering, she told herself she was lucky and she stared across the lake, past the steel-colored water to the opposite shore where houses were tucked in the evergreen forest.

"Nikki?" Trent's voice whispered on the wind. She turned and found him approaching, his hair ruffling in the breeze, his familiar leather jacket open at the throat. "What're you doing here? I saw your car and…" His voice drifted away as his gaze caught and held in hers.

"I thought we had some unfinished business," she said, feeling the ridiculous urge to break down and cry. Lord, she seemed to fall to pieces whenever she was around him. Blinking against that sudden rush of tears, she walked to him and linked her arm through his. "Come on, let's not stay here."

They followed the path to a point that had been unspoiled by the evil and malevolence that had trailed them from Salvaje to Seattle. "I, um, I've been thinking," she said, still holding his arm as she turned to face him. The wind caught her hair, blowing it over her face, brushing it against her cheeks.

"When have you had time?"

So he'd seen her on the news. Kept track of her busy life. "Things have been hectic," she admitted, "but I've had a lot of hours to do some heavy soul-searching."

"Have you?" He wasn't buying her story, obviously. "I heard you got a commendation and a promotion."

She shrugged. "I quit."

He didn't say a word, just stood there woodenly, not taking her into his arms, even when she was silently begging him to.

"It was time to change."

"Got another job?"

She shook her head. "Not yet."

"Seems to me you could have your pick."

"Doesn't matter." She felt his hand stiffen and held his fingers more tightly in her own. "I don't want a new job, Trent. I just want you." When he didn't respond, she took his face between her palms and forced him to stare into her eyes. "Those hours I spent soul-searching I was alone. In my bed, crying my eyes out. I decided if I wasn't going to wallow in my own misery any longer, I had to face the truth and that is—" she took in a shuddering breath, ready to bare her soul "—I love you, Trent McKenzie, and I want to marry you." His jaw clenched tight. "If you'll have me."

Swallowing the lump of pride that filled her throat, she reached into her purse and withdrew a packet. "Tickets to Salvaje," she said. "For you and me."

His lips cracked into a small, skeptical smile. "You want to go back there?"

"Mmm-hmm."

"When?"

"Right after we stop down at the courthouse and tie the knot."

His smile kicked up a little higher. "What if I don't want to get married?"

Pain sliced through her heart, but she tilted her chin upward defiantly. "Then come with me as my lover."

He barked out a short laugh and stepped away from her. "You're too much," he said, resting his hands on his hips and shaking his head.

Disappointment curdled her insides.

"I thought you never wanted to see me again."

"I had a change of heart." When he didn't respond, she tossed her hair out of her face. "Damn it, Trent, this wasn't easy for me, you know. I've swallowed my pride, told you that I love you, nearly begged you to marry me and you don't have a thing to say?"

"Oh, sure I do."

Here it comes. "And what's that?" she demanded, feeling fire leap in her eyes.

He slid a finger into the pocket of his jeans and withdrew the slim gold band, the very band that had been her wedding ring on Salvaje. "I just wondered what took you so long."

She let out a long, agonized breath. "You've been waiting for me to come back here. You knew I would, didn't you?"

"Thought you might."

"You arrogant, self-important—"

He cut off her insults with a kiss that caused her blood to turn to liquid fire. "Will you shut up a minute?" he asked as he slipped the ring that he'd sized to fit perfectly onto her finger. "I need to get this right this time." He looked down into her eyes and cradled her face in his hands. "Marry me, Nikki," he whispered, feeling the tremor of her body as it molded to his.

Wrapping his arms around her, he pressed anxious lips to hers and knew that now and forever Nikki would be his special woman.

* * * * *

NEW YEAR'S DADDY

CHAPTER ONE

"I GOT A letter for Santa Claus!" Amy sang out as she burst through the door. A four-year-old dynamo with black curls that had fallen from her ponytail and were now dusted with snowflakes, she torpedoed into the cabin as she peeled off her jacket and backpack.

Through the open door, Veronica spied her sister Shelly's huge Chevy wagon idling near the garage that they'd converted into a warehouse. In the paddock nearby her horses sniffed at the snow covered ground searching for a few blades of grass.

"Gotta run, Ronni, the twins are starving," Shelly yelled, waving through the open window of her car. Her boys, Kent and Kurt, were arguing loudly enough to wake the dead.

"My turn tomorrow," Veronica called and in a plume of blue exhaust the old station wagon lumbered out of sight. Closing the door behind her, she saw her daughter delving into the front pocket of her backpack. "What's this about a letter?"

"For Santa," Amy repeated, retrieving a single sheet of paper with a Santa sticker in one corner and a four-year-old's uneven scrawl across the page. "Come on, Mommy, we gots to put a stamp on it and mail it."

"First take off your boots and tell me about preschool today, then we'll mail the letter in the morning." Veronica poured a cup of coffee and settled into a corner of the couch, where she patted a worn cushion to indicate a spot for her daughter.

She was glad to have Amy home. It was early December and all afternoon she'd felt ill at ease on the mountain where she worked as part of the ski patrol. There had been record-breaking snowstorms in the Cascades this year and more skiers than ever were gliding down the slopes, challenging the mountain. Thankfully, despite her premonition, there hadn't been a serious accident on the mountain today. Still, she was cold deep in her bones, though she'd left Mount Echo nearly an hour before.

Amy's eyes, so like her father's, sparkled. "Promise you'll mail it?"

"Cross my heart," Veronica replied with a laugh as she dragged a finger over her chest in an exaggerated motion. No matter how melancholy Ronni felt, Amy had a way of making the gloom disappear.

"Okay!" The little girl dashed across the room, her stockinged feet sliding on the hardwood until she reached the braided rug. The cabin they lived in had no formal rooms, just living areas separated by sparse furniture groupings. Everything on and around the blue-and-white rug was considered the living room, the rest of the downstairs was the dining room and kitchen. A small half bath was located on the far wall and the loft above supported a bedroom, full bath and open den area where Veronica slept. The mountain home was small, but cozy, and big enough for the two of them. "Miss Jennie helped me with it."

Miss Jennie was Amy's preschool teacher. A patient woman of about twenty-five, Jennie Anderson was a godsend on the days that Veronica worked in her small mail-order shop in her garage-warehouse, shipping a variety of Northwest items to eager customers.

"So, I suppose you told Santa what you want this year," Veronica prodded, her gaze straying to the boxes of ornaments and lights that she'd hauled out of the attic and stacked near the bookcase. Christmas. It used to be her favorite holiday, but ever since Hank's death... She closed her eyes for a second, refusing to dwell on the past.

"I want a puppy," Amy said, climbing into her mother's lap while the fire crackled and hissed behind an ancient screen.

"Oh, now there's a surprise!" Veronica teased as she kissed the curly hair of Amy's crown. "You're like a broken record when it comes to a dog. We've already got the horses."

"But I want a puppy!"

"I know, I know." Ronni tried a different tack. "Anything else on your list?"

"A daddy."

"A what?" Veronica silently prayed she'd heard incorrectly.

"A daddy, like all my friends have." Amy said the request matter-of-factly, as if her mother should be able to see the perfect logic of it all. "Then you wouldn't have to be alone."

"I'm not alone," Veronica protested. "I've got you." She squeezed her daughter and Amy giggled, then squirmed off her lap to run to the bathroom.

Veronica was left with a cooling cup of coffee and a Christmas wish list she couldn't hope to fill. She stared at the crayon-written letters and sighed. Sooner or later this was bound to happen, but she'd been counting on later. Much later. She'd been married to Hank, her high school sweetheart, three years when she'd learned she was pregnant. Their happiness had been complete. Tears shimmered in her eyes when she remembered Hank's reaction to the news that they were going to have a baby, how his handsome mouth had stretched into a smile and the sound of sheer joy when he'd laughed out loud, grabbed her and twirled her off her feet. She'd counted herself as one of the truly blessed people in the world. Amy's birth had been incredible. Hank had been with her in the delivery room and when he'd first held his little daughter, he'd cried silent tears of joy.

Then, within a year, he was dead, her life shattered with no way to put the jagged and crumbling pieces together again.

Veronica closed her eyes. Maybe no one was supposed to be as happy as they'd been. Maybe everyone was supposed to suffer, but it wasn't fair. It just wasn't fair. Big, blond, strapping Hank should have lived until he was in his nineties. Instead, he'd been cut down at twenty-six. Almost four years ago. Four long, lonely years.

He was simply irreplaceable.

She blinked rapidly and told herself that it didn't matter. Even if Amy wanted a daddy, they could do very well without one. Veronica had long ago determined that she could be both mother and father to her little girl. She held her cup to her lips and grimaced when she noticed she was shaking.

Amy was back quickly and scrambling onto the couch.

"Did you wash your hands?" Veronica said automatically.

Amy nodded and Veronica saw that her daughter's fingers were still wet. One thing at a time. They'd tackle drying those little fists another day.

"Hey, lookie!" Amy was standing on tiptoe on the cushions of the couch, leaning against the back pillows, her nose pressed against the glass as she stared outside. Veronica twisted to squint through the frosted panes. Icicles glistened on the eaves of the porch and snow touched by silvery moon glow blanketed the ground. "Lights," Amy said. "New lights."

She looked through the branches of the trees and noticed the warm glow of lamps shining from the house across the lake. "Well, what d'ya know? Someone must be staying at the old Johnson place." That thought bothered her more than it should have, she supposed, but she couldn't help her dream of someday owning the old lodge by the lake and converting it into a bed-and-breakfast inn. The lodge had special memories for her, memories she knew she would cherish to her dying day. Her father had been caretaker of the grounds and she'd grown up swimming in the smooth water of the lake and chasing her sister through the long grass of the shoreline. In winter, her father would let them build camp fires on the beach and cross-country ski along the old logging roads.

"It's creepy there!" Amy shuddered theatrically at the mention of Johnson's property.

Ronni laughed. "No," she said, squeezing her daughter, her melancholy chased away by Amy's analysis of a place she found absolutely charming. "It's just that the house is big and rambling and has been vacant for a long time. Believe me, with a lot of money and a little bit of elbow grease, it would be the nicest place around for miles."

Amy wrinkled her nose. "Elbow grease?"

"It means hard work. The old lodge needs TLC—that means tender loving care."

"I *know* that. But it has cobwebs and broken windows and probably snakes and bats and ghosts!" Amy said, obviously remembering the walk they'd taken down the winding lane that ran past their property and ended up at the Cyrus Johnson estate.

Veronica had ignored the No Trespassing signs and helped Amy over the gate so the little girl could observe ducks and geese gather on the private lake. It had been early morning, they'd watched in awe as the sun rose over the mountains, chasing away the shadows of the land as a doe with her speckle-backed fawns drank from the water. An eagle had soared high overhead and on the ground chipmunks had scurried for cover.

But Amy remembered the spiders and imagined the ghosts of the rambling old lodge. She'd never wanted to go back to the lake again, and Veronica, hoping her daughter would outgrow her fears, never mentioned that it was her secret dream to buy the place someday—to create the same haven for Amy that had sheltered her. Even the old caretaker's house could be rented out—maybe to Shelly.

The Johnson property had been on the market for nearly a year and no one had shown any interest. A real estate agent and friend of Veronica's, Taffy LeMar, had promised to call if she heard any gossip about a serious buyer.

Not that Veronica had any real hope of owning the hundred-plus acres. As rundown as it was, the lodge and property were worth over half a million dollars. Financially she was doing all right but she couldn't hope to secure such a large mortgage.

"I wonder who's inside?" Veronica thought aloud. Apparently not anyone who was taking up permanent residence, or Taffy would have called her. But Veronica was left with an uneasy feeling—that same inexplicable sense of dread that had clung to her all day.

"Ghosts and witches," Amy insisted. "That's who lives there!"

"I don't think so." Rubbing her chin, Veronica tried to imagine who would move into a drafty old lodge in the middle of winter. They were probably just renting it for a week or two—an eccentric couple looking for a rustic retreat for the holidays. Or they could be trespassing. The electricity wouldn't be turned on but they could use kerosene lanterns for light, a camp stove to cook on and camp fires for warmth. Water would be the only problem as the pump was probably fueled by electricity, but they could always carry buckets from the lake. She gave herself a swift mental kick for letting her imagination run away with her—she was as bad as Amy.

"Creepy," Amy said again before being distracted by the sparkling ornaments. She dashed across the room and searched through two boxes of Christmas decorations before dragging out a piece of red tinsel and draping it around her neck like a glittery feather boa. "Look at me, I'm a Christmas tree."

Veronica grinned widely. "No way. You're an angel."

"Not an angel." A look of sheer vexation crossed Amy's small features. "A tree."

"You need a star on top, don't you?"

Amy's eyes rounded. "Do we have one?"

Shaking her head, Veronica said, "I can't remember. Seems to me it broke last year when I was putting it away. We might have to buy a new one." That thought brought her no joy. All the Christmas ornaments she had she'd bought with Hank. Their first tree had been a little tabletop pine with one strand of lights and a few red balls that reminded them both of the animated tree from "A Charlie Brown Christmas," and each year they'd purchased a larger tree and picked out new decorations. Each Christmas Eve, they had opened a small gift in their stockings, which traditionally had been a special ornament with the date inscribed across it. Once the stockings were empty, they hung their new little decorations on the tree, sipped mulled wine and made love beneath the branches. With only the light of a few candles on the mantel and an old afghan and each other for warmth, they had stayed awake until midnight when it was officially Christmas Day.

A deep, grieving sadness stole through her heart as it always did this time of year. If it weren't for Amy, she'd chuck all her Christmas traditions. Oh, Shelly would probably demand their little, fragmented family still get together. But Veronica was certain that were it not for her daughter, she would probably just give Shelly, her sister's husband and the boys each a gift certificate to their favorite store, forget the cards, decorations, stockings and tree, fly away for the holidays and spend the last two weeks of the year soaking up the sun somewhere, lounging around a tropical pool, sipping iced tea and pretending that the Christmas season had never existed.

"Can I buy the new star?" Amy asked, dragging her back to the here and now.

"Sure you can. Whatever star you want," Veronica replied, forcing a note of gaiety into her voice. "I bet we'll be able to find one at the church bazaar. Now, come on, you can help me make dinner."

Amy followed her into the kitchen area, tinsel dragging on the floor after her like the train of a bridal gown.

"Can we have macaroni and cheese tonight?" Amy had asked the same question every night for the past five.

"I was thinking about turkey soup and hot bread. See, I was cutting up carrots when you came home."

Amy wrinkled her nose. "Don't like—"

"We'll even add this pasta I bought," Veronica added quickly, forestalling her daughter's protests. "Here, take a look." Reaching into her cupboard, Veronica pulled out a wrapped package of red, green and yellow pasta shaped like miniature Christmas trees.

Amy's mouth rounded into a gasp of pleasure. "Can I do it?"

"You bet. When the broth's boiling and if you're very careful so you don't get burned, you can help me by tossing in a handful or two."

"I can do it," Amy vowed. She threw another loop of tinsel around her neck and pushed a chair near the counter all the while singing the first few words of "Oh, Christmas Tree" over and over again.

"I can't believe there's no cable," Bryan grumbled for the dozenth time. At fourteen, he seemed to think it was his God-given right to watch MTV around the clock. He adjusted his Seattle Mariners' cap, twisting it so that it was on backward, the bill pointing down his back, his brown hair poking out around the edges.

"No TV, period," his father reminded him as he lugged a basket of kindling and set it near the river-rock fireplace which rose two full stories to the ceiling. The place was dusty, drafty and needed so much work that Travis second-guessed himself for the first time since moving from Seattle. The rooms were barren and the moving van wasn't scheduled to show up for a couple of days so he and Bryan planned to work together—kind of a father-and-son project—to put the old house in order before their things arrived. So far, the son part of the team couldn't have been less interested.

Travis had decided they'd shore up the sagging porch, clean the floors and windows, determine how much rewiring and new plumbing was needed and just spend some time getting to know each other again—to make up for lost time.

Bryan dropped his basket onto the hearth and glanced up at the chandelier, which was constructed of deer antlers that supported tiny lights, most of which had probably burned out years ago. "This place stinks. It looks like something out of The Addams Family!"

"You don't like the haunted-house ambience?" Travis asked, smiling and dusting his hands. The kid needed to be jollied out of the bad mood that he'd hauled around with him for the past week.

"I hate it, okay?"

Boy, Bryan was pushing. Travis told himself not to explode and tell his son to find a new attitude. "It'll be great if you give it a chance."

"Are you crazy? It's a pit! Beyond a pit! Should

have been condemned fifty years ago. Probably was."
Bryan flopped down on one of the two mattresses they'd
brought. He propped his head on his rolled sleeping bag
and scowled at his new surroundings as if he'd just been
locked into a six-by-twelve prison cell.

"Give it a rest, Bryan," Travis warned, even though
he, too, saw the problems with the old lodge, maybe
clearer than his son.

Cobwebs trailed from the ceiling and the leftover
meals of spiders—dead, drained insect carcasses—vied
with mouse pellets for space in dark corners. The pipes
creaked, the lights were undependable and all the old
linoleum would have to be replaced. Toilets and sinks
were stained and the grout between what had once been
beautiful imported tile had disintegrated. Fixing the
place up would probably cost him as much as his original investment, but it would be worth it, he silently
told himself, stacking kindling on ancient andirons.
Any amount of money spent would be cheap if it meant
saving his boy.

He glanced over his shoulder at Bryan and saw the
sullen expression in his son's eyes, the curled lower lip,
the ever-present baseball cap on backward and tattered,
black clothes that were three sizes too big for him. His
fashion statement wasn't really the problem, nor did Travis object to Bryan's earring or the streak of bleached-
blond hair that contrasted to his natural deep brown, but
Bryan's general attitude needed an overhaul, and fast.

"You're gonna love it here," Travis said, striking a
wooden match on the hearth. Sizzling, the match flared
and Travis touched the flame to bits of old newspaper
wadded beneath the firewood.

"In your dreams."

"Give it a chance, Bryan. I've heard that you can see eagles and deer, maybe even elk and rabbits."

"Big deal."

The fire began to crackle. "We both agreed that we needed to change—"

"No, Travis," he said, rarely calling his father anything but his given name ever since the divorce. Jabbing a thumb at his chest, he added, "*I* didn't agree to anything. This was your deal. Not mine. I would have stayed in Seattle, with my friends."

Travis bit down hard on his molars so that he wouldn't make some snide comment about the friends Bryan chose, not necessarily bad kids, but the kind that seemed to scare up trouble wherever it was hiding. Bryan's choice of friends had been one of the reasons that had prompted this move to Oregon. One kid had been caught smoking marijuana several times; another had convinced a few pals to skip school, which ended in a joyride cut short when he wrapped the car around a telephone pole, sending several boys to the hospital; and a third had attempted suicide. Not a healthy environment. "Staying in Seattle wasn't an option."

"Yeah, because I don't have any say in anything that happens to me."

"Not true, Bryan."

His son's lips folded over his teeth in annoyance and he popped his knuckles. "Did anyone ask me what I wanted when you and Sylvia got divorced?"

"Your mother and I—"

"Got married 'cause she was pregnant with me and then you found out that you didn't love each other. The only reason you stayed together so long was because of me." He made a sound of disgust in his throat and glared at the ceiling. "I don't know why you bothered."

This was getting complicated. Travis walked to the vacant mattress, which lay only a few feet from Bryan's. He sat on his rolled sleeping bag and clasping his hands together, hung them between his legs as he looked his boy straight in the eye. "Your mother and I weren't the greatest match, it's true, and yes, she was carrying you, so that pushed up our wedding plans, but we'd already committed to each other. We were going to get married and have kids, one way or the other. It just didn't work out."

Bryan's lips tightened.

"We tried."

"Who cares?"

"You do, I think, and I feel badly that you got hurt."

"I'm *not* hurt, okay?"

Travis felt like giving up, but he gritted his teeth.

"I just want to move back home," Bryan said.

"This is home now."

"Never," Bryan muttered.

"Look, Bry, it's complicated and hard, I know, but you have to realize that Sylvia and I each love you very much."

Levering himself up on an elbow, Bryan stared straight at his father, his gaze, so like Travis's boring into him. "So that's why she took off for France."

"She needed time and space."

"It's been three years!"

"She likes it over there."

"So she can be away from me. Doesn't have any responsibility then, does she? She can hang out with that gigolo—you know, Jean Pierre or whatever his name is."

Damn! Travis had to bite his tongue. His ex-wife

wasn't a bad person, just incredibly self-centered.
Half of what Bryan was saying about her was true.
Sometimes it was impossible to explain that whimsi-
cal woman who thought more of herself, her "freedom,"
than she did of her family. But then she alone wasn't to
blame for the divorce. Travis, in his own way, had neglected her and their son. "Your mother's just uncon-
ventional. Always has been."

"Does that translate to basket case?"

"No."

"Then it must be a fancy way of saying she doesn't
give a damn about me!"

"Bryan, listen—"

"Oh, just forget it." He flopped back on the sleeping
bag and stared at the ceiling again. Making an angry
motion with one hand, he said, "I don't want to think
about her, anyway. I don't want to think about anything."

"Things have a way of working out," Travis said,
cringing inside at the patronizing ring to his words.
"You'll get used to living here, maybe even like it."

"Why? Why would I want to live in some little
Podunk town?"

"You needed a change."

"You mean you did." Bryan eyed his father disdain-
fully and Travis was suddenly painfully aware of his
jeans and flannel shirt as opposed to the suits that Bryan
had seen him wearing since the day the kid was born.
He couldn't deny the fact that he'd been little more than
a part-time father at best, spending more hours with his
fledgling businesses than with his son in the first few,
formative years of the boy's life. He'd kicked himself
to hell and back for his mistakes, but it didn't make any

difference. The past was the past. Now it was time for a new start.

"Look," Travis said, climbing to his feet. "We worked hard today. Let's spoil ourselves and go skiing tomorrow afternoon."

"What? No more chopping wood? Splitting kindling? Mopping floors?" Bryan sneered.

"Careful, or you'll find yourself doing just those things," Travis warned, though he smiled. "We'll check out Mount Echo. May as well since it's practically in our backyard. What do you say?"

"*Anything's* better than hanging around this place," Bryan growled, but Travis had noticed a spark of interest—the first since they'd moved here—in his son's sullen eyes.

The next day Travis and Bryan headed to Mount Echo. After skiing together for a while, they split up and agreed to meet at two o'clock. Now, Bryan was looking down a very steep run. He had heard about Devil's Spine from Marty Sinclair, a friend of his in Seattle who had bragged about "getting twenty feet of air," by jumping off the spine. Marty had bragged and laughed as he'd rolled a joint and offered it to Bryan, who had declined and been rewarded with a cloud of smoke exhaled in his face. Bryan had determined for himself that if Marty could make the jump, so could he. Never mind that he was already late meeting his dad at the lodge, never mind that the run was obviously closed and he'd had to cross-country it over to the ridge, never mind that he was cold and tired and was, deep inside, a little bit chicken about doing this. He had a point to prove. To Marty. To his dad. And especially to himself.

He'd eyed the jump and it was nowhere near twenty feet. Maybe six or eight, but twenty? No way. Poised at the top of the narrow canyon that wound steeply between trees and cliffs on either side, he screwed up his courage, planted his poles and took off. Tucked low, faster and faster he sped, his skis skimming over the trail. The snow was glazed with ice, bumps carved into the pack so hard they sent shock waves through his legs as he raced through the narrow channel. But there was no turning back. Fir branches slapped at his face, but he didn't care. He took the final turn and the world seemed to open up as the trees gave way and there was nothing in front of him but cloudy sky. With a final push, he was airborne, soaring through the frigid air, wind rushing at his face, his entire body free and sailing through the sky.

Adrenaline charged through his bloodstream as he looked over the tops of trees. His heart nearly stopped when he finally glanced down, preparing for his landing. He braced himself, keeping his knees loose. *It'll be okay. If Marty can do it, so can I!* But his heart was pounding in fear. His mouth was dry. What if he didn't land right? What if he turned an ankle. What if—

Bam!

His skis slammed into the ground. His body jarred. He was speeding downhill. He'd done it! Exhilaration swept through him just as his right ski caught an edge. He tried to right himself and overcompensated. Before he knew what was happening, he was falling, head over heels. One binding released. His ski flew off and he was tumbling ever faster toward a small fir tree. The second biding broke free. He tried to break his fall, but couldn't dig in. The sky and ground blurred. "Oh, God," he yelled, snow filling his mouth.

He careered into a tree, his body jerked by the force. With a yowl, he felt pain—intense, blinding and hot— scream up his leg and he realized that he was all alone, on a part of the mountain that was closed, where no one would find him. He tried to yell, but blackness swirled in front of his eyes and he had to fight to stay awake. He screamed before the darkness surrounded him again and this time, though he struggled, he passed out. His final conscious thought was that he was going to die. Alone.

Not that his parents would care....

CHAPTER TWO

VERONICA ANGLED HER skis, cutting the edges into the fresh snow as she glared up at the summit of Mount Echo, a jagged, craggy peak nearly concealed by the clouds that clung to its uppermost reaches. *A terrain of savage beauty,* one journalist had written. *Treacherous. Unforgiving. Cruel.* "Damn you," she whispered, then snapped her goggles over her eyes.

This is crazy, Ronni! You can't keep blaming the mountain for Hank's death! It's been four years. Enough time to heal. Time to move forward with your life.

Then why did she feel that she couldn't breathe sometimes, that the need to get back at someone or something was so great it suffocated her? She'd suffered through a grief support group, cried on her sister's shoulder, forced herself to smile for her child's sake, but had never completely come to terms with the fact that Hank was gone—irretrievably and forever.

"Get over it," she told herself, dismayed that she'd actually sworn at the mountain. Adjusting her straps, she turned her back to the wind that whistled above the timberline and planted her poles. Expertly she skied down a wide, tree-lined bowl. Most of the skiers seemed to be handling the gentle slope of North Alpine Run without much difficulty, though a few hotdoggers and snow boarders barreled at breakneck speeds past their more cautious counterparts.

Veering to the left, Ronni steered down a narrow cat track that headed into rougher territory, where the steeper grade of Redrock Canyon usually took its toll on less experienced skiers. As part of the rescue team, she patrolled the slopes, helping stranded or injured skiers get back to the lodge safely. Years ago, before the accident, she and Hank had worked the slopes together and after his death, she'd continued her association with the rescue team, helping the injured, vowing to prevent Echo from taking more victims, hoping to assuage the guilt that still kept her awake some nights. It was her personal quest—her vendetta against Mother Nature.

She spied a little girl in a pink ski outfit who seemed alone and lost. The child, around twelve, judging by her size, was standing on the edge of Jackpine Run, a trail that changed from softly rolling terrain to a steep mogul-filled slope. Veronica was about to see if the child needed help, when a man—probably the kid's father—swooshed up to her and together they tackled the difficult terrain.

All in all it had been a quiet day, thank God, but the temperature had dropped, the wind had picked up and on the east face even the groomed runs were icy. *Treacherous. Unforgiving.* She plunged her poles into the snow and started downhill. For years she'd told herself to give up this part-time job. Between managing her growing mail-order business and being both mother and father to Amy, she had her hands full. But she couldn't stop. It was as if she was compelled to tackle Mount Echo, to try to save lives, to help the injured, all the while spitting in the face of the mountain that she loved and hated.

She probably needed to see a psychiatrist, she thought, someone to help her quit blaming herself and the mountain for Hank's death.

Skiing down a final slope, she weaved easily through the throng that had collected around the base lodge. Skiers and snowboarders were moving in all directions, heading for the warmth of the lodge, the lift-ticket lines, the chairlifts, rope tow or parking lot. On the back deck of the lodge a crew was still barbecuing chicken. Black, fragrant smoke curled to the sky, and each time the lodge door opened, the sound of music added a throbbing backbeat to the general hubbub.

Maneuvering to the emergency hut, she was just pushing out of her bindings when Bobby Sawyer threw open the door. "We've got two new ones, Ronni," he said as he stretched his fingers into his gloves. "Both on the north side. One on Double Spur, the other in Devil's Hollow."

"Let's go." She snapped off her skis, held them against her and together they climbed onto a waiting snowmobile. Bobby drove and Ronni tucked her head against the wind. The snowmobile roared up an icy cat track, away from the skiers.

Yelling to be heard over the noise of the engine, Bobby filled Veronica in on the details. "I'll go up to Double Spur, that's where a little girl slammed into a tree. There's a possible head injury and we may have to life-flight her."

Ronni's heart sank. No! No! No! This mountain couldn't claim another life, not that of a child.

"The other injury is a kid who was taking a jump off the rocks on Devil's Spine. I think he ended up tangling with a tree. From the reports it sounds like leg problems. Tim's already coming with the sled."

"When did it happen?"

"Someone saw him less than ten minutes ago."

"I thought the spine was closed today."

"Either the guy can't read or he ignored the warnings."

There was always some fool who didn't think the rules applied to him and took off on his own. Bobby dropped her off near the empty chairlift that linked the base lodge with all the runs shooting off Devil's Hollow and Veronica snapped on her skis. She sped under the lift, shot through a narrow trail that cut through the trees to the ridge of boulders and run that was known as Devil's Spine or just the spine. Icy and treacherous, the mountain wasn't giving an inch on this side. She caught a glimpse of the downed skier lying in the snow beneath the rocks. Both skis had been thrown off. One lay split near the protruding red boulders that formed the vertebrae of the spine; his other ski was tangled in the broken branches of a small fir tree.

"Hang in there, kid," Veronica said under her breath as she skied down to him. "Hey, you all right?" she said when she reached him.

He didn't move.

"Oh, God."

First-aid training swept through her mind.

She was out of her skis and next to him in an instant. "Hey, are you all right?" she repeated. "Can you hear me?"

Eyes, a startling blue, blinked open and focused. A good sign.

"How do you feel, hmm?" she asked, watching as consciousness slowly returned.

"Like hell," he finally whispered. He tried to move and winced.

"I'll bet that was quite a fall you took," she said, just talking to keep him awake. He lifted his head, then closed an eye.

"Just lie still."

"My leg," he whispered, blinking rapidly as the tears started to form in those incredible eyes.

"Shh. Let me look at it."

He tried to move again. "I can't get up," he said with an edge of panic to his voice.

"Don't worry about it. I'll take care of you. All you have to do is relax and don't move."

"It hurts," he said, then uttered an oath under his breath. He had the look in his eyes of a wounded, cornered dog and Veronica's heart went out to him.

"I'm sure it does," she said, offering him a smile. "Hang in there, we've got a basket coming and we'll get you down. Do you hurt anywhere else?" She was touching him gently, looking for signs of injury. He had a bruise forming on his chin, but thankfully there were no signs of other head injuries.

"No."

"No headache?"

"No."

"But you did pass out?"

"Yeah—" He looked around and blinked again, "I guess I did."

Aside from his leg, he didn't appear to have sustained

any other injuries, but she had to check and the fact that he'd lost consciousness earlier wasn't a good sign. Either he'd hit his head or nearly scared himself to death. "How about your back, neck or arms?"

"Just my leg, okay?" he shouted, then clamped his mouth shut and looked guilty as sin. "Sorry."

"Don't worry about it," she said quickly, realizing how scared he was. He was big, five eight or nine and probably somewhere between the ages of twelve and fourteen, but he still resembled a little kid. "How long have you been here?"

"Don't know. Not long."

Good. He was dressed warmly, so he shouldn't have any frostbite. But he couldn't move his leg without biting hard on his lower lip. She glanced at the sky, ever-threatening, and noticed the wind was too fierce for any snow to collect on the branches of the surrounding trees.

"My skis—"

"We'll take them, too." *Or what's left of them.* "What's your name?"

"Bryan."

"Got a last name?" she asked, watching carefully for any signs of shock setting in. *Come on, Tim. Hurry up.*

"Keegan," he said.

"Okay, Bryan Keegan, I'm going to untangle you from this Douglas fir and if anything hurts too bad, you let me know, okay?"

"'Kay." He didn't utter a sound as she worked him gently away from the branches of the trunk. Tears filled his eyes and he brushed the drops aside with the back of his gloved hand when he apparently thought she wasn't looking. She had seen the tears and the look of embarrassment on his face, and her heart went out to the hurt boy. Somewhere nearby, she heard a snowmobile rush by and in the distance was the wail of an ambulance. Above both sounds was the disturbing sound of a helicopter's rotor. The little girl on Double Spur hadn't been as lucky as Bryan.

Ronni thought of Amy and sent up a silent prayer for the injured child, then she looked at her new charge. "That's not for you," she assured him. "I think it's about time for formal introductions, don't you?" Before he could answer, she said, "My name's Ronni Walsh and, if you haven't guessed yet, I'm part of the ski patrol," she said, even though her red jacket and name tag said as much. "Are you skiing here alone or are you part of a group?"

"My dad. He's here somewhere. I, uh, was supposed to meet him at the lodge."

"Good." She hoped to sound reassuring. "We'll find him and let him know what's happened. That way he can meet you in the clinic. What's your father's name?"

"Travis."

"Keegan? Same as yours?" These days she didn't want to assume anything.

"Yeah."

"Okay." He was finally untangled from the tree and some of his color seemed to be returning. Rocking back on her heels, she asked, "What day is it?"

"Sunday."

"Do you know where you are?"

"Mount Echo. Devil's…Devil's Bowl?"

"Close enough." He didn't seem to have any kind of memory loss, which heartened her. "As soon as my partner gets here, we'll take you down to the lodge and find your dad. Sound like a plan?"

"I guess," he said warily, but offered her the faintest of smiles.

Tim Sether arrived pushing the basket-sled, which was shaped like a canoe with bicycle handles and runners. Together they helped Bryan into the sled, covering him with a plastic thermal blanket before strapping him in tightly. Kneeling beside the rig, Tim laid a comforting hand on the boy's shoulder and explained the procedure. "I'm gonna take you down the hill. Just relax and go along for the ride. I'll do all the work. Ronni, here, she'll try to find your dad. Okay?"

"'Kay," the kid mumbled, his teeth chattering.

"Let's do it," Tim said to Veronica as he tugged on the edges of his knit cap.

The going was rough, the wind a blast of arctic air that blew across the snow. Veronica skied down first and Tim followed behind, never losing his grip on the sled as he guided it, plowlike, down the hill. At a path, they cut across the face of the mountain, back to the protected area and groomed runs. Within minutes they were at the basement of the lodge where the small emergency clinic was housed.

An ambulance, lights flashing, was already waiting at the double doors and a little girl wearing a cervical collar and strapped to a gurney was being hauled into the back.

"It's going to be okay, Jackie," a man in a black jumpsuit was saying as he leaned over the stretcher. His goggles hung around his neck, his face was ashen and his eyes were worried.

A middle-aged woman in a purple jumpsuit who was

fighting tears cleared her throat. "That's right, honey, you just hang in there."

"Don't worry," the doctor, Syd Fletcher, was saying. "I've called Dr. Bowman in Portland. He's a good man, been to him myself. He'll be able to help you get back on your feet again, Jackie."

The woman blinked rapidly. "But a crushed pelvis—"

"It'll be fixed. Come on, let's go." They didn't have time to argue and the mother climbed into the back of the ambulance before an attendant slammed the door and the vehicle tore out of the parking lot.

Veronica stepped out of her bindings. "Are you all right?" she asked Jackie's father.

He was still standing where his family had left him, his eyes fixed on the brake lights of the disappearing ambulance.

"What? Oh, yeah. Yeah, fine," he said brusquely before letting his mask of bravado slip a bit. "It's just that Jackie's our only child and if anything happens to her..." Kneading the stocking cap he was holding, he let his voice trail off. "Damn it all, anyway." He shook his head and seemed to snap out of it. "I don't know what I'm doing standing around here like a dime-store dummy, I've got to get to the hospital."

"Maybe you should have a cup of coffee first—give yourself a little time to pull yourself together."

"No time," he said as he gathered skis and headed across the parking lot and disappeared behind a bus.

Dr. Fletcher turned his attention to the boy on the stretcher. "What have we got here?"

"Right leg—though the injury seems to be confined to the knee," Tim said. He'd already stepped out of his skis and was unstrapping Bryan from the sled. "Possible head injuries, he was knocked out, but he's stabilized, no sign of concussion."

Fletcher frowned. Bending down, he ran expert hands over Bryan's head, examined his eyes and asked him a few questions. Apparently satisfied that Bryan wasn't injured more seriously than Tim had said, he smiled at the boy and clicked off his penlight. "Knee, is it, son? Haven't had one of those today." Fletcher gave Bryan his famous relax-and-let-me-take-care-of-you smiles which people always said reminded them of an old-fashioned country doctor who made house calls. In truth, Syd Fletcher was a sought-after internist whose thriving practice in Portland was more than enough to keep him busy. A skiing enthusiast who spent every other Sunday working in the clinic, he spent as much free time as possible on the mountain. "You'll be my first this afternoon. Kind of an honor."

From the looks of him, Bryan didn't think so.

"What's your name?"

"Bryan...Bryan Keegan."

"His father is somewhere on the mountain," Veronica said to Fletcher, then smiled at the boy. "Okay, Bryan, hang on to Tim and me and we'll carry you inside to a wheelchair."

"'Kay." He didn't argue and within seconds they'd maneuvered him into a chair.

"Now, about your father. Any idea where I can find him?" Ronni asked.

"Probably in the lodge," Bryan said with a shrug, but beneath his nonchalance and the pain that caused his skin to be the color of chalk, there was hint of guilt in his eyes as he avoided looking directly at her. "I, uh, was supposed to meet him."

"Don't worry, we'll find him."

The nurse on duty, Linda Knowlton, was a friend of Veronica's. With a "Well, what have we got here?" she wheeled Bryan through a maze of stainless-steel equipment, desks and occupied beds to an area behind a heavy door where an X-ray machine was located.

Once Bryan was out of sight, Veronica used the phone mounted on a wall near a cupboard containing first-aid equipment and called the information desk. She asked the receptionist to try to find a male skier by the name of Travis Keegan who might or might not be in the lodge. If located, Travis was to be sent to the clinic to pick up his son, who, though injured, wasn't in any medical danger.

Now all they could do was wait for the father to come looking for his missing boy.

After a few minutes with Linda in the X-ray room, Bryan was lying on one of a series of hospital beds that were crammed against one concrete wall of the small clinic. His boot was off, his leg in a brace. "Nothing's broken," Dr. Fletcher told his patient. "You were lucky this time."

"Don't feel lucky."

Fletcher chuckled. "Well, no, I imagine not."

Veronica felt a measure of relief for Bryan though she couldn't help remembering the little girl that had been rushed away by ambulance. The mountain had a way of taking its toll on young and old alike.

Unforgiving. Savage.

Gritting her teeth, she noticed the other patients. One woman in her sixties had twisted her ankle and seemed to think it was a snowboarder's fault for cutting her off and causing her to fall. "They shouldn't be allowed on the mountain," she asserted. "Dangerous, reckless wild kids who have no place on ski runs! I've been skiing for forty years and never seen the like. Rude. That's what they are. Should be barred!"

"Hey, I board and it's safer than skis," a teenage boy with long bleached hair and a splint on one arm chimed in.

A little girl wearing a thumb splint was waiting for her parents and a man in his twenties was being given pain relievers. His right arm was in a sling and the preliminary diagnosis was that his elbow was broken. An ambulance had already been called. "When's it gonna get here?" he demanded as Bryan stared at the ceiling.

There was something about the boy that tugged on Veronica's heart strings. Beneath his macho I-don't-give-a-damn attitude was a scared little kid. She could read it in his eyes whenever he glanced in her direction.

"Look, I've been here for half an hour," the twenty-year-old complained.

"The ambulance will be here soon," Fletcher remarked without looking up from the chart on which he was scribbling.

"I'm dying here."

"I don't think so."

"But there was already a vehicle."

"Which took away a little girl who was in worse shape than you," Fletcher snapped. "This isn't a cafeteria line where it's first come first served. Everything here is done by priority—the more serious the injury, the faster you get medical attention."

The patient rolled his eyes. "I'll never get out of here."

The nurse, Linda, a blond woman with a patient smile, said, "I know it feels like it, but it will be just—"

The doors burst open and two attendants stormed into the room. With a cold rush of air and the smell of exhaust was a glimpse of an ambulance, lights spinning eerily as it idled next to the clinic. "Here you go," Linda added, and without the least bit of wasted motion, the two attendants, dressed in ski coats and caps, hustled their charge into a wheelchair and out the door. Within seconds they were gone.

"Thank God," Linda muttered.

"So how're you doing?" Veronica asked Bryan.

"Fine," he mumbled and wouldn't look in her direction.

"You up here for the day?"

His gaze flattened as if he was bored. She could hear the words, *What's it to ya, lady? Buzz off!* though he hadn't uttered a sound.

"Well, good luck," she said. It was four o'clock and she was officially off duty. She could pick up Amy from the Snow Bunny area where the little girl had taken toddler ski lessons earlier. After the group lesson, Amy was fed lunch, then encouraged to nap on one of the cots placed around the play area. She spent what was left of the afternoon in a special day-care area of the lodge where she played with kids her age under supervised care.

Ronni had just started for the double doors when they flew open and banged against the wall. A tall man, mid-thirties from the looks of him, with harsh, chiseled features and dark hair dusted with snow, strode into the room as if he owned it. His mouth was turned down at the corners, his gray eyes dark with worry, his thick, unruly eyebrows slammed together in concern. "I'm looking for—" He stopped suddenly when he saw Bryan lying on one of the beds. "Thank God," he said, relief softening the hard angles of his face. His gloved hands opened and clenched in frustration. "Hell, Bryan, you gave me the scare of my life. I thought you might be dead or unconscious somewhere."

"May as well be," the boy responded. He glanced sullenly around the room, disdain radiating from him. "This place is about as lame as it gets."

"But you're okay?"

"He'll walk again." Syd extended his hand. "I'm Dr. Fletcher—"

The phone rang shrilly.

Linda answered it and waved to Fletcher. One hand over the receiver, she said, "It's Dr. Crenshaw. He wants information on the little girl who came in this morning with the injured spleen. Her name was—" She searched for a chart ——————————————. Excuse me for a second." Dr. Fletcher took the phone from the nurse's outstretched hand and turned his back on Bryan while he concentrated on the conversation. Meanwhile, Linda attended the older woman who was asking for a pain pill while she waited for her husband.

Keegan turned his attention to his son. "I thought I told you to meet me at the lodge."

Bryan scowled deeply. "I lost track of time."

"You've got a watch and the lifts have clocks at the bottom as well as the top."

"Yeah, I know, but I said I lost track of time," Bryan repeated sullenly.

Keegan rubbed a hand around the back of his neck in frustration. "It doesn't matter. You're all right and that's what I really care about, but why don't you fill me in? Tell me what happened, how you ended up here."

"I caught a little air and landed wrong."

"Where were you?"

Bryan didn't answer.

Veronica thought she had to step in. She didn't want to get the kid into trouble with this large man who looked as if he was barely hanging on to his patience, but it was important that they both realize how dangerous it is to ski in closed areas, how lucky Bryan was not to be in worse shape.

"I found him on Devil's Spine," she said, stepping to the other side of Bryan's bed.

"Devil's Spine?" the man echoed, seeing her for the first time. His troubled gaze centered on her face, hesitated, then dropped for an instant to skim her chest where her name tag was pinned.

"I'm Veronica Walsh, one of the rescue team."

He was staring into her eyes—flinty gray, the of storm clouds gathering over an angry ocean. "*You found Bryan?*"

"Yes." She bristled slightly as she always did when she came up against someone who didn't seem to think a woman could handle the job. But she held on to her temper as she realized he was upset about his son. Maybe he wasn't a first-class chauvinist.

"Where on earth is Devil's Spine?"

"North canyon," Bryan said.

"That's right. Because of the windy and icy conditions today, parts of the north side weren't groomed and the area around the spine, which is an expert run, was closed today."

"Closed?" Keegan repeated and his son's face hardened.

Feeling like a rat, Ronni did her duty. "I think Bryan might have been jumping from the top of the spine to the bottom. That's a drop of nearly ten feet." She stared at the kid. "Am I right?"

Bryan shrugged.

Keegan's mouth thinned into an unforgiving line and Ronni couldn't help comparing him to the mountain. *Fierce, savage, challenging.* Keegan's fingers tightened over the rail of the hospital bed as he stared at his son. "For the love of God, Bryan, what were you thinking?"

"Look, Mr. Keegan, people do it all the time, but not when the run's closed," she said, trying to soften the blow. Bryan's father needed to know that his son had broken the rules, but she didn't want to get the boy into big trouble. She touched Bryan on the shoulder and he flinched. His gaze was hard and accused her of being a traitor. "It turned out all right," she added. "Bryan was lucky."

"Lucky?" Bryan grumbled under his breath. "Lucky?" He rolled his eyes. "Why does everyone keep saying that? I've been so *lucky* lately, I can barely stand myself."

"That's enough," Travis said, embarrassed by the boy's lack of gratitude, even though this woman was getting under his skin a little. She was pretty, with all-American looks and a smile he found beguiling, but he didn't need her, or any woman, for that matter, messing with his mind. "The least you could do is thank these people for helping you," he said to his son. Then, despite his best efforts to hold his tongue, he added, "Geez, Bryan, what was going through your head? Why were you skiing where you shouldn't have been when you were supposed to meet me?"

A defiant light flared in his son's eyes and Travis gave himself a hard mental shake. The boy was hurting already and Travis needed to remember that Bryan was just a kid.

"Mr. Keegan?" a woman in a lab coat asked. Slightly overweight with short, straight, blond hair, she was sliding X rays into a large manila envelope.

"Yes?" His attention returned to the nurse.

"Hi, I'm Linda Knowlton and I've been working with Bryan." She grabbed a clipboard that hung suspended from the foot of Bryan's bed. "We have a few forms for you to fill out."

"Can I just get outta here?" Bryan complained.

"In a minute," Linda said patiently. Winking broadly, she clucked her tongue. "You're going to make me feel like you don't love us."

"I don't love...geez—" Bryan flopped back on the bed. "Nothin's busted. I don't see why we just can't leave."

"We will, once the doctor gives you the okay," Travis said, too relieved to be angry. When he'd split up from his son on the mountain a couple of hours ago, he hadn't panicked. Bryan was a good skier and they'd planned to meet at the lodge for a snack at two. He'd gotten in early, drunk a cup of coffee and when Bryan was late, Travis wasn't worried. Hell, the kid still let time slip away from him, but after an hour had passed, Travis had become concerned, and was on his way to the information desk when he'd been paged. His heart had nearly stopped. In his heavy ski boots, he'd sprinted through the carpeted hallways, shouldering past slower-moving people. In terrifying mind-numbing images, he'd imagined his son's broken and bent body, even his death.

Fletcher hung up the phone and walked back to Bryan's bed. "As I was saying, I'm Dr. Fletcher." Travis yanked off his ski glove and shook the shorter man's hand. About five-ten, Fletcher had lost a good amount of his hair. What remained was a clipped horseshoe of red blond strands which matched his thick moustache. "Your son's going to be fine, but I'm afraid he'll be laid up for a while." Quietly, while the nurse looked in on the patients in the other beds, Fletcher explained his concerns for Bryan's knee, the possible torn ligament and cartilage damage, though no bones appeared to be broken. "You might want to have an MRI on the knee and check with your orthopedic surgeon," he said. "If you don't have one, I recommend any one of these...." He opened the desk drawer, withdrew three business cards, including one of his own, and offered them to Travis. "I have a clinic in town myself." Winking at Bryan, he added. "I just moonlight up here."

"Thanks." Travis took the cards, then noticed Ronni stepping away from the bed.

She patted the top rail. "I'll see ya, Bryan." Smiling, she waved to the other people in the room. "Linda... Syd...that's it for me for the day. Someone else will have to bring you your next victims." Winding her rope of braided hair onto the crown of her head, she tugged on a ski hat. "See you next weekend."

"Not me, Ronni, I'm off, till after Christmas," the

nurse, who was placing a plastic cover on a thermometer, said. "Nancy and Cal are rotating through the holidays, so the only way you'll see me is if I need help getting down the mountain or medical assistance."

"Don't tell me you're going to spend your honeymoon back here?"

Linda shook her head and for an instant her eyes, behind her oversize glasses, gleamed. "Nope. Ben and I are going to Vegas and then spending a week at Timberline on Mount Hood, in the old lodge."

Ronni couldn't help smiling at the blush of romance in her friend's cheeks. Linda was forty-five, her children grown, her first husband a man who had walked out on her and the kids when they were still toddlers. Linda hadn't dated much over the years. All her time and energy had been devoted to her kids. But two years ago, she'd met Ben through a mutual friend. Now they were going to run away and get married. It almost made a person believe in romance again. Almost.

"So, if you're patrolling on Hood next weekend and see a downed skier in a hot-pink jumpsuit and a wedding veil—"

"Don't even think it," Ronni said, zipping up her jacket. "I guess I should say merry Christmas, as well as congratulations." She was tugging on her gloves.

"You, too. I hope little Amy gets everything she wants."

Ronni's smile faltered slightly before she managed to pin it back into place. "She wants a puppy. I think I'm doomed."

"I know someone who's got a litter. Blue Heeler and spaniel, I think. Call me if you're interested."

"I'm not, but Amy is. Give my best to Ben. Tell him he's lucky to have you for a bride."

"I remind him every day," Linda assured her before being summoned by the woman who was complaining about snowboarders ruining the runs for the skiers.

Ronni tossed a look to the boy with the sad eyes. "You, too, Bryan, have a good Christmas, and the next time you're up here, be sure to check the signs so you know which runs are open and which are closed." She glanced at the kid's father, an imposing man if she'd ever seen one. She'd give ten to one odds that he was a corporate big shot—all take-charge energy and impatience. An out-of-towner, coming to the mountain to unwind. Now, with his son injured, he was rattled. "Have a great holiday."

"It's not starting out so great, is it?" he asked, motioning to Bryan.

"Then it's bound to get better, right?" She offered him a smile that Linda had once told her could melt ice.

"Let's hope."

"'Bye."

Travis watched her leave. There was something about her that he found damnably fascinating. He, a man who had sworn off women. He, who had been through a gut-wrenching divorce that he still found painful. He, who didn't trust any female.

Suddenly hot, he unzipped his jacket and found his son staring up at him. "You want to tell me why you were skiing on a closed run?"

Bryan lifted a shoulder. "Not really."

"I'd like to know."

With a grunt, Bryan moved on the bed then winced. "What's the big deal?"

"It was unsafe. As you found out. The only reason they close a run is—"

"Yeah, I know, it's dangerous. I already heard the lecture. From her." He jutted his chin toward the empty spot where Ronni had stood only moments before.

"Fine." This was no place for an argument. From the corner of his eye, Travis watched Ronni shoulder her way through the double doors that swung slowly closed as she passed through. She didn't bother looking over her shoulder as she found her skis and poles, which had been propped against the outside of the building. Then the doors swung shut.

"How are you doing?" Dr. Fletcher, looking harried, was back at Bryan's bedside.

Shrugging, Bryan mumbled, "Okay, I guess."

"I've prescribed some pain pills, just enough for the next couple of days. You might not even need them." He looked at Travis. "Bryan's young and strong. This will slow him down for a while, but he'll be up and around and probably be able to ski by next season."

"Next year?" Bryan said, closing his eyes in disappointment. "Oh, man."

"And you might be prescribed a special brace to wear when you're involved in sports."

"No way!"

Fletcher grinned. "They're not too bad, really. I wear one myself."

Glowering, Bryan's eyes silently accused the doctor of having to resort to such a device because Fletcher was old.

Fletcher didn't seem to notice. "Let's not jump the gun. Wait and see what your orthopedic doctor suggests."

Bryan swallowed and blinked.

"Feelin' rough?" Travis asked, laying a hand on his son's head.

"Like sh—horrible." Bryan slid away from his touch.

"It'll get better."

Suddenly, the doors swung open and a woman, dressed in a silky aqua jumpsuit, hurried into the clinic. Her nose wrinkled in disgust at the concrete floor and tight quarters. "I'm Wanda Tamarack. Is my daughter, Justice—"

"Mommy!" The girl nursing her sprained thumb sent up a wail loud enough to wake the dead in another continent.

"Dear God." Wanda hurried past the desk and around a curtain to spy her daughter stretched out on one of the beds. "Oh, honey, what happened?" Wanda asked.

"Sprained thumb," the nurse replied. "I have some forms you'll have to—"

"We've got to get you to a specialist. Oh, baby, does it hurt?" The woman went on and on, and her daughter, under control a few minutes before, began to fall apart. Her lower lip quivered and tears drizzled down her cheeks. "Oh, sweetheart, don't cry. Mommy's here and we'll get you out of this awful place." The woman's diamond earrings flashed in the wavering light from the fluorescent tubes mounted high on the ceiling.

Bryan rolled his eyes at the woman's flair for the dramatic—so like Sylvia, his mother.

"See, it could be worse," Travis whispered into his son's ear. "Wanda could be taking you home with her."

"Ugh!" Bryan almost cracked a smile before he tried to move his leg and sucked in his breath in a hiss of pain.

"We'll take care of that," Travis promised. "You'll be okay."

"You think so?" Bryan retorted. Scowling down at the brace surrounding his knee, Bryan gritted his teeth. "No matter what you say, Travis, this Christmas is going to be the pits!"

CHAPTER THREE

"WATCH OUT, MOMMY." Amy gave the toy tugboat a push and it plowed through the high mounds of bubbles surrounding Veronica as she soaked her tired muscles. Amy was standing on tiptoe on the bath mat, leaning over the side of the tub, precariously close to falling face first into the suds and drenching herself all over again.

"*You* watch out," Ronni warned.

Already bathed, her hair still damp from her recent shampoo, her body snug in red-and-white elf pajamas that Ronni had found on sale, Amy was happily splashing the warm water.

"You're getting soaked!"

Amy giggled.

"Come on, let's get out of the bathroom." So much for the relaxing bath. "How about a hot cup of lemonade?"

"With strawberries?"

Ronni plopped a mound of suds onto Amy's tiny nose. "If that's what you want."

Amy's impish grin stretched wide. "Hurry, Mommy, get out!" Amy cried, already scampering into the living room, the red-and-blue tugboat forgotten.

Ronni pulled the plug and reached for a towel. She rubbed the water and suds from her body and called after her daughter, "First the lemonade, then will you read me a bedtime story?"

Footsteps echoed from the hallway and Amy stuck her head around the corner. "You're silly, Mommy."

"And so are you." Rotating the kinks from her neck, she dropped her towel into the hamper and stepped into a thick terry-cloth bathrobe. Amy was off again and Ronni heard the distinctive click of the refrigerator door opening.

"Wait for me," she called as she cinched the belt of her robe. Barefoot, she followed Amy's trail of forgotten and dripping toys. Scooping up each sodden piece of plastic, she smiled. Amy was so innocent; such a joy. Ronni couldn't imagine her growing up and developing into a teenager with an attitude like the boy, Bryan, who'd been injured today. Not that he was all bad. Veronica had seen through his bravado and witnessed the pain in his eyes, the fear contorting his features when she'd helped him off the mountain.

His father was a different sort, she thought as she lifted her hair away from her neck and tied it with the ribbon she kept in the pocket of her robe. It was clear he'd been torn between anger with Bryan for his rude remarks and relief that the kid was in one piece. There was something about him that nagged at her and it wasn't just the fact that he was so sensually masculine. Though she'd tried to deny it earlier, she couldn't lie to herself. He was tall and lean, with wide shoulders, thick neck and blade-thin lips. His hair, unruly from a stocking cap, was a deep brown and straight, his nose slightly crooked, his eyebrows thick and harsh over intense eyes. Handsome, yes. Sexy, undeniably. And trouble of the worst order. He looked like the kind of man who barked out orders to underlings.

But he did care about his kid. That much was obvious and that won him points with Ronni. Big points. Not that she'd ever see him again. So what was it about him that was so disturbing, so fascinating, if that was the right word? For what had remained of the afternoon, she'd thought about him, unable to shake his image from the corners of her mind. Had she seen him before somewhere? Certainly she would have remembered such a take-charge individual. What was it about him? "Stupid woman," she muttered. What did she care?

"Who's a stupid woman?" Amy asked, her cheeks flushed as she made the drawers into stair steps and climbed onto the counter.

"Your mama, she's the stupid woman, but only sometimes. Hey, you know you're not supposed to do that. I'll get the lemonade." She reached for the tin and spooned healthy tablespoons into a couple of mugs before adding water and placing both cups into the microwave.

Travis Keegan had been all business, worried about his son and seeming a bit lost with this aspect of fathering, as if he was more at home at the head of a boardroom table than dealing with a teenage boy.

She plucked a couple of last year's strawberries from a bag in the freezer and, once the lemonade had heated, dropped the frozen berries into the now-steaming cups. "I'll carry," she said to her daughter. "You go pick out the book."

Amy was off, sorting through a basket of toys and books as Ronni settled into a corner of the couch. She placed the lemonade on the coffee table as Amy returned dragging five of her favorite bedtime stories.

"We don't have the tree decorated yet," Amy complained as she stood on the couch and pressed her nose to the windowpane. The tree they'd picked out from a local stand was propped against the rail of the porch. Amy's breath fogged the glass as she peered at it.

"I know. We'll do it tomorrow."

"Now."

"Not now. I just got clean from taking care of the horses. If I started fooling around with the tree, I'd probably get pitch all over me, and so would you. Besides, you wanted some strawberry lemonade."

Amy wasn't really listening. Once she got an idea in her head, that particular notion was set in concrete. "Katie Pendergrass's daddy did theirs after church on Sunday."

"Do you think he'd come and help me with ours?" Veronica teased, touching her daughter on her crown of silky curls.

"Why not?"

Veronica laughed, then sipped from her cup. "He probably has a dozen reasons."

"You could call him."

"No way, José. Tomorrow we'll put up the tree and we'll manage alone."

Amy's face fell in on itself and a sly look came into her round eyes. Veronica braced herself. Though not yet five, Amy had already learned about feminine wiles and how to wheedle to get what she wanted. It was annoying—being manipulated by a four-year-old. "But I want a tree."

"You'll have one. That one." Veronica tapped on the window with her fingernail and pointed at the rugged little fir. She couldn't help noticing that the lights were on in the Johnson place again and she wondered if she had permanent neighbors or people who were just hanging out at the old lodge for the holidays. She still thought they might be trespassers, people camping out and gaining free rent. *Or maybe they're here to stay.*

"I want one today," Amy insisted, drawing Ronni back to the conversation about the Christmas tree. She picked up her lemonade, took a sip and lost interest again.

"Tomorrow," Veronica said firmly. "I'll tell you what, though, we can put up the stockings tonight."

"Can we?" The storm clouds in her daughter's eyes suddenly disappeared.

"Mmm. See if you can find them."

"In one of the boxes?" Amy said, already squirming from the couch, her feet in motion as they hit the floor.

"That's right."

Amy started rummaging through the old cardboard crates. Ronni took a final sip from her cup, then stepped into her slippers and cinched the robe a little tighter around her middle. By the time she crossed the room, there were ornaments, tinsel, strings of lights and tissue paper all over the floor.

"Hey, slow down," she admonished, eyeing the decorations and frowning. "I know they were in a white box with—"

"Here they are!" Amy yanked two stockings out of a box and held them up proudly. One was red with felt-and-sequin angels, holly and hearts on it, the other green and decorated with a miniature baseball bat and glove, Santa face and reindeer.

Veronica's heart wrenched painfully. Memories assailed her and she remembered Hank had worked overtime for two months each evening that first fall after they had married. While dinner was simmering on the stove and she was waiting up for him, she'd spent her evenings watching television and working on her secret projects, lovingly sewing the felt pieces and sequins together by hand. The red stocking was hers, the green had belonged to Hank. She'd never had the heart to throw his away. "Oh, honey…well, isn't there another one—white, I think?"

Amy dropped the first two on the floor and tossed out the Christmas-tree skirt before discovering the third stocking—white felt decorated with a rocking horse, teddy bear and mistletoe. Sequins glittered under the lights. "Here's mine!" Amy cried, waving the stocking like a banner while Veronica picked up the scattered decorations.

"Let's hang yours and mine on the mantel," Veronica suggested, her voice thick as she placed Hank's stocking back into the box. She closed the lid and her memories of their first Christmas with Amy, who, barely able to sit up, had stared at the lighted tree with wide, wondrous eyes.

Together, Veronica and Amy draped the stockings from the nails that were permanently driven into the mortar just below the mantel and Veronica tried not to notice that one nail was vacant, a reminder that their family was no longer three.

She tucked a damp curl behind her ear. Maybe Amy was right. They could get a puppy this Christmas and in the coming year she could construct the dog's own stocking so that it wouldn't be quite so obvious that there was a void in their lives.

"They're beautiful, Mommy," Amy said proudly as

she gazed at the glittery socks, their toes nearly touching the curved top of the fireplace screen.

"And think how nice they'll look when we put the fir boughs and holly on the mantel. Come on, now, time for bed."

Amy went through her ablutions, standing on a stool while brushing her teeth, wiping her face and extra toothpaste onto a wet towel, then climbing the stairs to the loft. At her bed, she fell to her knees and began to pray, saying the usual "God Blesses" for Aunt Shelly, Uncle Vic, her twin cousins and Veronica. She paused a moment, then added, "And please, God, bring me a puppy for Christmas and a new daddy so my mommy won't be so sad. Amen." Scrambling off her knees, she climbed into bed and slid between the covers.

Veronica didn't move. Her heart felt like lead in her chest. "Oh, honey," she whispered around a lump of tears caught in her throat. "Mommy's not sad. I've got you."

"But you miss Daddy."

"I'll always miss him," she said, kissing Amy's crown of dark curls, "but that's okay. Besides, you remind me of him every day. Aren't we happy together?"

"Happy," Amy repeated around a yawn as she threw an arm around her one-eyed stuffed tiger.

"I'll see you in the morning." Veronica smoothed a hair away from Amy's face and sighed. It was time to stop grieving, time to let go. Hank was gone, his life lost on the slopes of Mount Echo, and for the past few years Ronni had held her grief and anger inside, blaming herself, blaming the mountain, blaming the company who'd sent him the new bindings and demo skis, trying to find a reason that her husband, not yet thirty years old, had been stolen from her.

Determined to start over and push the pain of losing Hank into a dark, locked part of her heart, she walked down the stairs from the loft and eyed the pile of paperwork on her desk. Letters to be answered, orders to be filled, invoices to be paid. She should be thrilled, she supposed; her cottage business was taking off. Ronni did most of the legwork finding new items, putting together the catalog, locating new outlets, while her sister Shelly handled the day-to-day business of boxing and filling orders. Between the business, her part-time job at the mountain and Amy, Ronni didn't have time to house-train a new puppy, let alone search for a new man. Not that she needed one. She could be both mother and father to her little girl.

Then why was Amy praying for a new daddy?

"He'll be okay," Travis said, assuring his ex-wife that their son was still in one piece. He'd made the call from the first phone booth he'd found near the hamburger joint where they'd had dinner. "The doctor on the mountain thought the injury was more serious than it was, but the specialist we saw tonight in Portland is more optimistic. Bryan will be laid up a week or so because the tendons are stretched and there's some damage to the ligament, but it's hanging together and the cartilage damage doesn't look as bad as was originally thought."

"You're not just trying to make me feel better?" Sylvia asked in her pouty, accusing voice.

Travis closed his eyes and didn't give in to the urge to ask her why a woman who'd walked out on her son and husband years before would feel guilty or bad about the kid's latest injury. "No. I just thought you'd want to know." God, what time was it in France? Why was she still up?

"Why didn't you call earlier? The accident happened, what—sometime yesterday?"

"I didn't want to worry you. Besides, we didn't really know how laid up he'd be."

"So you wait until the middle of the night?" she said around a yawn.

"Sorry." Travis glanced to the dark sky. He couldn't explain that he'd been too busy to call. Things had changed since Bryan's injury; the old "fixer-upper" lodge was no longer quaint. He'd spent hours with contractors and movers, making the house as livable as possible.

"Can I talk to him?" Sylvia asked.

Rain pounded on the small, open telephone booth. Travis gauged the distance to the Jeep and nearly laughed. "Not right now. I'm in a phone booth and he's in the car, but I'll have him call you as soon as the phones are installed at the house."

"Tell him I love him," Sylvia ordered.

"Will do." Travis hung up and sighed. Ducking his head against an icy gust of wind, he strode to the Jeep and climbed inside where the radio was blasting some bass-throbbing hard-rock song. Bryan sat slumped against the passenger window and was staring through the glass. Traffic roared by, splashing water and dirt into the parking lot of the fast-food restaurant where they'd stopped for burgers after a lengthy session with the orthopedic surgeon. Though he would have to take it easy for a few weeks, Bryan would heal quickly. Things were looking up—or should have been, though Bryan had slipped back into his sullen you-can't-make-me-care-about-anything mood.

"Okay, cowboy, let's go," Travis said, turning the volume-control dial of the radio so that the riff of an electric guitar didn't threaten to burst his eardrums. Twisting in his seat, he watched for other traffic as he backed the vehicle out of the lot. Shifting into first, he nosed the Jeep into the steady stream of cars, trucks and buses heading east toward the ridge of mountains that weren't visible in the dark. "Your mom sends her love."

Bryan made a sound of disgust in the back of his throat.

"She wants you to call her when the phone's hooked up."

"She can call me."

"Bryan—"

"She took off. Not me," he charged angrily.

"It's ancient history," Travis said, but didn't add anything else. Obviously, Bryan still felt abandoned, though his perspective wasn't quite on the money. True, Sylvia had packed up and moved to Paris, but she still cared about her son—in her own, odd way.

"And I'm not a cowboy," Bryan grumbled.

Travis wasn't about to argue as he concentrated on the drive. Red beams of taillights smeared through the wet windshield as the traffic cruised along, steadily climbing through the forested foothills and across bridges spanning icy rivers. They drove through several small towns along the way and eventually the rain turned to snow that stuck to the pavement and gave a white glow to the otherwise black night.

Traffic thinned as vehicles pulled off at two ski areas that were lit up like proverbial Christmas trees. Night skiers were racing down the slopes, one of which was visible from the highway.

Soon they were nearly alone on the road. The quiet, snow-blanketed hills were soothing to Travis and he wondered why he'd clung to big-city life for so long, why chasing the dollar had been so damned important to him? When, exactly, had he lost touch with what was really meaningful in life?

"Tell me about the woman who helped you down the mountain," he said, wondering why he'd thought about her several times in the past couple of days.

"What about her?"

"Her name is Veronica, right?"

Bryan scowled. "Ronni." He reached for the volume-control dial, but a sharp look from Travis caused him to settle back against the cushions. A permanent scowl was etched across his face. "Why do you want to know?"

"I think I owe her a thank-you."

"So send her a card."

"I'd like to talk to her."

"Oh, brother. Why?"

Good question. One that had been bothering him ever since she'd flashed that blinding smile of hers in his direction. "Just curious, I guess."

"Don't tell me you've got a thing for her."

"A thing?" Travis couldn't help the amusement in his voice.

"She's not your type," Bryan muttered.

"My type?" Travis grinned in the darkness of the Jeep. "Who's my type?"

Bryan glared through the glass, watching as snow-flakes were batted away by the wipers. "You know, Dad, I don't really think you have a type. Or maybe you shouldn't. Your track record with women isn't all that great."

Travis couldn't argue the point. The few dates he'd had since his divorce from Sylvia could only be described as nightmares. But then, he wasn't looking for a woman to go out with. He just wanted to tell Ronni Whatever-her-name-was that he appreciated her helping his injured son. That was all there was to it. Nothing else and certainly nothing romantic.

He'd learned long ago that romance, if it existed at all, wasn't for him. No woman, not even one as intriguing as Veronica with the thick rope of dark hair and a smile as warm as morning sunshine could change that one simple inalienable fact.

"So we can count on you and Amy for Christmas?" Shelly asked as she shoved the final box into the back of her battered old station wagon. She and Veronica had spent the past twelve hours packing the last of the orders to be shipped for Christmas, while Amy had "helped" stuff packing into boxes or sat coloring or played in the snow-covered yard between the house and garage-warehouse.

"Sure," Veronica said. "Why not?"

"Because you hate the holidays," her sister said as she searched in her purse and pulled out a heavy ring of keys. Three inches shorter and twenty pounds heavier than her sister, Shelly was blessed with the same dark hair and eyes, but a more rounded, softer face, larger breasts and more than the start of a belly that she'd never lost after her pregnancy with the twins, who were now six and hell on wheels.

"I love Christmas," Ronni argued.

"Sure you do. That's why you're always vowing to go to Mexico or Brazil or the Bahamas every year."

"Idle threats."

"I know, but I just wanted to make sure you'd be around. Vic and I are counting on you, and the boys would die if Amy wasn't coming."

"Sure. I'll bring the rum cake and spiced cider and molded salad."

Shelly grinned. "Just bring Amy. And maybe a date."

"A date?" Veronica laughed at the absurdity of it. Just like Shelly to suggest something so silly. "On Christmas Eve? Oh, sure. Just let me check my little black book."

"Come on, Ronni." Shelly slammed the tailgate and climbed into the front seat. "You must meet lots of cute, eligible bachelor types up on the mountain."

"I do. But they're usually wearing casts and using crutches," Veronica teased.

"Think about it."

"Oh, right. Long and hard," Veronica said as Shelly buckled her seat belt and closed the door.

Shelly twisted the key in the ignition. The old car wheezed, sputtered and died. Pumping the gas several times, Shelly winked at her sister and tried again. A plume of blue smoke shot from the exhaust and Shelly rolled down the window. She patted the dashboard fondly. "Hasn't let me down yet."

"Knock on wood."

"See ya tomorrow." Shelly shifted into first and was off, the station wagon gently coasting along the lane that wound through the trees.

A date? Trust Shelly to come up with some lame-brained idea. Veronica smiled as she watched the blue car disappear past a thicket of fir trees. No matter what her troubles, Shelly always looked on the bright side of life. Though her husband, Victor, who had been a sawyer for a mill that had shut down last winter, was still unemployed, Shelly refused to worry. Victor managed to make a little money doing odd jobs. He chopped and hauled firewood or helped out at the gas station in town when the crew was shorthanded. Right now he spent his time down at the D&E Christmas Tree Lot, helping Delmer and Edwin Reese sell natural, flocked and even some artificial trees. Shelly just wasn't one to dwell on her troubles. "As long as there's bread on the table and gas in the tank, we don't need much more," Shelly was fond of saying. "The Lord has a way of providing for everyone."

Ronni crossed her fingers and hoped Shelly was right. She spied Amy drawing in the snow with a stick. "Come on, let's go feed Lucy and Sam," she said, motioning in the direction of the barn. Both horses were standing outside, their winter coats thick and shaggy, their ears turned back as they stood beneath one of the fir trees in the paddock.

"Can't we make a snowman first?" Amy said, her little face crumpling in disappointment. "You promised."

"That I did," Veronica said, even though she was dead-tired.

"And put up the tree?"

"Another promise that won't be broken." If only she had her daughter's seemingly endless supply of energy. "Come on, we'd better get started."

They spent the next half hour rolling snowballs, piling them on top of each other and sculpting Mr. Snowman's face and belly. The result was a decent enough

Frosty, especially when he was given a stocking cap, carrot nose and stones for eyes.

Setting up the tree proved more difficult. After the horses were locked into the barn and fed and watered, Ronni and Amy struggled with the little fir tree. Veronica had to keep biting her tongue to keep from swearing as she tried to adjust the trunk in the stand while attempting to keep the tree standing as close to straight as possible. "You know, when Uncle Vic sold us this tree, I thought it was straight," she grumbled. "I don't know what happened." When she was finally finished, she decided to prop the tree in a corner so that it wasn't so obvious that it still listed.

For dinner they ate home-baked pizza and after the dishes were done, Ronni took a quick shower. Amy helped her string lights, popcorn and ornaments. The red tinsel that Amy had used as a boa a few nights earlier was draped in the appropriate places. But there was no star or angel for the top of the tree. "We'll find one at the bazaar." Veronica promised as she turned out all the overhead lights. Amy was sitting in the big wooden rocker—the one Hank had built before his daughter was born—and staring at the tree as Veronica plugged in the electrical cord. Hundreds of miniature lights sparked to life.

"Oooh," Amy breathed, clapping her hands together. "It's *sooo* pretty." Her face glowed in the reflection of the tree lights.

"That it is. You did a good job."

The doorbell chimed and Veronica nearly jumped out of her skin. "Who in the world…?" she asked, glancing out the window to the porch. Travis Keegan, holding a bag, one shoulder propped against the door frame stood under the porch light. Snowflakes clung to his hair and the shoulders of his battered aviator jacket, and his expression was set, grim and determined, no hint of a smile in his beard-shadowed jaw. For a second she thought that something was wrong, that something must have happened to his injured son and her heart leaped to her throat. That poor kid—then Keegan's gaze touched hers through the glass and her heart jolted. His eyes were intense and bright and his expression softened a bit.

"Who is it, Mommy?"

"A man I met last Sunday."

Amy scampered across the room but Ronni barely paid attention. She was struck by the same feeling of power in him that she'd recognized in the clinic. His features were large, chiseled, all male, and the tiny lines near the corners of his mouth indicated he'd frowned too many times in the past few years and a deep-seated harshness had developed. Yet there was something in his eyes that suggested a kinder man who wanted to learn how to smile again. Never, since Hank's death had she been attracted to another man. Travis Keegan seemed about to change all that. She couldn't help but notice the way his faded jeans hugged his hips, the wayward lock of hair that fell forward over his forehead or the tiny scar near the corner of one eye.

So what was he doing on her porch?

There was only one way to find out. Bracing herself, she yanked open the door. Wind, cold and raw, swept into the room.

"Is something wrong?" she asked.

"Wrong? No." Black eyebrows slanted together.

"But—" She sounded like a ninny. "Then why are you here?"

For the first time, a hint of a smile pulled at the corner of his mouth. "Everything's fine, it's just that I thought I owed you a thank-you…or something for seeing that Bryan got down the mountain safely. Everything happened so quickly, I didn't have a chance earlier." He hesitated, shook his head and smiled.

So he did have a kinder side.

A blush climbed up his neck and Ronni swallowed a smile of her own. Keegan didn't look like the kind of man to show any kind of embarrassment. "Now, to tell you the truth, I feel like a damned fool," he said.

"That makes two of us. No one ever stops by here at night, and when I saw you, I thought that something might have happened to your son, though why you'd be on my porch—" She tossed back her head and laughed. "Forgive me. I've been accused of being a pessimist, worrywart, you name it." She stepped out of the doorway, "Come in, we were just admiring our work." Still holding the door, she motioned to the little tree with her chin. "And before you say anything, the Christmas tree is straight, it's the house that's crooked."

By this time, Amy, curiosity being one of her primary personality traits, was hiding behind her mother like a skittish foal, while peeking around her legs and sizing up Travis, who was still standing on the other side of the threshold.

"So who are you?" Keegan said, bending a knee so that he could look Amy square in the eye.

"Who are *you*?" Amy repeated, refusing to answer.

"I guess it's time for formal introductions," Ronni said. "Travis Keegan, this is my daughter, Amy. And

Amy, this is Mr. Keegan. He has a son, Bryan, who was hurt on the mountain a couple of days ago. I helped take Bryan to the clinic."

"You can call me Travis."

Amy's eyebrows drew together in concentration and cold air swirled into the house. "Where's Bryan?"

"At home," Travis replied as he straightened and his gaze touched Ronni's again.

"Come on in before we all freeze." She stood aside to let him pass, only then noticing that there was no truck or car parked anywhere nearby, though the snow was broken by a steady path of footprints leading into the woods. For the first time, she felt a drip of fear slide down her spine.

Still on the porch, he stomped the snow from his boots while Veronica kicked herself for asking a total stranger into the house, one who'd appeared on her doorstep like a vagabond, one whom she knew nothing about other than he had a son, could afford to go skiing and wore expensive jeans.

"You walked here?" she asked before softly closing the door. Surely she could trust him. If not, there was Hank's old deer rifle. But it was unloaded and locked in a crate in the attic. Not too handy. But then, Veronica didn't believe in owning a gun. She just hadn't been able to sell any of Hank's beloved personal belongings, including the rifle his father had bought him for his sixteenth birthday.

"It didn't seem to make much sense to drive," Keegan said. He opened the bag and withdrew a chilled bottle of wine—chardonnay—which he handed her. "To say thanks," he explained. "And to get better acquainted, I guess. We're neighbors."

"Neighbors? I don't understand, where do you…?" she asked, but a sense of dread told her she already knew the answer.

"I bought Cyrus Johnson's old place a few weeks ago. Signed the papers and picked up the keys on the tenth and Bryan and I moved in just last week."

CHAPTER FOUR

TRAVIS WATCHED AS Ronni's face drained of color.

"Ick!" the little girl, Amy, said, staring up at him with round, horrified eyes. "It's creepy there!"

"Creepy?" Travis smothered a smile because the imp was so vehement in her appraisal of his new home.

"Shh!" Ronni sent her daughter a glance meant to hold the girl's tongue, but it didn't work. The precocious kid had to get in her two cents' worth.

"It's scary. Gots bugs and snakes and—"

"Amy! Please." Forcing a tentative smile, Ronni shook her head as Amy rambled on.

"Probably ghosts, too."

Some of Travis's doubts about hiking over here disappeared. He'd argued with himself long and hard about visiting the intriguing woman who had helped save his boy, and in the end rational thought had lost to curiosity and a desire to get to know more about her. No woman had interested him, really interested him, in a long, long while. "Ghosts?" he repeated, raising his eyebrows. "At my house?"

Wide-eyed Amy nodded with the heartfelt conviction of the young. "Lots of 'em!"

Keegan winked at her. "Haven't seen any yet."

"So you bought the old Johnson place," Ronni said, and he imagined a note of discouragement in her voice.

Amy made a big production of rolling her eyes. "You'll see," she predicted.

"There are no ghosts!" Ronni said as she set the bottle of wine on a side table in the cozy little house.

"It doesn't matter if the house is haunted or not," Travis said as he stuffed his gloves into his jacket pocket. "Even if there was a battalion of ghosts and goblins, Bryan's in such a black mood these days, he's probably scared them off." Frowning to himself, he unzipped his jacket.

"Mommy said no one would buy the old lodge 'cause it was too 'spensive."

Ronni let out a little gasp, then in an effort to change the subject, said, "Why don't you tell me how you found me since I don't remember giving out my address to anyone?"

He felt a grin tug at the corners of his mouth. "That required all of my detective skills, I'm afraid. It took hours, and I finally was forced to take drastic measures. I had to look you up in the telephone directory."

Chuckling, she tightened the belt of her robe around her slim waist. "Sometimes I think this town's too small." She was nervous and he didn't blame her. Aside from having to deal with the little girl, she had to make small talk with a virtual stranger who had trudged through the snow and appeared on her doorstep. Walking over here tonight was a mistake, a half-baked idea that had entered his head and wouldn't be dislodged, no matter how hard he'd tried to talk himself out of it. From the moment he'd seen her leave the clinic, he'd hoped to meet her again. And he wasn't the kind of man to sit idly by while time slipped away. He was and always had been a man of action.

"I think I should apologize for my daughter," she said as Amy played with some ornaments on the tree and yawned loudly.

"Why?"

She gazed fondly at the little girl. "Sometimes Amy is a little forward, if you didn't notice."

"She's just a kid," he observed. "Remember, I've got a teenage son." He offered her a knowing smile. "Believe me, it only gets worse."

"Great!" she said sarcastically. "And I was hoping with maturity, things would improve."

"Not for a long, long time." He eyed her speculatively. Her hair, piled onto her head, was damp and curling around her face, her skin flushed as if she'd just stepped out of the shower. The thought of her naked body caused a tightening deep in his gut and he shifted his gaze away from her face and the wicked turn of his mind. "But if I were you, I wouldn't do too much apologizing for that one." He motioned toward Amy. "I'd rather meet a kid who wasn't afraid to talk to adults, to ask questions, to speak his or her mind. It's the quiet ones I wonder about."

The little girl yawned again and Ronni took her cue.

"Just let me put her to bed and we can have a glass of wine or, if you'd prefer, hot strawberry lemonade— Amy's favorite."

"I'm not tired," Amy complained, her heavy-lidded eyes belying her words.

"You never are. Come on, I'll read you a quick story."

"No night-night." Amy started to scramble away, but Veronica scooped her up and carried her, protesting loudly, up the stairs. He heard voices, Ronni's calm and even, the little girl's louder and more insistent as he removed his boots and jacket. His conscience pricked at him because he knew he was disturbing their night-time ritual that Ronni, dressed in the soft bathrobe, was ready to settle in for the evening rather than entertain. But he hadn't been able to keep himself away, especially when he'd learned they were neighbors.

Within minutes, she was hurrying down the stairs, but she'd taken the time to replace her robe with a sweater and pair of black jeans. "You didn't have to change," he said, feeling even more like an intruder.

"No problem. I was just being lazy because I took my shower so early. Come on, I'll get a couple of glasses and we'll have a drink by the fire." With a fleeting smile, she padded barefoot into the kitchen area where she searched in a drawer and muttered to herself. "I know it's in here somewhere. Ah—*Voilà!* I've captured the elusive beast!" With a flourish, she held up the corkscrew. Dark eyes assessed him and her full mouth curved into an easy, heart-stopping smile. "Half the battle is won. You can do the honors while I find glasses." She tossed him the corkscrew.

As he uncorked the bottle, he wondered if this is what his subconscious had planned when he'd stopped by the little deli down the road and bought the wine.

"I guess I should explain about my daughter's comments earlier," Ronni said as he worked the cork free. "Amy and I walked over to the lake last summer and Amy didn't think much of the lodge. She let her imagination run away with her."

"The house does need a lot of work."

"Mmm, but it's beautiful over there. I remember when the Johnsons lived there. My dad was the care-taker for a while." Was there a touch of regret in her voice? She stood on tiptoe while trying to reach the wineglasses gathering dust on an upper shelf. "We lived in the cottage on the south side of the lake. It's still there, but in worse shape than the main house."

"Here, I'll get those." He was close enough to smell the scent of soap clinging to her and noticed the way her sweater hugged her breasts as she reached her hands over her head to pluck the glasses from the shelf. Clearing his throat, he handed her two glasses, which she rinsed quickly in the sink and then dried with a clean cloth.

"I, um, haven't used these in a while." A trace of wistfulness crossed her features and he caught her coffee brown gaze in his. Quickly glancing away, she poured the wine, then touched the rim of her glass to his. "To new neighbors?" she asked.

He nodded. "And no more skiing accidents."

"Amen." Again that note of muted misery.

As he sipped, he took stock of the house. A tipsy Christmas tree glowed with the colored lights strung through its boughs, and stockings—two of them—hung from the mantel. A fire warmed the grate and Travis, while drinking his wine, looked for signs of a man on the premises. But the coatrack held only two ski jackets—one for a woman of Ronni's size, the other for a small child. The same was true of the skis mounted near the back door. No oversize male boots warming by the fire, no magazines targeted for men spread on the coffee table, no hunting trophies displayed on the wall or baseball bats or other sporting equipment tucked in any corners, no newspaper lying open to the sports page.

If there was a Mr. Walsh, he'd definitely made himself scarce.

Feeling out of place, Travis sat in an old rocker and she settled into a corner of the couch. "So, you've lived here, I mean in Cascadia, a long time," he remarked, remembering her comment about the caretaker's house.

"Born and bred here. I'm a native and so's Amy."

"Family nearby?"

If she thought his questions were too personal, she didn't show it. "Just my sister, Shelly. She lives closer to town with her husband, Victor, and their two boys. Twins, a couple of years older than Amy. They keep Shelly hopping." Leaning back, her dark hair falling in restless tangles that tumbled over her shoulder and curled over the swell of her breast, she studied the wine in her glass as if it held the secrets of the universe. "My folks are both gone," she said sadly as she twirled the stem of her glass between long, ringless fingers. "Dad had a heart attack years ago and didn't survive. Mom eventually remarried, moved to California and died a few years later. Breast cancer."

"I'm sorry."

"So am I," she said, growing contemplative. "So am I."

"What about Amy's father?"

She started, then stared at him as if he'd trespassed on private property. "Hank?" Sighing softly, she glanced up to the mantel where a photograph was mounted. Captured by the camera's eye, a handsome blond man in a plaid shirt, worn jeans and hiking boots was holding an infant and grinning proudly as he stood backdropped by snow-laden fir trees.

"He died." Amy's voice floated down from her hiding spot on the landing. Clutching a beat-up stuffed animal that might have—considering the yellow-and-black stripes—once been a tiger, she peered through the rails.

"What are you doing up?" Veronica asked, her voice firm as she cleared her throat and seemed to chase away the melancholy thoughts that had gathered around her at the mention of her husband. But the sight of her child caused her eyes to twinkle and Travis suspected that the imp could get away with murder.

"He asked about Daddy."

"I know," Ronni said quickly.

Amy pointed a chubby finger in Travis's general direction. "Mommy misses Daddy. She cries sometimes—"

"Amy!" Horrified, Ronni set her glass on the table. "It's way past your bedtime. Tell Mr. Keegan goodnight." Her cheeks burned bright and she blinked rapidly as she hurried up the stairs. Amy scrambled ahead of her and Travis was left with a half-full glass of wine and an inkling that he'd stepped over an invisible and very private line, one he should never have crossed.

"I don't want to sleep!" Amy cried, her voice trailing down the stairs.

"I know, but it's time. Settle down, honey."

Restless, Travis climbed to his feet. He walked to the tree, lit so brightly and decorated with unique ornaments that were, for the most part, hand-crafted. Strings of popcorn and cranberries were woven between the branches, so unlike the trees they'd had in Seattle.

Sylvia had always called an interior decorating company that had supplied the tree—usually a gargantuan noble fir decorated with a theme and sporting shiny ornaments, metallic bows and glittery tinsel. One year, every decoration had been gold on a white flocked tree; the next year had been red balls and ribbons on snow-dusted bows. But the most memorable had been a flocked blue tree with navy and silver ornaments that had fascinated Bryan when he was about six. He'd played with the ornaments until several broke and then he wasn't allowed in the living room until Christmas morning, after the annual office staff party where everyone from the company was invited to their house to ooh and aah over the elaborate decor and pick at catered trays of hors d'oeuvres and fill their rented glasses from fountains of champagne.

As Travis thought about it now, he cringed. The holidays had come and gone but they'd held no soul. Christmas had been a time for spending a lot of money and putting on a show. New Year's Eve had been a day to hand out bonuses and party long into the night. All that was about to change. This year was going to be different. In the extreme.

Veronica, blowing her bangs from her eyes, hurried down the stairs. "It's official. Amy's down for the night. Exhaustion won over curiosity, thank God."

"I should probably get a move on, anyway." Standing, he reached for his jacket. "I don't want to leave Bryan alone too long."

She didn't argue, just walked him to the door. "Thanks for the wine," she said after he'd slid into his boots and zipped his jacket. "It wasn't necessary."

"I know, but, to tell you the truth, I wanted to see you again."

"You did? Why?"

He stared at her a moment and her brown eyes seemed to reach into his and search past his soul. "I wish I knew," he admitted with a shake of his head.

"I wish to God I knew." He grabbed hold of the door-knob, then hesitated. "Stop by sometime. I'll give you the grand tour and maybe then we'll be able to show Amy that the lodge isn't haunted."

She laughed softly. "I don't think that's possible."

"Wrong, Veronica," he said, thrusting open the door. "Haven't you learned yet that anything's possible?"

"Keegan? Travis Keegan?" She shook her head. "You know, that name sounds familiar...but...no, I've never heard of him." Shelly said as she poured another cup of coffee from the pot on Ronni's counter. This morning they'd shipped out a few late orders that had to be rushed to the nearest express mail company and were taking a break at the kitchen table.

"He's not from around here." Ronni straightened the napkin holder and salt and pepper shakers—Christmas elves in honor of the season.

"Oh." Shelly eyed her sister skeptically. "You—and a new guy?"

"Don't get any ideas. He's just someone I met and you'll get to meet him, too. He bought the Johnson place."

"*Bought* it? But I thought you were interested."

"I was."

"Wasn't the real estate agent supposed to call you if anyone had a serious offer?"

"Taffy told me she would, but it's not like I could have bought it if I'd known anyone was interested. I couldn't scrape up a down payment if my life depended upon it."

"Still, she should have phoned. Taffy LeMar was al-

ways a flake. A flirt and a flake. Even in high school.
I never liked her much."

"She wasn't obligated to let me know about the house
selling, she was just going to call as a favor. Besides, it
was probably just a pipe dream, anyway."

"I believe in pipe dreams." Shelly walked to the refrigerator, pulled out a carton of cream and added a
thin stream to her cup. "But then, I guess I have to."
Biting her lower lip, she shoved the carton back onto
the shelf and closed the fridge door. "I have some news
of my own."

"Good or bad?" Ronni asked, puzzled by her sister's change in attitude. Shelly was always so happy-
go-lucky, a person who was known to fly by the seat of
her pants and somehow make everything turn out right.
Now her brown eyes were dark and serious.

"Depends upon who you ask. Me or Vic."

Ronni's stomach knotted in apprehension. "What?"

Resting a hip against the counter, Shelly watched the
clouds of cream roll in her dark brew.

"Uh-oh. Shelly?"

Blowing across the top of her cup, Shelly stared at
her sister. "I'm pregnant."

"What?" Thunderstruck, Ronni nearly dropped her
mug. *Pregnant?* "But—"

"I know, I know, I don't need a lecture." Tears starred
Shelly's lashes and she blinked rapidly. "This couldn't
have come at a worse time with Vic's being out of work
and all, but you know something, Ronni, I'm happy
about it. We've always wanted another baby and I guess
we're going to have one." She was smiling despite the
tears drizzling from her eyes.

How in the world were they ever going to make it?

Financially strapped as they were, another mouth to feed was the last thing they needed. On the other hand, the thought of a new baby was invigorating and uplifting. Maybe a new member of their family was just what they needed.

"I think this calls for a celebration!" Ronni said, though she was stunned. Not only was Vic out of work but Shelly was already run ragged. Between working for Ronni and dealing with the twins, Shelly barely had a minute to herself. How could she squeeze in any extra time for an infant?

"Vic doesn't think so." Shelly wiped her eyes with the back of her hand, smearing streaks of mascara that were already running down her cheeks. "He—well, he's in a state." When she read the horror on her sister's face, she held up a hand. "Don't get me wrong, he doesn't want me to do anything to jeopardize the pregnancy, but—"

"But he's not happy."

"And he blames me."

"Didn't a wise man once say that it takes two to tango?"

Shelly laughed a little and dabbed at her eyes with a napkin. "He knows that, but he's just having a little trouble adjusting. He'll get used to the idea."

"He'd better," Ronni said, her hackles up a bit. She liked Victor, he was a great guy, but he had a tendency to place blame and come up with excuses when things didn't go exactly as he planned. Though Ronni didn't doubt for a minute that he'd be as good a father to this new baby as he was to the boys, another child was a burden as well as a joy.

"Vic's worried, and, really, I don't blame him. We

don't have insurance, you know, and if there are any complications, like last time with the twins and the C section...it could be devastating." Taking a deep breath, she straightened her shoulders. "Look, I didn't mean to bring you down, I just wanted you to know that you're going to be an aunt again."

"And I'm thrilled," Ronni said from the bottom of her heart. Sliding out of her chair, she crossed the room and hugged her sister fiercely. "There's nothing so special as a new little person."

"I knew you'd feel that way," Shelly said, her eyes filling with tears once more. A broken little sob escaped her throat. "Oh, look at me, blubbering and going on. You know how emotional pregnant women are."

"So when's the blessed event going to occur?"

"Middle of July. I suspected that I might be pregnant last month, even took one of those in-home tests, but I didn't want to say anything until I'd seen the doctor."

Ronni was disappointed; while growing up, and even as adults she and Shelly had shared their deepest secrets. "I don't blame you," she lied. "And really, you couldn't have chosen a better time of year to have the baby. No worry about not being able to get to the hospital because of the weather in July." She squeezed her sister's shoulders again. "Well, come on. We just have time for me to take you to lunch before I have to pick up Amy."

"But we should work."

"Nah. The shipping's done for the day and I can clean up tomorrow. I'm closing down the shop at the beginning of the week anyway and I think we—" she glanced pointedly at her sister's belly "—all three of us, need a break. Come on, get your jacket, Hamburgers on me."

Shelly brightened. "Okay, but just this once. The doctor's already worried about my weight."

Ronni grinned. "Good. Then I get your fries."

Shelly took a look at her sister's slim figure. "You're disgusting," she said with a grin.

"Yeah, but I work hard at it." Ronni tossed Shelly's thick jacket to her. "You know, Shell, I think this is the best news I've heard in weeks."

Ronni wrapped a scarf around her neck as they trudged through the snow to her van. The snowman was still standing, looking a little heavier with a fresh layer of snow dusting his features, and the tracks where she and Amy had rolled the snowballs were covered with white again.

The old Ford started without a fuss and as they drove passed the turnoff to the old Johnson place—now the Keegan lodge—Ronni bit her lip. She'd envisioned the huge old lodge as a bed-and-breakfast inn that she'd own and manage, and Shelly and Vic could move into the caretaker's house and out of their small duplex in town.

Snapping on the radio, she heard the first strains of "White Christmas." She'd had a lot of silly dreams, she realized, but they'd all changed in the past few days. All because of Travis Keegan.

"Come on, come on," Travis growled, glaring at the fax machine and waiting for a report that was supposed to have been transmitted. For the most part, everything was working correctly. He'd had to call an electrician whose crew had worked the better part of a week rewiring the old house, bringing it up to code, making sure that there was enough power to accept the strain of the additional equipment such as the microwave, satellite dish, three televisions, extra telephone lines, computer, modem, fax machine, printer and on and on.

He'd converted a small first-floor bedroom with a bay window overlooking the lake for his private office, which was linked electronically to the factory and home office just northeast of Seattle. His vice president, Wendall Holmes, was in charge of operations. When Travis had decided to move to Oregon, he and Wendall had worked a deal and now Wendall was buying shares of the sporting goods company. Eventually, if everything worked out over the long haul, he and Travis would be equal partners in TRK, Inc., which was the umbrella corporation for all his businesses.

For his part, Travis was glad to be this far away from the rat race.

The fax finally whirred and pages started spewing forth, a memo from Wendall and sales reports, accounting information, employee reviews, everything. Satisfied that the electronic linkup was working properly, Travis began reading through the latest proposal from the advertising firm handling his company's accounts, the newest marketing strategy to sell more skateboards, snowboards and ski equipment. The new line of apparel called Rough Riders was selling well in the Northwest and as far south as Sacramento. Yes, Wendall was doing a more than respectable job and this setup hundreds of miles away was working.

He worried a little because just two days ago this room was cold enough for ice to sheet on the inside of the windows. He'd contacted a local contractor who'd helped him with some preliminary remodeling and revamping of the place. Storm windows had been added and a new furnace and duct work was scheduled to be installed at the beginning of next week. A plumber had already given his estimate to replace the ancient pipes and fixtures. Some walls would have to be broken into and it looked as if there was no chance of a simple re-modeling job, but maybe that was good. Travis had envisioned Bryan working with him to restore the old lodge. Trouble was, Bryan wasn't interested. He was still grousing about missing his friends in Seattle and now that he was laid up, the father-and-son bonding would have to wait for other projects.

At that moment, he heard his son hitching himself across the huge room they'd designated as the living area. A few seconds later, the rubber tips of Bryan's crutches came into view and he was leaning against the door frame.

"I called Marty today."

"Did you?"

"So that he would have my new number."

"Good idea." Travis tried not to show any sign of emotion though he didn't trust Marty Sinclair, a friend of Bryan's from Seattle. The kid had been in and out of trouble for the past six or seven years, his latest stint involving driving under the influence of alcohol with a suspended license. There had been another incident with stolen compact discs and then the trouble with vandalism. Bryan had been in on that one. All these "incidents" and Martin was barely sixteen. He'd only escaped being sent to a juvenile center because his old man had money and a bevy of lawyers at his command. "What did Martin want?"

"For me to fly up and spend the weekend with him."

This was the part he hated. Saying no. It was harder

than any kid could ever imagine. "I think you'd better stick around. You've got another appointment with the doctor on Monday and sooner or later we've got to register you for school."

"Yeah at Backwoods High. What do they teach here—whittling, tobacco spitting and log rolling?"

"Those are just electives," Travis replied, managing to keep a straight face while consternation crossed his son's features. Obviously, Bryan was in no mood for jokes.

"Sure, Dad. Look, I don't see what going back home would hurt. It's just a couple of days," he whined.

"This is home now. Marty can come and visit."

"Here?" Bryan gestured broadly, taking in the entire lodge with its rough cedar walls and sparse furniture.

"Sure, he could think of it as camping, you know, roughing it."

"Travis, get serious!"

"I am."

"This is *Nowhere,* U.S.A. Marty's not going to want to come here."

"He would if he's a good friend."

"Yeah, and if I were a good friend, I'd go up there."

"The answer is no."

"You hate all my friends."

"No, Bry, not true." Travis snapped out the lights in the den and walked down the short hall to the living room with its dying fire and tall windows, all of which would be eventually replaced with double panes. Bryan followed after him, his crutches moving jerkily over the old wooden floors. "I like all your friends, including Marty. But I don't think he's a very good influence right now," Travis said.

"Just 'cause we got caught ripping off a couple of hood ornaments."

"Right. Stealing and vandalism all wrapped up together."

"The car belonged to Marty's uncle. The guy's a jerk."

Travis raised a hand. "Good thing he wasn't enough of a jerk to swear out a complaint against you. Do you realize how lucky you were that he let you pay for the damage and get off without dealing with the police?" Bryan had spent four weekends stacking boxes in Travis's sporting goods company's warehouse in order to earn the money to pay off his debt. "Look, call Marty back and invite him to come spend some time over the holiday break, but don't count on going to Seattle."

Bryan wanted to argue; Travis saw all the classic signs, defiant light in his eyes, chin thrust forward belligerently, fists opening then closing over the handholds of his crutches, but he didn't argue. With a sound of disgust, the boy turned and headed back to his room on the first floor. It was small, originally some kind of servants' quarters, Travis suspected, but until the remodeling was finished and Bryan could mount the stairs, there was no reason to move him to the second floor.

Bryan's door slammed, the noise echoing through the high-ceiling rooms.

He'll get over it, Travis told himself. He looked around the big, empty lodge and thought of Ronni's cozy cabin just down the lane. With a lumpy snowman standing guard and a string of lights on the front porch, the little cottage seemed more like home than this cold, empty behemoth. But all that would change—he'd see to it.

Walking along the hallway to Bryan's room, he called loudly, "Come on, Bryan, I'll buy you dinner, then we can pick out a Christmas tree."

No answer. Just the pounding sound of rock music.

Travis rapped sharply with his knuckles, and pushed open the door. "I said, let's find ourselves a tree."

"Can't you have one delivered?" Bryan was lying on his makeshift bed, his hands stacked behind his head as he stared through the window to the moonlit night. Some hard rocker was screaming through the speakers of the stereo.

"I suppose, but we can pick one out."

"Oh, sure. Next I suppose you'll want to pull a Paul Bunyan routine and chop down your own!" He slid his father an ungrateful look. "If only I could remember where I put my ax and blue ox. Get real, Travis."

"Lose the attitude."

"I don't have an attitude, I'm just bored."

"Well, it's time to change all that." Travis snatched a pullover from a wrinkled pile and tossed it onto his son. "Let's go, Bry. I'll buy you a pizza and a rootbeer, too, but not one more word about going north for any part of the holidays."

"You just don't know what it's like," Bryan grumbled as he struggled into a sitting position and reached for the hooded sweatshirt. "This is a big adventure for you. Throw away the suit and tie, put on flannel shirts and jeans and move to Oregon. Play Dad for a while. Don't you know that I don't know anyone here—not one stupid person? How do you think I'm gonna feel walking into that school the day after New Year's, huh? You know how embarrassing it will be to be introduced to each class—to have the principal or the teachers tell the kids to welcome me, that we all should become fast friends?" He blinked against tears blurring his vision. "It's gonna be hell, Travis," he said, swallowing hard. Jerking to his feet, he sniffed loudly. "Good thing I know just who to blame."

CHAPTER FIVE

RONNI SLID HER skis into the back of the van and slammed the back doors. She was tired. It had been a long, hard day on the mountain. Strong winds and whiteout conditions had closed down the upper lifts and she'd had to deal with lost skiers and too many injuries. Finally, the storm had abated and the sun had dared to peek through the dark clouds, even as a few final flakes floated to the ground. But the damage had already been done. Rubbing the kinks from her neck and finding her keys in her pocket, Ronni was thankful the day was over. She envisioned a hot cup of tea and a warm bath.

Then she spied Travis Keegan leaning against the driver's door of her van, his arms folded over his chest as if standing in the middle of the parking lot of Mount Echo's base lodge was the most natural thing in the world. Wearing aviator sunglasses, old jeans and a rawhide jacket, he managed a thin replica of a smile when he saw her.

"Fancy meeting you here," she quipped, yanking off her cap and shaking out her hair.

"I was looking for you."

She couldn't help the silly little jump in her pulse when his gaze, hidden though it was, sought hers. "Why?"

"I think I need your help." Sunlight refracted against his dark lenses and he scowled as if the admission was difficult. It probably was. Keegan didn't appear to be the kind of man who asked for assistance. While everyone else was wearing down coats and parkas, ski pants and woolen hats, he stood bareheaded, snow catching in the dark strands of his hair, the arms of his jacket shoved up to his elbows, his big hands bare.

A horn honked as a four-wheeled pickup roared past. Ronni waved to Tim and his son before turning her attention to Travis and quieting the unsettling feeling that played with her mind whenever he was around. There was something about him that put her on edge, made her restless, though she didn't know why.

Because he's attractive, sexy and a take-charge kind of guy, the first man who's interested you since Hank. Oh, God. She nudged that wayward thought back into a dark corner of her mind where it belonged.

"What kind of help?"

"I need your expertise," he admitted.

Laughing, she said, "My expertise? Let me guess— how to tie a four-year-old's shoelaces?"

"Nothing quite so complicated," he drawled and behind his tinted lenses his eyes sparked. "Why don't you let me buy you a cup of coffee or a drink while I plead my case?"

Tilting her head to the side and sizing him up, she decided it wouldn't hurt. Hadn't everyone she knew told her it was time to start meeting people again, time to start letting go of the past? "Why not?" She checked her watch. "I have to pick up Amy in about forty-five minutes, but until then, I'm free." The errands she was going to run before she stopped at Shelly's to collect her daughter could wait until later.

Travis Keegan interested her and it had been long, too long probably, since she'd spent any time alone with a man. Maybe Amy was right. Maybe she was lonely. No, she told herself as they walked carefully over the icy ruts of the parking lot and climbed the metal-grate steps to the lodge, she just missed Hank.

They found an unoccupied booth near the window of the café where they each ordered cups of Irish coffee. Floor-to-ceiling windows provided a panorama of white snow, tall evergreen trees and skiers racing down the runs.

"How long have you been a part of the team?" he asked, motioning to her red jacket with its patch proclaiming her part of the ski patrol.

"Ever since I was eighteen," she admitted with a smile. "*Years* ago."

"You must be quite a skier."

"My dad had my sister and me up on skis about the time we learned to walk," she admitted. "He was part of the patrol and a ski instructor part-time, so it was pretty natural that Shelly and I would follow in his footsteps—or ski tracks, I guess."

"Shelly—your sister?"

"Yeah. She still lives in town, too."

"You're close?"

"Best friends." Ronni nodded as the waitress brought glass cups filled with coffee and topped with whipped cream. A drizzle of green crème de menthe added a bright spot of color that melted into the cream. "You said something about needing my expertise," she prodded, expecting him to ask her to teach Bryan the finer points of skiing. She was wrong.

Travis scowled and took a swig from his mug. "I can't believe I'm here doing this."

"What? Doing what?"

"Asking you to help me organize the house for Christmas... I realize it might be an imposition, and believe me, if you don't want to help, I'd understand. And I'd pay you for your time—"

"What time? What are you talking about?"

"The tree. Some garlands. A strand or two of lights, I guess." He leaned closer and took off his sunglasses. "Look, I can't believe I even care about anything as trivial as Christmas decorations, but after I stopped by your place the other night, I decided that drafty old lodge could use some sprucing up for the holidays. This is Bryan's first Christmas away from his friends and...well, he's apart from his mother and laid up and I thought...hell, I don't know what I thought," he admitted, looking up at the high cedar ceiling in frustration. "This is all fairly new to me—this single-parenting business and you're so good with your daughter. I tried to talk Bryan into picking out a tree with me the other night and you would've thought I'd asked him to rip off his toenails. Anyway, it didn't happen, but I think... well, some kind of decoration would help make the place feel more like home."

She stared at him in wonder. "You want *me* to help *you* organize your house for the holidays?"

"Something like that." Shaking his head as if he was disgusted with himself, he lowered his eyes so that his gaze touched hers. In that single heart-stopping moment, she felt a spark, a connection, as if his soul was reaching for hers…but that was silly. Good Lord, what was wrong with her? He rimmed the top of his mug with one finger. "To tell you the truth," he told her, "I haven't been much of a father to Bryan. Too many years spent in the office, at meetings, trying to make a bigger profit, expand the company, make more money." He spewed out the words as if they tasted bad. Another swallow from his mug. "I missed a lot, didn't spend as much time with Bryan as I should have and I'm now trying to…"

"Make up for lost time?"

"So to speak."

She stirred the cream into foam that melted into her coffee. "And you think throwing up a few lights and strings of tinsel will change all that?"

"No," he admitted with a sound of disgust. "I can't change the past. That's the way we lived our lives, like it or not. I made a helluva lot of mistakes, so did my ex-wife, but I'm trying to make it up to Bryan now."

"And be a real father rather than an absentee?" she said, unable to keep her tongue from being harsh. She'd seen a lot of men who didn't have time for their families, who were so concerned about chasing after the dollar or other women that they ignored and neglected their wives and children. Oftentimes, they ended up divorced, with a new, younger wife and no relationship with their kids whatsoever. And then there were men like Hank, a man who would have done anything for his newborn baby. A man who was snatched from life far too young. Bitterness climbed up the back of her throat. "You can't make up fourteen years in one Christmas."

His jaw tightened. "I know that."

"And you can't hire a stranger to come in and expect her to toss some glitter around the house, throw up a Christmas tree and hang a few sprigs of mistletoe in the hopes that the spirit of Christmas will see fit to touch your home."

"I'm just trying to get started on the right foot," he said, his voice rising in pitch. "Look, I was hoping you and Amy would come over and we'd...I don't know, have a tree-trimming party or whatever you want to call it."

"And you would pay me?" she asked, sick inside.

"Right."

It all seemed so callous, so unfeeling, so crass and commercial. So *un*Christmassy. "No thanks." She stood, reached into her wallet and found a couple of dollars, which she slapped onto the table.

"I offended you." He seemed surprised.

"Bingo." She placed both hands flat on the table's surface and leaned forward so that her nose was close to his. Staring deep into his eyes, she noticed the varying shades of gray and the thick spiky lashes that refused to blink. "Look, Keegan, I know you're used to the city, to the boardroom, to giving orders and expecting everyone to hop to them. You're one of those corporate executives who flies around in a private jet, sleeps at the best hotels and thinks that he can buy anything he pleases, including a merry Christmas for his son, but you're wrong. Christmas, real Christmas, comes from the heart not the pocketbook.

"Now, whether you want to hear it or not, I'm going

to give you some advice," she continued, holding his stare, feeling the heat radiate from him, sensing the anger that caused his chin to tighten and his nostrils to flare. "Cascadia is a small town, the people are close-knit, they help one another because they want to, not because they feel obligated or because they expect to be paid. That's why it's so special here. That's why I live here and that's why big-wheels from the city sometimes have trouble fitting in.

"Goodbye, Mr. Keegan. Thanks for the company."

She turned to leave but he caught her wrist in a quick motion. On his feet in an instant, he pulled her body close enough that her breasts nearly brushed his chest. Almost—but not quite. "Look, lady, I didn't mean to insult you."

"Well, you did."

"I—"

"Leave it alone, Keegan," she said, yanking her hand from his. "We're just neighbors, we don't have to like each other." Spinning on her heel, she walked stiff-backed out of the café and sensed him watching her every move.

"You did what?" Shelly said, dipping her French fry into a pool of catsup in the paper-lined burger basket. They were sitting in a booth at a local hamburger den and an old song from the Righteous Brothers was play-ing over the sound of the loudspeaker for the drive-up, the rattle of French fry baskets, orders being yelled to the cooks and the scrape of spatulas on the grill.

The restaurant, a hangout for teenagers ever since Ronni and Shelly had been adolescents was about half-full. Their children were in the next booth arguing over how Santa could possibly finish his rounds and slide down everyone in the world's chimney on Christmas Eve.

Ronni swirled her straw in her soda. "I guess I told him to get lost. Not in so many words, maybe, but he got the message."

"Are you out of your mind? Why?" Shelly snapped up her French fry and munched blissfully.

"I didn't like his attitude."

Rolling her eyes, Shelly wiped the salt and oil from her fingers on a paper napkin. "The most interesting bachelor to show up in town in years—at least that's the way Taffy LeMar describes him—and you tell him to get lost? You know, Ronni, sometimes I think you should have your head examined."

"So you talked to Taffy?" Ronni said, still disappointed that her friend hadn't let her know that the old Johnson place was going to be the new Keegan estate. As many times as she reminded herself that there was no way she could have bought the land and the old, rambling lodge on it, she wished she'd had the chance to put some kind of deal together. *With what?* She'd saved twenty-five thousand dollars from the insurance money when Hank had died, but that money was earmarked for Amy's education and so far she hadn't touched a dime of it. Not that it would have helped all that much.

"Yeah, I talked to Taffy and she was lit up like the proverbial Christmas tree, all atwitter about Keegan, saying he's tall, dark, handsome and single." Shelly slid a glance toward her boys, then said, "I reminded Taffy that you were interested in the place and she mumbled something about being sorry but that this guy just swept into the real estate office, told them what he wanted, how much he wanted to spend and within twenty-four hours the deal was done."

"That sounds like Keegan," Ronni said.

"How would you know?"

"As I said, it's the man's attitude."

"Men," Shelly said, shaking her head as her eyes clouded over. "Sometimes..." Her voice faded off.

"How's Vic these days?"

Shelly sighed and leaned an elbow on the table. "Trying to buck up, I think. He says he's excited about the baby, but he's worried. I can tell. He's started talking about moving to California again. His brother would hire him, but what does Vic know about computers?"

"He could learn," Ronni suggested. "Vic's only what—thirty-five?"

"I know, I know, but he hates to be cooped up. An office job would kill him." She frowned, then heard the boys' voices begin to rise. "Kurt, Kent, hold it down," she ordered.

"But he stole one of my chicken nuggets," Kurt complained.

"Don't you each have your own?"

The thought of Shelly moving away was depressing, but Ronni would never show it. She and Shelly had been best friends all their lives except for a period in high school when they'd pretended not to know each other. Now they saw each other every day and Amy thought of the twins more as brothers than cousins. Shelly had been Ronni's strongest support when Hank had been killed and the thought that she might be moving away was devastating.

"Has it really come to that—to leaving?" Ronni asked.

Shelly's eyes were dark with worry. "I hope not," she said, "but Vic needs to find work, permanent work, to make him feel good again." As quickly as the concern had crossed her features, she chased it away with a smile. "I tell him not to worry—things always have a way of working out, but you know Victor. If he didn't have something to fret about, he wouldn't be happy."

Ronni laughed, because that much was true. Ever since Ronni had known him, Victor Pederson had been a guy who stewed about the future, while the wife he'd chosen barely looked past the end of the week.

"You know, Shelly, if things are bad, I've got money—"

"Amy's inheritance? Forget it. We've been over this before, Ronni." She picked up the tray. "Now, forget about me for a second and think about your new neighbor. The way I see it, the man just asked for a favor. He needs help decorating for Christmas, so he offered to pay you. Is that such a crime?" She turned her head and shot out of her chair. "Kurt, stop it! Now." Kurt had his brother in some kind of headlock and Kent was screaming. "I think it's time we took off," Shelly said as the boys, red faced and hurling insults, squared off. "I'll call you later. Come on, boys, let's go. Now!" She grabbed each one by a tight, grimy little fist and shepherded them out of the restaurant.

"Come on, Amy," Ronni said, gathering up the trash. "I think it's time we left, too."

"Why do they do that?" Amy asked, her little face a knot of vexation as she stared through the swinging glass doors to the parking lot where her cousins were climbing into Shelly's big car.

"What? Oh, you mean the boys? Why they fight? It's just natural, I guess. Aunt Shelly and I used to fight."

"No!"

"All the time. It drove Grandma nuts." She tossed the trash into one of the containers near the door, then paused to help Amy zip her jacket.

"You don't fight anymore."

"Oh, but we did, like cats and dogs, even though we were really each other's best friend. I know it sounds silly, but it's true. Kurt and Kent will get over it, too. But not for a long, long time."

"It's a pain," Amy said as Ronni tied her hood in place.

"I'll second that."

"If I had a sister, I'd never fight with her."

Ronni laughed as she searched for her car keys.

"So why don't I?" her daughter demanded.

"Have a sister?" Ronni asked as she pushed open the door. "I thought you wanted a puppy."

"I do!" Amy said with a grin, her attention derailed from the subject of a sibling, a painful subject that came up every once in a while. Long ago, Ronni had promised herself she'd never have an only child, that because of her close relationship with her sister, she'd want Amy to have a brother or sister. Hank had agreed, for the opposite reason. He'd had no brothers or sisters and thought he'd missed out.

But then fate had stepped in and taken him and any plans for another baby.

"Come on," Ronni said, refusing to dwell on the past. She planned to make it her New Year's resolution that she'd start living her life for the future, not for the past. And she didn't have to wait until New Year's— she could make that resolution today, even though there were several weeks of this year left.

They stepped into the parking lot just as Shelly's car eased into traffic. Ronni tried to envision her sister with another baby and she smiled. Shelly was cut out to be a mother—she was right, things would work out. "Have faith," she told herself.

"What?" Amy screwed up her face and stared up at her.

"Nothing, sweetheart. Hey, let's go see what they've got in there," she said, pointing across the street to the variety store that had stood on the corner of Main Street and Douglas Avenue for as long as she could remember. The display window was filled with Christmas decor— lights, ribbon, tinsel, everything a person would need to decorate their house…or an old hunting lodge. Ronnie held on to her daughter's hand and walked briskly to the cross walk. Shelly's words followed after her, accusing her of misinterpreting Keegan's offer, and Ronni decided there was no time like the present to right a wrong. Or to eat humble pie. Gritting her teeth, she pushed open the door of the little shop and heard Jake, the owner's parakeet, whistle out a throaty, "Come in, come in."

"Ronni and Amy!" Ada Hampton, the proprietor, grinned, showing, perfect, if false, teeth. A woman with wide hips and a wider smile, she'd stood behind the same cash register since her husband died thirty years ago. "What a nice surprise." Wearing a crisp red apron, she waddled through a narrow opening in the counter. "What can I do for you?"

"I wish I knew," Ronni replied, not really knowing where to start.

Ada reached into a voluminous pocket and pulled out a green sucker. "This is for you," she said to Amy. "You know, I used to give suckers to your mother and her sister when they were about your age," she said. "But that was a long time ago."

Jake, hopping from one perch to the other, whistled out a sharp, "Hey, honey, what'cha doin'?"

"What're you doin'?" Amy responded, licking on her sucker and staring up at the green-and-yellow bird.

"Come in. Come in," Jake said.

"Silly bird!" But Amy giggled and Jake bobbed his little head wildly.

Ada chuckled and reached for a tissue. Dabbing eyes that were always running from her allergies, she said, "Now, is there anything special you want today?"

"Lights, ribbon, garlands, the works," she replied, wondering if she was out of her mind. She only had a vague notion of what she planned to do, but it included landing on Travis Keegan's doorstep with a small fortune in Christmas decor. She only hoped he still wanted it. After their last conversation, there was a good chance she might end up with a door slammed in her face. "Do you have anything on sale—like last year's stuff?" she asked while mentally calculating what she had in stock at home and in the warehouse. Most of her mail-order

Christmas inventory had been sold, but there were still a few garlands, bells and spools of ribbon. She could cut boughs of holly and cedar from some trees in her backyard. With a little money, a lot of imagination and some work, she could make the old lodge look like a Christmas picture postcard.

"I've still got a few things," Ada said, leading her to a sale table where most of the items had already been picked over. "Not much left, I'm afraid, but what's here is at bargain-basement prices."

"I think I can find what I need." Ronni picked up a large spool of red-and-white gingham ribbon that had been marked down to half price. "This'll do just fine."

Over the thrumming beat of hard rock, Travis heard a buzzing. He listened, heard the noise again and put down his screwdriver. He'd been trying to fix the bathroom door as it wouldn't latch, and pieces of the lock were strewn across the counter. "What the devil?"

The noise quit again and suddenly there was a loud pounding on the front door. The doorbell! Of course. Something was wrong with it and the chimes were reduced to a static-laden, irritating buzz.

Thinking one of the contractors had returned to pick up a forgotten tool, he threw open the door and found Ronni and her daughter on the front porch. Involuntarily, his throat tightened at the sight of her. Wearing oven mitts, Ronni was holding a white pan, covered in aluminum foil. The scents of tomato sauce and cheese seeped out in the steam rising from a slit in the foil. "I, uh, think I owe you an apology," Ronni said quickly. "I didn't mean to come unglued this afternoon when you asked me to help you, you just kind of blindsided me and…I overreacted. I brought a peace offering." She held up the pan and more tantalizing odors wafted from the dish.

"So you're here to…?"

"Boy, I wish I knew," she said, shaking her head. "How about to eat a little crow?"

"Crow?" Amy, bundled in a yellow snowsuit, wrinkled her nose and acted as if Ronni had lost her mind. "It's lasagna, Mommy."

"That it is." She winked at her daughter. "I guess I forgot." She took in a long breath and squared her shoulders. "Look, you can't imagine how awkward I feel— this is really not my style, but here goes…" Meeting his gaze squarely, she said, "I thought we should start over and I'm going to try and be more neighborly, so Amy and I brought dinner and some Christmas decorations and if the invitation's still on, we'll have that tree-trimming party you wanted."

He couldn't stop the smile that crept from one side of his mouth to the other.

"Unless you've already eaten or have other plans," she added hastily.

"No plans and we're starved." Thoughtfully rubbing his chin, he pinned her with a stare he knew was sometimes disturbing. "You know, Ms. Walsh," he drawled, "I don't know what to say."

"'Come in' would be nice or 'Gee, thanks. Apology accepted' would do. I'd even go for, 'Woman, I'm starving. Thank God you showed up!'"

Travis laughed. Seeing her standing on the porch with her face upturned, her cheeks rosy with the cold, he felt an unlikely stirring deep in his heart that was completely out of line. She was here offering food, for crying out loud. "Okay, here goes. Woman, I'm starving. Thank God you showed up."

"That's much better." As he stepped out of the way, she strode into the house. Amy wasn't going to be left on the porch, and clutching a bag full of some kind of tinsel, she followed her mother.

"Can I help?" he asked Ronni, a little bewildered by her change of heart. Why was it he felt as if he'd just won a major battle?

"I thought you'd never ask," she teased. "The van needs to be unloaded."

"You brought more things?"

"A few," she said, then laughed lightly and the sound seemed to echo through the house. Her dark eyes sparkled and she shook the snow from her hair. "When Amy and I are asked to trim a tree, we come prepared, don't we?"

Amy nodded, but stuck close to her mother, eyeing the high ceilings and mantel as if she expected ghosts, goblins and an assortment of demons to fly down the chimney and, cackling evilly, snatch her away.

"You've done a lot with the place," Ronni said as she stopped at the step leading down to the living area and gazed across the polished floors to the bank of windows stretching along the back wall. Beyond the glass, the lake, dark and serene, was visible through snow-dusted strands of hemlock and fir trees.

"We've still got a long way to go, though. I'd like to restore it the way the original architect would have liked it—well, as much as possible, and still bring it up to the local building code. But that's going to take a while and now that Bryan's laid up, all those father-son projects have become just father jobs."

Her eyes seemed to search every nook and cranny, exploring the floor-to-ceiling bookcase, now empty, each stone of the large fireplace and every exposed beam in the ceiling. "It really is beautiful," she said, placing her warm pan down on a small table and using an oven mitt as a pot holder. Running a finger along the time-smoothed banister leading to the second floor, she gazed up at the railing of the reading loft. "I remember when there used to be huge parties thrown here and my sister and I would hide in the shrubbery and watch expensive cars line the driveway." She walked to the windows and stared into the chilly darkness where soft moon glow played upon the inky waters of the lake. "Sometimes the Johnsons would hire a singer, other times a piano player or a band and they always strung Japanese lanterns down the path and along the dock into the lake."

"Dock?"

"It's gone now," she said. "No one's brought a boat in here in years." She cleared her throat, but a trace of sadness seemed to linger in her eyes. "Oh, well, ancient history." She managed a smile as she grabbed the steaming pan again. "I'd better take this down to the kitchen or it'll get cold."

"I guess I'll unload the van," he offered, wondering what she had brought and feeling guilty that she had obviously spent not only time but money in her attempt to apologize and be neighborly. Somehow he'd have to make it up to her, but he doubted, from her reaction in the ski lodge earlier, that she'd take a check. "The kitchen's down that hallway and through—"

But she was already on her way, walking swiftly along the corridor as if she was as familiar with this drafty old lodge as she was with her own snug little cabin. Her daughter was right on her heels, never letting Ronni out of her sight and sometimes glancing nervously behind her.

Travis stood at the door a second, watching her swing down the hall. Black jeans hugged her hips and a red vest and white blouse peeked out from beneath a short woolen jacket. A scarf was wound around her neck and her black hair bounced and gleamed beneath the lights. Her back was ramrod straight, her footsteps determined—a no-nonsense lady with a vulnerability that she tried so hard to hide. He wondered what it was about her that he found so very fascinating?

A cold gust of wind reminded him that he was standing in the middle of the hallway, gaping and practically drooling, like some sex-crazed adolescent with a bad crush. "Damn it all," he muttered, not bothering with a jacket as he broke a trail through the snow to her van.

He was used to attractive, aggressive women. He'd met them in the workplace. Usually trim and sleek, always well-groomed and well-spoken, they could be bold and brash, or quiet and sedate, but they were all determined and came with their own agendas—hidden or otherwise. He'd dealt with them on a daily basis before and after his divorce. Some of the women were aggressive not only in their jobs but in their personal relationships, as well.

He'd been chased, propositioned and almost seduced by strong-willed women who, beautiful though they had been, hadn't interested him. Nor had he been attracted to the few homebodies he'd met through mutual friends, often desperate women who looked at him as if he were an answer to their prayers—a wealthy man who could help them quit chasing after deadbeat ex-husbands for child support, a means to get rid of their boring jobs.

He'd never been tempted, hadn't even started an affair that he knew would only end badly. In fact, he'd convinced himself that he was now a confirmed bachelor.

Until now.

Until he'd seen Veronica Walsh deal with his injured boy.

Until he'd seen how she handled her imp of a daughter.

Until he'd looked into those dark, knowing eyes that could penetrate all his defenses or twinkle with laughter.

She'd started to change his mind about women because she'd been so different. Strong, yet vulnerable, with a quick tongue and sharp wit. But there was something more, something deeper   a sadness—that touched him and made him feel as if he wanted to fold her into his arms and tell her everything would be all right. Hell, he was losing it. He didn't even know her, for crying out loud, and here he was fantasizing about her.

The back of the van was stacked with boxes and sacks. For the love of Saint Peter, she must have spent a small fortune. His guilt started eating at him. She was a single mother and she couldn't afford whatever it was she'd come up with.

Gritting his teeth, he carried in two boxes, then returned for four more sacks, which he set in the living room. He paused once to knock on Bryan's door and let himself in. While the beat of some grunge band was throbbing through the room, Bryan was lying on his back lifting weights.

His son slid a glance his way when he turned the volume of the stereo down several decibels.

"Hey!" Bryan complained.

"You're going to go deaf with this so loud."

"Who gives a rip?" Bryan was still giving him the cold shoulder and hoping to back Travis into a corner of guilt so that he'd break down and let him spend some of the holidays in Seattle.

"We've got company."

Bryan tried hard to keep his gaze flat and his expression bored, but he couldn't quite hide the curiosity that rose to the surface.

"Ronni Walsh and her daughter."

"The *three-year-old* you told me about?" Bryan pulled a face and pushed the weights off his chest.

"Actually, I think she's four."

"No difference. Still a little kid." He lowered the bar.

Travis wasn't going to argue with him. "Just put on a clean shirt, wash your hands and come into the kitchen. Ronni brought dinner."

"Why?"

"I asked her to help us decorate the house."

"Oh pleeease, Travis. You didn't." Again he lifted the bar and weights away from his body, his muscles straining.

"I did and it's going to be fun."

"Yeah, a blast," Bryan grumbled.

"I'll see you in five minutes," Travis said and closed the door behind him. He could only hope that Bryan's appetite, which had been phenomenal of late, would force him to comply so that they wouldn't have to get into another one of their knock-down-and-drag-out arguments.

Delicious aromas drifted from the kitchen and as Travis pushed open the swinging doors, he found Ronni tossing a salad and Amy standing on a chair beside her. The table was already set. Two candles were already lit and dripping wax down the sides of old wine bottles. The flames reflected in dozens of flickering lights upon the mullioned windows surrounding the table.

"I *hate* cucumbers," the little girl was saying.

Ronni wasn't intimidated. "Too bad, I like 'em."

"And I *hate* tomatoes."

"Not tomatoes. These are red peppers, and they're good for you."

"Then I *hate* red peppers."

"Fine, pick around them."

"I *hate* salad."

"I know, I know, but I don't really care. You're going to eat some, anyway." Ronni blew her bangs out of her eyes but looked up when the door creaked shut. With an exasperated smile, she said, "We're in a negative mood tonight. Sorry."

"Don't be. I'm used to it. Negativity seems to be a way of life around here these days. Remember, I told you it doesn't get any better."

"Thanks for reminding me." She sprinkled an oil

and-vinegar dressing over the salad greens and he was taken with how natural it seemed for her to be bustling around the kitchen. "I assume Bryan's joining us?"

"He is if he doesn't want to be grounded for the rest of his life."

"I'm here," Bryan announced as he hitched himself through the swinging doors and scowled at the crowded room.

"Good. How're you feeling?" Ronni asked.

"Compared to what?"

"Well, compared to, 'Gee, I feel great, I think I could run a marathon,' that's a ten—"

He snorted derisively.

"Or 'I feel so crummy—like I've been run over by a steam roller and I think I'll curl up and die,' that's a zero."

"About a minus six, okay?" he grumbled and Travis felt the familiar tensing of his jaw.

Ronni's eyes glittered merrily. "Funny, you don't look near death's door, but then it's been said that looks can be deceiving. I was going to ask you if you wanted to come over and exercise my horses, but, if you're too sore—"

"Horses?" Bryan's head snapped up.

"Mmm. Quarter horses. Loose Change—we call her Lucy—and Sam," she said and Travis noticed the boy's bored expression changed slightly. "Amy and I ride them whenever we get the chance, but it would be nice if someone came over on a regular basis. It doesn't have to be right away, we're doing fine, but in the spring when your knee's healed and the doctor says it's okay, it would help me out."

Bryan glanced at his father, then rolled out his lower lip as if he didn't really care. "It's up to you," Travis said.

"I'd pay you, of course." She shot Travis a knowing look. "You could ride them around the lake over here, if your dad doesn't mind."

"Fine with me," Travis said. "As long as the doctor agrees." He could barely believe the transformation in his son. Try as he might, Bryan couldn't hide his interest. Somehow, Ronni had known how to get through to the kid when no one else— teachers, school counselors and certainly not he—could pierce Bryan's emotional armor.

Ronni screwed the cap back on the vinegar bottle. "We've got time, just think about it. Now, Amy, why don't you show Bryan what we brought?"

The little girl scrambled off her chair and rushed to the refrigerator where she found a bottle of sparkling cider and hoisted it proudly into the air over her head.

Ronni placed the salad bowl on the table between the two candles. "We usually save this for special occasions like birthdays, Christmas and New Year's, but I figured this was close enough since it's the holiday season."

"You like it?" Amy asked the teenager, her eyes round with anticipation.

"It's okay." A dismissive shoulder raised.

"Let's open it," Ronni suggested. "Bryan, why don't you do the honors? And Travis, I brought a bottle of Chianti, it's—"

"Got it," Travis said, spying the green bottle resting on the counter and scrambling through the top drawer where he thought he'd placed his corkscrew. He pushed aside spatulas, spoons, a potato peeler and a wire whisk before he located the opener. "Here we go." As Ronni placed the pan of lasagna and a basket of garlic bread on the table, he poured them each a glass. "It looks great," he said and she grinned under the compliment.

"Let's just hope it tastes as good as it looks!"

She didn't have to worry. Everyone appeared to be hungry, and by the time the dishes were carried to the sink, most of the food had been devoured. Even Bryan, though trying to maintain an image of being cool and disdainful, ate as if he hadn't seen food in a week. When they were finished, some of the tension had eased and Amy seemed to have forgotten that the house was supposed to be haunted and inhabited by all manner of creepy-crawlies.

"Bryan and I will tackle the dishes," Travis announced and the boy didn't bother hiding his shocked look.

"Women's work," he grumbled.

"You think so?" Ronni asked, amused.

"In Seattle, we had a maid—"

"I hate to be the one to tell you, kid, but we're not in Kansas…er, Washington anymore."

"What?" Bryan looked at his father as if he thought Travis had lost his mind.

"An old joke, comes from the movie *The Wizard Of Oz,* I think. Never mind, you're too young, but the point is, as many of us males have learned rather painfully over the past twenty years or so, there is no such thing as women's work versus men's."

"There should be," Bryan argued.

Travis picked up his dish and carried it to the sink. "Okay, I'll grant you that men and women are different, physically, mentally and emotionally, and there have been some heated debates on the subject, lots of tempers flared, but I believe deep in my heart that men, if they wanted to, could clean the dinner dishes just as well as their wives. If only someone would give them the chance," he said.

His son rolled his eyes to the ceiling. "Oh, Travis. But maybe they don't want to."

Ronni couldn't leave it alone. "Okay, okay, you two, bring out the white flags and declare a truce. Tonight I'm going to do you a favor, Bryan. Since you're on crutches, I'll cut you a break. You show Amy around and I'll handle the pots and pans." She glanced at Travis, half expecting him to argue with her, but this time he held his tongue, and Bryan, after looking at Amy and sizing her up, made good his escape, moving out of the kitchen faster than any person on crutches should. Amy, realizing she was about to be dumped, hurried after him.

"If he thinks he can outrun her, he's got another think coming," Ronni said fondly.

"Where did you learn to handle teenage boys?" Travis asked, studying her so intently that she wanted to squirm.

"I gave ski lessons for years. Dealt with all kinds." She carried the plates and stacked them in the sink. "You're worried about him, aren't you?"

Deep furrows etched the skin between his eyebrows and he glanced at the door to the kitchen, still swinging slightly. "You know, there was a time I thought I could do anything. Didn't matter what it was. Form a company, hit a baseball, climb Mount Everest if I wanted to. I guess I was a little full of myself." Smiling in self-mockery, he shook his head and closed his eyes. "Damn but I was wrong. I never realized how trying teenagers could be."

"You'll work it out," she predicted, turning on the faucets and listening as the old pipes squeaked and groaned.

"I hope you're right," he said, unconvinced.

The phone rang and Travis snatched the receiver. After a short pause, he grimaced, glanced at his watch and swore under his breath. "What time is it over there?" he demanded, then said, "I don't think I even want to know." He paused and listened, all the while his fingers clenching the receiver in a death grip. "No, no, he's fine, Sylvia. Better every day. I told him to call… oh, please, don't cry."

Ronni recognized Travis's ex-wife's name and wished there was a way she could graciously back out of the room. She didn't need to be a part of the emotional turmoil that was suddenly reeling through the room like a tornado.

"Pull yourself together, okay? I'll get him. Hang on."

All the animation had left his face. Turning on the heel of his boot, Travis stormed through the swinging doors and within minutes Bryan hobbled back through the room. His lips were pursed and his jaw tight. Before he could pick up the receiver, Ronni decided she didn't want to eavesdrop on a private conversation. Turning off the taps and grabbing a towel for her hands in one swift motion, she pushed open the swinging doors with her hips and nearly collided with Travis striding back to the kitchen.

"Oh…look, maybe this is a bad time. Amy and I can come back later."

"No!" he nearly yelled, then let out his breath slowly.

Touching her lightly on the arm, he said, "It's just Sylvia. She's into theatrics, and right now she's ticked at me because I haven't called her every day with a progress report on Bryan."

"At least she cares—"

He cut her off with a look that silently called her a fool. "When it's convenient, that's when Sylvia cares." He opened his mouth as if to say something more, then, seeming to think better of it, snapped his teeth together. "Forget the dishes, I'll handle them later. Let's start in on the rest of the project."

"Okay, uh, I guess we should begin with a tree. You said that you and Bryan went out looking for one, but that—"

"It was a bust. A major bust. We ate dinner and by the time we were finished, it was too late. The lot was closed. Which was just as well, considering both of our moods."

"Uncle Vic will help you," Amy said.

One of Travis's dark eyebrows quirked. "Who's Uncle Vic?"

"My sister's husband. He works at a lot in downtown Cascadia for a couple of his friends."

"Then that's where we'll go." He started for his jacket just as Bryan appeared in the doorway. His face was red, his gaze distant as he leaned on his crutches.

"I think you'd better call Mom in the morning, Travis," he said, biting his lower lip.

"Why?"

Bryan's jaw tightened in a younger whisker-free imitation of his father's. "Because she wants me to come to France."

"What? For the holidays?" Travis muttered something under his breath. "That woman doesn't know what she wants."

"No, Travis," he said and his voice quivered slightly. "You're wrong. I think this time she's serious. She says she wants me to come and live with her. And not just for a few weeks. She's talking about marrying Jean Pierre and she wants me to move in with them. Permanently."

CHAPTER SIX

"DAMN THAT WOMAN," Travis said, shoving one hand through his already-rumpled hair. "Why can't she make up her mind?" Then as if suddenly realizing he had an audience, he shook his head. "She's going to marry Jean Pierre?"

"What's it to you?" Bryan wondered.

"Nothing. Nothing. She can marry whomever she pleases, but when it affects you, then I care."

Bryan's fingers clenched nervously over the smooth metal of his crutches. "Maybe it wouldn't be so bad."

"You *want* to live with your mother?" Travis demanded, pinning his son with a gaze that would make a grown man shudder. "In Paris?"

With the aid of his crutches, Bryan stood his ground and elevated his chin. "Don't know."

"You don't even speak the language."

"Couldn't be much worse than here," the boy said, his eyes slitting in anger. "You won't even let me go up and see my friends, so what does it matter if I live in Podunk, Oregon, or Paris, France?"

"I told you Martin could come visit."

"That's not what I asked for, though, was it?" Bryan threw a scathing look around the room and started for the door. "Mom said to call her tomorrow and let her know what I want to do."

"She wasn't going to talk to me?"

"She's ticked at you," Bryan yelled over his shoulder.

"Why?"

"Because of these." He lifted one crutch. "She thinks that if you were keeping better track of me, I wouldn't have gotten hurt."

Travis's neck burned red with rage but he didn't answer, and Ronni, feeling like an outsider, said, "Maybe Amy and I should come back another time."

"No!" Travis was vehement. "Bryan, we'll talk about this later, okay?" When the boy didn't reply, Travis repeated, "Okay?"

"Yeah. Fine. Okay," he agreed, obviously none too pleased as he managed his way across the room to stand at the tall windows and stare outside at the serene waters of the lake. His shoulders were slumped and Ronni's heart went out to the boy. Though both parents loved him, he was obviously torn and missed his mother. The rebellion he aimed so pointedly at his father was in direct response to Travis's authority, though Bryan probably didn't realize it.

"Okay, so what now?" He motioned to the boxes and sacks and Ronni tried to turn her attention away from Sylvia—the mystery woman who lived half a world away from her son and ex-husband—to tackle the job at hand, a job she now wished she hadn't started. She and Amy didn't belong here in this tense room, intruding on a family with problems they needed to solve between themselves.

"I thought you didn't have a tree, from what you'd said at the ski lodge, but I didn't pick one out for you." She began unpacking the sacks and boxes. "I think choosing the tree is a personal decision."

"Who cares?" Bryan said from the corner of his mouth. "It's just a stupid tree."

"It's not stupid!" Amy planted her little fists on her hips.

"Of course it's not," Travis said. "Bryan—"

"So let's go down to the lot," Ronni cut in, trying to forestall an argument that seemed ready to explode again between father and son. "I told Vic we'd stop by, so he's expecting us."

"Can't I just stay here?" Bryan complained. "It's such a hassle with the crutches and everyone stares at me."

Travis looked about to disagree, but didn't. "Yeah, fine. Whatever," he said.

She saw the father, frustration etched across his features, and the son, a look of defiance across his, and her heart went out to them both.

They drove into town in Travis's Jeep. Cascadia was deep in the throes of Christmas. Nativity scenes were on display at both churches, lighted candy canes were supported by lampposts and the D & E Christmas Tree Lot was doing a banner business. Cars and trucks were wedged into the few parking spaces surrounding the rows of trees. Colored lights, suspended around the perimeter of the lot, bounced in the wind, and the smell of fresh-cut cedar and pine mingled with the tantalizing scents of coffee and cinnamon. Everyone who walked onto the lot was given a free cup of coffee or spiced cider and entire families strolled through the rows of newly-hewn trees while sipping from paper cups.

Vic, in his plaid jacket and hunter's cap, was ready to haul the chosen tree, chop off any unwanted branches and bind it to a car, or offer advice to potential customers. He was a big, rugged man, blond and blue-eyed, evidence of his Danish ancestry. He'd been raised in Molalla, a small logging community in the foothills of the mountains, and had moved to Cascadia when he was in high school. He'd worked in the sawmill from the time he was seventeen until recently when the local mill had shut down and he'd been forced to look for another means to support his family. Reduced to scavenging for odd jobs, his once-carefree face had begun to line and weather, his honey-gold hair showed strands of gray.

"Ronni!" He spied her and clapped her on the back. "I was beginning to think that you'd stood me up."

"No way."

Amy scampered through the trees and Vic caught her, spinning her off her feet. "How's my favorite niece?" he said and she giggled. It didn't matter to her that he had no other nieces, Victor Pederson was the only father figure she'd ever known. He plopped her back to the ground and said, "I think I've got just the animal you want."

"A Christmas tree isn't an animal!" Amy said, giggling again.

"Isn't it? Well, I guess you're right." After quick introductions, Vic showed them a fourteen-foot noble fir, so large it was propped against the side of the next building—a vacant warehouse. "If you want this one, I'll tie it to the back of the pickup and bring it over," he offered. "No delivery charge."

Travis gave a curt nod. "Can't beat a deal like that. How about a stand? You sell 'em?"

"Absolutely!" Vic said. "Over here." In a lean-to tent he showed a couple of different styles of tree stands that could support a large tree. Within minutes, the decision was made and the men shook hands. "I'm off in half an hour. I'll bring tree, stand, the whole ball of wax, over to the Johnson place then."

"Can I ride with you?" Amy asked, clinging to her uncle and showing him her dimples.

Victor was easy. "You bet, pumpkin. If it's okay with your ma."

Ronni wasn't convinced. Amy, if the mood struck her, could be more than a handful and Victor was already busy. "You sure you want her?"

"Heck, yes, I'm sure. When do I ever get a little girl to spoil?"

"All right," Ronni said, caving in to her daughter's wishes yet again. "But Amy, you be good, do just what Uncle Vic says."

"I will," she called brightly as she dashed off through the rows of trees propped against lines of sawhorses.

"She'll probably get you fired," Ronni said worriedly.

"Not a chance. Delmer and Edwin think I'm the god of Christmas-tree sales." Laughing, he adjusted the brim of his hunting hat. "Now, don't worry about Amy-gal. She and I will get along just fine."

Ronni believed him and secretly prayed that Shelly's unborn baby was a little girl for Vic to spoil and love. Travis paid for the tree and shook Victor's hand once more. He helped Ronni into the Jeep, then climbed behind the wheel.

"Seems like a nice guy."

"Vic? Yeah, he is," she agreed as the Jeep lunged forward, rocking over potholes in the old, cracked pavement. She tried not to think about the fact that she was alone with Travis, or that his knee was only inches from hers and his hand on the gearshift knob was near enough that his fingers could easily graze her thigh. She shifted slightly, huddling closer to the passenger door even though she told herself she wasn't intimidated, that just because he was more purely animal male than she'd been around in a long time, she had no reason for the nest of butterflies that seemed to roll and flutter in her stomach.

The silence stretched between them and she blocked her mind to his scent, a mixture of soap and leather, and refused to notice the way his lips compressed in a sexy, blade-thin line. She didn't want to be reminded of how starkly male he was. He was a complicated man, she decided, and right now she didn't need or want any complications in her life.

"What do you do when you're not rescuing idiots who get lost on the mountain?" he asked, shifting down to take a corner as the streetlight changed from green to amber. They passed the old theater building, built like a World War II Quonset hut and now boarded over. "You have some kind of shop on your property, don't you?"

"It's a warehouse, really. A few years ago, I started advertising in some magazines about items unique to Oregon—items I sold through mail order. I got a handful of orders, found some new inventory, advertised again and each year I sold a little more."

"More what?"

A service station, its lights dimmed for the night, flashed by and then they were on the outskirts of town where the once-thriving sawmill was now shut down. The gates of the fence were chained and padlocked shut and a single tall security lamp gave off an eerie blue glow. Her brother-in-law had spent most of his adult life working at this very mill and now it seemed, with the restrictions on old-growth timber, environmental concerns and forest depletion, the sawmill would never reopen. And Victor would take Shelly and the boys and move away.

She realized then that Travis was waiting for an answer. "Oh. What do I sell?" she said, shaking away her case of melancholy. "A little of this and that, odds and ends that I think are difficult to find anywhere else. Myrtle wood, that's big here and hard to get in other places. And specialty jams and jellies made from native fruits. Books on Oregon. Some Native American art— mainly from Northwest tribes, jewelry, handcrafted pieces, even chain-saw sculpture and kits for tying fishing flies indigenous to Oregon. It's all kind of a hodge-podge. Some of the Christmas decorations I brought over are last year's stock."

"Sounds like a big operation."

"Bigger by the year. I hired my sister to do the secretarial stuff and handle some of the orders and when it really gets busy, I call a temporary agency in Portland. It's not a huge operation by any means, but it's grown so that I make enough money to support myself and Amy without having to worry too much."

"But you're still part of the ski patrol and search-and-rescue team?" The town had given way to the forest and only a few lights from hidden cabins sparkled warmly through the thick stands of fir and hemlock.

"Have been for a long time," she admitted, looking out the window and touching the fogging glass with a finger. She wondered how much she should tell him, or if she should bother explaining at all.

"You must love it."

Sighing, she glanced over to him and his gaze

touched hers for just an instant. Even though she knew little about him, she sensed that he was trustworthy, a man who cared. "My husband, Hank, was killed on Mount Echo nearly four years ago—a few months after Amy was born."

His jaw tightened. "I didn't know."

A pang of the same old sadness stole into her heart and she felt as if the temperature in the Jeep had dropped twenty degrees.

"I'm sorry."

"Oh, God, so am I," she admitted. "So am I." She focused past the front end of the car and the dual splashes of light offered by the headlights. "He and a partner, Rick, were up on the ridge, setting off charges to make the mountain avalanche-safe before the runs were opened. But something went wrong. A charge went off early, though no one can tell me why. Hank and Rick tried to outrace the snow but Hank's bindings failed. It didn't really matter anyway; Hank and Rick were both killed, buried in the snow." She shuddered at the thought.

"I'm sorry," he said as if he meant it.

"It's not your fault."

He wheeled into the long tree-lined driveway of the old lodge. "It sounds like it was no one's fault, that it was a freak accident."

"Maybe." She closed her eyes a second, trying to dispel the horrid image of Hank, her beloved Hank, caught in the rage and terror of thousands of pounds of snow.

"There's something else," he said as if reading her mind. They passed through the open gate to the lodge. Snow was beginning to fall again, sticking to the windshield before melting. Through the trees, from the windows of the lodge, soft, golden patches of light welcomed them.

"Hank shouldn't have died that day," she said, her throat closing.

"Of course he shouldn't have."

"No, you don't understand," she said, feeling that painful gnawing in her insides, that raw scraping of guilt. "I mean, he wasn't supposed to be on duty that morning." She rubbed a drop of condensation from the window as he parked in front of a dilapidated garage. Swallowing hard, she said, "It was my shift. I was the one that was supposed to be up there that day."

She felt rather than saw him move, and when his hand reached forward and his finger hooked beneath her jaw, she didn't fight him, just turned her head to look into dark, caring eyes. "You've been blaming yourself," he said, shaking his head, his breath whispering across her face.

"No, not just myself. I spread the blame around."

"But deep inside, you think you were at fault."

"Yes."

"And do you also think you should have been the one to die?"

She nodded, feeling the heat of his curled finger on the soft skin near her chin.

"You can't beat yourself up over an accident you couldn't have prevented." Travis stared at her long and hard. "I didn't know your husband, but I'm willing to bet that he wouldn't have traded places with you."

Squeezing her eyes shut, she tried not to think of Hank or the pain.

"Let it go," Travis advised, and when she opened her eyes, his face was nearly touching hers and the fog clouding the inside glass of the idling Jeep seemed to cut them off from the rest of the world. His fingers slid around her neck to her nape and with just a little pressure, he drew her close. "It's over, Ronni." His eyes searched her face. "He's gone and he wouldn't have wanted you to shroud yourself in guilt and grief forever."

His words were a soft balm on her old scarred wounds. "What do you know about it?" she asked, her voice hoarse.

But he didn't answer. Instead, his lips brushed over hers in a feathery kiss that brought goose bumps to her skin and an ache to her heart. She didn't want him to kiss her, or so she told herself, but she was unable to resist the sweet, delicious pressure of his mouth when it found hers again. Her breath was lost somewhere deep in her lungs and her heart was knocking wildly against her ribs.

She should stop, she should break away, but when his arms surrounded her, she felt her body yield and soften against him and she sighed willingly, opening her mouth against the touch of his tongue.

How long had it been? Years. Since Hank. Tears were hot against the back of her eyes and her throat clogged.

When he lifted his head, he brushed a strand of hair off her cheek. He looked about to say something, seemed to think better of it and switched off the ignition.

Ronni's fingers scrambled for the door handle. She needed to put some distance between herself and this man. "I, uh, think we'd better go inside. Vic will be here with the tree soon."

Travis stared at her a second, then pocketed his keys. "Right."

Opening the passenger door, she slid to the ground and silently called herself a fool. What had come over her? She hadn't kissed a man since Hank, never once wanted another man to get close, and yet in the Jeep, she'd felt the old stirring of lust and longing that she thought she'd buried along with her husband.

He caught up with her at the porch and his fingers curved over the crook in her arm. "Ronni—"

"What?" She turned and his arms wrapped around her. As she gasped, he kissed her again, this time with more urgency, his lips hard and strong, hers soft and pliant. Her pulse thundered and her legs seemed to turn to liquid.

His tongue slid into her open mouth and she felt a thrill of anticipation spread through her bloodstream, warming her from the inside out, creating a hunger she'd thought she would never again experience. With a groan, he leaned closer, the kiss deepened and his hands tangled in her hair. "Ronni," he whispered hoarsely when he finally lifted his head.

He tucked her against him and she felt the strength of his arms surrounding her, the tickle of his breath as it swept over her crown. Her heart was pounding like a jackhammer.

"I—I can't get involved with anyone," she said, cringing at the breathy tone of her voice.

"Me neither." Tipping her chin with one hand, he stared into her eyes. "But if I could…"

"Don't even think about it, Keegan," she teased, even though her own thoughts were racing ahead to what it would feel like to make love to him, to sleep in his bed, to wrap her arms around him and wake up in the morning smelling his scent. She bit down on her lip at the wayward turn of her mind. She was a woman who had no interest in a relationship, a person who had pledged her life to her child, someone who had tried to defy gender by being both mother and father to Amy.

"You can't blame yourself forever," he said.

"Why not?"

"And you can't go on punishing yourself."

"I don't!" she snapped. She was too sane, had her feet planted too firmly on the ground to fall into the trap. Or did she? "So who do you think you are? Sigmund Freud?"

"It was just an observation."

"What do you care?" she asked and the question hung between them like ice crystals gathering in the cold night air.

"I wish I knew," he said, holding her close. "I wish to God that I knew."

Headlights flashed and Vic's old half-ton pickup rolled into the driveway. Travis dropped his arms, and Ronni, embarrassed though she didn't really understand why, stepped away from him. She thought she saw a movement inside the house, a flutter of a curtain, but it could have been a trick of light combining with her hyperactive imagination.

Amy flew out of the truck, while Vic, careful of a bad knee he'd injured hauling wood a few years back, was a little slower. While Ronni carried in the stand, the two men wrestled with the tree and finally managed to get it upright without its leaning much. Bryan, though clearly loathe to admit he was interested, hobbled out of his room to watch the endeavor.

Spying his son, Travis said, "Don't we have some fishing wire around here—heavy-duty stuff like twenty-pound test? Why don't you see if you can find it, Bryan?"

"I'll help," Amy piped in.

Bryan, an unfriendly scowl set on his features, took off in the direction of the kitchen with Amy scampering after him. Travis located a ladder in a closet under the stairs and by the time the ladder was snapped open, Amy was dashing back, a spool of clear plastic fishing line in one hand. "We found it," she announced and Bryan hobbled back into the room.

Vic steadied the ladder while Travis drove nails into the wall and anchored the uppermost branches. Ronni helped Vic hold the tree steady and noticed the way Travis's sweater stretched upward as he pounded, allowing a glimpse of his flat abdominal muscles above the waistband of his jeans. He jammed the hammer into a back pocket and the faded denim slid lower. Ronni's stomach tightened and she bit her lip. Hard, lean muscles moved as he pulled the fishing line taut.

Realizing she was staring, she dragged her gaze away only to find Bryan's suspicious eyes fixed on her.

"You got Nintendo?" Amy was asking, obviously fascinated with him.

He didn't bother to answer even when she repeated the question.

"That should do it," Vic said, testing the stability of the tree. "I think one of Ronni's fool horses could come stampeding through here, hit the tree and the thing would still stand."

"Oh, right," Ronni said, grinning.

"Good." Travis hopped to the floor

"I'd better be shoving off." Vic eyed the tree and nodded to himself. "Shelly will be startin' to worry."

"Let me pay you for your trouble," Travis offered and was rewarded by a sharp look from Shelly's husband.

"It was part of the deal."

"Then, how about a drink? Or a cup of coffee."

"Another time, maybe, but now I'd better get home before the twins are in bed." He squared his hat upon his head and Travis extended his hand.

"Thanks."

"Don't mention it."

"I think we should be leaving, too," Ronni interjected as she caught her daughter, still pestering Bryan as she tried to hide a yawn.

"Nooo!" Amy protested. "We gots to put the lights on the tree."

"Not tonight, kiddo. It's waaaay past your bedtime." And Ronni didn't want to spend any more time close to Travis. Not until she'd sorted out the jumble of emotions that being around him evoked.

"But we have to—"

"She could sleep in one of the guest rooms," Travis offered, his eyes suddenly dark and serious, his voice soft as a caress. Ronni's heart kicked into third gear.

"But I'm not tired!" Amy said.

"I think it would be better to get her home." *For her, for Bryan and especially for me,* she added silently as she searched for her purse and jacket.

"So you're abandoning us to this mess?"

"We'll come back and help," she said, finding her leather bag near the fireplace.

"We can handle it." Bryan was still glaring at her as if she were the embodiment of all things evil. She didn't have to ask why he'd suddenly turned on her; obviously, he had watched his father kissing her on the porch. No one else had been home and the curtains had moved. So Bryan had seen them embracing, which was difficult for any teenager, and Bryan was going through a rough enough time as it was. Between the move and his mother's demands, the last thing he needed was his father to be distracted by another woman.

Travis didn't seem to hear his son. "How about tomorrow evening?" he suggested. "And this time, Bryan and I will cook dinner."

"Oh, brother," Bryan said, rolling his eyes.

"Can we?" Amy, finally accepting the fact that her mother wasn't about to budge on her decision to return home, jumped all over the suggestion.

Ronni hesitated for a second, but when her eyes found Travis's again, she managed a smile. "Sure," she replied. "Why not?"

There had to be a million reasons—a million good, sound reasons—but at that moment, staring into Travis's eyes, Ronni couldn't think of one.

CHAPTER SEVEN

"OH, JANICE, THEY'RE adorable," Ronni said, stepping closer to the pen and eyeing seven wiggling puppies. Six weeks old with bright eyes, wagging tails and high-pitched yips, they scrambled over one another in an eager attempt to reach her. Some brown, others black, still others with gray-and-white markings on their fuzzy coats, they staggered on unsure legs across old newspapers that had been spread across the floor of the Petrocellis' garage.

"We're not really sure what they are exactly," Janice admitted, running fingers through her spiky blond hair. As she moved her hand, her bracelets jangled, causing more excited yips. "I'm afraid they may have had more than one dad—that's possible, you know." A heater in the corner kept the shell of a room warm enough for the inhabitants of the huge pen. "Our Fangette, here," she said, motioning to the tired-looking mother dog, "she's part German shepherd, Lab and golden retriever, and a sweetheart, aren't you, baby?"

She patted Fangette's wide head and was rewarded with a sloppy pink tongue washing her palm. "She escaped once while she was in heat and this is the result. Seven of 'em, five males and two females. Near as I can tell, some of them look like they have some husky blood in them—see the ones with the curly tails and white markings—and the others could be anything. I don't think Fangette was particularly discriminating—kind of like some women I've met." She chuckled to herself.

"Well, she certainly ended up with some beguiling pups," Ronni said.

"Her first and last litter, believe me. We're going to get Fangette fixed pronto. It's not easy finding homes for these little guys."

Ronni petted all the eager, upturned faces, watching little curly tails whip with excitement. One brown puppy with black-tipped ears was the most playful of the bunch. She growled and lunged at her brothers and sister and the spark of devilment in her eyes touched Ronni. "This one," she said, picking up the wiggling bundle of fur. "Will you keep her until Christmas Eve? She'll be a surprise for my daughter."

"Will do." Janice seemed relieved to have found an owner. "Just hold her there a minute." She walked to a cabinet, opened the cupboard door, and amidst the fertilizer, insect spray and camping equipment, found a bottle of red nail polish. "I'll paint her toenail so that we don't give her away to anyone else by mistake."

The puppy licked the underside of Ronni's chin.

"Hold her still." Janice applied a dab of quick-drying polish and then blew on the tiny foot. "There ya go, darlin'," she said to the pup, and reluctantly, Ronni placed the little dog back in the pen with her brothers and sister. "One down, six to go. If you hear of anyone else interested in a puppy, please tell them about Fangette's litter."

"I will," Ronni promised and cast one last look at the puppy who was happily chewing on one of her brothers' ears. Smiling, she headed to the van. Amy would be in seventh heaven when she found the furry little pup under the tree on Christmas morning.

Travis had cut his teeth on tough negotiations. When he was expanding his business, buying out smaller corporations, dealing with union officials, talking to lawyers, accountants and sales representatives from all walks of life, he'd prided himself on his ability to usually, through minimal concessions, get his way.

But bargaining with Bryan was more difficult than anything he'd ever been through. Because his heart was involved. Because he cared. Because if he messed up with his son's life, he would never get a second chance. And the kid seemed to sense it.

They sat on the floor of Bryan's room amidst the clutter of compact discs, magazines, baseball cards and clothes, staring at each other as if they were mortal enemies. Travis leaned against the bed for support, Bryan sat cross-legged and was sorting through a stack of baseball cards that he hadn't looked at in over two years.

"Okay, let me get this straight," Travis said, feeling manipulated by his own adolescent son. "You're willing to give up this idea of moving to France if you can spend a weekend with Martin in Seattle?"

"That's it." Bryan's defiant eyes met his father's. Daring. Challenging.

"One weekend for the rest of your life."

"Yeah." He shoved the baseball cards aside.

"I don't think so."

"Fine." Stretching out on the floor and leaning on one elbow, he said, "Then I'm going to live with Mom."

"In a pig's eye. You'd no sooner get over there and

you'd be on the phone to come home. You tried living with your mother once before, remember?"

"That was different."

"Yeah, she still lived in Seattle and you could see your friends anytime you wanted. You went to the old school, lived in our house. It still didn't work out."

"Thing's have changed," Bryan argued glumly.

"That's right." Travis drove the point home, even though it was bound to hurt a little. "Now your mother's in a foreign country and you wouldn't know anyone there. You'd be isolated in some American school, if you were lucky, and get to hobnob with the sons and daughters of diplomats and the like. You think life here is hard, just you wait."

Bryan's lips rolled over his teeth and he stared at the floor. Travis gambled. "But if it's what you really want, if you think you'd be happier in Paris, then go. With my blessing. Just remember two things."

"What?"

"First and foremost, I don't want you to go. I want you to live with me." He stared at his son long and hard. "I love you, Bryan, and even if it's not a guy thing to say, I want you to know it."

A growl of disbelief.

"Now the second thing, and it's important, too." He folded his arms over his chest. "If you decide to go to France, then you can't come back until summer. You've got to learn to commit, sport, and if you want to live with Sylvia, then you can't play this same game over there that you're playing with me now. You can't use me, or living with me, as a bargaining chip to get what you want from her, because even though your mother might buy into that kind of blackmail, I don't."

Bryan drew his finger in a circle on the faded carpet. "Then you're a liar, right. If you really loved me—"

"I'd do exactly what I'm doing because it's the best thing for you and that's what matters."

"Bull!"

"I guess you don't understand, Bry. When you love someone, really care for them, you don't use that love as a weapon, or a wedge, or a trump card. You don't use it against them at all. It's a gift."

"Geez, Travis, listen to yourself! Talk about sounding hokey! All you need is a pulpit and you could open your own church." His finger quit moving on the carpet. "You never were this way before."

"I know." Travis picked up a barbell and wrapped his fingers around the cool metal. "I'm trying to fix that."

"If you ask me, you're getting weird. What happened to you?"

"I looked in the mirror one day and didn't like what I saw." Travis lifted the weight over his head.

"Oh, sure. It didn't have anything to do with Mom deciding to 'find herself' or whatever it is she thinks she's doing."

"It happened about the same time."

Bryan chewed on his lower lip a second, then he raised his eyes and pinned his father in his troubled gaze. "You ever gonna get married again?"

"Me? No," he said quickly. Then the image of Ronni's upturned face, her lips parted, her brown eyes warm and inviting chased through his mind, and for the first time in years, he doubted himself. "At least I don't have any immediate plans."

"You're sure?"

"Why?"

"No reason," he said quickly, then added, "Me neither. I'm *never* getting married!"

"You're a little young to be saying that."

"Yeah, but girls are trouble."

"I think that's what makes them so damned fascinating." He transferred the barbell to his other hand and started a series of repetitions.

"What about you and that Ronni?" Bryan asked, his eyes narrowing suspiciously.

The muscles in the back of Travis's neck tensed. "What about us?"

"She seems to like you a lot."

"We're friends." *Liar! It's more than that. Much more. Even Bryan's picked up on it.* "I barely know her."

"Her kid's a pain."

"Amy?"

"Yeah. Always askin' questions and gettin' into my stuff! Messin' it up."

"How can you tell?" Travis asked, eyeballing the clutter that was strewn everywhere. Bryan's bedroom looked like a cyclone had stormed through, turned around, decided enough damage hadn't been done and swept back the way it had come. But Travis wasn't riding him about the mess. At least not yet. There were bigger, more important issues to deal with. Until his son was off crutches, in school, had made some new friends and felt more comfortable living in Cascadia, Travis had decided not to sweat the little things, such as a messy room.

"I can tell, okay? The kid was only here a few hours and most of the time stayed out of my way, but boy, when she was in here, she trashed the place. She bugs me."

"She's only four."

"Well, she can be four someplace else."

"Not tonight. They're coming over. We're cooking."

"You and me? I thought that was just a joke."

Travis rolled his eyes to the ceiling, then lifted his hand solemnly, as if he were about to take the most important oath of his life. "I swear on my honor. It's the truth."

With a sound of disgust, Bryan flopped onto the floor and stared at the ceiling. "Well, that's great, Dad. Just…just great."

"You don't know the half of it. We're going to barbecue."

"What?" Bryan glanced to the window where snow was settling against the lower panes. "It's freezing outside."

"We've got pretty big porches."

"But—but you barbecue for the Fourth of July or… what's wrong with you?" Bryan stared at his father as if he'd completely lost his mind, and Travis couldn't really blame him. The idea of a barbecue had just popped into his head.

"I don't even think you can do it in the winter," Bryan said. "It must be against the law or somethin'."

"They cook outside up at the lodge on Mount Echo all the time."

Bryan leveled his father a look that silently called him a lunatic, but he held his tongue.

"It's going to be fun," Travis assured him.

"Since when do you care about fun?"

Good question. For years he'd avoided any activity that wasn't business-related, including seeking out a good time. He'd been single-minded and with only serious purposes in mind. "Since I decided that living inside a boardroom was a waste of time—mine and yours. So this is the start, and we're going to do a lot of fun things in the future."

"Like what?"

"Camping, trail riding, fly fishing, maybe even mountain climbing." Travis set the weight down and climbed to his feet. "Now, I'd better go locate some charcoal and a grill in the middle of winter in Cascadia."

"While you're at it, you might try to find the rest of your brain," Bryan said, but there was a twinkle in his eye that Travis hadn't seen for weeks.

"Very funny. You coming?"

"I don't know why," Bryan grumbled, but grabbed his crutches, propped them against the bed and struggled to his feet. He followed his father to the hallway and as Travis checked to make sure he had his keys, his son asked, "Hey, Dad, what are the symptoms of a guy who's going through a second childhood?"

"I don't want to be a wise man," Kurt announced, crossing his arms over his chest as Ronni, on her knees in the dining area of her house, tried to adjust the hem of his costume. "They're dorks."

"Stand still," Shelly ordered around a mouth of pins. "And remember that the wise men were *not* dorks. They were very important kings. That's right, isn't it?" she asked Ronni. "Kings, right?"

"I think so."

"Well, dressing in towels is dorky," Kurt stated emphatically. The costume, cut from two old striped beach blankets, draped over his body and touched the floor.

"How about sheets?" Kent twirled, sending his shepherd outfit of muslin billowing. "That's dorky, too."

"They didn't have malls back then, or big department stores," Shelly said as she made a final tuck in one sleeve. "This will have to do."

"I hate the pageant," Kurt muttered under his breath.

"Don't they go to church to learn how *not* to hate?" Ronni asked her sister.

"That's the way it's supposed to work."

"I hate church, too."

"Stop it, Kurt, you do not."

"Do, too."

Shelly rolled her eyes to the ceiling as if searching for God and hoping that He would intervene. "The pageant will be fun. Now, come on, boys, settle down, we're just about done."

Amy fluttered through in the garb of an angel. "I like being an angel," she said, her tinsel halo bobbing as she talked, her wings stiff.

"You would," Kurt observed.

"I was an angel last year," Kent said.

"Yeah, who ever heard of a boy angel?"

"How about Gabriel?" Shelly asked. "He's a man, right?" Again she looked at her sister. "Maybe I'd better brush up on my Bible study."

"Who cares?" Kurt complained.

Ronni stood and dusted her hands. "Okay, that does it. Take off your costume—carefully, now," she added when Kurt began to rip off the offensive robe. "You three can play outside for a while, if you want, run off some of that restless energy."

Towel-robes, sheets, wings and halo went flying as the kids grabbed their jackets and headed out the front door. Ronni had to help Amy with her zipper, hat and boots, but the little girl was out the door in a flash, chasing after her older cousins. From the window, Ronni watched Kurt hurl a snowball that smashed against the back of Kent's jacket. With a squeal, Kent scooped up a handful of snow and the fight was on.

"Victor told me about helping set up a tree for you over at the old lodge," Shelly observed as she draped the shepherd's outfit over the end of the ironing board.

"It wasn't really for me. I'm just helping decorate it."

"For Keegan?"

"Mmm." Ronni nodded and adjusted the pins on the sleeves of Kurt's costume.

"How does the old place look?"

"Good," Ronni admitted, despising the wistful tone that stole into her voice. "The lodge is still pretty drafty and there's lots more work to be done, but what he's done so far is nice and he's trying to refurbish it rather than remodel it." She snapped the pin box closed and stretched her arms over her head. "He didn't say too much about it, but it seems as if he's not going to do anything as stupid as modernize it—except for the needed repairs and necessary updates to bring it up to code."

"Did you ever talk to Taffy—ask her why she didn't tell you someone was interested in buying the place?"

"Nah." Ronni wound measuring tape between her fingers and frowned at the mention of her old school friend turned real estate agent. "What would have been the point? I couldn't have afforded the place anyway."

"I know the feeling," Shelly said. "I'm afraid it's going to have to be a spiritual Christmas this year."

"That's the best kind."

"I think so, too, but tell it to a couple of six-year-olds

who want everything they see on television. Kent's list is two pages and he keeps coming up with more ideas."

"How about a puppy?" Ronni suggested. "I know where there's a great litter."

"We rent, remember? No dogs allowed. And if we have to move—"

"You're not moving. Don't even talk like that," Ronni said, but saw the worry in her sister's eye before Shelly changed the subject back to Travis.

"So tell me about your new neighbor."

"Not much to say."

"Oh, come on. Vic wouldn't say a word, just that he seemed like an okay, regular kind of Joe. I told him that was crazy. Regular guys don't buy old lodges and lakes and hundreds of acres of woods. The guy's got to be loaded."

"Or in debt."

"Nah. The banks only loan money to you if you don't need it. Believe me, I know." She placed her hand near the bottom plate of the iron, decided it was hot enough and started pressing the wrinkles out of Kent's shepherd costume. "So what does Keegan do?"

"He's never really said." Ronni, glancing through the window over the sink to make sure the kids were okay, reached for the coffeepot and turned on the water while watching Kurt climb onto the fence and try to lure the horses to the side of the paddock with a handful of oats. The animals, standing in the shelter of a fir tree, pricked their ears forward and flicked their tails, but weren't enticed. Loose Change, nicknamed Lucy, snorted in disdain and her tail flicked over her rounded belly.

"Well, he must earn a living some way, or else— God forbid," she mocked, "he's independently wealthy."

Ronni chuckled as she rinsed the glass pot and scooped coffee into the maker. "I think he owns some sporting goods company in Seattle and it runs itself or he has a manager who does all the legwork. I don't know." She looked up at her sister and noticed a gleam in Shelly's eye as she leaned across the counter. "Why?"

"You seem to be spending a lot of time with him."

"Not a lot."

"So come on, tell me, what's he like, what's he look like...? Vic wouldn't fill me in on the details."

Coffee started to drizzle through the filter and the scent filled the room. "What's he like?" Ronni said, pulling down cups and saucers from an open cupboard. "Well, he's in his mid-thirties, I'd guess, and he's tall, about the same size as Vic, but he's got dark hair and gray eyes and...a great smile, very sexy, but he hardly ever shows it off." She set the sugar bowl on the table along with a small creamer filled with half-and-half. "Oh, and he's got a son. Fourteen going on twenty-five."

"You don't like his boy?"

"No, that's not the problem," Ronni said, watching Loose Change finally deign to amble through the snow and nuzzle Kurt's mittened hand in search of grain. "He doesn't like me."

"Oops."

"Yeah. He's a little mixed up and needs to settle in with his dad before he should have to deal with a woman...." She let the words trail away. What was she thinking? Bryan would never have to deal with her, not permanently. She was just Travis's neighbor, potentially a friend. *Who are you trying to fool?* a tiny voice in her mind nagged. *Do you tell your neighbors your darkest secrets? Fantasize about them? Stay awake all night remembering what it felt like to kiss them?*

"So you're interested," Shelly said with a matchmaking glimmer in her eye.

"Not really."

"Sure you are. Look, he's new in town, doesn't know anyone and lives up in that rambling old place with just his son. Why don't you invite him to have Christmas dinner with us?"

The coffeemaker sputtered. "Christmas?" Ronni repeated.

"Why not?"

"Look, Shelly, don't start with this, okay? It's not like we're dating or anything. I'm just having dinner with him—"

"Twice." Shelly held up two fingers and wiggled them before she turned off the iron and hung up Kent's costume. "When's the last time you went to dinner with a man, hmm?"

"I'm not inviting him to Christmas dinner," Ronni said firmly as she poured them each a cup of coffee and they settled into their usual chairs at the table.

"We'll see," Shelly murmured, undeterred.

"Don't do anything stupid, Shell."

"*Moi?* Of course not."

"Don't you go around my back and invite him."

"Wouldn't dream of it." But a sly smile curved her lips, and before Ronni could say another word, the door burst open. Kent, holding his mouth, ran into the room. He was crying and sobbing and slipped on the floor.

Shelly was on her feet in an instant and scooping him up. "What is it, honey?" she asked.

"K-Kurt, he tagged me—"

Shelly pulled his hand away from his mouth. Blood was smeared on the lower half of his face and his glove. He let out a terrified howl of pain. Shelly's face drained of color.

"I'll handle this," Ronni said. "Let's see." Kent clung to his mother as Amy and Kurt, looking sheepish, slid into the room. "Close the door," Ronni ordered while taking a clean cloth from a drawer, soaking it in warm water and washing Kent's tear-streaked and blood-soaked face. "I think you'll live," she said as she studied the scratches around his mouth and looked inside where one of his front teeth wobbled precariously and blood still ran. "You'll probably beat your brother in the tooth-loss department, though. My guess is the tooth fairy might come before Santa Claus this year."

"Really?" Kent blinked against the tears standing in his eyes.

"No way!" Kurt complained. He'd been born ten minutes before his younger brother and seemed to think, as eldest son, he had all sorts of privileges.

"Really. Here, let me get a mirror and you can see for yourself. Amy—" But her daughter was already dashing through the dining and living area, her boots squishing as she left a trail of water on her way to the bathroom.

"Got it," she cried. Back in an instant with a hand mirror, she nearly stumbled in her attempt to hand it to a sniffing Kent. "Lookie," she said as the boy tried his best to eye his injuries.

Shelly's color returned. "Now, since no one has to be placed permanently on the injured reserve list, what happened?"

They all started talking at once, but near as Ronni could tell, Kurt, bored with petting Lucy's soft nose, had packed a snowball with pieces of ice he'd picked up from the frozen mud puddles. He'd hurled the icy snowball at Kent, whose back was turned, but a second before the moment of impact, Kent had turned and the hard-packed missile had caught him in the face.

"I think I'd better take my warriors home before anyone else gets hurt in battle," Shelly said. She glanced longingly at her cooling cup of coffee. "I'll see you tomorrow. Come on, boys." Kent refused to walk—Shelly had to pack him into the car—and Kurt hung his head, probably because he knew that during the drive home, he was sure to receive a long lecture on playing safely.

"Kurt wanted to hurt Kent," Amy announced as she watched the boys struggle with their seat belts.

"No—"

"Yes, he did, Mommy. Kurt's mean."

"Just rambunctious."

"'Bunctious and mean." Amy flounced back into the house and Ronni hesitated on the front porch. Dusk was just beginning to settle and the forest seemed dark and gloomy, but through the trees she caught a glimpse of colored lights at the old Johnson place and her heart warmed. What was wrong with her these days? she wondered as she closed the door and looked forward to an evening with a man she barely knew and a boy who seemed to hate her.

Bryan, obviously coached by his father, was on his best behavior. Beneath the surface was the same sullen boy, but he was outwardly friendly. After a meal of grilled steaks, salad and baked potatoes, they finished decorating the tree. Travis had already strung lights through the branches, so most of the hard work was done. The ladder was necessary again and when the last ornament was hung and the final length of tinsel draped, they lit candles, turned out the lights and plugged in the tree.

Amy gasped as hundreds of tiny, winking lights blazed, lending the huge room a cozy glow. "It's beautiful," she breathed, her eyes shining in wonder. "But it needs a star."

Ronni shrugged. "We've got the same problem and thought we might find a homemade star or angel at the church bazaar."

"Church bazaar?" Bryan snorted. "Don't tell me, there's a Christmas pageant, too."

"Are you coming?" Amy asked eagerly and Bryan rolled his eyes.

"No."

"Why not?"

"A dumb pageant?"

"It's not dumb," Amy said, her lower lip trembling. "I'm an angel."

"Then it will be great!" Travis said, bending on a knee so he could look her squarely in the eye. "We'll be in the front row."

"No way!" All of Bryan's pretenses shattered and fell away. "I'm not going to some stupid show about Jesus getting born. I've seen it a hundred times."

"We'll be there," Travis said, rumpling Amy's hair and shooting his son a look that brooked no argument.

Bryan grabbed his crutches and hitched himself out of the room. A second later, the door to his bedroom slammed shut.

"Why did he say it was dumb?" Amy asked, wounded.

"Because he's fourteen," Travis said, "and sometimes he has a hard time remembering to be polite."

Amy started off in the direction of Travis's room, but Ronni caught her by the shoulder. "Why don't you give him a few minutes to cool off, honey? He'll probably change his mind."

"No doubt about it," Travis said, his jaw set.

Amy fell asleep on the couch watching a Christmas special and Ronni covered her with a hand-pieced quilt Travis found. "This looks like an antique," she said, tucking the faded blue squares beneath Amy's chin.

"My grandmother's. I think her great-grandmother made it—or maybe it was her great-great-grandmother, I can't remember. Anyway, the story is that it came over on the wagon train—Oregon Trail—and then when the family moved north a generation or so later, it traveled along with them.

"My grandmother thought I should have it and so now it's back in Oregon. Come on." He took her arm and guided her back to the kitchen where he made hot coffee, infusing it with a shot of brandy. They put on their jackets, walked to the back porch and watched as lacy snowflakes fell, powdering the boughs of trees and collecting on the ground.

"So you have a lot of family in the Seattle area?"

"Some. A sister, a few cousins and my folks, but my parents live in Arizona in the winter."

Funny, she'd never imagined him as part of an extended family. He seemed like such a loner, a man who was used to doing things for and by himself. "Is your sister coming down for Christmas?"

Frowning, he gave a curt shake of his head. "Nah. I don't see much of her."

"Oh." She didn't want to pry and yet there was so much she wanted to learn about him.

"She resents me." A simple statement of fact. No emotions tangling it down.

"Why?"

"I don't really blame her," he admitted with a crooked, humorless smile. "She was firstborn and smart as a whip. Excelled in school, studied abroad, a real academic."

She watched the steam rise from her coffee cup and blew across the cup, waiting for him to continue.

Leaning a hip against the top railing, he said, "I, on the other hand, was a screwup. Always in trouble. Never studied, barely passed, hated school. Despite all the grief I gave them, my parents, both of them, treated me as if I were the golden child. I was the boy, my father's only son, the last Keegan of his line. My sister, no matter how hard she tried, was always second best. It wasn't that they didn't love her in their own way, it was the fact that I was supposed to excel, be the best." He took a long swallow. "My sister never forgave me."

"But that wasn't your fault," she protested, trying to reconcile the image of the rebel teenager with that of the successful man staring into the winter-dark night.

"Maybe not, but when you're hurting, you try and hurt back. When she couldn't gain my folks' attention through achievement, she found other means, married someone they disapproved of and moved to L.A. She's divorced now, no kids and barely speaks to me." He shrugged, then drained his cup. "The ironic part was, about the time she started rebelling, I'd finally grown up, finished college and started working for a computer software company. A couple of years later, I was married, a father and had moved into sporting goods and equipment. All of a sudden, I had to live up to my parents' expectations, and by the time I stopped to take a breath, my marriage was falling apart and my son was a stranger who was starting to get into some of the same kind of trouble I got into as a teenager. I decided to change things."

"So you moved here."

His smile flashed in the darkness. "Sounds like I was running away, doesn't it?"

"No, just making a change."

He made a sound of disgust in the back of his throat. "Let's just hope it was for the best."

She set her cup on the windowsill and he linked his fingers through hers. Snow crunched beneath their shoes as he, tugging on her hand, led her through a copse of trees to the lake. Inky water lapped at the shore where ice had formed between the rocks.

At the edge of the lake, he turned to face her, his features in shadows, his eyes as dark as the night. Ronni felt that new feeling, the sizzle in her blood, the anticipation in the beat of her heart. With snow drifting around them, he pulled her against him and his mouth found hers in the darkness. He tasted of coffee and his lips were firm and hot, demanding. The feminine part of herself she'd buried so long ago responded and she linked her hands behind his neck. A cool winter breeze caught in her hair and lifted it from her nape. Snowflakes drifted from the sky.

Ronni felt her insides quiver as the kiss deepened. Her heart pounded so loudly she was certain he could hear it. Slowly he lifted his head and touched his forehead to hers. "Who are you, Veronica Walsh, and what are you doing to me?" he whispered.

"I—I was going to ask you the same thing." She swallowed hard, trying to get a grip on her equilibrium, but his lips claimed hers again, slashing across her mouth with enough force to shatter all thoughts of resistance.

Inside she shuddered. It was she who knew nothing about him—just a few comments about a sister and parents and a grandmother's quilt, about a troubled son and complicated ex-wife. But still he was a stranger, a man she'd only recently met, a man she didn't know well enough to trust.

Not that he was part of some sinister plot, that was silly, but the way he made her skin quiver when he kissed her, the power of emotions swirling and fighting in her being, the racing beat of her heart, all were signs that she needed to know more about him. He wasn't like Hank, a boy she'd grown up with and trusted, a man she'd loved, a husband she'd adored and been faithful to.

His hands slid beneath her jacket and farther, past the hem of her sweater to her skin. She sucked in a breath as his fingers grazed the stitching of her bra, moving sensually over the cup, heating her flesh beneath the thin layer of silk and lace.

Warning bells clanged in her mind. *Stop! Ronni, use your head! You don't love this man. You barely know him. Think!*

But it had been so long. So very long. Endless, restless, sleepless nights had stretched from that time she'd last felt a man's touch, last realized what it was like to be wanted. His hand lowered, settling at the curve of her waist, fingers warm and supple.

His tongue touched hers, delving, retracting, toying with her until a dark warmth curled slowly in her belly. Liquid heat radiated from deep inside.

She felt the jacket being stripped from her, heard the soft thud of denim sinking into the snow. A breath of wind touched her flesh as he lifted her sweater over her head and her long hair fell back on her bare skin. Slowly he unhooked her bra, letting the scrap of lace fall into the white powder at their feet as he watched snowflakes melt against her skin.

She was breathing with difficulty, all too aware of the tightening of her nipples, the dark points high and proud and aching. His eyes touched hers and she licked her lips nervously as he traced one long finger along the cleft of her breasts and lower to hook on the waistband of her jeans.

"Veronica," he whispered across her open mouth. "Let me…"

"W-what?"

"Love you."

She squeezed her eyes shut.

"No, darlin'," he said, his breath tantalizing her ear. "We both go into this with our eyes open or we don't go at all."

Swallowing with difficulty, she forced her eyes open. His hands moved up her rib cage slowly, achingly, until they reached her breasts and then he cupped them both, rubbing his thumbs across her nipples, staring into her eyes and kissing her lips. She didn't resist as he dragged her onto the snow, pulling her on top of him as he kissed one dark, proud point. Icy snowflakes settled against her back as he licked and teased, tasted and toyed. She moaned, arching her back, settling her hips against his and he suckled wildly, one hand lowering to grab her buttock and hold her firmly against him as he pleasured her.

Old sensations, new emotions, a storm of heat and fire and passion swept through her blood and she lost control, moving against him, her flesh yearning for his. All thought of restraint was caught by the passing wind and carried away. She wanted more of him, of his magic touch.

His mouth was moist and warm and wondrous and when he kissed her abdomen, she trembled with want. Her zipper slid down with a quiet hiss promising more and her body was on fire.

Don't think, just feel, her wanton mind cried.

"Oh, Ronni, no!" Suddenly he stopped. His hands quit moving and his entire body tensed. "No," he said, his words muffled against her skin. "Hell, no."

"Travis?"

Strong arms wrapped around her, holding her close for a second before he rolled over and still embracing her, swept a long dark strand of hair from her shoulder. "I...I... Look, Ronni, I think we should slow down."

Her laugh was brittle. So he thought she was easy—that it was common practice for her to fall willingly and naked into a man's arms. A hot blush climbed up her back as she tried to scramble away. What could she say? She hadn't acted like this for years. Not since Hank. Oh, what had she been thinking? "You're right," she agreed, trying to break away. "I don't know what got into me."

"Into us."

"I feel like a fool."

"Why?"

"Why?" She stared at his eyes, deep gray in the darkness, and shook her head in frustration. "Because, believe it or not, despite what just happened between us, it's not my usual practice to try and seduce a near stranger in the middle of a snowstorm—"

"We're not strangers."

"Nonetheless."

"And I was the one doing the seducing." His voice was tinged with self-condemnation and he cast an angry glance at the moonless sky. "I lose my head when I'm with you."

"Don't blame yourself." She extracted herself and, suddenly self-conscious, reached for her sweater.

"I'm not blaming anyone."

"Sounded like it to me." She jerked her sweater over her head, then scooped up her jacket, shaking the snow from the folds of the denim. "Look, let's just call it a mistake and move on."

"Is that what you think?" he asked, his mouth tightening. "That being with me was a mistake?"

"Wasn't it?"

"No." He grabbed her arm. "Look, Ronni, I don't know what's happening between us and to be honest it scares me, but I don't believe for a second that it's wrong."

She tried to step away, but he held her fast, his fingers tightening possessively. "I just don't want you to get the wrong impression," she said.

"Have I?"

"I—I haven't dated much since my husband died and I've never even kissed another man since—" At his shocked expression, she added, "I know, it sounds unbelievable, but I wasn't…I mean, I'm not ready for any kind of relationship. I never expected anything like what happened between us and I think it would be best if we… Oh, Lord, I can't believe I'm having this conversation, but I think it would be best if we didn't…"

"Didn't what?"

"Get too involved."

"And what does that mean?" he asked, his eyes narrowing in the shadows. "That we shouldn't see each other?"

"No, not that, but—"

"That I shouldn't kiss you."

"Probably."

His laugh was harsh. "A few minutes ago, you were just about to—"

"I know what I was about to do and we both realize it would have been a mistake," she said, stung, her cheeks flaming in the darkness. "But nothing happened."

"Yet. Nothing's happened yet," he told her. "Look, things were heating up too fast for both of us, but that doesn't mean we shouldn't still see each other. We'll just take things slower."

"I think it's time for us to leave," she said, stuffing an arm down one sleeve of her jacket. "I'll just pack up Amy and—"

"Don't," he said, his voice a soft command.

"Don't what?"

"Don't leave angry."

"I'm not—" She clamped her mouth shut and silently counted to five. "I'm not angry with you."

"No, you're angry with yourself."

"So now you're a psychiatrist." She started for the house, half expecting him to try to stop her, but he followed after her at a slower pace and she was inside the kitchen by the time he'd caught up with her. He didn't say a word, just leaned one hip against a battle-worn butcher-block counter.

"So where do we go from here?"

"I don't know," she admitted, confused by the conflicting emotions that tore at her soul. "This is…it's all new to me…well, new the second time around."

"Since your husband?" he asked, his eyebrows drawing together.

"Yes."

"But you've dated."

"Look, I'm not trying to play the virgin's role here. I was married and have a child, but it's been…it's been a long time since Hank and—"

"Since Hank?"

She was startled by the accusation in his voice. "My husband."

"I know who he was," he snapped, the corners of his mouth tight. "But you're a young, vibrant woman. You don't expect me to believe that in the what?—nearly four years since his death, you haven't been involved with another man."

She inched her chin up a notch. "I don't care what you believe."

"But—"

"I was in love with my husband, Travis, and just because he died doesn't mean that my feelings for him disappeared, that I was ready to jump right back into the dating scene. Thanks…thanks for tonight," she added and pushed through the swinging doors and down the hall to the living room where Amy, in the glow of the Christmas tree, was still sleeping soundly.

Without a word, Travis helped her gather her purse and, over Ronni's protests, wrapped Amy in the old quilt that his grandmother had given him.

Bryan, at his father's insistence, stumbled out of his room. Earphones surrounding his neck, he managed to mumble a quick good-night before Ronni strapped Amy into the van and drove the short distance home. In her sideview mirror, she caught a glimpse of Travis, legs apart, arm folded over his chest, watching her leave as the colored lights strung across the roof of the porch winked cheerily.

She waved despite the small hole she felt tearing her inside. "Don't be a fool," she muttered aloud. He was her neighbor—no more than a casual friend.

She worried her lip as she drove through the ice-spangled gates of the his newly acquired estate and reminded herself that casual friends didn't nearly make love on the snow-covered shores of a winter-dark lake.

CHAPTER EIGHT

TRAVIS DIDN'T CALL. Not the first night, nor the second, nor the third. Not that he should, Ronni told herself as she waxed her skis in a lean-to area off the back porch of her house. Pink shavings littered the concrete floor beneath the sawhorses that Hank had set up years ago for just this purpose. His skis hung on an interior wall and in their upstairs closet she'd kept his boots, jumpsuit and poles.

She hadn't realized how many reminders of her husband she'd kept around the house and wondered for the first time in nearly four years if she was clinging to the past, unable or unwilling to let go. She'd told herself that it was important for Amy to know who her father was, to have some tangible evidence of the man he'd been, but now she considered the very real possibility that she'd never come to terms with his death. Not that she'd spent the past few years moping around, drinking wine and sighing over could-have-beens, but there was a part of her that hadn't been able to face the heartrending truth and the pain.

Stiffening her spine, she told herself that a new year was coming and no matter what else happened, Ronni Walsh vowed that she was going to put the past behind her, once and for all.

Through the open door to the house she heard the

phone ring and her heart jump-started. *Travis!* "Oh, for the love of Saint Mary, Ronni, you're acting like you're sixteen again!" she reprimanded herself as she climbed the two steps into the kitchen and accepted the receiver from Amy's outstretched hand. "Hello?"

"Ronni?" Shelly asked, her voice sounding oddly strangled. "Do you think you could watch the boys this afternoon?"

"Sure, Shell, what's up?"

"Vic's going to run me to the clinic and I, um, think it would be best if the twins were with you."

"The clinic?" Ronni repeated, dread drizzling through her blood.

"Yeah. To see Dr. Sprick. It's, um, probably nothing but…well, I'm spotting a little and I think it should be checked out."

"Oh, Shelly," Ronni said, leaning back against the refrigerator and closing her eyes. "Sure. I can come and get the boys in fifteen minutes."

"No—we'll bring them by. Vic's already warming up the car."

A hard lump settled in the pit of Ronni's stomach and when she heard the rumble of Shelly's old station wagon, she dashed across the yard. The twins, more subdued that usual, clambered out of the backseat and ran into the house, but Ronni paused at the open passenger window.

"You're going to be all right," she said, managing a smile.

"I know it." Shelly's voice didn't have its usual lilt and Vic stared through the windshield, barely glancing in her direction.

"Don't worry about the boys. If they have to spend the night, it's no big deal."

"It shouldn't be that long," Vic said, and for the first time Ronni noticed the cigarette burning between his fingers. Victor had given up smoking seven years ago, before the twins had been born, and to Ronni's knowledge hadn't lit up since. Until today. He avoided her eyes.

"Okay, well...I'll see you later."

Shelly's chin wobbled and tears glazed her eyes. "Yeah." As Ronni patted the car door and stepped away from the time-worn station wagon, Victor slipped it into gear. They drove away in a cloud of blue exhaust, and Ronni, sending up a prayer for her sister, hurried into the house. "Come on, you guys," she said to the kids who were already jockeying for favored positions as they huddled around a cartoon show on television, "let's bake Christmas cookies." She touched her nephews on their shoulders, hoping to lift their spirits. Even though Shelly probably hadn't told them what was wrong, they'd obviously picked up that there was some kind of problem. "By the time your mom and dad get back, we'll have a plate just for them."

"Can we?" Amy was on her feet and dashing into the kitchen without a second thought to the cartoons.

Kent followed after her but Kurt rolled his eyes. "I don't cook. Dad says it's women's work."

"Now where have I heard that before?" she said, thinking of Bryan. "There must be some new macho conspiracy that I don't know about. Come on, Rambo." Sometimes, God love him, Vic could be such a throwback to some unenlightened generation.

"I don't wanna."

"Hey, sport, think about it. You've been into the bakery a million times."

"Yeah?" He continued to stare blankly at the television.

"And you've met Mr. Schmidt."

"So?"

"He's the baker, isn't he?"

Kurt scowled and scratched his head. "Maybe he's a sissy."

"I wouldn't tell him that, if I were you," she said with a smile. "Someone told me he was a pro wrestler for a while and he can outski me, so you'd better be careful what you say about him. Anyway—" she rumpled her wayward nephew's hair "—you decide what you want to do, but the rest of us are going to cut out cookies and decorate them."

Pasting a smile on her face, she went into the kitchen and tried not to concentrate on Shelly or stare at the clock and wonder what was happening to her sister. After all, as Shelly had told her dozens of times, worrying wouldn't help anything. Ronni went through the motions of mixing butter, sugar and flour, rolling out the dough and even cutting out shapes of Santas, reindeer and Christmas trees. Kurt, after only a few stubborn minutes, joined his cousin and brother at the table, and despite the flour and sugar spread over every inch of tabletop, counters and floor, the crisp results were soon cooling on a rack, ready to be frosted.

In the middle of the melee, Travis and Bryan appeared at the front door, and Ronni, sugar and flour dusting her apron, hair and face, felt as if a great burden had been lifted from her shoulders. The sensation was ridiculous, of course, but she couldn't help the rush of relief at the sight of him. "Come in, come in," she said, standing out of the doorway so they could join the general chaos.

"Want a cookie?" Amy asked. She was standing on a chair and placing red heart candies and green sprinkles on several works in process.

"Nah," Bryan said, then catching a pointed look from his father, looked at the floor and muttered, "Sure, why not?"

"They're Christmas trees," Amy exclaimed as if he couldn't see the obvious. With a flourish she handed him a finished cookie and found a second for Travis.

Untying her apron, Ronni quickly introduced the boys who, tired of standing at the table, had resumed their positions in front of the TV. Kent was creating some kind of fort with plastic snap-together blocks, and Kurt, one eye on the television, was fashioning a weapon with them.

"Why've you got crutches?" Kurt asked, obviously in awe of the other boy.

"Fell down skiing. On the mountain."

"Can I try 'em?" Kurt was on his feet in an instant, the plastic blocks forgotten.

Bryan glanced at Ronni and his father with the worried look of someone who's looking for a means—any means—of escape. "A teenage boy's nightmare," Ronni said, watching the exchange. Even Amy gave up decorating cookies and scurried into the living room where she planted herself near Bryan, as if staking her claim.

"How about some coffee?" Ronni offered.

"I can only stay a minute."

"Oh?"

"Bryan and I were talking. He'd like to take some

skiing lessons or…snowboarding lessons, either alone
or with a group of kids his age when he gets better—
probably next season unfortunately—and I suggested
you or someone you know."

"I don't know how good I am with a board," she admitted. "I've only tried it a couple of times and I wasn't
that great, but I can get him in touch with someone up
on the mountain who's worked with kids and could
place him in the right class."

"Would you?" Travis said, seeming relieved. "I'd
like him to meet some boys his age."

"No problem."

"Thanks." He shifted restlessly from one foot to the
other and then, casting a look at the kids to see that
they were all occupied, he grabbed Ronni by the crook
of the elbow and shepherded her onto the back porch.
The horses were huddled together near the fence line
and a solitary hawk swooped through the sky, but otherwise the day was still. "Look," he said once they were
alone outside, "I know I blew it the other night. I pushed
too hard. I thought—er, I was hoping…oh, hell, I don't
even know what I'm trying to say here." Frowning, his
eyebrows beetling over his steady eyes, he cleared his
throat. "I thought maybe there was a chance that we
could start over."

"Start over?" she repeated, curling her hands over
the railing and staring at the snow-covered remains of
her vegetable garden. A soft mist gathered in the trees
and a few solitary flakes fell from the darkening sky.
"You mean, go back to square one?"

"I wish I knew what I meant." Impatiently, he shoved
a hand through his hair and muttered something unin-
telligible.

"Let me guess," she suggested, unable to resist goading him. "You want to be friends? You know, wave when we meet at the mail box, feed each other's pets when one of us is out of town, work out the fence line and…oooh!"

He yanked her close to him and this time she knew she'd pushed him too far. His mouth was razor thin, his speech clipped with a patience that seemed to forever elude him. "What I want, lady," he said, the intensity of his stare laser bright, the fingers of his hand curved over her forearm in a white-knuckled grip, "is downright indecent. If you want to know the truth, what I want is to kiss you until you can't think straight and then carry you to bed so that I can make love to you all night long." His expression was stark with strain, his skin stretched tight over high, bladed cheekbones and there was a desperation in his voice that he failed to hide. "What I want, very simply put, is you. All of you."

Ronni's throat went dry and she tried to back away, but he caught her and squeezed her up against the door. "Ever since I first laid eyes on you, I've wanted you and I've tried to be patient and play the game, be the friendly neighbor, but it's just not my nature and—" he gazed at her lips so hard that she licked them nervously "—and you seem to have a way of bringing out the worst in me." Before she could argue, he pressed the length of his body against hers and kissed her with a fever that spread from his lips to hers and slid through her bloodstream to melt her very bones.

Breathing was difficult, pulling away impossible and she gave in to the hot impulses that fired her blood. She sagged against him, and as desperately as a starving person, she kissed him back, her pulse thundering in her ears, her breathing ragged and short. Her arms wound around his neck of their own accord and when he fit his legs between hers, his fly rubbing against hers, she felt a warmth begin to flow.

Somewhere in the distance bells began to ring and Ronni was vaguely aware of the noise. Travis lifted his head and cocked it to the side.

Another sharp ring and the scramble of anxious feet on the hardwood floor as she heard Amy race for the phone.

"Expecting a call?"

"No—" *Shelly!* "Oh, yes. It could be news about my sister."

It was. Victor, still at the hospital, was on the other end of the line and he gave her the sketchy news—that Shelly was all right, though still spotting. The doctor had ordered her to bed, no work, no frantic Christmas shopping and complete rest until the crisis resolved itself. There was still a chance she could lose the baby, early as it was in her pregnancy, but if she took care of herself, the risk was lessened.

"The boys will stay here." Ronni decided when Vic finished telling her as many details as he could remember. What she was going to do with two rowdy six-year-olds she wasn't certain, but somehow she'd figure it out.

"Oh, no, I can handle 'em," Vic told her. "They'll be with me at the lot and when I need a break, Mandy, our neighbor—she's divorced, you know—offered to help out. I figure we can trade off. I'll stack some cordwood for her and fix her kids' bikes in trade."

"But the boys are more than welcome here," Ronni insisted.

"I know, I know, and believe me I'll probably be

askin' for your help, but now that Shelly's…well, laid up, you won't have a secretary or worker in the warehouse and you've already got your end of the business, the ski patrol and Amy and…Lord, girl, I think you're plate's about full, as it is."

"But Shelly—"

"She's right here. Hang on."

A few seconds later, Shelly's voice, filled with a falsely cheery ring, sang over the wires. "How are the boys? Have they worn you out yet?"

"Don't worry about them. How are you?" Ronni wound the cord in her fingers and glanced at Travis who had walked into the living room and was having a discussion with his son.

"I'll be fine. It's just the baby—they're not sure if, well…if I can go to term or even to the next trimester." Her voice cracked and she cleared her throat. "It's scary, Ronni," she admitted. "I know this baby wasn't planned and it's poor timing and everything but—"

"Shh. It's all right. The baby's going to be fine."

"I hope so," she whispered. "Anyway, I'm just about on my way home. Vic will come by and get the boys—"

"No way. Tonight they're staying here. We'll talk more tomorrow morning. Go home and take it easy, Shell. You can call me when you're awake."

Shelly started to cry and Ronni wished she could console her sister. Obviously Shelly was worried sick and Ronni, too, felt a dull ache in the middle of her belly, a pain that she could only describe as dread.

"Problems?" Travis said once she'd hung up. She felt cold to the bone and rubbed her arms to shake the chill that had started in the middle of her heart.

"A few." She gave him a sketchy rundown of what

was happening in her sister's life including Shelly's pregnancy and worries about having to move in order for Vic to find a steady job. All the while Ronni tried to keep her voice low enough so as not to be overheard by the boys.

While she spoke, Travis found a mug in the cupboard near the refrigerator and poured her a cup of coffee. "I could help," he offered, handing her the steaming brew.

"You? How?"

"Well, not with the baby, obviously. That's up to the doctors and nature. But Vic could work for me."

Ronni leveled him a look that was meant to convey, *Don't tease me on this one, Keegan.*

"I'm serious." He poured the remains of the coffee-pot into a cup and snagged a finished cookie from the drying rack.

Sighing across the top of her mug, she said, "I've seen the equipment you've got set up. Vic wouldn't know a fax machine from a word processor, and as for linking up to the Internet, forget it. He's a sawmill man. Born and bred for generations. He's not a three-piece suit kind of guy."

"I was talking about helping me get the house reno-vated and updated. I've had to hire contractors and subs for the tough jobs that require a lot of expertise and li-censes and such, but there's a lot of work that I'd hoped I could share with Bryan which isn't going to happen for a while—at least not until he's off crutches—and some of the jobs won't wait."

She wavered as she sipped her coffee. It slid in a warm path to her stomach and chased away some of the cold fear that had settled there. Travis was offering a much needed helping hand to a man he barely knew.

"Vic's proud, almost to a fault. He won't want your pity or accept anything he construes as a handout."

"I think that can be managed," Travis replied, a mischievous light gleaming in his eyes. "Would you feel better if I promised to work off his behind?"

"Not me, but Victor would. A proud, stubborn, hardheaded man, that one," she said as if to herself, but inside, the wheels of her mind were turning ever-faster. Travis's plan might just work. Business at the tree lot had slowed. With only a week before Christmas, sales had fallen off drastically and it was only a matter of days before her brother-in-law would be unemployed again. Tilting her face up, she eyed this complex man who could be hard-hearted and seemingly ruthless one minute, compassionate the next, and sexy as all get out, to boot.

"You don't know Vic."

"I met him the other night. Seemed conscientious enough to me—personable to the customers at the tree lot and someone who wasn't afraid of hard work. Unless he was just putting on a show for me by delivering the tree and sticking around to see that it fit into the stand."

"Don't be ridiculous."

"Then he's got a job if he wants one."

She was stunned. "That's how you hire people? From meeting them once?"

A small smile twisted his lips. "It's one way. When you can't get a résumé or don't have time to do background checks, then you have to rely on gut instinct." He lifted one shoulder. "Usually, it's right on."

"Oh?"

"It was right about you."

She squinted up at him. "How's that?"

"Pretty. Intelligent. Serious, with a wild side that needs to be explored."

"Oh, right," she mocked just as Kurt, struggling on tiptoe, crutches stretched out in front of him to accommodate his small size, fell into the room. He let out a yelp, then held his tongue as his brother, who was forever getting the short end of the stick, in Ronni's estimation, started to laugh.

"Kurt! Oh, be careful," she admonished, then picked up her nephew and hugged him. For all his bravado, he was just a little boy and he sniffed loudly, though she suspected his pride was injured more than any part of his body.

Bryan sent his father a baleful look and Travis took the hint. "I promised Bryan he could rent some movies this afternoon."

"What? And give up entertaining the troops?" she said with a teasing grin. "I can't imagine why he'd want to do that."

Travis was suddenly sober, his eyes dark with emotion, his voice low enough so as not to be heard over the television. "It's all part of our new deal—peace treaty really. Bryan's agreed to spend the rest of the school year here, with me, then if things don't work out, he's moving to Europe to be with his mother."

"Oh, Travis." She read the pain in his eyes and knew that only a child could wound so deeply.

"I just hope he gives Cascadia a chance," he said, finishing his coffee. "Come on, Bryan, we've got money to spend at the video store." In an aside to Ronni, he added, "I could take the rest of the kids, too, if you want to go visit your sister for a while."

The truth of the matter was that she was itching to

see Shelly, but she wasn't about to dump the load of kids on Travis. "I'll see her in the morning," she answered. "She needs to rest now and we've—that's a collective we, meaning the children as well as me—have a kitchen to clean."

"I'll call Vic," Travis promised. "Now, about those lessons?"

At that point, Bryan hobbled over to the front door.

"When do you get off the sticks?" Ronni asked.

"Probably next Monday," Bryan answered curtly.

"Two days before Christmas? Good."

"Yeah and I'm gonna try snowboarding that day!"

"I don't think so," Travis said.

"I'm not waiting a year!" Bryan insisted, glowering. "No way."

"We'll see what the doctor says. Hopefully snowboarding will be better on your knees. There's less chance of reinjuring yourself when you get good enough not to fall all the time. The problem with learning something new is that you're bound to fall over and over again. When you fall and lose control, that's when there's the danger of reinjury."

"Not me. You don't know, I could have a natural ability," Bryan said.

"It's possible, I suppose, but my guess is that you might land on your backside more often than not on the first day," Travis told him, setting his empty cup in the sink.

Bryan rolled his eyes.

"Don't forget what I promised about the horses," Ronni said, hoping to cheer the boy. "Anytime you're ready."

"I'll see you later," Travis said, touching her arm in a familiar gesture that caused her pulse to race.

"I'd like that," she admitted, surprised at her reaction. How could this man she barely knew make her heart thunder, her mind wander to long-forgotten fantasies, her lips curve into a smile? She wondered fleetingly if she was falling in love, then gave herself a quick mental shake. Love was an emotion that had to be nurtured over the years, that came with respect and trust. No, what she was feeling was lust—basic primal chemistry between a man and a woman. Travis was a sexy man with an easy smile, quick wit and quiet charm. She'd just been too long without a man—that was all there was to it. Nothing more. She stood on the porch, letting the cold winter air swirl around her as she watched him drive away. Silly though it was, he seemed to take a piece of her heart with him.

"I'm going to be fine and the baby's going to be fine, too. Just quit worrying," Shelly scolded from her worn plaid couch. From her position, she had a clear view of the side yard and the swing set where all three kids, despite the snow, were playing. Dressed in snowsuits, boots and stocking hats, they ran in crazy circles around the slide and teeter-totter.

"Worrying is what I do best," Ronni admitted as she set a red poinsettia on the coffee table near the platter of cookies the kids had baked.

"This is too much, you shouldn't have," Shelly protested, but she smiled as she fingered a silky scarlet petal.

"No way."

"It's not as if I can't do anything for myself, you know."

"I know, I know, but let me pamper you, okay?" Ronni hesitated at the front door. "Besides, I owe you. There was a time when I was a basket case. If it wasn't for you and Vic, I don't know what Amy and I would have done," she said, her heart squeezing when she remembered how Shelly, mother of two rambunctious two-year-olds, had put her own life on hold to help Ronni find herself in those brutal, dark days after Hank was killed. Vic, too, had stepped in awkwardly to provide whatever emotional support he could. "You just stay there on the couch for a second while I put a few things together," Ronni said.

She made a trip to the car and carried in a casserole dish filled with meat loaf and potatoes. After setting the timer and temperature, she shoved the dish into Shelly's small oven on timed bake. "That should do it. There's a green salad in the fridge, rolls in this basket and a chocolate cake on the counter."

"You're too much," Shelly said, her voice clogged with emotion.

"I just want you to get better and, with that in mind, I brought you my own special brand of medicine."

"Uh-oh."

"Oh, believe me, you'll love it." She ran out to the car and returned with the latest edition of Shelly's favorite movie magazine.

"You know my weakness," Shelly said, her eyes crinkling at the corners in delight. She'd given up her subscription when Victor had first been laid off.

Ronni handed her the slick magazine and sat on the

corner of the coffee table. "Now, the truth, how are you feeling?"

Absently, Shelly thumbed the magazine, then looked across the room to a spot only she could see. "The truth?"

"That's right."

"Okay, I'm scared. I hate to admit it, but I am. I want this baby desperately but I can't afford to be off my feet, and Vic—he needs me healthy. He's coming around, though. The thought of losing the baby frightens him." She glanced down at the magazine cover with a picture of one of her favorite stars. "He's made a couple of calls to guys he knows who moved to California, because once the tree lot closes, he's out of work and his unemployment benefits ran out a long time ago." She let out a long sigh. "It's just a rough time right now, but I tell myself that we're all healthy—well, everyone else is, and this—" she motioned toward her belly "—it's in God's hands now, I guess."

"I might know of a job," Ronni ventured, unable to hold her tongue.

"For Vic? Around here?"

She hated the hopeful sound in her sister's voice. "I talked to Travis Keegan last night. He came over in the middle of our cookie-baking adventure." She went on to describe most of her conversation with Travis and Shelly's eyebrows drew together in concentration.

"It sounds good—too good," she finally said. "And if Keegan's doing this because he's seeing you, there's no chance it will work. You know Vic, he's prideful to a fault."

"Just have him talk to Travis."

Shelly rubbed her chin. "I still can't figure out why

his name sounds so familiar, but it does, every time I hear it, I feel like I should know something more about him, that I *do* know something, but I just can't put my finger on it."

"If it's important, it'll come," Ronni said. She spent the next hour chatting with her sister.

By the time she was ready to pack Amy back in the car, Victor had returned from the tree lot with his check and word that he wasn't needed any longer, at least not until next year. "Decent of Delmer and Ed," he said, though his eyes gave him away and frustration clenched his jaw. "At least I'll have a job next December."

"Maybe you won't have to wait that long," Ronni said.

"Not if we move. Let's see, what's it gonna be? San Francisco or Seattle?" He found a coin in the pocket of his bib overalls and flipped it into the air.

"Talk to Keegan," Ronni advised.

"Why?" Victor was immediately suspicious and Ronni felt as if she'd been caught meddling. He scowled as she told him the work Travis needed help with. He felt in his chest pocket for a pack of cigarettes that didn't exist and scowled angrily. "I've always taken care of my family," he said when she'd finished her spiel. "Haven't taken a handout in my life."

"I know, I know. But just talk to him. If you think the job's bogus, then forget it, but see what he has to say," Shelly said, and the stubborn set of Victor's jaw softened as he stared down at his wife.

"All right," he reluctantly agreed.

"What have you got to lose?" Ronni asked.

"My pride. And when a man's pride and dignity are

gone, he's left with nothing." He took off his old hunting hat and scratched his head.

"Victor," she reprimanded quietly.

"Okay, okay," he growled, snapping his hat against his leg. "You win. I'll see what the man has to say."

"So I'll need someone to help me with some of the refurbishing and cleanup," Travis told Victor as they walked through the third floor of the old house. It was filthy, some of the windows were cracked and rain and snow had blown in, destroying the hardwood floor. There were three dormer-style rooms tucked under the eaves and on the second floor, five bedrooms and three bathrooms. The interior in all cases was knotty pine, yellowed with age and battered by the elements where the wind and rain had permeated the old timbers. "The roof needs to be fixed, the moss killed, the gutters replaced. I could have a contractor do some of the work but I'd like to take a hand in it myself."

"I thought you were a businessman," Victor said, running the tips of his callused fingers on the old railing that wound down the stairs.

"I am…was, but I needed a break. Wanted to start a new life for Bryan and myself."

"This house is pretty big for just a man and a kid," Victor observed, and Travis was vaguely uneasy. His wealth had come through hard work, but it was there just the same, where a man like Victor worked day in and day out to scrape together a living for his family. The house, if it hadn't been in such disrepair, would have been ostentatious.

"Yeah, I know, but I fell in love with it. I wanted

something different with enough acreage that we wouldn't feel cooped up."

"I don't think you'll have much worry about that."

The walk ended up in the front hall and the telephone rang. Travis excused himself and took the call in his makeshift den. Wendall was reporting in, offering suggestions on a new employee-benefit and health-care package and explaining about one of the smaller skateboarding companies that TRK, Inc. was planning to buy. He listened, offered his advice and glanced at his watch. He was too young to retire and yet the business had started to bore him. He needed something new and fresh in his life, something he expected to find here.

Something or someone? his mind taunted. *Someone like Ronni Walsh?*

He hung up, feeling restless and frustrated. Trapped in a skin he was anxious to shed. Whenever he was reminded of his life in Seattle, he was disturbed and he longed to just cut the whole damned thing loose. His life here with Bryan seemed so far removed from the rat race he'd left.

He found Victor in the living room, staring through the windowpanes at the lake. "Just one thing I want to know about this job, Keegan," he said, frowning in concentration as he worried the brim of his hat in his work-roughened hands. "I'll work for you, do whatever it is you want done, but I have to know that I got the job because of me, not because you're interested in Ronni."

"This has nothing to do with her," Travis said. "This is business. I just happened to have met you through her."

Victor tugged on his lower lip. "All right then."

They discussed the terms of his employment and a smile of relief crossed Vic's features.

"Thanks, Keegan," he said, extending his hand.

Travis clasped his fingers over Vic's callused palm and gave it a shake. "I'll see you tomorrow at nine."

"I'll be here." Victor Pederson whistled as he left the old lodge and Travis ignored that irritating voice in his head that called him a fool for hiring Ronni's brother-in-law. His relationship with her was rocky already. What would happen if he was forced to fire Vic? He'd hedged when he'd confided to Ronni that he was hiring Victor on gut instinct. It was more than that. He'd hired the man because of her, because he wanted to get closer to her, because he wanted to look good in her eyes.

Damn it all, what was happening to him? In years past, he'd hired and fired men and women because of their qualifications and performance, nothing more. Sure, people had given him names, but he'd always been careful, aware that by hiring the friend of an employee he could inadvertently cause problems between the two employees or with him. Oftentimes, professional jealousy developed or worse, and one of the two had to be let go. He'd rarely ever hired one person on the recommendation of an acquaintance unless that person was in the business.

But in one fell swoop of wanting to erase the silent worry in Ronni's eyes, he'd given up his objectivity and hired her brother-in-law.

He only hoped he didn't live to regret it.

CHAPTER NINE

"A PUPPY FOR me and a new daddy for my mommy!"
Amy announced. Clutching a candy cane in one fist, she
balanced on the mall Santa's lap and cast her mother a
superior, knowing look. Ronni wanted to fall through
the tiled floor and die of embarrassment. Her face flaming, she grabbed Amy's little hand and led her away
from the crowd that had gathered at the bench labeled
North Pole at the south end of the shopping center in
east Portland. She felt the eyes of other mothers watching her as she joined the clog of last-minute shoppers
that bustled anxiously through the wide hallway outside one of the major department stores.

Shifting her parcels into her other hand, she said,
"I think we should get something straight, Amy." She
glanced down at her innocent daughter who didn't seem
to understand what she'd done wrong. "I don't want or
need another husband."

"Why not?"

"Because…because Daddy was special." Jostled by a
group of teenage boys, she automatically said, "Sorry,"
even though the bump wasn't her fault. The kid that actually bumped her was six feet tall with shaved hair up
the sides of his head, multiple earrings and a fluff of
blond frizz on top. As he marched away in his army-

style boots, he didn't bother turning around or acknowledging her.

Ronni ignored him.

Amy wasn't to be put off. "Just because he was special doesn't mean we can't have another daddy. Katie Pendergrass has two daddies, one that lives with her and one that lives…somewhere else."

"I know, but I just haven't met anyone who could replace your father," she said, cutting across the wide mall and through the undergarment department of one of the anchor stores. What was she doing having this conversation in the middle of a frantic throng of shoppers? "Come on, sweetie," she said, tightening her hold on Amy's hand as she shouldered open an outside door to the gray day. She searched the lot, trying to remember in which row her van was parked. Fortunately, the vehicle was big enough to stand out even in a filled parking lot and she dashed through the rain, keys in hand, packages rattling, Amy's little legs flying as the little girl kept up with her. By the time she'd gotten her daughter into the front seat, she was soaked and a woman in a small import was holding up traffic, waiting for Ronni's parking space.

Somehow, today, in the gray drizzle of Portland, the Christmas spirit eluded her. Slate-colored skies, pushy shoppers, picked-over merchandise and the continual clink of coins and cash registers reminded her how commercial the most sacred holiday of the year had become.

Easing out of the parking lot, she headed east, toward the mountains and home. Her shopping was done and, of course, the puppy, now weaned, was waiting to be brought home. Shelly had agreed to let Ronni put on Christmas dinner and she'd arranged her schedule at the mountain so that she had both Christmas Eve and Christmas Day off. Things wouldn't get hectic with her mail-order business until after the first of the year when people already started ordering items for Valentine's Day, but if Shelly wasn't able to help her, she'd have to hire extra staff.

Shelly. Ronni sent up a silent prayer for her sister and unborn baby. So far, Shelly was still pregnant and Vic had started working for Keegan. Things were working out, or so it seemed.

Suddenly, Taillights flashed in front of her. Tires squealed. A black dog came out of nowhere, galloping across several lanes of traffic up ahead. Automatically she stood on the brakes. The van fishtailed in the rain, its tires screaming in protest. The van stopped just before she collided with the car in front of her. She braced herself as she checked the rear view mirror and caught a glimpse of a silver sports car skidding sideways on the pavement behind her. "Watch out," she cried and the car missed her by inches.

"Thank you," she whispered in prayer. Adrenaline pumped through her and her heartbeat, normal only minutes before, began to throb wildly. "Oh, Lord."

"What happened?" Amy, round-eyed, her candy cane a sticky mess on her lap, asked.

"I think a dog ran out in front of one of the cars up ahead. The first car stopped and the next one nearly ran into it starting a chain reaction."

"Is the dog okay?" Amy's lower lip trembled and her worried eyes searched frantically through the foggy glass.

"I think so. He took off through those houses." Ronni pointed to the development just off the shoulder of the four-lane highway. Amy wiped away the condensation and her eyes searched the brush and path between the houses. "It's not his fault," Ronni said. "His owners should keep him leashed or fenced."

"But is he hurt?"

"I don't think he got hit."

"How do you know?"

"I don't, honey, but I saw him run past that fence. I think he'll be all right."

Traffic started moving again and the silver sports car roared into the lane beside Ronni. The driver laid on his horn, and when she looked at him, he glowered at her and used an obscene gesture before speeding away.

"Merry Christmas to you, too," Ronni muttered.

"You know him?" Amy peered through the drizzle and approaching darkness to stare at the car's bright taillights as they blended into the long stream of red beams ahead of them.

"No, and I don't want to know him. He's rude."

Amy picked up her candy cane and started working on it again. Ronni was about to protest as the sticky peppermint was already on the child's jacket and pants, but she kept her mouth closed and concentrated on the road that wound through the steep foothills. The suburbs gave way to rolling farmland dotted with smaller towns, then eventually the highway grew steeper and cleaved to the thick forest of the mountains. Rain turned to snow in a matter of miles and soon white powder piled high on the shoulders gave the dark night a small cast of illumination.

Amy glanced at her mother. "I still want a puppy for Christmas."

"I know you do, sweetie."

"And a daddy."

"Oh, honey, I don't think—"

"What about Bryan's dad? He gots no wife."

Travis. Funny, when she thought of marriage, his image always came to mind. "I don't think he's ready to tie the knot again—I mean, get married—either."

"Why not?"

"Oh, honey, I'm not sure." How did they get on this crazy subject? Amy seemed almost obsessed with thoughts of a father these days. The one thing Ronni couldn't give her.

With a theatrical sigh, Amy drew on the passenger window again, her small finger sliding through the condensation. "Everybody else has a daddy."

"Everybody? Like who?"

"All the kids in school and I told you about Katie."

"Yes, I know. She's got two." The lights of Cascadia loomed in the horizon just as the snow began to stick to the road. "I guess she's lucky."

"She likes one better than the other one."

"See, she's got problems, too."

"But Travis is nice."

Back to him again. "Yes, he is."

"He likes you."

"And I like him but that's not enough reason for people to get married, okay?"

"But—"

"Subject closed." She drove past the welcome sign and old, empty sawmill near the railroad tracks. She could understand why Amy would try to pair her with Travis. They'd had dinner together the past three nights and had visited Shelly while Bryan watched Amy. They'd finished decorating the old lodge and celebrated by kissing under the mistletoe that Travis had hung in the foyer. Ronni had struggled with the idea of buying him a Christmas present, then decided to give Bryan and him a housewarming gift instead. It seemed safer and less personal. As each day passed, she and Travis were becoming closer. Just thinking of him caused a warm feeling deep inside, and whenever they were alone, the sparks flew.

She now knew the name of the company—TRK Inc., the holding company for smaller corporations—that he'd started and built into the empire that it was today. She'd also gained a little more insight into his marriage and why it had failed. Though he still blamed himself, it sounded as if his wife was as much, if not more, at fault for their union's slow and painful demise. Yes, Ronni and Travis had grown closer, emotionally as well as physically.

Never, since Hank, had she been tempted to make love to a man. She'd been a virgin when she and Hank had started dating and hadn't slept with anyone since her husband's death. She'd always just assumed she would never make love again, never wake up to the smell and feel of a man's arms around her, never experience a man's touch on her breasts or spine or—

She brought herself up short. Lately, her thoughts had a way of turning wanton, and she knew where to lay the blame for that. If Travis weren't so damned sexy...but it was more than his looks. There was the strong man with the soft center that appealed to her and touched her deep inside.

With a sigh, she wheeled the van into the parking lot of a local mom-and pop grocery store and steadfastly pushed Travis Keegan out of her mind. She just didn't have time for a man in her life—no matter how fascinating he was.

"That's it then," Travis said, handing his son the thick sheaf of papers that had come from the school. Aside from health, registration and fee forms, there was information for all of the classes in which Bryan was enrolled. "Looks like a lot of work."

"Looks like a disaster!" Bryan corrected, eyeing the pages as if they were his death sentence. He hobbled over to the fireplace and sat on the raised hearth.

"They would have been here sooner, but they were sent to our address in Seattle and forwarded here."

"Great. Just goes to show you how on top of it the school is."

"Give the school a chance, Bryan."

"Why? So I can look like a freak to all the other kids."

"You won't look like a—"

"What about these, huh?" Lifting a crutch and swinging it in the air, he added, "What if the doctor doesn't let me get rid of them? I'll look like a geek. A weirdo—"

"A kid who had an accident," Travis said, trying to understand his son and yet remain firm. "I know it'll be difficult going to a new school, trying to make new friends, hoping to fit in, but you'll do just fine." He offered Bryan a smile. "You're worrying this to death."

"Because it's my life!"

"Your new life."

"I liked my old one."

"Did you?" Travis asked softly.

"Yeah, I did. And I liked living with Mom."

That was a lie, but Travis wasn't about to call him on it. Not while the boy was so upset.

"You know how weird it is living with your dad?" Bryan asked.

"No." Travis sat on the edge of a couch and let his clasped hands drop between his knees. "Why don't you tell me."

"It's way beyond weird. Guys live with their parents or their mother but no one lives with his dad."

"So that's it. You want a mom?"

"I've got a mom." He made a dismissive motion with his hand and bit his lower lip. "She's just not here."

"There you go, guys." Ronni shook forkfuls of hay into the manger and two velvet-soft noses began plucking at the dry blades. Contented snorts and the swishing of coarse tails contended with the rustle of straw as the horses shifted in their stalls.

Lucy, the white mare, was round with the foal she would deliver in the next couple of months, and Sam, the sire, a gray stallion with a black mane and tail, nuzzled her out of the way.

"Greedy," Ronni admonished. Liquid brown eyes blinked, dark ears flicked, but he kept on chewing and snorting, determined to get his share and then some. "Just like a man."

Ronni hung the pitchfork on two nails driven into the interior walls, dusted her hands and was ready to snap off the light when she saw the shadow. Her breath caught in the back of her throat and she reached for the pitchfork again as Travis stepped out of the doorway and into the lamplight.

She gasped, then shook her head. "You scared the devil out of me!"

"Sorry, just got here. I knocked at the house, but no one answered."

"Oh, well…" She had trouble catching her breath and her heart beat a little faster than it should.

"Amy's had a big day—shopping, Santa and all that—she's already asleep and I'm late with feeding the horses, so that's why I'm not in the house…." Why did she feel the need to explain herself? Why couldn't she tear her gaze away from his mesmerizing stare? Why did her blood still race stupidly?

"How's your sister? Her husband's kind of tight-lipped about what's going on." In the shadowy light he looked more handsome than ever as he shoved his hands into the pockets of his jacket.

Ronni cleared her throat as it didn't want to work. "Vic's worried about her, of course, and the baby, but she's hanging in. Between her neighbor and me, she gets a little relief with the twins, but I think she's still on her feet more than she should be." She tightened the lid on the oat barrel, trying to regain some of her fast-fleeting composure. "But at least Victor's working and that's helped relieve some of the stress." She glanced past him to the darkness and prayed he couldn't hear the ridiculous hammering of her heart. "Are you here alone?"

Nodding, he said, "I finally got a packet from the school with information on Bryan's classes and they're different from the ones he was taking in Seattle, so he's doing some catch-up reading—Charles Dickens." His gray eyes touched hers again and lingered for a second. "Well, that's what he's supposed to be doing."

"So…you decided to take a walk," she guessed. Dear

Lord, were her palms sweating? It was cold as ice out here, yet she felt a warm flush.

His smile was positively wicked as he snapped off the lights and the only illumination was the reflection of moonlight that bounced off the snow to shaft through the small windows and open door. "Actually, I decided to see you," he admitted with an edge of reluctance to his voice.

"Should I be flattered?" she asked, unable to stop flirting a little even though her heart was beginning to knock crazily in her chest.

"Definitely." He pulled the door shut behind him and they were suddenly alone. More alone than they had been.

"Why's that?" she asked, her pulse leaping wildly.

"Because it's been a long time since I wanted to be with a woman," he said, walking slowly up to her. "Maybe too long." Stopping just inches from her, he wound his finger in the long braid that had flipped over her shoulder to curl around her breast. "You know, Ronni, I just don't know what to do with you."

"No?" she asked, the barn suddenly seeming to close, the air hard to breathe. "Why not?"

"You're not like any woman I've ever met."

"Is that bad?"

"Maybe...maybe not." She licked her lips nervously and a muscle worked his jaw. "I don't want this," he said.

"Want what?" But she knew. They both knew. Desire, new and frightening, yet as old as time, hung in the air.

Resting his forehead against hers, he whispered, "I don't know what it is about you, woman. Can't put my

finger on it, but there's something damned irresistible."
His arms circled her waist. "I just can't fight it," he said,
"though God knows I've tried."

His lips brushed over hers and though she knew she
was wading in dangerous waters, she couldn't stop.
Wouldn't. It had been too long and Travis touched her
like no other man. Ronni's breathing was already shal-
low, her heartbeat fluttering like the wings of a frightened bird. She gave herself without hesitation, kissing
him, holding him, feeling his weight drag them both to
the straw-strewn floor.

His lips were warm, the air cool and the quiet nicker
of the horses in counterpoint to the soft hoot of an owl.
Ronni closed her eyes and reveled in the feel of him, the
way his lips touched the shell of her ear, the pressure of
his hands as his fingers found the zipper of her jacket.
She sensed the cold whisper of air caress her skin as he
lifted her sweater over her head, and then, with weak
moonlight filtering through the windows, unhooked her
bra, letting her breasts spill into the night.

He kissed the deep cleft, breathed fire across the
goose bumps that raised on her skin and touched a nipple that puckered and strained until his tongue encircled the taut point.

Writhing in sweet agony, she arched upward, her
blood on fire, a dark need unfolding deep within. His
hands reached behind her, pressing intimately on the
naked small of her back, tracing the long depression
of her spine as his lips surrounded one nipple and he
began to suckle, creating a whirlpool of desire deep in
the most feminine part of her.

"Travis," she cried when he delved beneath her
jeans, his fingers grazing her buttocks, his hands hot

and ready. The buttons of her fly opened in a sharp series of pops and soon, still making love to her breasts with his mouth, he skimmed the jeans down her legs, discarded her shoes and socks and she was suddenly naked in the dark barn. Burning and anxious and naked.

When he lifted his head, she cried out, but then he moved lower, his tongue tracing a path along the center of her abdomen. She bucked, her hips rising off the floor with the want of him and he whispered, "Slow down, honey. Just slow down and enjoy."

She knew she should stop, that she was crossing an invisible and dangerous line, but she couldn't find the words and her voice was dry and hoarse as he continued kissing her and stroking her, spreading her legs gently, slowly finding that sensitive part of her that she'd sworn no man would ever discover again.

But she didn't stop him and as he touched her, slowly at first and then more rapidly, she found his rhythm and moved furiously with each magic stroke, inviting more, wanting more, gritting her teeth with the need of him, all of him. His hands and mouth were exquisite and she felt herself soaring ever higher like a shooting star careering across the sky until the release, when it came, rocked her so hard she would have sworn the heavens split and the world shattered.

Only when it was over, when he was holding her in his arms and kissing away the tears of relief, was she able to slow the beating of her heart and hear the soft sigh of the wind over her own ragged, desperate breaths. How could one man affect her so? How could she ever let him touch her again—how could she not? In a few short weeks, she'd come to rely on and trust him as she had trusted no one since Hank.

"Travis, I—"

"Shh, honey. No need for words." But his eyes had darkened as if there were unspoken gestures hanging between them.

She nestled in his arms for a minute before becoming aware of the sharp tensile strength of his muscles, the hard planes of his face and the very noticeable bulge in the front of his jeans.

Turning to him, she held his face in her hands and began kissing him, slowly at first and then more feverishly until he moaned with pleasure. With fumbling fingers she stripped him of his jacket and sweatshirt, her fingers playing softly in the swirling hair of his chest.

Strong and sinewy, his flesh was hot and firm. She kissed him on his bare skin, rimming one of his nipples with her tongue and letting her fingers explore him, the ridges and planes of his muscles, the slope of his back, the rounded firmness of his buttocks.

When she opened his fly, he didn't stop her and as she pushed off his jeans, he groaned in some kind of male ecstasy. Her fingers glided over the hard muscles of his thighs and she moved lower, but before she could pleasure him as he had her, he kissed her and his knees parted her legs. Eyes, seeking and dark, stared at her breasts as he poised over her. "You're sure about this?" he asked, sweat beading his upper lip.

"Yes," she lied. How could she be sure of anything? But she wanted him…maybe even loved him….

"No regrets?"

"None," she promised.

Biting his lower lip, he fumbled in the dark, found his jeans and shook out his wallet. Deep within the leather he found the foil packet and opened it quickly.

Ronni was still breathing hard, her abdomen rising and falling, her breasts full and wanting as he kissed first one nipple, then the other. He lifted her hips with his hands. Eyes locked with hers, he entered her, so slowly she thought she would die in ecstasy, and then he withdrew just as lazily, as if he had all the willpower in the world. She would never have thought she could be ready so soon after being satiated, but her need was great and she moved with him, accepting his thrusts, yearning for more, wanting all of him.

His tempo increased. She moaned and cried out as he fell to his elbows and joined her in a fierce, ancient dance that caused the earth to shatter and the seas to part.

"Travis," she whispered, his name familiar and right. "Travis, oh, please—" And then it came, that sweet spasm of delight that caused him to collapse against her, crushing her breasts and jarring her to her very soul. This was how it was supposed to be.

She held him close, her heart pounding wildly, and a new sensation akin to love surrounded her in its gentle blanket. The horses snorted as if in disapproval, but she didn't care. For the first time in nearly four years, she felt like a woman, a full, complete woman.

"You're beautiful, Veronica," he said, his voice rough with emotion. He brushed a strand of hair from her face and when he stared at her, she saw deeper emotions in his eyes, as if he too felt the change in their relationship, he too realized there was no turning back, he too knew their lives would never be the same.

Levering up on one elbow, he stared down at her and touched the hill of her cheek with one long finger.

"I...I..." He stopped, took in a deep breath and shook his head. "Look what you've reduced me to, woman."

A tightness was forming in her throat as she realized how serious he'd become. How sober. How intense.

A heartbeat, then his gaze locked with hers. Her throat turned to sand. Oh, God, she knew what he was going to ask before the words, those beautiful, frightening words whispered through the barn.

He took her hand in his as if afraid she might pull away, "I want you to marry me."

CHAPTER TEN

"I…I DON'T KNOW what to say," Ronni whispered as Travis plucked a piece of straw from her hair.

A smile split his jaw and some of the tension drained from his face. "How about, 'Oh, Travis, I never thought you'd ask, I'll marry you and bear your children, clean your house, wash your clothes, kiss the ground you walk on and be devoted to you for the rest of your life?'"

Ronni, close to tears a moment before, laughed. "Oh, sure, that's what was on the tip of my tongue." Kissing him, she saw the merriment in his eyes and she hugged him closer. Marriage. To Travis. "I—I want to be sure," she said as the reality hit her.

"You aren't now?"

"For the moment, yes, but for the rest of our lives…? I barely know you."

He smiled, his teeth flashing white in the darkness as he stared at her. "I feel like I've been looking for you all my life."

"Really?" she asked and he laughed. "Be serious for a minute."

"I am. Dead serious. I want you to be my wife."

"I though that after your divorce you were through with marriage."

"But I didn't count on meeting you."

Sighing, she said, "I don't know if it would be fair—to you."

"I know what I want."

"Do you?" Still reeling from his proposal, she sat up and felt the cold air chill her skin. Never once had he said that he loved her, nor she him. It was just too soon, too early in their relationship. She'd known Hank for years before she'd married him and even now, almost four years after his death, she felt as if she was betraying his memory.

"I'm willing to take a chance."

"But I don't know if I can," she admitted. "There's Amy—"

"Who's crazy about me and Bryan."

"That much is true." Wrapping her arms around her legs, she stared at this wonderful man. Her first impulse was to say yes and throw herself into his arms and make love to him over and over again, but she had to be practical. She was a mother; he, too, had a child. It wasn't just the two of them, they weren't impetuous teenagers.

"How do you feel about my son?"

"Oh, that's not it," she said, reading his thoughts. "Bryan's a little on the surly side sometimes, but that's just the nature of the beast. A teenager suddenly thrown into a new situation—new home, new school. Then he wracks up his knee and feels like a fool so he covers it with bravado."

"Thank you, Dr. Freud."

"You disagree?" She arched a dark eyebrow high.

"Not at all, and I think you're just what he needs—a no-nonsense woman who likes kids."

"So that's what this is all about."

"No," he said quietly. "I'm not just looking for a new

mother for my son. If that were the case, there are several women in Seattle who would have gladly done the honors." He looked away from her and she experienced a jab of jealousy for these faceless women who wanted him. "But they were more interested in becoming Mrs. Travis Keegan than being a companion to me or my son. I had the feeling that each of them had the same agenda—their first act as my wife would be to banish Bryan to a boarding school as far away as possible."

Had they slept with him? Shared his bed? Said they loved him? Had he promised them marriage? Told them he cared? "Then they were fools. Bryan's a great kid."

"You really think so?"

"I know so. He just needs some of his rough edges filed down, but it will all come in time." Reaching in the straw for her jeans, she added, "Look, I'd better go inside. If Amy wakes up—"

"You're ducking the issue."

Flinging her sweater over her head, she said, "I just can't make a quick decision like that. I mean, I never thought I'd marry again...."

"Because you were still married to Saint Hank."

The accusation stung, but it was true. Years before, she'd believed that she would marry Hank, have his children, experience the joys and worries of parenthood, look forward to their grandchildren and eventually grow old holding each other's hands. Emotion clogged her throat. "When I took those vows, I was serious."

"But they ended with the 'till death do us part' bit." There was a trace of anger in his voice and he glared at her with hard, unforgiving eyes.

"I know. I've finally accepted it." She stuffed her bra into the back pocket of her jeans. "But it's taken a while.

A lot longer than it should have." Only recently had the stones in her heart lightened. Only recently could she think of Hank's death and not be angry. "Come on," she said, shaking her hair loose, "I'll buy you a cup of coffee and you can try and persuade me that becoming the next Mrs. Travis Keegan is the sane, sensible and only path to take."

She started for the door but he tackled her and drew her down to the floor with him once more. "All right, Ronni, we'll play this game your way," he said, his nose touching hers, his eyes, bright and intense as he stared at her. "But I'm warning you, I'm not a patient man."

"Funny you should bring up your lack of that particular virtue," she replied with a giggle, "because I've been accused of the same thing."

"See. We're perfect for each other."

"Convince me."

"Gladly," he whispered and kissed her until the breath was trapped in her lungs and the world began to spin again.

"You're kidding!" Bryan said as he walked from one side of the room to the other. He was without crutches now and his gait was even and strong, with no hint of any lingering damage. The doctor had told him to take it easy, no strenuous running or jumping or skiing for a few weeks, but he was healing well and it looked as if he wasn't going to need surgery. He threw his hat onto a sofa in the living room and glowered at his father. "I'm *not* going to any dumb little Christmas pageant, Dad."

"Amy's expecting you," Travis said and swallowed a smile. Recently Bryan had begun to call him Dad again, though when it had first occurred eluded him.

"Geez!" Bryan flung one hand into the air in disgust. "Why'd she have to invite me?" he wondered aloud.

"Because she likes you."

"She's a runty little kid."

"Doesn't matter. She thinks you're great."

Bryan rolled his eyes and sighed theatrically. "She thinks everyone's great and I'm tired of her hanging around bothering me. Why is it we spend so much time with them, anyway?"

"Because I like her mother. And I like Amy and Ronni's going to be over here any minute, so try and paste a smile on your face, okay?"

He'd no sooner said the words than Ronni's van pulled into the driveway. She'd worked all day at the mountain and her face was still flushed from the cold as she entered the room without her daughter. Travis spun Ronni under the mistletoe, then as she giggled, kissed her lightly on the lips.

Bryan, witnessing his father's affection, looked out the window and glowered. He was talking about moving to France again and Travis figured he'd have to put up with the boy's insecurities and worries for a while longer. No doubt Bryan would be upset until he started school and then, hopefully, once he realized that he would be accepted and find friends, all this angst would abate.

"Look at you," Ronni said a trifle breathlessly when Travis set her on her feet. She was staring at Bryan as she stepped into the living room and tossed her purse onto the hearth. "No more crutches."

"Nearly a clean bill of health," Travis said.

"Yeah, but no basketball, skateboarding or skiing," Bryan grumbled.

"All in good time."

He made a sound of disgust as if he believed he'd never get to do anything the least bit fun again.

"So how were things on the mountain today?" Travis asked.

"Relatively calm considering it's Christmas break," she replied. "A few injuries, but not many, thank heavens."

Another deprecating noise from Bryan's direction.

Ronni ignored the boy's foul mood. "I wanted to make sure you know how to get to the church. The pageant's at seven, but I have to be there earlier since I'm in charge of the angel choir and getting the twins into their costumes."

"And Shelly? Vic seems to think she wouldn't miss this if she were on her death bed."

"She's coming. But just for the performance. Supposedly she's forgoing the party afterward that the parson always throws. She's even going to avoid the bazaar." Ronni's eyes clouded. "I hope she'll be all right." Forcing a smile, she attempted to hide the fact that she was worried sick. Shelly was still spotting lightly and Dr. Sprick was considering hospitalizing her.

Declining a soda or cup of coffee, Ronni explained that she had to pick up Amy who was playing over at her friend Katie's house this afternoon. "I'll see you at the church," she said as the doorbell rang and she ducked around the edge of the fireplace to retrieve her bag.

Travis opened the door and found Taffy LeMar, dressed in a business suit and high heels, smiling brightly as she stood on the porch. "Hi," she said to Travis and handed him a basket filled with sprigs of holly, two fluted glasses and a bottle of expensive champagne decorated with a wide gold ribbon. "From the firm. Just a thank-you for doing business with Mountain West Realty." A dimple creased her cheek. "And from me, too, I guess. I'm sorry I didn't deliver this earlier, but I've been out of town on business and…well, now I'm back." She forced the basket into Travis's hand.

"Thanks. This wasn't necessary."

"Of course it was," she said, touching his arm familiarly while her gaze, all blue and shiny, stared up at him. She walked into the entry hall without an invitation, and whether she realized it or not, stopped beneath the chandelier decorated with ribboned pieces of mistletoe. "This is a small town, Travis, and we're glad for new neighbors—especially someone who might bring his business here and revive a town that was so timber-dependent. Dear God, this house is so beautiful. I knew you could—" Her words clipped off when her gaze slid around the room to land squarely on Ronni still standing near the fireplace. "Veronica!"

Ronni experienced a hard pang of jealousy.

Color washed up Taffy's neck. "I didn't expect to find you…but then you're neighbors, aren't you?" Recovering quickly, she said, "I tried to reach you, you know, to tell you about the impending sale, but with my schedule and yours, we never seemed to connect."

"It's all right," Ronni replied, gritting her teeth. Looking over Taffy's shoulder, she noticed Travis, still standing in the raised entryway, his expression drawing into a thoughtful frown.

"But I know how much the place meant, er, means to you," Taffy said, obviously flustered. "And I figured it was impossible for you to come up with a down payment on a place this size,…oh, God…" She was digging herself a deeper and deeper grave and seemed to realize it. "Well... Oh! You must be Travis's son!" Apparently anxious to change the subject, she crossed the living room and clasped Bryan's hand between both of hers. "Don't you just love it here?"

"I hate it," he said simply.

"Oh, well, I don't see why. It's so gorgeous by the lake, and inside, well, the decorations are fabulous."

"Ronni helped," Travis explained. He crossed the room and stood next to Ronni.

"Did you?" Taffy seemed to notice Ronni with new, calculating eyes. "Been here often?"

"Not as often as I'd like," Travis said, draping a familiar and possessive arm over Ronni's shoulders.

"Oh, well, I see...good. Since you're neighbors and all. How perfect." She leveled a surprised look at Ronni. "It's good you're finally getting out and seeing people. I was concerned, well, we all were, that you'd never snap out of mourning."

"It just took time," Ronni said evenly. "It was hard."

Travis's arm tightened around her as if offering her silent strength and she resisted the urge to sag against him.

"Well, merry Christmas to you all," Taffy said, making a hasty exit, her heels clicking loudly on the hardwood floors. "And a happy New Year, as well."

"And good riddance," Travis muttered under his breath once she'd closed the door behind her. "That woman's a barracuda."

"She seemed to think you liked her."

"I did business with her. Period."

"You wanted to buy this place?" Bryan asked, eyeing Ronni suspiciously. "Why?"

"Sentimental reasons."

"Such as?" Travis prompted, his hand dropping to his side.

"Growing up here in the caretaker's house, I guess." She hoisted the strap of her purse to her shoulder. "I always felt at home here and I loved this old house, not that I was in it much, but it seemed special. I...well, it was silly really, because I never could afford it, but I always thought the estate would make a great bed-and-breakfast inn for skiers in the winter and sailboarders or hikers in the summer. Just over the mountain in Hood River, a town on the Columbia River, the sailboarders come by in droves. I thought Shelly and I could run the place and her family could fix up and live in the caretaker's house. It's empty now, but wouldn't take much..." Suddenly embarrassed, she added, "Oh, well, just a pipe dream."

"That I spoiled."

"It could never have happened. Really. It's better that I let it go and deal with reality, which is—" she checked her watch "—that I don't have much time before I have to pick up Amy. So, I'll see you at the church and don't forget there's a party and bazaar after the pageant."

"Whoop-de-do," Bryan muttered.

"We'll be there." Travis walked her out to the van and as she started to climb in, he caught hold of her arm. "It's been a few days, Ronni," he reminded her. "Have you given any thought to getting married again?"

She laughed. "If it makes you feel any better, it keeps me awake nights."

His sexy, crooked grin slid into place. "I'd like to think *I* keep you awake nights." His gaze slid to her lips. "You seem to have that affect on me."

She grinned and kissed him lightly on the mouth. "Dreamer."

"Am I?" Gathering her into his arms, he kissed her. Instantly her blood was on fire, and desire, that beast that had slumbered within her for nearly four long years, was restless and ready to be awakened with just a touch, a smile or a sidelong glance.

When he lifted his head, she waited to hear the words, the declaration of his love, the vow that he couldn't live without her, but he just stared at her and gave her a quick little kiss to her forehead. "I can't wait forever," he warned her as she climbed into her van.

She rolled down the window. "Three days is *not* forever."

"Seems that way to me." He touched her face with his fingers and she started the engine. Could she really marry him? Trust him to learn to love her? Maybe a good marriage wasn't necessarily founded on love, but on mutual respect, on a shared sense of humor and compassion, on like ideas. Maybe the hot-as-a-branding-iron kind of passion was close enough to true love. No way, she told herself. Ever since she was a teenager, she'd known the difference between love and lust, and what she felt for Travis was a blending of the two. True she wanted him physically and emotionally, but did she love him? Would she throw down her life for his? Walk through fire to be with him? Accept his son as her own? Have children and grow old with him? Yes! Yes! Yes!

But did he love her or did he want to marry her to add some stability in his life? Did he think of her as a stepmother to Bryan, a woman who would become an instant wife and mother? He now knew she'd hoped to buy the old lodge, maybe he thought living there would be an enticement. Maybe she was silly to hope to hear those magic words of love.

As she drove across town, maneuvering through the streets by rote, the nagging questions racing through her mind, she knew she'd come to a crossroads in her life and she couldn't take both paths without being ripped in two. What she'd wanted all her life was now in question. The past was the trail she'd already taken and to her left was a path she'd started down, a road of loneliness and devotion to a dear, dead husband; the second path stretched to the right and it was a brighter future, one with Travis and his son.

Without realizing what she was doing, she headed east and through gates on the outskirts of the city that opened to the cemetery. She parked, letting the engine idle and cool, then walked up the hill to a grassy spot with a simple headstone. Beloved Husband and Father, she read and felt hot tears well in her eyes. A blast of icy wind whipped around her and blew her hair into her eyes. "I loved you," she said to the plot where her husband lay buried. "I loved you with all my heart. I never wanted to let go. Never. But it's time, Hank. Way past time, and I think…no, I *know* that I've got to get on with my life, with the living part."

She waited, almost as if expecting an answer, but the only noise was the rush of the wind that blew through the surrounding trees. A few snowflakes swirled in the air and she shivered. "I'll never forget and you'll always be Amy's father, but there's another man, one I think I might be able to love and…and he wants to marry me." She sighed and lifted her face to the cloud-covered sky, as if she could glimpse heaven through the thick curtains. "I'm going to do it." Her fingers, frozen and bare, curled into determined fists. "By God," she vowed, "I'm going to marry Travis Keegan."

The pageant was a delightful fiasco. The angel choir sang the wrong song and the boy who played Joseph kept forgetting his lines. Fortunately, the girl who played Mary prompted him and when it was all over, the audience was smiling, the kids were relieved and they all celebrated at the party and bazaar.

Shelly managed to sit through the performance, but Vic whisked her and the twins away before she could get bogged down in any of the festivities. Amy was in her element, laughing and talking, still wearing the costume that she adored. She drank cup after cup of cranberry punch that drizzled down the white folds of her angel outfit and still managed to put away two slices of rum cake. By the time the party was over, she was pooped and Bryan was trying hard to look bored out of his mind.

"Let's go home," Ronni suggested.

"But you said we'd buy a star for the top of the tree." Amy's face, so sweet only seconds before, clouded over and her chin jutted stubbornly. "Or an angel or—"

"We will—"

"Tomorrow's Christmas Eve," Amy said.

"You're right. Let's look through the bins and see what we can find." She glanced up at Travis who was smothering a smile. "You've heard of the angel Gabriel, well you just met the angel Groucho."

Travis laughed and they followed Amy past tables laden with everything from gooseberry pies to quilted Advent calendars. Some of the local crafts were so intricate that Ronni made a mental note of them and thought they would make wonderful additions to her next year's winter catalog. She knew most of the local artists and craftsmen and women already but there were a few new and interesting pieces, created by artisans she had yet to meet.

"Here it is!" Amy found a table laden with hand-crafted ornaments and chose an angel made of a cone, netting, a hand-painted doll's head and gossamer wings. Pearly white beads and a loop of gold ribbon caused the angel's dress to glimmer and sparkle.

"Isn't she beautiful?" Amy breathed, holding the decoration as if it were made of spun gold.

"Gorgeous."

"Can we get her, Mommy?"

Ronni winced as she read the price tag, but realizing that half the proceeds went to the church, she agreed to make the purchase. "I think we'd better get out of here before we go broke," she said to Travis. "Oh, wait. I think you should meet some people who have kids about Bryan's age."

"No way," Bryan insisted, but Ronni wouldn't take no for an answer and within minutes she'd introduced Travis to the Carters and their son, Jake, and the Hendersons with their daughters, Becca and Sherrie. Bryan stared at the floor as if he found the yellowed linoleum fascinating, especially when he had to say something to the Henderson girls, but Travis and Ronni lingered, forcing the kids to interact.

Jake was interested in horses, skiing and basketball players and talked without seeming to take a break. The girls told him what to expect from his teachers at school. Bryan was nearly mute, answering in monosyllables, eyes nailed to the floor, but, Ronni figured, it was a start, a little inroad in that swamp of teenage relationships. The preacher's daughter, Elizabeth, joined them and encouraged Bryan to join their youth group, which met every Wednesday night and combined Bible study with fun, usually in the form of pizza parties, dances and trips skiing in the winter and swimming in the summer.

By the time they got into the parking lot, Bryan didn't even bother saying good-night, just slunk into the passenger seat of his father's Jeep and showed too many signs of teenage rebellion. "I hope he's all right," Ronni said.

"He will be," Travis assured her. "It's just going to take a while for him to change his mind-set."

"Good luck."

He kissed her lightly on the lips, then she walked to her van. Amy was yawning as Ronni helped strap her into the seat. "Is Travis gonna be my new daddy?" she asked, trying to keep her eyes open.

Startled, Ronni asked, "Would you like it if he was?"

"Mmm. Would you?"

Before Ronni could answer, the little angel with the cranberry-stained gown fell asleep.

"A puppy!" Amy squealed in pure delight. All the presents had been opened, and while Amy was playing with a new doll, Ronni had hurried out to the barn where she'd hidden the pup since five o'clock in the morning. Before that, she'd been up with the frightened little dog half the night as the animal had whined and howled and threatened to wake Amy. "You got me a puppy!" Amy fairly danced a special little jig and wiggled as much as the dog to get her fingers on the wriggling ball of fluff. "Oh, Mommy, he's beautiful!" Amy cried, entranced.

"She. It's a girl."

"So she can have more puppies someday!"

Ronni laughed. "I don't think so. One dog's going to be more than enough, I think."

After nearly squeezing the life from him, Amy let the pup down and the dog ran in circles, sped around the Christmas tree, under the table, into the kitchen and back again. Amy, in four-year-old heaven, raced after her and slid on the hardwood floors.

Ronni tried to drink a cup of coffee throughout the chaos. This—early Christmas morning—was their time together alone before Travis and Bryan and Shelly's whole family descended for Christmas dinner later in the afternoon. She couldn't believe how her life had changed in the past few weeks and she eyed the little Christmas tree under which the presents were spread. She'd even broken down and bought something for Travis and Bryan as they seemed already a part of her family.

"Let's name her Snowball."

"But she isn't white."

"Does it matter?"

"No, honey, I don't suppose it does. You can name her anything you like."

While Ronni picked up the litter and discarded wrapping paper from the Santa gifts, Amy busied herself by making a bed for the dog.

Once the house was cleaned and the pup was relegated during nonplay hours to a newspaper-strewn laundry room, Ronni turned on her favorite Christmas CDs and started stuffing the turkey. After plopping it into the oven, she even danced a little as she put together a molded salad, peeled white potatoes from her own garden and washed the yams. Yes, it was a time of new traditions, a new beginning. A new dog and a new extended family.

It was nearly four before she had time to dress Amy and get changed. Sitting at the vanity, slipping silver hoops through her earlobes, she heard the doorbell ring. "Coming," she called, following Amy down the stairs.

Travis and his son stood on the porch, their arms laden with packages. Ronni's heart kicked into double time at the sight of Travis in black slacks and a cream-colored sweater, his hair rumpled by the wind. Bryan, for the first time in ages, was without his baseball hat and wore clean jeans and a gray shirt tucked in at the waist. He managed a tight smile and Ronni was taken with how much he looked like his father. Once the soft flesh of youth gave way to harder planes and angles, he'd be as handsome as Travis.

"Come in, come in," she invited. "We have someone we'd like you to meet." From the laundry room, the pup gave an excited yip and Amy ran to get her.

"Lookie!" she cried, running with the little dog. "Her name is Snowball! Mommy got her for me."

Snowball wriggled and tried desperately to wash everyone's face. Travis and Bryan exchanged glances. "Uh-oh," Bryan whispered.

"What?"

"Well—" Travis rolled his eyes. "What is it they say about great minds thinking alike?"

"Oh no," Ronni whispered, fingers to her lips as she caught his meaning.

"What?" Amy asked, befuddled.

"May as well bring our surprise in now," Travis said and handed the keys of his Jeep to Bryan.

Ronni's gaze locked with Travis's. "I don't believe it."

"Believe."

A few minutes later, Bryan returned to the house carrying a half-grown pup.

"Wow!" Amy's eyes rounded.

"We got him at the local animal shelter," Travis explained. "His name is Rex."

"Is he mine?"

"If it's okay with your mother."

Ronni skewered him with a knowing look. "Oh, great, make me the bad guy."

"Can we keep him, Mommy?" Amy was dancing again, her eyes sparkling in anticipation, her cheeks rosy.

"I suppose."

"Yippee!"

Rex, black and white and looking suspiciously as if he had a Border collie in his family tree somewhere, bounded through the door as if he knew he was home. The smaller pup let out a worried woof, then dashed away to cower under the table.

Travis grinned sheepishly. "He's housebroken."

"That's the good news. One down, one to go," Ronni said. Yesterday she owned no dogs, today she had two. Unbelievable.

Travis kissed her cheek. "You'll survive," he predicted.

When Shelly, Vic and the boys landed, Ronni pointed a wooden spoon in her sister's direction. "Tell me you didn't buy a dog."

"I didn't," her sister swore, looking drawn.

"And you didn't pick up one at the animal shelter, humane society or a stray walking down the street."

"Scout's honor," Shelly said, hiding a smile as she held up two fingers.

"Good, then you can stay, but only if you promise to take it easy and put your feet up in Hank's recliner." Ronni wagged the spoon in front of her sister's nose.

"Yes, ma'am," Shelly replied with a mock salute. "But I thought you couldn't bear the thought of his chair empty in the living room. Wasn't it stored away?"

"I decided that was silly. Along with a lot of things," Ronni explained. "Besides, I wasn't really acting rationally, was I?"

Shelly didn't answer and plucked a cracker from a small bowl, then dipped it into the cheese spread.

"I mean, some of his things I kept around to remind me of him and others I hid away because I didn't want to think about what I'd lost." She shook her head. "I didn't realize how much of a basket case I was."

Shelly cocked her head to one side and munched on the cracker. "And now?"

"Now is tough, but I'm better. My New Year's resolution is to become whole again. To start over."

Folding her arms over her chest, Shelly motioned with her chin toward Travis. "I don't suppose this has anything to do with him."

"A little, probably," Ronni admitted, "but I'd decided it was time to rebuild just before I met him."

"And your war with the mountain?"

"Oh, it goes on forever," Ronni said. "As long as there are skiers trapped up there, I'm going to bring them down. Mount Echo will still win sometimes, but I'll fight her all the way."

"Her?"

"Her, it...does it matter?"

At that moment, both puppies galloped into the room, yipping and giving chase to each other. "My Lord." Shelly laughed. "What happened?"

"I think we're experiencing Amy's vision of heaven."

"And mine of hell," Shelly whispered with a chuckle.

Ronni laughed, too. This Christmas—the one she'd dreaded—was turning out to be the best ever.

They all ate around the table, though it had to be extended with a folding card table at one end and the tablecloth looked a little lumpy where the two tables butted up to each other. Candles graced the centerpiece and Christmas music filled the room. Ronni poured wine for the adults, though Shelly declined, then filled the children's glasses with sparkling cider. Travis was given the honor of carving the turkey and after everyone had eaten until they couldn't take another bite, they left the dishes and turned their attention to the Christmas tree and gift exchange between the families.

Kurt and Kent were thrilled with the new video-game system Ronni had bought for them. Even before the wrapping was totally off the package, they were fighting for the opportunity to play the first game. Shelly ended the argument by stating that if anyone was going to have the honor of using the new equipment first, it would be she.

Amy was so distracted by the puppies, she could barely concentrate on the intricate rag doll her aunt had sewn for her. "Just don't let any of those mongrels near it," Shelly teased. Bryan seemed, or at least pretended, to be interested in the instructional movies on skiing and snowboarding that Ronni had given him and Travis grinned over the books about the history and favorite recreational sports in Oregon. By the time everyone headed home, Ronni was exhausted and the house looked as if it had been hit by a hurricane.

After the first load of dishes was running in the dishwasher, she took the horses a Christmas treat of apples and carrots, then returned to clean up the rest of the house. Amy was so tired she could barely move, but she insisted on camping out on the sofa to be close to the puppies, who, now that they had each other, were curled in a ball of fur and fluff on a blanket in the laundry room.

Ronni had just hung up her apron when she noticed Travis on the front porch. His breath fogged in the air and his face was awash with color from the exterior lights. Catching her attention, he waved her outside and Ronni slipped through the door. After the warmth of the fire, the outside air ripped through her in a fierce gust of raw December wind. Nonetheless, her pulse raced at the sight of him. "Brrr," she whispered, rubbing her arms against the cold. "What are you doing here? Where's Bryan?"

"Back at our place watching the movies you bought him. I told him I'd be home in about an hour and he barely even said goodbye he was so engrossed."

"That's good, I guess, but it still doesn't answer my first question."

"I forgot to give you your present."

"No," she said, shaking her head. "I distinctly remember you handing me a leash, flea powder and twenty-pound bag of dog food."

His laugh was deep as it rumbled through the trees.

"I know. That was your personal, intimate gift. Just for you."

"Thanks so much," she mocked.

"But I thought you needed something a little more practical."

"Like a shovel for scooping the you-know-what?"

His teeth flashed white. "No, something a little less personal than that."

"Oh, great."

He fished into the inner lining of his jacket and withdrew a long white envelope. "Careful," he said as she took it from his hands, her eyebrows knitting in concentration.

"What's this?" she asked. "Airline tickets?" She looked at him before fanning out the tickets and squinting to make out the destination.

"Lake Tahoe," he said. "For the four of us. You, me, Bryan and Amy. We take off tomorrow night."

"But why?"

He reached into the front pocket of his jeans and withdrew a small black box.

A lump the size of a golf ball filled her throat and she found it almost impossible to breathe. "It's not—"

"See for yourself."

Heart thudding almost painfully, she opened the velvet-lined case and stared at a diamond ring that winked softly in the glow of the Christmas lights. "I—I don't know what to say," she whispered and Travis withdrew the ring from its softly lined container.

Taking her left hand in his, he said, "Tell me yes."

Her eyes searched his face, and she bit her lip for a second, "I—I Yes!"

"You'll marry me?" he repeated, seeming astounded.

She flung her arms around his neck. "Of course I'll marry you."

Laughing, he twirled her off her feet and kissed her head. "I was worried you'd say 'no.'"

She grinned and shook her head. "Oh ye of little faith," she teased. Again he kissed her, his lips filled with a sweet, gentle pressure. When he finally lifted his head, he sighed. "We'll elope tomorrow. Fly down to Tahoe and tie the knot, spend a few days there and come home just before New Year's."

"But—I can't leave. Shelly, my business, the dogs—"

"I've already talked to Victor. Shelly's doing as well as can be expected. It's just a matter of time and rest now and you can call her every day if you want to. Vic will look after the dogs and the horses. You already told me that your business is slow this time of year. As for the ski patrol, I talked to Tim Sether who said he could find someone to fill in for you."

"You were pretty sure I'd say yes," she said, still spinning in a rush of emotion.

"No, but I knew what I wanted." His voice deepened and his eyes were suddenly serious. "And what I want is you, Veronica Walsh. Now and forever."

She almost cried tears of happiness. "You've got me, Travis Keegan, and if you ever try to get rid of me, you'll regret it for the rest of your life."

"Never," he vowed, and with his arms wrapped around her protecting her from the cold, she believed him. He slipped the ring onto her finger, kissed her until she no longer felt the cold night air. Then, once her bones had begun to melt, he lifted her off her feet, carried her over the threshold of her little house, locked the door, and while Amy slept soundly on the couch, mounted the stairs to Ronni's bedroom where, for the next hour, they celebrated Christmas alone.

CHAPTER ELEVEN

"YOU MAY KISS the bride!"

The preacher, Reverend Randy, as he insisted upon being called, lifted his hands as if he were addressing an entire congregation instead of the two witnesses Ronni had never met before, his wife on the piano and Bryan and Amy. The tiny chapel was wedged between two casinos and decorated more like an arcade than a church, but it didn't matter. Travis pulled her into the possessive circle of his arms and kissed her in that same breathtaking way that always caused her heart to skip a beat.

Amy, on cue, tossed confetti and rose petals into the air, and Bryan, trying hard not to glower, managed a grim, hard smile. Being his new stepmother wasn't going to be easy, Ronni told herself as she stared into the eyes of her new husband. Marge, Reverend Randy's wife, began to play and music filled the chapel. Ronni was ready for the challenge. Even if Travis didn't love her, she was certain he cared about her and Amy. Love would come later. It had to. They walked down the tiny aisle together and stopped at the back of the chapel when Marge stopped playing. A top-heavy lady in a polka-dot dress, she scurried to the camera that was already poised upon a tripod and took some pictures of Ronni and Travis, the kids, even one with Reverend Randy.

Outside, the sun was just setting, and they walked the

few blocks to their hotel. Sprawled along the shores of the lake, the hotel reminded Ronni of the old Johnson lodge—the place that would finally be her home with Travis. Living in and restoring the old lodge had been her dream for the past several years, except that in her dreams she'd never once thought she would share the premises or her heart with a husband and a stepson.

"Can I call you Daddy?" Amy, holding Travis's hand as they walked into the hotel lobby, wanted to know.

Travis grinned down at his new stepdaughter. "Sure. Why not?"

"Because you're not her daddy," Bryan said, the edges of his lips white.

"We're a family now—"

"No, Travis, we're not a family and this isn't the Brady Bunch. I've already got a mother." He glared at Ronni as if she were the devil incarnate.

"I wouldn't presume to try and take her place—"

"You couldn't, okay? No one can." With a furious glance at his father, he stormed across the lobby and through French doors to the deck.

"I'd better handle this," Travis said. "I'll meet you upstairs." Ronni, still holding her bridal bouquet and feeling like a wretched fool, watched as Travis followed his son. "Come on," she said to Amy. "Let's get changed."

Once she and her daughter were in the suite, she peeled off her ivory-colored suit. Catching a glimpse of herself in the mirror, she remembered her first wedding, complete with a white silk and satin dress, long train, veil and Shelly as her matron of honor. The church in Cascadia had been filled with friends and good cheer, a long reception had followed wherein the timeless rituals of toasting each other, cutting the cake and taking the first dance together had been honored. This time, the wedding had been without all the trimmings—just the four of them, a pieced-together family who still weren't sure how they each fit with each other.

"Bryan hates us," Amy stated as Ronni hung up her clothes.

"No, honey, he's just not sure what to think of all this. It's happening too fast, I think. We should have waited until after the new year."

"I don't see why. I didn't have a daddy for Christmas and now I have one for New Year's and we're going to have a big party." Amy struggled to yank a barrette from her hair.

"Here, let me get that," Ronni said, helping her daughter and laughing a little. "A party? Now, where'd you get that idea?"

"Travis—er, Daddy said we could."

"Oh. Then we will." Sitting on the edge of the king-size bed, Ronni kicked off her heels and massaged the aches from her feet. She thought about her friend, Linda, who was on her honeymoon at Timberline. Wouldn't she be surprised that she wasn't the only new bride working on Mount Echo? "You know what we should do," she said to her daughter.

"What?"

"Call Aunt Shelly."

"And find out how Rex and Snowball are?"

"Well, that's one reason." Rolling to the side of the bed, she reached for the phone on the nightstand. She punched out her sister's number and waited. The phone rang six times before an answering machine with Shelly's voice responded. After waiting for the tone, she said, "Hi, Shell, it's Ronni…I mean, Mrs. Travis Keegan. Can you believe it, I'm actually married again? It's so…strange…but so right." Stretching the phone cord to the window, she gazed past the snow-dusted branches of towering pine trees to the deep blue waters of the lake. "I just thought I'd share some of my happiness with you and I'll call you later—" She was about to hang up when Amy ran up to her.

"Ask about the puppies!" she demanded.

"Oh, and Amy would like an update on her new pets," Ronni said with a smile though she felt a vague sense of unease. Why wasn't Shelly answering? "She's going to want a full report."

She hung up telling herself that she was borrowing trouble again. Shelly had probably needed to get out of the house and had gone with Vic to take care of the horses and dogs, or the entire family had gone out for pizza or hamburgers. Being the vivacious person she was, Shelly couldn't very well lie on the couch day after day.

"Where was Aunt Shelly?" Amy asked as Ronni slipped into a pair of tan jeans.

"I wish I knew." She donned a cream-colored blouse with billowy sleeves and a leather vest. "Come on, let's get you into something a little less dressy."

Within minutes, Amy had transformed from an angel in pink velvet to a tomboy in a red jumpsuit who was not about to let Ronni comb out her hair. "It's okay this way," she said and Ronni decided it wasn't worth the trouble of chasing her daughter around with a brush.

"Fine, who cares?" Ronni said, tossing the brush onto the bed. "Let me know if you change your mind."

A key clicked in the lock and Travis, still in his black

suit, walked into the room. Ronni's heart jolted. This man—this handsome man—was her husband. From now until forever. A flood of happiness swept over her until she spied Bryan, hands in his pockets, head slouched between his shoulders. "I—I'm sorry," he said, glancing at his father as if for approval.

"You don't have to apologize for stating your opinion," Ronni said.

"No, but he can't be rude. That's the rule we're going to have in this family. No one can be rude or cruel to anyone else."

Bryan winced at the word *family* and Ronni's heart went out to him. Obviously, his father's new marriage was tough on him, tougher than any of them could imagine.

"All right," she said. "But we all have to agree to listen to each others' opinions because I think it would be impossible for us all to think the same way. And—" she looked pointedly at her new husband "—everyone's opinion counts."

"Equal?" Bryan wanted to know.

"As equal as it can be," she replied. "For example, you might think you should be able to drive the car, and we don't—you'd have to give in. There are laws to consider and sometimes wisdom does come with age."

"I knew it."

"On the other hand," she said, wagging a finger at the two new men in her life, "your father and I promise to remember what it was like to be a teenager and will try to put ourselves in your place."

"As if you could."

"It won't always work," she admitted with a shrug.

"But I'm willing to give it a shot. It's the best I can offer."

Bryan looked at her as if he wished she'd evaporate on the spot and Ronni gritted her teeth. Being a stepmother was going to take a lot of determination, but she decided right then and there she'd be the best secondary mother any kid could ever want.

Scratching the back of his neck, Bryan asked, "Is the deal still on with the horses? Will you let me ride them if I take care of them?"

Finally, common ground. "You bet. And if your father says it's okay, you can have Sam—he's the stallion. Lucy is Amy's mare, but Sam, he was my husband's. Now he's yours."

"Are you serious?" Bryan asked, all pretenses dropped, his expression one of stunned disbelief.

"'Course."

"Wait a minute—" Travis tried to intervene, but Ronni wouldn't hear of it.

"Consider him yours, Bryan, but remember to take care of him."

"Wow." He studied her for a moment, as if he was trying to determine if she was out of her mind, then shrugged and walked over to the window ledge where he'd left his CD player. Within seconds, he'd clipped on his earphones again.

From the corner of his mouth, Travis said, "You can't reward that kind of behavior."

"He just needs to know that he still belongs," she said, winking at her new husband. "Besides, Sam needs more exercise than I give him. It'll be all right."

"Will it?" he asked.

"Promise."

"You know what they say about promises," he teased, one hand touching her shoulder.

"What's that?"

"That they're made to be broken."

"Not this one."

Travis took them to dinner and a show and by the time they returned to the suite it was after midnight. Amy fell into bed and was asleep before her head hit the pillow. Bryan, rather than sleep in the same room with her, took refuge on the couch in the living area and plugged into the headphones of his CD player. Glowering darkly at the ceiling, he didn't bother to say goodnight.

"Maybe this wasn't such a good idea," Ronni said as Travis closed the door to their bedroom and bolted the lock. A fireplace gave off the only light in the room and flickering shadows seemed to climb up the walls and reflect in the windows.

"What? Getting married?"

"So soon, I mean. Bryan wasn't ready."

"Do you think he ever would have been?" Travis asked, stripping off his sweater and shirt. Firelight gleamed gold against his bare skin.

"I don't know."

"Give him time, he'll get used to it."

She worried her lip as his arms surrounded her. Travis pressed a kiss to her temple. "Bryan will be fine," he said. "He has a lot to work out, but we'll help him along the way. Come on, wife," he whispered suggestively against her ear. "Let me take you to bed."

"But—"

"Shh." He pressed a finger to her lips, then lifted her from her feet. Kicking off his shoes, he carried her to

the bed and together they tumbled into the downy soft-
ness of the comforter as man and wife.

"I just don't understand it," Ronni said the next
morning as she hung up the telephone in frustration
and chewed distractedly on her fingernail before catching herself. "Why isn't Shelly home?"

"Haven't got a clue." Travis, barefoot in low-slung
jeans and no shirt, was leaning over the sink in the
bathroom as he shaved. Fascinated, Ronni watched him
scrape the foam and whiskers from his chin and wondered why it seemed so sexy. As if reading her thoughts,
his gaze met hers in the foggy mirror. "Are you worried about her?"

"A little," she admitted, thinking of the baby. *Please
see that she and the baby are all right,* she prayed. "I've
called three times and she's supposed to be resting so it
seems a little too coincidental that every time I phoned,
she was out."

"Or in the bathtub, or picking up the mail, or running
the twins somewhere or buying groceries—"

"I know, I know, but the doctor told her to take it
easy." An ugly nagging thought crept through her mind,
but she steadfastly tamped it down.

"We're going home this afternoon. You can see her
and catch up then." He shook the razor under the fau-
cet. "Have you ever heard that you worry too much?"

"Only about a million times, but don't you start in
on me, too."

"Are you ordering me around, woman?" The razor
dropped to the counter.

"Me?" She spread a hand over her chest and angled

him her most innocent look. "Wouldn't dream of it," she teased.

Toweling his face dry, he stared at her and her pulse jumped at the raw energy in his eyes. Tossing the towel to the floor, he grinned wickedly. Slowly he advanced on her. "I hope not," he whispered as his fingers twined in her hair.

"Why not?"

"Because I want a woman who knows her place." He kissed the shell of her ear.

She shivered as delicious little bursts of desire spread through her. "Do you? And…and where's that?"

His arms encircled her and his mouth was hot as it hovered over her lips. "Maybe I should show you." He brushed his lips across hers and her bones turned to jelly.

"Maybe you should," she murmured into his open mouth, and with the smile of a devil, he lifted her from her feet only to drop her back onto the bed again.

"You're wicked, Mr. Keegan," she said, suppressing a laugh.

"And so are you, love," he said as he kissed her. "So are you."

Amy was in seventh heaven. Her wishes had come true and she'd found herself a new daddy. Not so, Bryan. He acted as if he'd found his own personal hell. While Amy chattered and laughed during the flight back to Oregon, Bryan slipped earphones onto his head and, scowling darkly, generally avoided talking to anyone. His responses to questions were polite, short, to the point and muttered with a don't-bother-me attitude.

"I don't think he's crazy about the situation," Ronni

said as they gathered their few suitcases from the baggage carousel and walked through the bustle of holiday travelers at Portland International Airport. Bryan lagged behind, listening to his music, making a point of not being a part of the family.

"He'll get used to it," Travis said. "He's just got to make a statement, but he'll come around."

"You're sure?"

"Positive." He kissed her temple. "I'll get the car." They walked through automated doors and then he was off, dashing through the rain to the long-term lot where his Jeep was parked. Amy, tired and bored with always being shepherded, let go of Ronni's hand and wandered down the sidewalk to stand next to her new stepbrother. Tugging on his shirt to get his attention, she said something to him that Ronni couldn't make out and he lifted one earphone to hear her.

For a fraction of a second, he smiled as if he enjoyed her precocious question, then glanced at Ronni, caught her eye and snapped the earphone back in place. Anger twisted his mouth and he ignored Amy, whose smile melted from her tiny face. Lower lip trembling, she wound her way back through stacks of luggage to take her place by Ronni. "Why does he hate me?" she asked, clinging to Ronni's leg.

"He doesn't."

"Yes—"

"No, honey." Ronni dropped her carry-on piece of luggage to the sidewalk as a jet roared overhead. Picking up her daughter, she sighed and hugged Amy. "It's not you he has a problem with."

"He's mean sometimes. Just like Kurt."

"Because he's hurting inside. You just keep being

nice to him and it'll all work out. Now, don't you worry about Bryan for a while. We've got some puppies who are going to be mighty glad to see you."

Amy's face brightened and she wiggled to the ground just as Travis's Jeep rounded the corner.

The ride back home was slow and tedious. Along with the usual crush of vacationers on the road, enthusiastic skiers were heading to the mountain as seven inches of new snow had fallen in the Cascades over the weekend. The roads were icy and treacherous, with snowplows and sanding crews unable to keep up with the dropping temperature and increased snowfall.

"Looks like a good night to build a fire and curl up on the couch with a glass of wine."

"Mmm," Ronni agreed, glancing at the backseat where both Bryan and Amy had fallen asleep. Bryan's head was propped against the window and Amy had slumped against him, her forehead touching his sleeve. "I'd feel a lot better if I could talk to Shelly."

"You could try using the cell."

"No, I'll wait. We're almost home."

"That we are, Mrs. Keegan," he said with a smile. "That we are."

They stopped at Ronni's house and a groggy Amy collected the pups while Ronni gathered a few more clothes and Travis and Bryan fed the horses.

Again Ronni tried to reach her sister and this time her brother-in-law answered. "Oh, Ronni," he said in a voice that was flat and lifeless. "How was the trip?"

"Fine, fine, I'm a married woman now," she said brightly, though the serious tone in Victor's voice was enough to scare her to death. "I tried to call a couple of times but no one answered."

"We were at the hospital," he admitted.

Ronni's heart plummeted. "The hospital?"

"That's right. Look, Shelly's not in the best of shape right now. She's home and physically she's gonna be fine, the doctor assured her that she could still have more kids but..."

"Oh, my God," Ronni whispered, clutching the receiver and bracing herself against the refrigerator.

"Yeah," he said, and his voice cracked a little. "She lost the baby."

"You go home," Shelly admonished, squeezing Ronni's hand. She was lying in bed, her face drawn, the sparkle missing from her eyes as Vic and the boys watched television in the living room. "You're a new bride and you need to be with your husband—keep celebrating your honeymoon."

"Don't be silly."

"Not silly, just practical," Shelly said with a weak smile that didn't add any life to eyes that were puffy and red-rimmed from tears. "I'm going to be fine. The doctor said to take it easy for a few days, but I'm not bedridden and I should bounce back in no time."

"But...I feel so bad." Ronni sniffed to keep from crying.

"We all do, and even though I've got two healthy, wonderful boys, this was...well, a loss. I just have to think of it that way and get over it." Dragging her gaze away from Ronni's, she cleared her throat. A tear gathered in the corner of her eye, but she quickly dashed it away with a finger. "I'm going to be fine. It'll just take a little time to get used to..." A long, heavy sigh escaped her. "Oh, damn, maybe I'll never get over it."

"You will."

"I hope. The good news is that Victor wants to try again—can you believe it, after his reaction when he learned I was pregnant?" She gave a short, brittle little laugh. "He's come around and wants another baby."

"Of course he does."

"I wouldn't have believed it, but then he was out of work and now, thanks to Travis, he feels better. They've talked, you know, about him staying on after the work on the house is finished, and about fixing up the old caretaker's house for us. Travis said that Vic could either be a caretaker of the grounds like Dad was or he could work for Travis's company in some capacity—I don't know exactly what, the vice president in Seattle sent Vic some information…it's there, I think, on the bureau." She waved at a small stack of papers tucked behind her jewelry box. "I guess you married a millionaire."

"Maybe," Ronni said, embarrassed that she didn't have a clue as to Travis's holdings, that she didn't really care. She realized he had money, of course, and plenty of it, but she hadn't worried about how much and he hadn't bothered with a prenuptial agreement.

"No maybes about it—your husband is loaded." Shelly sighed dramatically. "It would be nice, but then again, money isn't everything." Tears filled her eyes once more as she absently touched her belly, but she pressed the silent drops back into her eyes. "Have you found that stuff yet?"

Ronni picked up the brochures and typed pages introducing Victor Pederson to TRK, Incorporated. Along with employee information, there were advertising sheets and lists of products with a letter of introduction signed by Wendall Holmes.

Ronni's heart nearly stopped.

Wendall Holmes!

She swallowed and stared at the signature. So bold. So precise. So damned familiar. "Oh, God," she whispered. She'd heard the name Wendall and once Travis had said something about Holmes, but she hadn't, until this very minute, put two and two together to get four.

"What?" Shelly sat straighter in the bed.

For a second, her vision blurred and she was sure that she'd made a mistake, she couldn't be reading the same name that had signed so many letters, but no matter how often she blinked, each time she looked at the letter, the name and the signature remained the same. Wendall Holmes.

"I've talked to this man before," she said, and her voice seemed disembodied, as if it belonged to another person in another time.

"Where? How?"

"Wendall Holmes was the vice president in charge of consumer relations for SkiWest," she said, her voice barely audible.

"Oh, Ronni, no." Shelly bit her lip.

"He was the guy I was writing to about Hank's equipment." The brochures balling in her fist, she sank onto the corner of Shelly's bed. "Those bindings…they were SkiWest 450's. Travis's company manufactured them."

"You don't know that," Shelly said, reaching forward and clasping Ronni's arm. "Holmes could have changed companies—"

Ronni shook her head. "No, I asked about him once. Travis told me they've worked together for years." Pain cracked through her heart and she bit down on her lip to keep from crying.

"Let it go," Shelly advised.

"I can't."

"You have to."

"Hank died, Shelly! He died!" Ronni said, shooting to her feet and reaching for the doorknob, but Shelly's silent, sad gaze held her in the room. "I can't just forget it."

"You have to put it aside."

"But he's dead."

Shelly's eyes lost all of their sparkle. "So is my baby, Ronni."

Travis drove the last nail into the new railing of the back porch. Bryan, against his better judgment, was helping out, using a square and a level, making sure that his father's work was precise. Ronni was visiting her sister and Amy was napping inside. "Better, don't you think?" Travis asked as he stepped away from the porch and looked at the bare fir two by twos.

A table saw screamed in the garage where Vic had set up shop and was cutting lengths for the next section of the rail. The old, sagging wood had already been hauled to the pile behind the garage and it was Bryan's job to take out all the old nails and stack the used lumber in the kindling pile. "It's okay."

"Just okay? Not terrific?"

Bryan stared sullenly at him. "Okay, it's terrific. Feel better?"

Travis's temper was already stretched thin. He hated walking on eggshells around his son and decided that it was now or never—time for another father-son showdown. "Are you going to tell me what's eating you or do I have to guess?"

"Whad'ya mean?" Bryan grabbed his hammer and tried to wiggle nails out of a piece of old railing.

"You've been in a bad mood since we moved here and every time things improve and I think you're settling in, we take a backspin."

The boy's jaw tightened. "So?"

This wasn't going to be easy. Travis straightened and rubbed the kinks from the small of his back. Frowning, he eyed the sky, a storm had been predicted, a big one with the promise of high winds and more snow. Already the tops of the taller trees were moving with the breeze. "You aren't very friendly to Ronni."

No answer. Another nail squeaked as Bryan yanked it out of the rotting wood.

"You know she's been nothing but nice to you. First she gets you down the mountain when you hurt yourself, then she offers to teach you to ski and now she's given you one of her horses. She's bent over backward to be friendly to you and all you've done in response is give her the cold shoulder."

"Big deal."

"That's right. It is. A very big deal. I assume you're not happy that I married her."

"What does it matter what I think?"

"A lot, Bryan."

"You didn't even ask me," his son mumbled, reaching for another rail. "You marry her and don't even ask me."

"I didn't know I had to."

"Don't I count?" Bryan wanted to know.

"Of course."

"And my opinion, too, right? That's what Ronni said."

"Yes, but—"

"Then what was all this talk about you and me being a family, huh? Just the two of us." In anger, Bryan threw the rail into the woods. "Was that all a bunch of baloney?"

"No, but—"

"What did we need her and her stupid little girl for? All they're gonna do is mess things up..." His voice trailed off and he looked away sharply. Travis heard a gasp and turned to find Amy standing in the partially open doorway. The puppy was in her arms and her face was twisted in silent agony.

"Amy," Travis said, but she ran away, the puppy yipping wildly. Travis turned on his son. "What were you thinking?" he demanded.

"You wanted to know," his son said. "I just told you what I thought."

"You hurt her feelings!"

"Yeah, well, you hurt mine." Bryan tossed another rail into the rapidly growing pile, and Travis, muttering under his breath, hurried into the house.

"Amy! Amy!" he called, walking through the lower level and up the stairs. If it weren't for the barking on the upper floor and the sound of dog toenails digging into wood, he might not have found her huddled in some old blankets on the floor of a closet in the attic.

"He hates me!" she said when Travis located her and the two dogs.

"He's just confused. Come here."

"Bryan," she said, her little jaw quivering. "He hates me."

"He's just not used to things the way they are right now."

"He's mean!"

"He's not trying to be." Travis gathered her into his arms and held her close. The dogs scrambled out of the closet and ran in circles through the pine-walled room. "This is hard for Bryan, too, honey. Being a new family isn't easy."

"I thought we were supposed to love each other." Crystal-like tears tracked down her face. She began to sob.

"We do all love each other, but sometimes…sometimes people inadvertently hurt the ones they love. They don't mean to, they're just shortsighted."

She sniffed loudly and the smallest dog bounded onto her lap to wash her face with her long tongue. Amy couldn't resist and giggled wildly. Travis's heart warmed at the sound and he wondered how he'd lived his life without hearing the happy ring of her childish laughter. One step at a time, he told himself, one step and one day at a time. "Come on, short stuff, let's take the mutts outside."

The lights flickered and Amy let out a whimper.

Travis hugged her. "Don't worry."

"Ghosts," she said, shivering.

"Just the wind, honey. Let's find some candles and kerosene lanterns in case the electricity decides to give out."

She carried the small puppy, he carried her and Rex bounded along behind as they made their way down to the main floor. Bryan, flopped on the couch and staring at the television, glanced their way and his eyes darkened in silent fury.

"I think we'd better scrounge up some flashlights," Travis suggested, but his son didn't budge. "Bryan?"

"Yeah?"

"You know where the flashlights are?"

"Yeah."

"Then find one before we lose power."

Bryan rolled his eyes, shot Amy a look that could kill and sauntered to his bedroom. Whistling to the dogs, Travis carried Amy outside and into the garage where Vic was just putting away his tools.

"Better get home," he said half-apologetically. "Shelly isn't happy when we don't have power."

"Don't blame her."

"But I'm leavin' early—"

"Doesn't matter. The weather service seems to think we're in for the storm of all storms, so you'd better get home before it breaks."

"Kind of ya," Victor said. "I'll be in early tomorrow." He unbuckled his tool belt and rumpled Amy's hair.

"Don't worry about it." Travis slid a glance to the slate-colored sky. Dark clouds skudded over the tops of the highest trees and snow had begun to fall in tiny, hard flakes. Victor turned his collar against the wind and strode to his truck. Still holding Amy, Travis watched him leave and hoped that Ronni would return home soon.

Thank God she wasn't on ski-patrol duty today. Against the horizon and through the thickening snow-flakes, Mount Echo loomed like a specter, tall and dark and threatening. "Come on, let's get you inside," he said, bundling Amy into the kitchen and calling for the dogs. The puppy, scared of the rising wind, didn't need any

encouragement. She dashed through the drifting snow
and scurried up the slick steps.

Rex, still sniffing trees in the forest, was more difficult to corral, but eventually he followed.

Bryan had found a couple of flashlights and Travis
gathered an old oil lantern, matches and a few candles.
He couldn't help glancing at his watch and then peer-
ing through the windows, all the while hoping Ronni
would return soon.

Obviously still miffed at her stepbrother's unkind
remarks, Amy stayed close to Travis and he was just
about to break down and call Shelly, interrupt his wife's
sister-to-sister talk when he spied Ronni's van rolling
slowly down the driveway.

Relief swept through him and he was at the front
door, holding it open, drinking in the sight of her running up the broken path in the snow, her hat pulled low,
snowflakes catching on the tips of her eyelashes, when
he noticed something different about her. Gone was
her easy smile and the twinkle in her warm eyes. Her
mouth was pulled tight, her nostrils flared, her expression grim as death.

Because of Shelly and her loss of the baby.

"I take it things didn't go well," he said, trying to
reach for her, but she stepped quickly out of his arms.

"Shelly's upset," she said, rubbing her arms. "I'm
upset. It's…it's not right."

Knowing instinctively that she didn't want to be pla-
cated, he held his tongue and didn't say that things
would turn out, that her sister would have more babies,
that it just took time to get over these things. She and
Shelly had to grieve.

"I'm sorry," he said softly and she stared up at him

with eyes that seemed to glisten in the night. Somewhere far away a horn honked and a lonesome dog barked. Closer to the house, the wind picked up, starting to whistle through the trees.

Again the lights flickered, this time causing darkness for a few seconds as the string of Christmas bulbs and the porch lamp died before blinking back on.

"There's a big one brewing," he said, reaching for her again as the lights winked again. "I've got a fire started, candles and flashlights ready. Come on in, I'll buy you a drink." Smiling, he touched her lightly on the shoulders, but she drew away and reached for the doorknob. Before shoving against the panels, she paused, her shoulders bunched tight, and she hung her head for a second, as if gathering the strength to fight a new battle.

"Ronni?"

"Wendall Holmes."

"What about him?"

She closed her eyes for a second. "He's worked for you for a long time, hasn't he?"

"Nearly twelve years." Was it his imagination or did her face wash of its usual color?

"I thought so."

"He's buying me out—"

Holding up a gloved hand, she nodded. "I know." Slowly she turned, and when she stared up at him, he felt something wither in his soul. "Then you were the owner and president of SkiWest Company?"

"Still am." Why did he feel as if he were signing his death warrant? Her eyes were full of silent condemnation and her lips were white as the snow that was blowing across the porch.

"I was afraid of this."

"What? What's wrong?"

"SkiWest bindings—450's were the kind that Hank was using—compliments of the company—when he was killed. The bindings didn't release." She reached for the door again but this time he caught her and grabbed her shoulders.

"You blame the bindings?" he demanded. "You think faulty equipment was the reason that your husband was killed?"

Sighing, she shook her head. "I don't know," she admitted and his heart felt as if it might crack. How much she'd loved Amy's father, how deeply she'd cared. He could never hope to fill the huge shoes left by Saint Hank and she'd never love him with the same fervor. "No...not really...but I just needed someone, *something* to blame."

"It was an accident. You said so yourself. The mountain reacted before they could make it avalanche-proof. He was unlucky, so were you. Even if his bindings had released, even if his skis had been stronger, even if he were the fastest skier in the world, he couldn't have outrun that wall of snow." Travis's throat twisted into a painful knot and his voice was strangled when he spoke. "Let it go, Ronni." He folded her into his arms and she shivered, burying her face in his neck, holding him, letting out the dry, wracking sobs that tore at her soul. "If I could change the past for you I would, but it's just not possible."

"I know," she said and it was as if the starch slipped away from her, as if an old dam she'd constructed had cracked and a tide of emotion swept through her. "I do know."

He kissed her hair. "I'm not the man he was, Ronni,"

he said and she let out a choked sound. "But I swear to you, I'll be the best husband and father I can be. I'll never leave you, never let you down." His arms tightened around her. "No one can bring Hank back."

"I know."

"He's gone and so is Shelly's baby. It's not fair, it's not right, but there it is. I can't promise you to be like Hank—I wouldn't even try."

"I wouldn't want you to."

"Are you sure?" He held her at arm's length and stared deep into her eyes.

"Yes."

The door opened. "Mommy?"

"Oh, sweetheart." Ronni dragged her gaze away and reached for her daughter who was still holding the pup.

Extracting herself from his embrace, she picked up Amy. In the semidarkness, she transformed from a grieving, unhappy woman to a concerned mother. "Let's go inside and light all the candles and have a party."

"A party?" Instantly Amy grinned, her fears forgotten as she squirmed to the floor and raced into the house.

Ronni stomped the snow from her boots and shook her hair out of her stocking cap. Travis was right, life marched on, and though she still grieved for Shelly's loss, there was nothing she could do but help her sister get well, both mentally and physically. As for Hank, she would always love him, there would always be a special spot in her heart for him and his family, but she was married to Travis now, her life was with him, and though she hated to admit it, she felt as if her love for him was deeper than it had been for Hank. Maybe because she was older and more mature, perhaps because her memories had faded over time. Whatever the reason, she loved Travis and, in his own way, he loved her.

She filled several kettles and the bathtubs with water as the pump for their well was electric and without power they'd have no water source for drinking, washing or flushing the toilets. Travis understood the problem, but Bryan, the city kid, lying on the couch and fiddling with an old Rubic's cube as he watched television, didn't pay much attention when she described what it was like in the mountains without any energy.

She heated soup and bread while Travis found down-filled sleeping bags that he brought into their bedroom, which had a lower ceiling than the living room and a huge fireplace for warmth. They'd just finished eating when it happened, the lights didn't even wink, just went dark. Amy whimpered, Ronni held her close and the wind howled around the house, rattling the window panes and screaming through the trees.

Travis snapped on a flashlight. "I think we'd better move into our room," he suggested.

"Why?" Bryan asked.

"To keep warm."

Bryan made a sound of disgust. "I'm not moving into your bedroom."

"Just until the lights go on."

"No way, Travis," he said, no longer calling him anything but his given name.

"Listen, we should stick together."

"Forget it. I'll hang out in my own room."

"There's no fireplace," Travis argued, but his son had already grabbed one of the flashlights, his blankets and headed off to his bedroom.

Ronni was about to protest, but Travis grabbed her

arm. "He'll be all right. We'll check on him later." They gathered the candles, lantern and flashlights and, after locking the dogs in their pen in a room off the kitchen, they headed for the bedroom. Amy, wrapped in her thick sleeping bag, her ratty stuffed tiger tucked under her chin, was asleep within minutes and Travis and Ronni snuggled close together, watching the fire cast warm golden light around the walls and on their faces. She sighed against his chest, resting her head in the crook of his neck, and they couldn't resist kissing and whispering to each other as the flames crackled and hissed against the dry oak logs.

Outside, the wind moaned and snow fell in a blizzard. Inside, the old lodge was warm and dry and cozy.

They fell asleep as the fire died, and over the howl of the wind, they didn't hear the footsteps in the hall, didn't realize their door was pushed open, didn't know they were watched for a few long minutes.

They slept on, uninterrupted as the front door opened and closed. And Bryan escaped into the night.

CHAPTER TWELVE

"Bryan's gone."

Travis's voice, deep and urgent, permeated her brain and Ronni roused herself from a deep sleep. Blinking, she found her husband dressing rapidly, stepping into ski pants and sweater, jacket and boots.

"What do you mean he's gone?" she asked, her mind still blurry with the soft cobwebs of sleep.

"Just that. He left sometime last night."

"Left? As in left the house?" Suddenly, she was instantly awake.

"I've looked everywhere from the attic to the cellar, even the out buildings and his backpack is missing along with his portable CD player. I think he took off."

"But how? Why?" she asked, throwing off the pile of covers that had been tossed over their king-size bed. But before he could speak, she knew the answer. "This is because of me, isn't it? He's run away because you and I got married and he feels like he doesn't have a place in the family anymore."

"I don't know why he left, I'm just sure he's gone."

Sick inside, Ronni threw on her ski jumpsuit and found her goggles. She glanced outside and saw that the storm was still in full force, snow blowing against the windowpanes, the wind screaming wildly. The power was still off and the temperature in the house had dropped, the fires mere embers. Fortunately, the phones still worked and Travis was able to get through to the sheriff's department. Every deputy was already on duty, trying to help people stranded in vehicles that couldn't get through the snow-covered roads and shut-ins without electricity.

"They'll start looking for him," he said as she lit the gas stove with a match and warmed water for instant coffee. He glared outside to the beauty and treachery of the storm. "What the hell was he thinking?"

"He wasn't."

The phone rang and Travis nearly jumped out of his skin. "Keegan," he answered curtly and Ronni watched as he steeled himself for bad news. The lines near the corners of his mouth and eyes deepened to crevices and his lips flattened into a worried scowl. "Just a minute." He handed her the phone. "It's your sister."

"Shelly! How are you?" Ronni asked, crossing her fingers and hoping beyond hope that there was word of Bryan. Maybe he'd made a friend of Victor and had walked the two miles into town. But when she asked about Travis's son, Shelly knew nothing.

"I was just calling to see if your power was out," Shelly explained, "and to tell you that I'm feeling better, but, no, we haven't heard from Bryan."

"I was afraid of that," Ronni said, her eyes meeting the distress in Travis's. "Look, we're worried sick and don't want to tie up the phone lines so that if there's any news, the sheriff's department can get through."

"Okay, but if you want a place for Amy to stay, bring her over and I'll watch her. Believe me, I need some distraction. Of course, Vic will help with the search.

Oh, Lord, I hope that boy wasn't so stupid as to take off in this weather."

"Me, too," Ronni replied as she hung up and tried to ignore the horrid feeling of desperation that burrowed deep in her heart.

While Travis searched the buildings outside again, Ronni started in the basement and looked in every nook and cranny in the old lodge, hoping Travis had missed a hiding spot during his first search. Closets, laundry chutes, cupboards, crawl spaces, stairwells, coal bins, every inch of floor space was inspected. But by the time she reached the attic, she was as certain as Travis that Bryan was gone.

She returned to the kitchen where Travis had poured himself a cup of coffee. His face was red from the cold, his hair wet with melting snow. "Nothing?" he asked and she shook her head.

"I found footsteps near the garage that look fresh, but they disappeared so quickly where the snow has fallen there's no way to know which way he went."

"I'll call the search-and-rescue team," she volunteered just as Amy, dragging her tattered blanket and stuffed tiger, bounced into the room.

"It's cold," she complained.

"That it is. How about a cup of hot cocoa?" Ronni offered and in silent agreement with Travis didn't mention that Bryan was missing. There wasn't any need to worry her. "I thought maybe you'd like to go visit your cousins this afternoon."

"Can I take the puppies?" Amy dashed to the pen where the dogs were playing with each other, growling and knocking over their water dish.

"Aunt Shelly can't have them at the duplex, honey,

but another time the boys can come here and play with them."

Amy's face twisted into a knot of frustration and she appeared about to argue, but Ronni handed her a cup of dog food and more water and, for the moment, Amy was distracted.

Travis was fit to be tied, pacing and glaring at the phone as if by staring at it long and hard enough, the telephone would ring. Ronni could barely think straight, her mind racing with images of Bryan in the snow, hitchhiking back to Seattle, walking through knee-high drifts, alone, cold, miserable. *Please keep him safe,* she silently prayed while going through the motions of fixing Amy breakfast and locating her clothes. Even though she'd been trained to deal with emergencies on and off the mountain, her calm fled when it came to her own family.

She dialed Tim Sether and explained the situation, then took Amy over to her sister's.

"Any word?" Shelly asked as she answered the door. Wearing jeans and a heavy sweater, she offered her sister a cup of tea or coffee, but Ronni couldn't stand the thought of sitting around and waiting. Outside, the temperature was barely twenty degrees and the winds and snow weren't supposed to let up for another day. Power outages were still widespread and a few of the smaller roads were closed. When Shelly asked about Bryan, Ronni felt an ache deep in her soul.

"We haven't heard anything."

"Fool kid," Shelly said, eyeing the sky through the window and shivering though a fire was blazing in the grate and the little duplex was warm enough. "Well, don't worry about Amy. She'll be fine here. Besides, I owe you, big time."

"You don't owe me anything. Are you feeling okay?"

"Right as rain," Shelly said with a sad smile. "Things have a way of working out. I'm still upset about losing the baby, but I've got to remember I've got the twins and they're healthy as all get out. If we want more kids later, we'll have another baby. Vic and I have already talked. Now, you find that boy of Travis's."

"I will," Ronni promised as she reached for the doorknob. She only wished she knew where to start looking.

Before returning to the lodge, she stopped by her house, the cabin she'd shared with Hank, then with Amy. Her life with her first husband seemed so long ago now as she stared at the hardwood floors, old couch and Christmas tree that had yet to be taken down. She picked up some camping gear, her snowshoes, skis and first-aid kit. Then she packed three bags of warm garments including her ski clothes and long underwear, loaded everything into the van and walked through the snow to the barn to feed the horses.

It was dark inside, but an anxious nicker called to her as she fumbled for the pitchfork and shone her flashlight around the barn. Lucy, always the more nervous of the two, whinnied softly. "How're you guys, hmm?" she asked, feeling as if something wasn't right, yet unable to put her finger on the problem. "Cold enough for you?"

Another nicker and she directed the beam of the light into the stalls. Lucy tossed her white head, then blinked against the glare of the light as she stood in the thick straw. Her ears twitched nervously as Ronni draped a red horse blanket over the Mare's back and snapped it into place. "You'll be okay," she said, moving to the next stall and stopping short. The enclosure was empty, the gate unlatched. "What the devil?" Sam had somehow escaped, and he hadn't done it alone. A bridle, saddle blanket and saddle were missing. Her heart lurched. It didn't take a genius to figure out that Bryan had walked over here last night, saddled the gray and ridden off on him.

But where?

And why in the middle of the worst storm in five years?

She was about to run to the house and call Travis when she noticed a piece of notebook paper, folded neatly and left in the manger. Heart racing, she smoothed the creases and began to read Bryan's sloppy scrawl.

Travis
I'm leaving. I know you won't understand, but I just can't take it anymore down here in the middle of nowhere and you don't need me, anyway. You've got your new wife and your new kid. I don't know how many times I heard Amy say she wanted a daddy for Christmas, well, it looks like she got herself one for New Year's. Don't tell Mom.
Bryan

"Dear God," Ronni whispered, her heart pounding, tears burning the back of her eyes as she dashed out of the barn, leaving a bewildered and hungry Lucy. In the house, she had to keep her fingers from shaking, then punched out the number for the lodge.

Travis was quick to answer. "Hello?"

"He's run away. On Sam. He left a note and took a saddle and bridle and—"

"Whoa, slow down." Travis's voice was grim. "Now, take a deep breath and start over. What's this about Bryan leaving a note and running away?"

Trying to stay calm, Ronni repeated everything, reading him the note and hearing the soft groan of denial from the other end of the line. "I'll be home in five minutes," she said.

"I'll call the sheriff again."

She hung up and felt the breath of doom on her neck. It was her fault Bryan had run away, her fault that at this moment he could be lying near death, freezing on the damned mountain. *Just like before. Just like with Hank.*

By the time she'd thrown Lucy two forkfuls of hay and driven to the lodge, a search party had formed. Tim Sether, Vic, Travis and a few other men and women who worked with her promised to gather volunteers and comb the surrounding woods. A deputy from the sheriff's department stopped by and helped organize the search.

Meanwhile, Travis read his son's note, once, twice, even a third time before crumpling the sheet of notebook paper in his fist. A muscle tightened in his jaw and his eyes narrowed in determination. "I'll find him," he assured Ronni. "Or die trying."

"Don't even say it."

"Let's just hope he sticks to the main roads," Tim said, his round face creased with concern. "What's he wearing?"

"I'm not sure, I didn't see him leave, but his navy ski jacket and pants are missing, along with the red stocking hat and face mask he wears up on the slopes." Travis's face was drawn, his eyes cloudy with worry.

"Hang in there," Ronni encouraged, though she couldn't force a smile. "He's going to be fine."

"Okay, everyone gather 'round." Tim laid out maps of the area on the kitchen table and Ronni heated hot water for tea and instant coffee. They discussed their plan of attack, called the weather service for conditions and coordinated the search with the sheriff.

Most of the searchers would start on foot, helicopters would be called in when the storm let up and snowmobiles and four-wheel drive rigs would be used where possible. They'd form a grid and work their way south, covering as much ground as possible with the men and women they had.

Ronni was elected to stay at the lodge near the phone and she protested violently. "No way, I know this mountain better than anyone."

Travis would hear none of it. "Someone's got to remain here."

"But he's my son now."

"And you've got a daughter who needs you. We can't risk losing you…" His eyes touched hers. "I can't risk that."

"I can help. Here I'm trapped," she whispered as one of the searchers raised an eyebrow and shot a look in her direction.

"I know, but I couldn't stand it if I lost you, too."

"Damn it, Travis, you can't force me to stay here."

"It's important that someone oversees the phones. What if Bryan calls? What if one of the searchers finds him? What if they need an ambulance? Someone's got to be here to receive and relay messages."

"It's best this way," Tim agreed and Ronni wanted to throttle him. She couldn't sit idle and twiddle her thumbs, staring at her watch and worrying herself to death.

"Please, Ronni, just this once, do as I ask." Travis's eyes searched hers and despite the clamoring in her heart that she was making a mistake, that she could help more by combing the lower slopes of the mountain, she nodded.

"If you think it's best," she said, hating the words.

He kissed her on the temple so gently, she thought her heart would crack.

"Okay, let's do it," Tim said. Everyone on the team carried flares and tracking devices, most had walkie-talkies. By nine o'clock, they left, fanning out from Ronni's place and the lodge, braving the storm and hoping to find a scared teenage boy in a whiteout.

Ronni wrapped her arms around her middle and stared outside. She couldn't shake a horrid premonition as she watched Travis leave. He was headed around the lake to search the forest around the base of Mount Echo and Ronni experienced a sickening sense of déjà vu, that this was the last time she'd ever see her new husband or his son, that the mountain would win again.

"Bryan!" Travis's voice boomed through the forest and echoed back at him. He stopped in his tracks, listened but only heard his own words over the force of the wind. He moved forward and with each step, his heart shredded. How could anyone survive in this? He could barely see four feet in front of him and the cold air froze against his nose. "Bryan! Bryan, can you hear me?" he yelled, trying to keep the edge of panic from his voice.

In his mind's eye, he saw his son's broken body, heard him whimper in fear, knew he could be dead. *"No!"* he yelled, and again his voice came back to him without an answer. He stumbled forward and for the first time in twenty years, he prayed.

"I couldn't stand it, just sitting in the house waiting to hear so I bundled up the kids and drove over. The car is stuck at the end of the lane. It couldn't make it up the last hill," Shelly explained as she walked through the front door, her eyes sweeping the dark interior of the lodge. Amy ran inside followed by her cousins and they made three beelines to the puppy pen.

"I'm glad you're here," Ronni admitted. "Now you can take care of the phones. I've called most of the teen shelters between here and Portland on Travis's business line, but none have taken in a boy of Bryan's description."

"He could have stopped by a house or a barn or anywhere," Shelly said. "Try not to worry."

"Impossible, but now that you're here and can handle the calls—"

"Me? What about you?"

"I'm going to join the search."

Shelly hazarded a glance to the window, where snow had drifted against the panes. "Wait a minute. Shouldn't you leave this to the men?"

As she began gathering her jacket, flares, flashlight and survival gear, Ronni shot her a look that could cut through the base of an old-growth fir tree. With a sound of disgust, she said, "The *men* need all the help they can get. And I think Beverly Adams, Maude Lindsay and JoAnne Rodgers would be offended if they thought you didn't think they, as women, were doing a good enough job."

"But—"

"All you have to do is be the information center. When a call comes in, you spread the word. Almost everyone in the groups have walkie-talkies and here's yours." She gave her sister quick instructions on how to run the equipment and before Shelly could put up any further protest, Ronni kissed Amy goodbye and was out the door.

Snapping on a belt, she tested her walkie-talkie and discovered she could hear the other groups of searchers. Much as she didn't want Travis to know that she'd gone against his wishes, she advised the other searchers of her plans. The only area that hadn't been covered when Tim's teams had marked their territory on his maps had been an old logging road, long overgrown, that wound up the lower slopes of the eastern face of the mountain. It was treacherous going, portions of the road had washed or eroded over the past twenty years, but it was the only unsearched spot. No one in his right mind would ride up that old trail, but then, she was dealing with a teenager unaccustomed to the mountains in winter.

She didn't think twice about saddling poor Lucy and, starting to ride the old trail. Although she was wearing her ski jumpsuit, goggles and a huge poncho, the wind pierced through her clothes, and her face above her ski mask was raw, but she rode by instinct, urging Lucy through the deep snow, her eyes straining as she looked for any trace of her stepson.

"Come on, girl, you can make it," she whispered and the horse kept plodding forward, ever upward, her breath steaming from her nostrils. Ronni brushed the snow from her goggles and tried to call other members of the rescue team on her walkie-talkie again but heard only static. Giving up on the device, she concentrated on her search. "Bryan," she called, crossing her gloved fingers as she held lightly to the reins. "Bryan?" And then more softly. "Where are you?"

The road narrowed and dipped but the old bridge that had once spanned the gully had long ago rotted through. Lucy picked her way down one steep slope and over a trickle of water that had iced over, only to slip while trying to climb the opposite side. "You can do it, girl," Ronni encouraged, squinting hard and searching the snow-covered undergrowth. Berry vines and ferns, brush and saplings were bent with the weight of their wintry blanket.

They kept plugging on, passing old, abandoned equipment, searching the trees. Once she stopped by an old logging camp that was deserted, the remains of the buildings only wooden skeletons. Bryan wasn't there.

By one o'clock, Lucy was breathing hard and Ronni stopped just a few minutes to rest the horse, then mounted her again and started through virgin forests of old growth that had escaped being eaten by the huge saws of the timber industry.

The afternoon wore on and Ronni's spirits sank with each of Lucy's plodding steps. It had been hours. How could he survive? She checked the walkie-talkie again but she couldn't hear much and what she did pick up suggested that the boy hadn't yet been found.

She thought about Travis and Amy and Bryan. If only she could turn back the clock forty-eight hours. Things would be different.

Lucy struggled to the top of the ridge where the wind was more fierce, the roar deafening. "Bryan?" she yelled and heard no response, but Lucy's ears pricked forward and she neighed anxiously. "Bryan?" Ronni screamed again, her voice hoarse. "Can you hear me?"

Lucy snorted and through the curtain of snow, Ronni saw a shape, a dark looming shape. Her heart leaped for a moment when she recognized Sam, her gray stallion. "Bryan, thank God—" Her prayer froze on her lips as the horse trudged through the snow and Ronni realized that his saddle was empty, the reins of his bridle dangling unattended to the ground.

Her heart plummeted. She'd held out a ray of hope that Bryan would be all right with his surefooted mount. Sam was familiar with these old mountain trails even if his rider wasn't. But the horse ambled forward riderless and now Bryan, lost somewhere in this frigid wilderness, was completely and utterly alone.

Dismounting, she snagged Sam's reins. She'd ride the stallion for a while, giving Lucy a break. "Let's go," she said, holding on to two sets of reins and turning Sam around. For as long as she could, she'd follow the trail Sam had broken in the snow. After that, she'd have to rely on luck.

"We're going to have to call off the search until the storm blows over," the deputy said over the crackle of static on his walkie-talkie.

Travis gritted his teeth. "No way. I'm in this until we find Bryan."

"I can't risk these people's lives. It's nearly dark and we're turning back. The storm's supposed to move north by tomorrow. We'll resume then."

Fear clutched Travis's heart in a stranglehold and wouldn't let go. In eight hours he could lose his son. "I'm not coming in. Tell Ronni I'll be back when I find him."

There was a pause on the other end, just the sound of crackling static. "Weren't you listening? Ronni's out here," the deputy finally said. "She called but something's wrong with her walkie-talkie. It looks like she took off after Bryan, too. Near as we can tell, she's on horseback. We're trying to reach her to call her in, but so far she hasn't responded."

His heart nearly clutched. "What?"

"You heard me. Took off and left her sister here to oversee the phones."

"Damn," Travis growled, his eyes searching the woods, his feet and hands nearly frozen despite his insulated boots and gloves. That hardheaded woman! Her image came to mind, her dark hair, warm brown eyes, smiling full lips. Oh, God, he couldn't lose her. Frantic, he plowed forward. Somewhere out here, somewhere in this damned wilderness, were his wife and kid. He only hoped they were still alive.

"Bryan!" Shivering from the cold, Ronni rode as darkness began to creep over the mountains. She had two choices—to keep searching or ride back. She couldn't stop for any length of time and build an ice cave because the horses wouldn't survive. She'd followed Sam's broken trail for over two miles, up a canyon and down a draw to the trickle of a creek flowing sluggishly between icy shores. When the trail had given out, she'd let Sam pick his way, hoping that the horse would understand and locate the boy. So far, it hadn't worked.

Be with him, please, keep him safe, she prayed, then squinted. For a second she thought she was seeing things, creating a happy mirage in her mind—a mirage of her stepson propped up against the spreading bows of a fir tree, but as Sam trudged through the drifts, she made out a navy jacket and a body… Swallowing hard, she yelled out. "Bryan? Are you okay?"

The body moved. She let out her breath. Bryan turned, waved frantically, and her heart soared.

"Oh, honey," she cried, jumping from Sam's broad back and taking the last steps through the snow on her own. "Are you all right?"

He managed to look sheepish though his teeth were chattering and his face was red from the cold. "Twisted my ankle when Sam spooked and I fell off," he admitted. "Can't walk and I was in so much pain, it hurt to ride, so, um, I, uh, stopped to rest and…Sam took off on me." His lip trembled, either from the cold or some strong emotion. "Guess I'm not much of a cowboy."

"That's not such a crime, is it?"

He stared down at his hands, his young pride bowed.

"Don't worry about it. You're all right now. We're going to get you home and warm and safe and…" She saw the doubt in his eyes and took his gloved hand in hers. "I know it's been rough and that your dad and I have been so wrapped up in each other that we inadvertently left you out, but you have to know that both of us love you so much. Your dad…he's frantic with worry and…" Rocking back on her heels, she looked him squarely in the eye. "I believe we can work this out—all of us. But if you're unhappy, if you think that

Amy and I don't belong in your family, well, then maybe something will change."

"Meaning?" he asked suspiciously.

"Meaning that I'd be willing to move out, at least for a while, until you and your dad figure out what's best for you two."

"You're serious?" he asked, disbelief threading into his hoarse voice.

Her heart nearly broke at the sound of hope in his words. "Yep," she admitted, then slapped him gently on the leg. "But first things first. We have to find a way to get you out of here. Can you ride?"

"I—I think so."

"Good, 'cause there's not much light left. We'll ride back close to the stream, follow it downhill and we should either end up in town or at some shelter, an old logging camp or mine or something." She paused to try to call on her walkie-talkie, but the battery had worn down and she couldn't reach anyone. She set off flares in the small hope that someone who was still searching the mountain might come across their trail.

"Okay, let's go." Helping him hobble to Sam, she acted as a brace. He winced as he climbed into the saddle, but eventually they were both mounted, the wind was at their backs and with the gray leading, they headed downward. Ronni crossed her fingers as they rode and hoped that they would find civilization before the horses or Bryan gave out.

Travis couldn't believe his eyes. The sizzling red light of a flare guided him and he shouted, his voice ringing through the woods. He followed the light from the small beacon, but when he reached the sputtering embers, he found himself alone. Gritting his teeth, he stared at the ground. There was a fresh trail broken by two horses. One that came down the ridge to the stream base, the other following along the dark, near-frozen water. With a flashlight he checked the depth of snow in the trails and decided to follow the stream. He plunged forward, yelling and hoping beyond hope that his family was safe. "Bryan! Veronica!"

"Travis?" Ronni's voice was faint but sure and he raced forward, plunging through the stream, running and mindful of nothing other than seeing his son and wife again. Tears burned in his eyes, the dark forest rushed past in a blur, and as he rounded a bend, he saw them, two dark shapes on horseback. Ronni was off her mount in a second, running to him, flinging herself into his arms, sobbing in relief.

"He's all right. He's gonna be all right," she said over and over again, and Travis, still holding on to her, approached his son.

With tears in his eyes, he looked up at his boy. "Don't you ever scare me like that again," he said, blinking and sniffing. "I was worried sick about you."

Bryan fought a losing battle with tears.

"Don't you know I love you?" Travis said. "That I'd do anything to make you happy? God, Bryan..." His words faltered and he felt Ronni slip out of his embrace.

"Dad—" Bryan's voice cracked as he slid off the horse. Travis held him close, afraid that his son would disappear again. The sheer terror of losing him washed over him in an icy wave.

"We're a family, son. All of us. Just because I love Ronni and Amy doesn't mean I love you less. If you only knew how scared I was, if you only knew how much I care about you and your happiness."

"I'm sorry—"

"Shh. We're gonna work this out." Travis looked at Ronni over his son's shoulder. "All of us."

Bryan nodded against his chest, then glanced over his shoulder to his new stepmother. Through his tears, he offered her a small smile. "Thanks," he said gruffly, his chin angling upward again. "I—I was stupid."

"I love you," she said simply and he squeezed his eyes shut. "I will love you as my own son, if you'll have me. And I won't stand in the way of your relationship with your dad or your real mom. Never."

He stared at her a second and then to Travis's surprise, he reached forward and hugged her. "I'm sorry for everything I said, everything I thought…I…"

"Shh, it's all right. Let's get out of here and get you home."

He blinked hard and nodded. "'Kay, Mom," he whispered, wiping the back of his glove under his nose, and Travis felt the scars in his heart begin to heal.

The surprise party was over, the guests, rounded up by invitation from Shelly and Vic, had long since left. Balloons and streamers still rose to the ceiling of the lodge and the Christmas tree was lit, but the surprise wedding reception/New Year's Eve party had ended and Ronni kicked off her shoes. Two bottles of champagne still rested in a bucket of ice. "Here's to us," Travis said, clicking his glass to hers. "All four of us."

"To us," she agreed and took a swallow. The past couple of days had been a whirlwind. The blizzard had ended and finally, they were a family again. Bryan had only sprained his ankle and didn't even have to use crutches. He'd finally accepted Ronni and Amy to the point that Amy tagged after him wherever he went. He'd quit talking about moving away and had even deigned to meet some kids from the local church group. There was hope, Ronni sensed, and there was happiness.

Travis slipped his arm around her waist. "So what's your New Year's resolution?" he asked and she smiled.

"Well, Amy's is that she's going to be good so she can keep you as her daddy." She reached into her pocket and dragged out a scrap of red paper with childish handwriting. "I think Bryan helped her with it."

"A smart girl," Travis said, his eyes misting as he read the note.

"And Bryan said he wanted to learn how to ride a horse, snowboard and play an electric guitar."

Travis winced. "*Electric?* Why not acoustic?"

"And he's agreed to visit his mother at least once a year. Maybe twice."

"That's progress."

"I think so. Vic and Shelly plan to have another baby," Ronni said.

"And you?"

"I thought I might go along with my sister. It sounds good, you know."

"What? To have another baby?"

"*Our* baby, half sibling to each of our kids. Kind of a knot to hold us together."

"Do we need one?"

She laughed and sipped the champagne. "Suppose not, but it would be nice."

"I guess so." He nuzzled her neck and caught a

glimpse of Bryan and Amy staring down at them through the rails of the landing.

"I'm not talking about right away," she said. "We need time to grow as a family, just the four of us."

A muffled bark from the area of the kitchen made her laugh. "Okay, just the six of us," she amended. "But, by the end of the year…"

"It could be a possibility." Travis's eyes sparkled.

"So right now I resolve that I'll be the best mother in the world to our two kids and the best wife on this earth to you."

"Hear, hear." He started to take a sip, but she caught his wrist.

"Not so fast, mister. What's your resolution?"

"Mine?" His grin stretched wide. "That's easy." He set his glass on the mantel and circled her waist with his strong arms. Intense eyes stared down at her. "I'm going to love you forever, Ronni," he vowed, saying the words that she'd longed to hear ever since first meeting him. "My resolution isn't for a year, it's for the rest of our lives."

EPILOGUE

THE CLOCK STRUCK twelve.

"Happy New Year!" Amy sang out, proudly displaying a front tooth that wobbled precariously on her bottom gums.

"Same to you," Ronni said with a yawn. She hugged her daughter as Bryan clomped down the stairs. The first signs of stubble covered his upper lip and his voice cracked whenever he talked. "Where's your father?" she asked. "I didn't think he wanted to miss this."

"In the bedroom," Bryan and Amy said in unison, then exchanged knowing glances.

"I should have guessed." Ronni pushed herself from the couch and walked past the embers of the fire in the grate to the master bedroom where Travis was reaching into the bassinet.

"You wake her and I'll strangle you," Ronni warned, but it was too late. Travis, fascinated with his two-month-old daughter, picked up the infant and held her close.

"Happy New Year," he whispered to Andrea and she made little sucking motions with her lips. With a proud smile, he looked up at his wife and winked. "You know she's the most beautiful baby in the world, don't you?"

Ronni grinned. "Don't tell Shelly. She thinks Kevin's got that award all sewed up."

"Well, she's wrong. Besides, he's bald."

"He's only two weeks old," Ronni said, but laughed when she thought of her sister and small family all tucked into the caretaker's house on the lake. Victor was working for Travis full-time and had added two bedrooms and a bath to the house where Ronni and Shelly had grown up. Now, all their lives had settled into a comfortable, contented routine. Ronni had moved from her little cabin and rented it to a young couple. She'd transferred her business to an old storage building near the lodge and the horses had moved, as well, to new stables Travis had insisted upon building. Bryan had learned to snowboard this season and had reconciled himself to having a stepmother and a few new siblings. He even called his mother in France every once in a while and planned to visit her again this summer, as he did last.

Amy, growing by leaps and bounds, was in seventh heaven with her new sister, two dogs and Lucy's half-grown colt, and Ronni was happier than she'd ever been in her life.

"I guess you're right," she admitted, gazing down at her infant daughter's precious face. "She's probably the prettiest baby ever born."

A thunder of footsteps announced Amy's arrival.

Andrea blinked and stretched a little fist, as her father, reached forward, grabbed the belt surrounding Ronni's waist and pulled her close.

"Aren't we gonna have champagne?" Amy demanded.

"Your mother and I are. You'll have to settle for sparkling cider. You, too," he added when Bryan poked his head into the room.

"I know, Dad," he said and Ronni smiled inwardly at the familiarity and love that had grown between father and son. Bryan was starting to talk about cars and getting his driving permit and some girl name Julie and Travis, bless him, was handling being a father of a teenager.

"We'll be there in a minute," Travis promised. "You guys find the corkscrew."

Amy was off on her new mission with Bryan in tow. "Now," Travis said, shifting the baby so that she wouldn't get squeezed, "I just wanted to make our private New Year's resolution."

"Oh? And what is that?"

"That we have a baby every year."

She laughed. "Only if *you* go through pregnancy, gain thirty pounds and then suffer with labor."

"Spoilsport."

"How about we have one this year and then decide?"

"As long as we can have at least one more."

"Mmm, I might be able to be convinced."

"I was hoping..." He loosened the belt of her robe and touched her breasts.

"Watch out," she warned, kissing him. "You might be getting yourself into big trouble."

"That's what I'm aiming for," he whispered, brushing his lips across her ear.

At that moment Andrea decided to wake up and let out a squawk loud enough to rouse the dead in three counties. Amy and her dogs thundered back toward the room. Ronni quickly adjusted her clothing.

"Later," she said, taking the baby from her husband's arms,

"I'm counting on it."

She grinned and winked. "Good. I think we'll both have to learn a little patience."

"No problem," he drawled. "The way I figure it, we've got the rest of our lives."

* * * * *

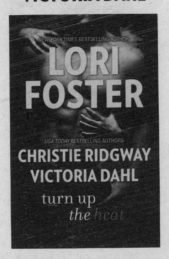

JILL SORENSON

Love is the most dangerous territory of all.

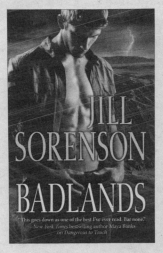

Every day, bodyguard Owen Jackson puts his life on the line. Assigned to protect Penny's father, a presidential candidate, Owen can't get emotionally involved. That is, until Penny and her young son, Cruz, are abducted and taken deep into the California badlands.

Owen knows the bleak territory from his childhood, and he knows the gang leader making ransom demands—his own brother. Owen has hidden the darkness in his past. Now his only chance of keeping Penny alive is to let her see the man he really is—even if it means losing the only woman he'll ever want.

Available now, wherever books are sold!

Be sure to connect with us at:
Harlequin.com/Newsletters
Facebook.com/HarlequinBooks
Twitter.com/HarlequinBooks

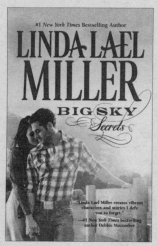

LISA JACKSON

77728	CONFESSIONS	___ $7.99 U.S.	___ $9.99 CAN.
77650	ABANDONED	___ $7.99 U.S.	___ $9.99 CAN.
77578	STRANGERS	___ $7.99 U.S.	___ $9.99 CAN.
77489	STORMY NIGHTS	___ $7.99 U.S.	___ $9.99 CAN.

(limited quantities available)

TOTAL AMOUNT	$ _____
POSTAGE & HANDLING	$ _____
($1.00 FOR 1 BOOK, 50¢ for each additional)	
APPLICABLE TAXES*	$ _____
TOTAL PAYABLE	$ _____

(check or money order—please do not send cash)

To order, complete this form and send it, along with a check or money order for the total above, payable to Harlequin HQN, to: **In the U.S.:** 3010 Walden Avenue, P.O. Box 9077, Buffalo, NY 14269-9077; **In Canada:** P.O. Box 636, Fort Erie, Ontario, L2A 5X3.

Name: _____

Address: _____ City: _____

State/Prov.: _____ Zip/Postal Code: _____

Account Number (if applicable): _____

075 CSAS

*New York residents remit applicable sales taxes.
*Canadian residents remit applicable GST and provincial taxes.

HARLEQUIN® HQN™
www.Harlequin.com

PHLJ0114BL

REQUEST YOUR FREE BOOKS!

2 FREE NOVELS
FROM THE SUSPENSE COLLECTION
PLUS 2 FREE GIFTS!

YES! Please send me 2 FREE novels from the Suspense Collection and my 2 FREE gifts (gifts are worth about $10). After receiving them, if I don't wish to receive any more books, I can return the shipping statement marked "cancel." If I don't cancel, I will receive 4 brand-new novels every month and be billed just $6.24 per book in the U.S. or $6.74 per book in Canada. That's a savings of at least 22% off the cover price. It's quite a bargain! Shipping and handling is just 50¢ per book in the U.S. and 75¢ per book in Canada.* I understand that accepting the 2 free books and gifts places me under no obligation to buy anything. I can always return a shipment and cancel at any time. Even if I never buy another book, the two free books and gifts are mine to keep forever.

191/391 MDN F4XN

Name	(PLEASE PRINT)

Address	Apt. #

City	State/Prov.	Zip/Postal Code

Signature (if under 18, a parent or guardian must sign)

Mail to the Harlequin® Reader Service:
IN U.S.A.: P.O. Box 1867, Buffalo, NY 14240-1867
IN CANADA: P.O. Box 609, Fort Erie, Ontario L2A 5X3

Want to try two free books from another line?
Call 1-800-873-8635 or visit www.ReaderService.com.

* Terms and prices subject to change without notice. Prices do not include applicable taxes. Sales tax applicable in N.Y. Canadian residents will be charged applicable taxes. Offer not valid in Quebec. This offer is limited to one order per household. Not valid for current subscribers to the Suspense Collection or the Romance/Suspense Collection. All orders subject to credit approval. Credit or debit balances in a customer's account(s) may be offset by any other outstanding balance owed by or to the customer. Please allow 4 to 6 weeks for delivery. Offer available while quantities last.

Your Privacy—The Harlequin® Reader Service is committed to protecting your privacy. Our Privacy Policy is available online at www.ReaderService.com or upon request from the Harlequin Reader Service.

We make a portion of our mailing list available to reputable third parties that offer products we believe may interest you. If you prefer that we not exchange your name with third parties, or if you wish to clarify or modify your communication preferences, please visit us at www.ReaderService.com/consumerschoice or write to us at Harlequin Reader Service Preference Service, P.O. Box 9062, Buffalo, NY 14269. Include your complete name and address.

SUS13R